VIRGINIA WINDS

A CIVIL WAR STORY OF A SCOUT FOR GENERALS,

BOTH BLUE AND GRAY,

AND HIS BATTLES, INTRIGUES AND LOVES

Author
C.R. Clark

Copyright © 2016 C.R. Clark

Submit inquiries to:
Plowshare Publishing Company
10511 Florence Ave., #88
Thonotosassa, FL 33592

All rights reserved.
ISBN-10: 1540562409
ISBN-13: 978-1540562401
Library of Congress Control Number: 2016963401

It is with the love of a father I dedicate this book to my son, Clark and my daughter, Ronnie. Each of you are so very different in personality, yet you both hold a most salient trait, commitment to your beliefs and work ethics, that have and will continue to pay great dividends. It is my hope and prayer that the both of you will see in this work, that as you age in life, new paths can be made in areas previously unthinkable. I love you both and each of you are most precious in my life.

Acknowledgements

It is with high regard and esteem that I hold these individuals that have seen me to the end of this book I started 8 years ago; and with little thoughts that it would ever be completed.

First, I must thank Dr. Dale Lick for his prodding and urging many years ago in his belief that I had the ability to write. In the end, his yeoman's work of editing and formulating my rough work into book form I shall be forever grateful. His friendship and love spans decades back to my parents. Without his efforts, all would have been futile in my desire to tell this story.

I also must thank ex-navy Commander Mike Stacy and his wife Karen for their love and belief in me in this effort. Their many hours of deciphering my handwritten chicken scratch to a type form for Dale Lick to refine. I can never repay their love of decades and firm belief in me. I cherish them dearly.

To Connie Swanson, Karen Stacy's sister, for her unique message to me of 'Get-r-done' in finishing the work when I was lazy!

To my Aunt Bev who inspired me for a character in the story! I love you dearly, dear Auntie Bev.

To Lisa Silver, my youngest sister, for giving special love and support for over a decade with especially difficult times. Your belief in my writings and me has blossomed. Dear Sis, I entrusted to you the final stage for presentation. I marvel at your skills in writing and to have you with me in this is most comforting. I love you dearly. A finer sister no man has ever known.

This concerted effort inspired me to this story's completion and on to write sequels and other efforts. To all, I thank you and love you dearly.

God's power and love has given to me a rebirth and a new heart. In Him I trust and believe. I have found the God of my father.

Chapters

1. A New Life
2. Together, A New Beginning
3. New Horizons
4. The help of a New Friend
5. Working for the Next Opportunity
6. A New Adventure Begins
7. Ned and Jake in the War
8. Success and Disaster
9. Lizza's Struggles
10. The Forceful Freeing
11. Facing Up to Unpleasant Realities
12. The Family and the Wedding
13. The Taylors and a New Allegiance
14. The Meanness of Prison
15. Preparing for Escape
16. Serious Trouble for Lizza
17. The Escape
18. A Surprising Family Relationship
19. Another Family Relationship
20. Healing and Moving On
21. Becoming a Union Captain
22. Molly at the Ball
23. Meeting with General Grant
24. The First Battle Under General Grant
25. Ned's Report and Grant's Next Maneuver
26. Finding Family
27. A Deadly Battle
28. Cleaning Up the Mess
29. Preparing for Grant's next 'Adventure'
30. Family Members' Crowing Concerns
31. Something in Common
32. Military Moves, Family Moves
33. A New Siege Begins
34. An Unexpected Reunion
35. A New Maneuver
36. Helping Bessie
37. Continuing the Battle

38. A Renewal with the Taylors
39. A Journey of Sadness
40. A New Command as Colonel
41. Trying to Regain Balance
42. A New Beginning
43. Another New Beginning
44. Unexpected Trouble
45. Beginning New Lives Together
46. More Trouble from the Past
47. The Possible Aid of a Friend
48. The Decision
49. Jake and the Jefferson Davis Family
50. Planning for Their Future
51. Moving to the Future

PROLOGUE

The Battle of Bull Run was but one month ago when Ned McDonald received word of his father, Clark, being killed. Two days after that his mother had succumbed to the fever. All alone now, on a barely profitable piece of land in Gloucester, Virginia, Ned knew he must move on and away from the only life and home he had ever known. Farming was a hard life. His mother and father had moved from Staunton, Virginia, to try a new life on the Chesapeake before he was born. He was the spitting image of his father, tall, long brown hair, with broad shoulders and a narrow waist. For being a farm boy, he was well read. His mother made sure of that. She schooled him in mathematics, science and, of course, the classics; all of this was interesting to him.

Ned was known around the Gloucester Peninsula for his horsemanship, skills learned and honed from his father. His prized horse, Jake, was a 17-hand chestnut stallion. Jake could clear a four-rail fence with ease, but was known most of all for his blistering speed. Ned had raced Jake against all comers and had never been challenged in his victories. They had even raced on land that George Washington had raced and wagered on some 100 years ago; the tavern, between the York River and Gloucester Court House, was a meeting place for such gaming.

Slavery was a prevalent sight all over eastern Virginia. Gloucester was no different. Even though it was so, Ned believed, as his mom and dad had, that it was against God's teachings and he believed in every word of the Bible!

With the passing of his parents, Ned had only three choices. He could stay and continue to work the land, the only land he had ever known, sell the land and move back to be with kinfolk in the Blue Valley in Staunton, or sell the land and commit to the Virginian Cause, protecting Virginia from northern invaders.

So, continuing what his father had given his life for, the path was clear to him, he chose the third option. Ned had found a buyer for the farm through a lawyer from the courthouse area and sold it for a good amount of money. He packed what belongings he could onto Belle, his families Belgian draft horse, saddled Jake and left Gloucester never to return.

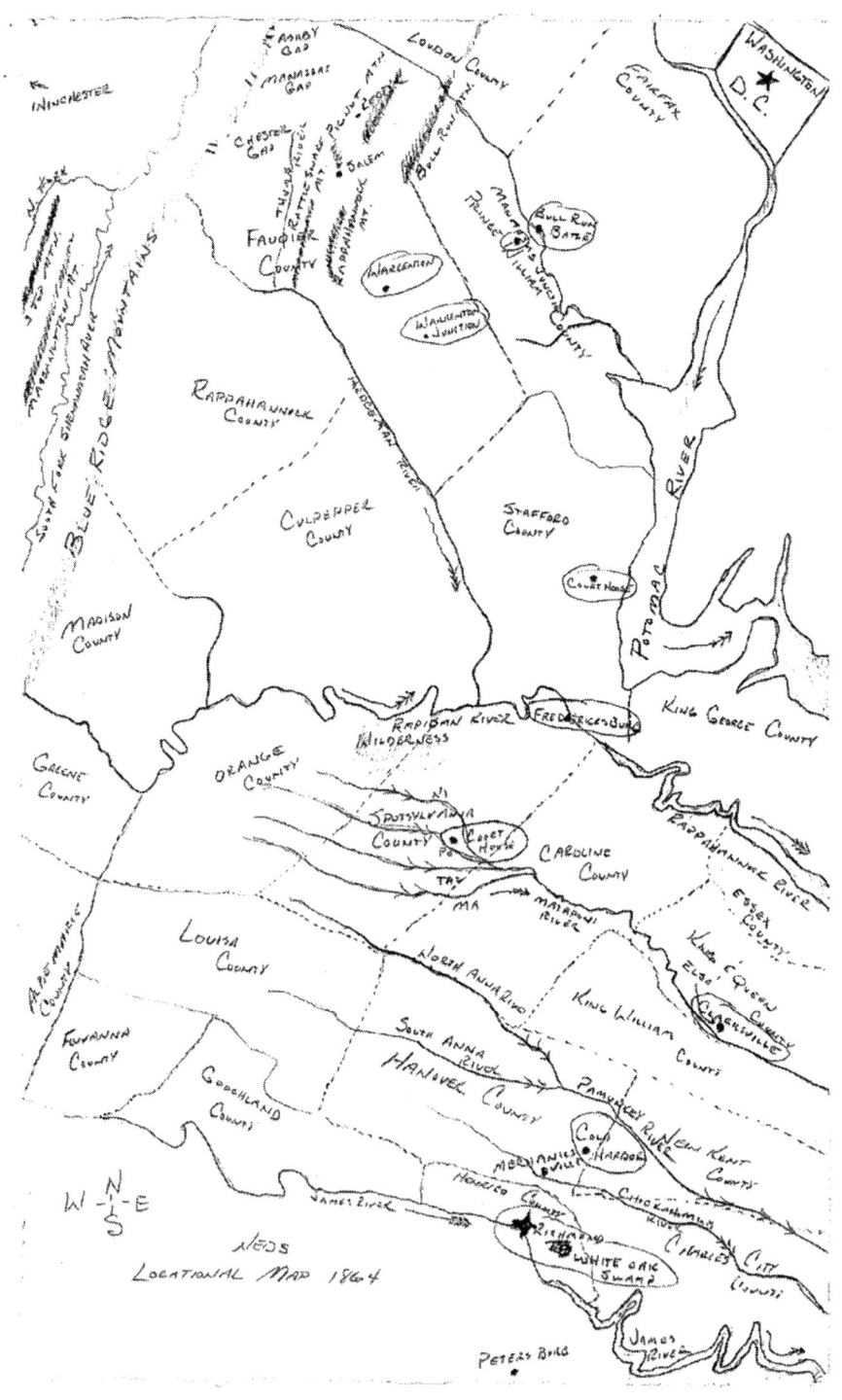

C.R.CLARK

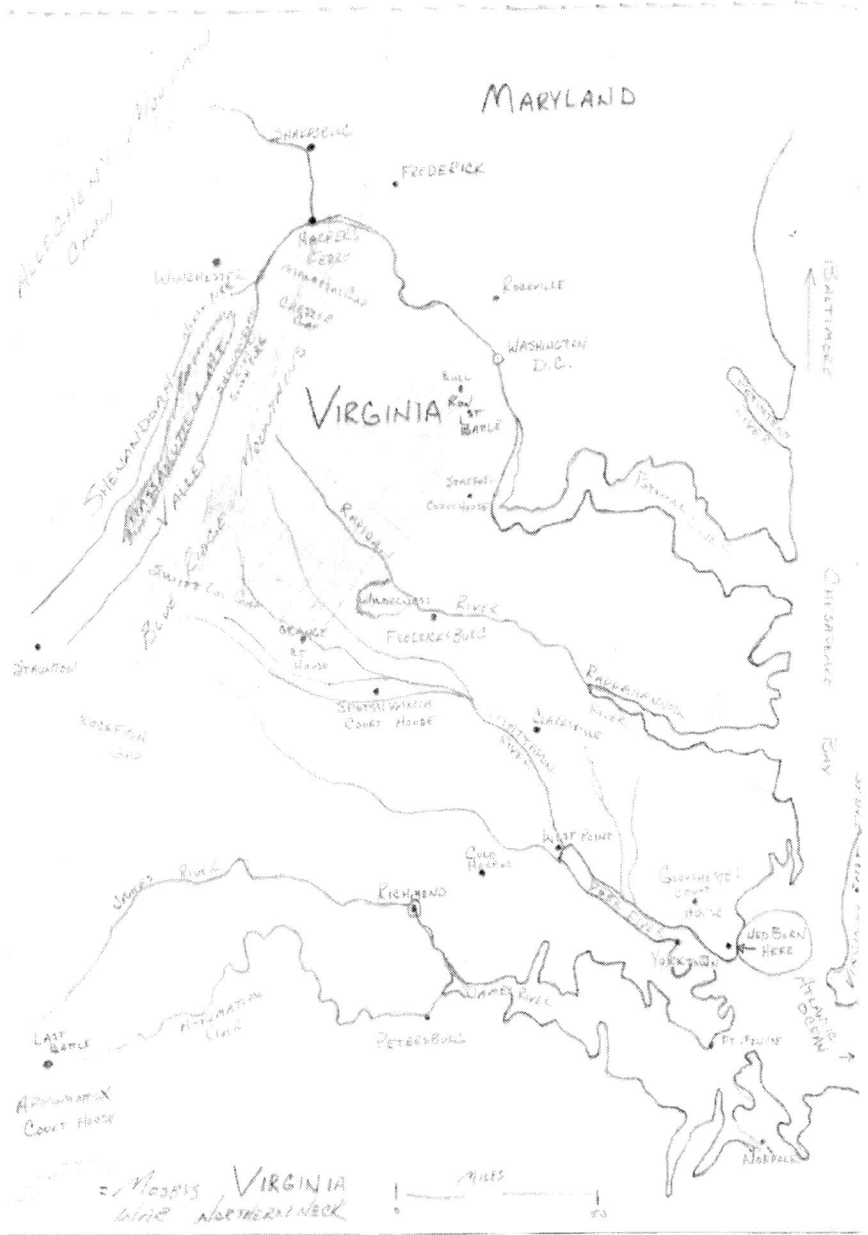

C.R.CLARK

Chapter 1

A New Life

Ned, his trusty mount, Jake, and Belle headed toward West Point, Virginia. West Point was at the head of the York River and was approximately 30 miles from Richmond. Upon reaching West Point, the trio would turn west toward Richmond to find his destiny in the Confederate Army, while protecting "Ole Virginie."

Ned knew this road well. He had traveled it countless times with his father over the years. It had no towns along its path and there were only scrabble type farms like the one he had just left behind. As the road grew to the west of Gloucester Court House, he came upon the plantation owned by a family named Foster. The Fosters were the largest plantation owners in the Peninsula; they had almost ten square miles of Foster land. Ned had seen Mr. Foster in the Court House area plenty of times along with his attendant slaves. He was infamously known for the hard, callus treatment of his slaves.

Ned had left his home around 10:00 a.m. and had only passed the most northern edge of the Foster Plantation by around 12:00 noon. The easy pace was more appropriate for Belle who shouldered the load, as a draft horse was used to a slow pace in order to toil all day long plowing, pulling and carrying loads.

It was a cool brisk morning when he started out, but by noon the temperature was beginning to rise. He came upon a tributary into the York River and before fording he decided to stop to water, rest and check over the horses. Rest, as his father had taught him, meant unloading completely, saddles and all loads. Ned lay down under the pines to look up at the clear blue sky. The temperature was continuing to rise, so he lingered for only an hour before loading up again. The threesome headed toward the stream preparing to ford, when the horses were startled even before Ned heard the noise of brambles breaking.

Into the roadway a breathless slave girl fell flat and sprawled out. She was as surprised as Ned was to see her. Quickly she turned over and crawfished away from him. She was terrified! Her green eyes were wide open and she was rapidly shaking her head and screaming, "No! No! Sir! I can't go back! Please sir!" This was clearly a runaway slave.

Ned dismounted and slowly raised his hand and spoke gently. "It's okay! It's okay! I'm not after you." The girl kept looking back in the direction she had just come from and then back at Ned. He spoke again, "It is okay, Miss! Please, what's this all about?"

Still out of breath, she said, "Mr. Foster's men are after me sir! I've run away again and if he catches me this time he will do more terrible things to me! Please, sir!"

Ned's mind was racing; what should he do? How could he help her? Then he heard it, the sound of hounds baying in the distance, perhaps only a mile or so away.

"Come quick," Ned said assuredly. "Come get on my horse with me!"

The slave girl looked at Ned searching for truth, and then she looked in the direction of the sounds of hounds baying.

Ned, smiling with his eyes, stuck out his hand and said, "Come quickly, we have to get some distance from them now!"

The girl jumped to her feet and before she could take two steps Ned had deftly mounted Jake and extended his arm to pull her up to sit behind him. Into a lope they headed north, northwest with Belle doing an admirable job of keeping up.

Ned surveyed their surroundings and noticed that to the west a thunderstorm was brewing. What a blessing! The storm would be to their advantage as it would throw off the hounds by washing away the scent of the girl.

Ned's new passenger was flopping all over Jake's back so, without stopping, he motioned her to sit up tight to him and wrap her arms around his waist. That way they would move together as one on Jake's back making it easier for the horse to move. She nodded in understanding and quickly took her place.

Soon after leaving the ford, the travelers came to a Y in the road. To the left was the road to West Point. To the right was Urbana, which sat on the Rappahannock River. Ned made a quick decision and headed right to Urbana. His plans had changed, at least for now.

Ned liked the winds out of the west. "I'll head downwind from the hounds," he said.

The pair had only traveled another two miles when they came to another Y in the road. This time Ned chose the north road, just as the storm was overtaking them. Soon, the pair and horses were drenched. However, chilling as the early fall rain was, the horses welcomed the cool cleansing of the lather they had built up.

The road bent back westward and from there Ned could see an old, and what looked to be, abandoned house and barn tucked in the pines. He reined Jake down the path.

Ned was right, it was abandoned. "There's our shelter for the night, we can rest the horses," he said.

Ned led the horses into the small barn. Perfect, there were two stalls! After getting the horses settled, without a word, the unlikely pair sat down at the barn's entrance for some rest, one on each side of the door. They were silent for some time as they watched the rain come down in buckets.

Ned looked at his new companion and was the first to break the silence. He asked, "So what's your name?"

"Lizza Johnson, sir," she said quietly.

"So, Lizza, how old are you?" he inquired.

"18 years old, sir," again she replied softly.

He responded, "Call me Ned. My name is Ned, Ned McDonald."

"Well, Ned, I thank you for helping me. You've given me a great blessing and I am much obliged."

He smiled and said, "How could I not help you, Lizza?"

Lizza responded, "Well, most men would have taken me back for the money Mr. Foster is prepared to give for my return. He calls me his belly-warmer. At that, Lizza leaned her head back and closed her eyes.

Ned continued to look at Lizza. He could not help but notice her beauty. She was about 5'5" tall, 125 pounds, broad shouldered with a narrow waist and her hair close cropped. She had a strong yet gentle jaw line, smallish nose and high cheekbones. She reminded Ned of a Nubian queen he had read about. Yes, he thought of her, as a queen, not a slave.

Lizza slowly opened her eyes and saw Ned staring at her, and for the first time, smiled and said, "What it is, Ned? Why do you look at me that way?"

"Please forgive me, Lizza. It's just that you are the most beautiful girl I've ever seen."

Puzzled, Lizza searched Ned's face and said, "I'm a Negro slave, Ned!"

Ned responded, "Yes, I know, Lizza, yet to me beautiful. Cannot a Negro be beautiful?" he asked.

Lizza,, then, positively said, "Yes, I suppose so. I, too, was thinking the same of you while my eyes were closed."

They both laughed.

Ned changed the subject and they were brought back to reality. He said, "This is very good. A long storm will surely throw those men off the trail."

Lizza quickly came back, "For now, but they will still come after me, Ned."

Ned quickly offered, "They will not find you if I have anything to say about it, Lizza."

"Are you my Knight of Old, Ned?" Lizza asked with a light laugh in her voice.

"Maybe," Ned smiled and continued, "Yes, I reckon I am, Lizza!"

"But how do you know?" Lizza quickly interjected.

Ned didn't reply. Instead he said, "We must get these clothes dry." He reached for his saddlebag, pulled out a clean nightshirt and gave it to Lizza. And said, "Here, take it till your clothes are dry. Here is a sewing kit. It looks as if the brambles had a go at your dress."

When Lizza returned from the back of the barn, Ned had his shirt off and a fresh pair of trousers on. Lizza's shape in the nightshirt was made known to Ned. Again, his mind thought of a goddess. Her breasts, full and heavy, swept outward; her legs were muscular and taut. She cut a beautiful sight.

Lizza, all the while, looked at Ned, his broad muscular chest, strong arms and long hair conjured up in her mind the mythical Thor, whom she had read about in secretive times. She commented, "You are Thor, Ned."

Ned asked, "How do you know of such things, Lizza?"

She confided that she had learned from the master's daughter who was about her age, and added, "The white girl taught me to read and write." Lizza had grown up on a plantation in South Hampton County, across the York and James Rivers, a few miles from North Carolina. It had been her home as well as her mother's and grandmother's.

Ned inquired, "Then, how did you ...?"

"Come to Gloucester, Ned?" Lizza finished his words. "My momma was a housekeeper, as was granny. As I grew the master had eyes for me and laid me down. The misses found out and had the master send me away to her brother, Mr. Foster. Then, Mr. Foster wanted me like my last master. So, I kept running away. The master said the last time that if I ran away again, he would crush my foot bones."

Ned could feel her pain as she caused her mind to recall these things. Tears rolled down Lizza's face as she told of her horrors.

Ned's face had traces of tears now and anger welled up in him as he said, "I'll be damned if they will touch you again! As God is in heaven, they will not!"

After regaining his thoughts, he told Lizza, "We will stay here tonight and move on in the morning."

"But what about the overseers, Ned?"

"I am quite sure they have stopped; no one can track in this, Lizza. With the dark, we will be safe."

With that Ned went to tend the horses and bring the gear to the house. Lizza had found a broom and swept a place clean on the floor to bed down. They both went separately outside to bathe briefly. The night air was quite cool. Lizza also scrubbed a dress she found in a trunk in the back bedroom. Ned stoked the firebox with dry wood from the barn and soon the night chill faded and the wet afternoon was a memory.

The twosome lay upon some blankets on the floor and they talked about their lives. Lizza talked mostly of freedom and having her own house, her own room, books, all the things white people had.

She went silent several times when talking about her momma, sisters and their plight.

Ned took note, as she spoke, of her manner of speech and intelligence; at times her manner spoke of privilege. "Again, Lizza, tell me how you came to read and write?"

Lizza began, "The master's daughter is Abigail. She was my age. We would secret away to play. As we grew older, I wanted to be like her, speak like her, and act as she did. As she learned, I did also. She would show and teach me. The secreted books for me to read were my escape. That is how I learned the lessons you learned, but much differently. I had to keep my knowledge from the whites and blacks."

Ned told her how his mother had made sure he got schooling and how his father taught him life skills of horsemanship, farming, carpentry and how to be a good man. He continued, "I've been brought up poor, Lizza, but I'm very lucky for my mom and dad, and their love and lessons of life. I, like you, miss my mom and dad."

Ned found himself opening up to Lizza like no other person before. He looked over at her lying next to him. She was still fixed on the ceiling as they had been for a couple of hours, just talking and bonding.

Ned then asked, "How is it, Lizza, that we are so much alike in so many ways, yet different?"

Lizza turned over on her side to look at Ned. They looked upon each other for a time, neither saying a word. Lizza broke the silence. "We are the same in the most important way, Ned." She paused, and then spoke again. "We are God's children. That makes us the same, don't you see. God's own one!"

He smiled, nodded and simply said, "God, yes! Sleep now, Lizza, we will need it for tomorrow." And soon they were asleep.

Chapter 2

Together, A New Beginning

At the break of dawn, Ned awoke. He found Lizza nestled up close to him as the fire had long gone out. The fall morning was brisk. He reached for her hand and squeezed it softly. He liked her next to him. She slowly awoke and squeezed his hand in return.

Ned leaned to kiss her forehead and said, "We must get moving, Lizza."

"Yes," she responded as she put her hand to his face, looked into his eyes and softly kissed his lips. "Ned, I feel safe, maybe the first time in my life."

Ned smiled and told her, "Safety is further down the road."

As they readied the horses then mounted Jake, Lizza quickly assumed a lesson from yesterday and moved in tight. Not just to help Jake, but to feel Ned and to feel safe. The closeness that the two were fostering was surprisingly deep.

Ned's plan was to get Lizza to Fredericksburg, Virginia, and, hopefully, even further north into Maryland. What neither of them knew was that the exact route they were on had been the path of the slave underground railroad for the eastern seaboard. This path had been used for decades and decades.

Ned reined Jake north on a road not 200 yards from the abandoned farm and then northwest at a crossroad. This road looked more traveled. It went straight up the middle of the Gloucester Peninsula between the Mattaponi and Rappahannock Rivers. The former ran right below the bluffs of Fredericksburg.

Ned told Lizza, "I hope to make Clarkston before dark. It's going to be a stretch, so we may have to bed down in the pines."

Lizza nodded, as she secured her seat against him.

After covering some ten miles or so, Ned reined Jake off into some secluded pines and unloaded his horses. He and Lizza drank what precious little was left in his canteens. The food was long gone. It had only been meant to get him to Richmond. He reluctantly allowed the horses to drink from some pooled water. He much preferred to give them fresh water as his father had taught him.

"I feel safer for you now, Lizza," Ned said.

She smiled, came to him and they hugged, enjoying being in each other's arms.

After only a few minutes had passed, he told Lizza, "We must move along."

The two mounted Jake after reloading the horses. They continued toward Clarkston as dusk closed in quickly with the shortened fall days.

Out of the blue, Lizza pulled at Ned's shirt. "Look! Over there," she said while pointing so Ned could see. "Go over there! See that house?" Ned looked in the direction she was pointing. There, barely visible, was a small house some 100 yards off the main drag.

"Why, Lizza?" Ned questioned.

"No! No! No! Ned, go over there," she quickly responded. See that piece of quilt hanging from the tree?"

He now saw it. It was only a two-foot by two-foot piece of quilt hung on the branch at the roadside.

"Yes," Lizza said, and added, "Ned, go to the house! It is a safe station house for slaves! Slaves moving north without conductors to guide them look for these signs."

"Lizza, are you sure?" Ned asked.

She quickly responded, "Sure as I am sitting behind you Ned, trust me."

Ned reined Jake up the road and as they neared the house an old woman came out of the door. He checked Jake up in front of the porch. The woman looked the pair over quickly and carefully. Then she smiled a grin of no teeth, save a few in front. It was the welcome smile that Lizza and Ned needed.

Quickly the woman told them, "Take the horses to the barn out back and you, child, come in the house," motioning to Lizza.

As Lizza entered the modest house, the aroma of the food cooking overtook her. It smelled so good. Food was something the two had not had enough of the past two days.

The woman spoke with a heavy German accent, but Lizza clearly understood her when she said, "My name is Elsa. Elsa Wildermuth. And you child, what is your name?"

"I am Lizza Johnson and he is Ned McDonald."

The woman said, "Well then, Lizza, I must say you two make an unlikely pair. Now tell me about yourself, child, and what has brought you this far on a seldom used track these days."

Lizza broke into their story as Ned came through the door after knocking.

"Well, young Ned, I'm Elsa. This here humble home is a safe house, do you understand?"

Ned nodded yes and explained that it was Lizza who recognized the house for what it was.

"Yes, well," Elsa continued, "Now-a-days the tracks north have moved west closer to Richmond."

It was then that Elsa remembered Lizza was telling her story. "I'm sorry child, continue."

Lizza instinctively moved closer to Ned as she told her story and of how she and Ned had met.

The threesome sat at the table in the kitchen while Elsa listened and filled plates with food, including potatoes, mustard greens, some cured ham and pumpkin pie. Ned and Lizza both ate heartily, filling very empty stomachs.

After hearing Lizza and Ned's story, while finishing their food, Elsa exclaimed, "Well, children, I've run my station for over 20 years and have never lost a passenger and I dare say never heard a story such as yours. Now I live here alone. My husband died last year. He was German also. Both he and I came over 30 years ago. We started helping the railway because we could not tolerate slavery. We have never been caught helping free slaves in moving north. Even the years that the tracks through here were busy! Now they have forgotten me, but I still post my flag every day just in case! And see, here you are!" she said excitedly while clapping her hands quickly.

Ned asked Elsa, "How far are we from Clarkston?" She told him they were located only two miles southwest of Clarkston.

"Good," he said, "We made good time then."

Elsa asked Lizza if she expected to find family up north.

Lizza responded, "No ma'am, I am the first of my family to try to get north. I don't know where I should go or how far."

Lizza had a sad look cross over her face. She moved even closer to Ned and put her hand in his. He smiled and reassured Lizza.

"First things first," said Elsa. For the first time since meeting the pair, she realized with folly what they meant to one another and she began speaking excitedly in German.

Lizza looked at Ned and then back at Elsa.

"Oh! Excuse me, I sometimes revert to speaking German when I am happy, especially when happily amused!" She spoke again. "You two fancy one another, yes?" They both sheepishly nodded their heads yes.

Elsa exclaimed, "Wonderful!" and again clapped excitedly. It was the first time the two young lovers acknowledged their feelings for each other, albeit nods.

"You must rest now children," Elsa said, "I have some straw mattress bags and blankets. You will be comfortable, no?"

"Yes," the two said together, and Ned added, "But I have to tend to the horses."

Elsa told Ned to use anything he may need in the barn. Upon his returning to the house, he found Elsa and Lizza had made the bedding ready.

Elsa then said, "Now rest children and we will talk more tomorrow about what you can expect and where you can go. Sleep well." Elsa went to her room for the night and shut the door. The small house was soon asleep.

Chapter 3

New Horizons

The morning came all too early. The travelers were awakened by the noise of the shoes of Elsa and the cool air from the front door as she exited. It was still a little dark as Ned stood to look out the window. Elsa was walking to the main road. She took down her flag from the branch and returned to the house. Ned and Lizza greeted her when she returned.

Elsa, in her jovial voice, said, "Ah! Good morning children, and how did you sleep? Good, yes?"

"Yes," they said in unison.

Elsa said, "Let's get some food in your bellies and we will plan the day and our next move!"

Breakfast of biscuits and gravy, coffee and some canned peaches was most satisfying.

Lizza, started to question Elsa as to there being a way in which she could stay in Virginia. Possibly, with forged papers that she had heard tell about on the plantations, ones that would confirm her a free slave.

Elsa exclaimed, "Why child? Why stay in Virginia?" What she did not know was that Lizza and Ned quietly talked before falling asleep the previous night and swore to stay close to each other if possible. Ned was compelled to stay in Virginia and Lizza would not leave Virginia without her new love. No matter the peril she might come into. Each was afraid they might not see one another again if Lizza continued north.

Elsa thought a bit while they looked upon her. Finally, she smiled that now familiar grin and said, "There was a man I knew in Richmond who owned a hattery. I am not sure he is still there. He was once mightily involved in the railway and the cause, but it's been three years since I last spoke with him or heard from him. His name is Frankie Porter. The establishment is called Porter's Hattery.

Lizza and Ned looked to one another. Ned spoke up, "Then I shall go to Richmond to find Frankie Porter. I'll go immediately. Elsa, can Lizza stay with you until I can find this Porter fellow and see if he can help?"

Elsa quickly responded, "As sure as spring will come, this child will be safe with me." She moved to Lizza and put her arm around her waist. "Besides, Ned, she will be great company."

Excited, Ned said, "Good, I will need to make Jake ready to travel! Is it also permissible for me to leave Belle in your care?"

Elsa offered, "She, too, will be safe with me. A good plow horse I know of and how to care for."

After Jake was ready and Belle was checked over, Ned returned to the house.

Elsa said strongly, "Now listen carefully, Ned. Upon finding Mr. Porter, it's extremely important, when greetings are over, that you ask him when the next train leaves north. He will say how many passengers and what's your destination. You must say, one to Buffalo. He will then know you are safe. He will take you aside and ask your needs."

"I got it, Elsa," Ned said. "Now, I must fly!"

"Fly then! I have work out back while you two say your goodbyes," Elsa said, as she left the room.

Lizza and Ned walked out the front door and up to Jake, who stood there quietly chewing and rolling his bit around. As they stood facing each other, they both searched each other's eyes and face.

Lizza spoke with a broken, sad voice. "Now you be safe, Ned. I will wait for word from you! I will pray, as never before, for your safety and return with good news."

The new lovers moved into one another and held each other, not wanting to pull away.

It was Ned's turn to speak up as he pushed away slightly and gazed into her eyes. Then he bent and kissed her, lingering softly, finally with resolve.

Then Ned said, "I must go,"

They hugged once more, then Ned swung up onto Jake and winked at Lizza. He reigned Jake 180 degrees and broke into a lope down to the main road.

Chapter 4

The Help of a New Friend

The town of Clarkston, Virginia, was 40 miles northeast of Richmond. Seeing that the day had already begun, Ned would have to sleep under the stars, but he would go as far as Jake would take him without straining him. It would be an easy ride into Richmond the next day and early enough to find Mr. Porter. And, if at all possible, get the results he and Lizza so desperately wanted. The first day out, Ned would cross the Mattaponi and Pamunkey Rivers and pass through the towns of Dunkirk and Aylett. In these two towns, he could water Jake.

As Ned disappeared down the road, a very sad Lizza walked around to the back of the house to find Elsa. She was busy hanging some wash.

"So my dear," Elsa started in, "you love him very much, don't you?"

Lizza cast her eyes to the ground. "Don't be shy now dear child, no need to be ashamed," Elsa said softly.

"Yes ma'am, I do, I do," Lizza responded.

"And he loves you, Lizza. It is plain as day," said Elsa.

Lizza smiled and said, "He touches my heart like no other."

"Yes, my dear," Elsa continued, "The right man will do that. Mr. Wildermuth did mine."

Showing some fear, Lizza asked, "Elsa what will we do if I cannot get the documents?"

Elsa positively responded, "It is best not to think that way, Lizza. If the time does come, then we will go another road. We will find a way, trust me child." At that, Lizza reached into the basket of clothes and helped finish the hangings to dry.

Ned had ridden until he lost daylight and then bedded down for the night in a small, secluded spot beside the road.

The next morning, Ned arose with the sun, readied Jake and continued toward Richmond. He passed the towns of Old Church and Mechanicsville. It was all good road now. He was on the Mechanicsville Turnpike, a straight shot into Richmond and only had a few more miles to go.

The Chickahominy River was now to his back. He entered Richmond by way of Shockoe Valley and Butcher Town. Shockoe Valley was an area just east of the center of Richmond that ran along the James River. Butcher Town was just that, the part of town that supplied meat to Richmond, the butchering of hogs and cattle and all the smells that come with the process.

Richmond was like that of an ancient Rome. It had seven hills. The city sat looking down upon the rapids that the James River created. Richmond was a formidable citadel, hills on all sides and all points of the compass.

As Ned came to Broadway Street and got his bearings, he headed down the street and then turned right towards the canal.

There it was! As he stood in front of the building, he read the sign. Sure enough it read, Porter's Hattery. He looked up and down the street before going inside.

After entering, he saw that the clerk behind the counter was buried in some ledger books. When it was clear the clerk was too busy to greet him, Ned spoke, "Excuse me, sir, could you tell me where and when to find Mr. Porter?"

The clerk, with his head still in his books, told Ned, "Mr. Porter will be back in about 40 minutes." He thanked him and told him he would return at that time. He turned, went out to the street and up to see Jake. He ran his hand over his stud. Finding no bumps or heat, he felt satisfied as to Jake's wellness.

Elsa and Lizza had been busy with some daily chores. Lizza was sweeping the main room when Elsa came out of the kitchen and said, "Quickly child, not a word, we have not a second to waste. Do not question me, Lizza." With that she firmly took the girl's arm and simply said, "COME!"

In the kitchen, she pulled the table and rug under it to one side and Lizza saw a trap door. Elsa swiftly lifted the door and pointed, "Down there, and not a word!" Lizza saw the urgency in Elsa's face and hurriedly crawled down into the darkness. She was shaking as she looked up at Elsa. Elsa's eyes briefly gave her the message, "It's ok; I'm here, look." Down came the door and the rug and table were dragged back into place at the very moment a knock came at the door.

Elsa had spied a twosome on horseback and quickly assessed who they were and what they wanted. She opened the door with the barrel of her long gun. She followed with a stern, "What is it you want?" The two men were taken back with the greeting of Elsa's gun. "Look here," Elsa continued, "I live here with my man who is due to return shortly. I know not of either of you."

The short fat stranger spoke first and was clearly nervous. "Ma'am, we're from down Gloucester way. We work for Mr. Foster, a very important man he is. He had a slave girl run away. One he paid handsomely for and we are charged with returning her. We wonder if you might have seen her or heard tell of her. We believe she is with someone on horseback."

Elsa responded, "No! No! I haven't, sonny. I keep to myself, as does my husband. We have lived here that way for decades and much prefer it that way."

Lizza could hear voices, but could not make out what they were saying. As the second stranger spoke up, Lizza immediately began to shake uncontrollably. She knew that gravelly voice. In her mind, she could see his scarred face and toothless sneer.

The overseer said, "May we come in, Ma'am? It's been a long ride." All the while, he was trying to look past Elsa into the house.

Elsa quickly responded, "No, you cannot! My husband is not home as I said. I will bring you some coffee or you may use the well for you and your horses. Then, I will ask you to move on."

The overseer said, "No coffee, ma'am. We will just get some water. Oh, and by the way, Mr. Foster is paying a tidy sum for the slave's return; so, if you see or hear tell of her, send word. It looks as if you could use a few extra dollars."

Elsa stayed in the door until the two had their fill at the well. Only after they had reached the main road did she release the hammer on her long gun. She closed the door and went to the front window before making her way to the kitchen window, which gave a clear view to the road.

"Lizza," Elsa said, "Knock if you are okay." Elsa heard one rap under the floor boards. "Good! Okay, child, now listen. You must stay there until dark and then I will bring you up. Those men were looking for you. Do you understand?" Elsa heard another rap. "Good! They are Mr. Foster's men. We must be wary for they may come back and you cannot leave the house for a few days. Do you understand?" Elsa heard yet another knock. She went on, "They may go to Clarkston and ask there about of you and of me. They will find no answers to help them for they are mostly sympathizers. If they do go to Clarkston, someone will give me news. It's been long standing in these parts about these things. So, you understand child?" Elsa heard yet another rap. "Good!"

In Richmond, Ned, having left the hat shop, was walking Jake northwest, down Main Street, three streets below Broadway. The city seemed to have doubled in people since he had come to Richmond with his father when he was but 10 years old. As he neared the center of Richmond, there were men everywhere, arms in slings, men bandaged on every body part, men on crutches, men with every conceivable injury, men sitting on benches outside buildings, sitting on curbs, even the open windows of hotels had men hanging out of them, yelling to women walking on the sidewalks.

The city had a stench to it. A mixture of sweat, hog slop and manure laced with faint hints of metallic. What he did not know, was that Richmond was busting at the seams with the stream of soldiers both injured and recruits. Hospitals were filled beyond capacity from the very battle that killed his father. Hotels were becoming hospitals along with homes. Any other building that had a roof made it viable hospital material.

Richmond was filled with hawkers and items of every description, as well, prostitutes who openly strutted their offers. On most street corners, manure was piled several feet high and wide waiting to be picked up. The Tredegar Iron Works, that had no equal in the South, was working several shifts seven days a week by hiring free blacks and German immigrants to make cannons, railroad rails and rifles. Richmond also had 52 mills and tobacco manufacturers.

Ned passed by the Ballard House and Exchange, hotels that had a covered walkway over the street to connect the two. The buildings sat between Main Street and Franklin. These two establishments were also filled with wounded Bull Run soldiers. For the noble city of Richmond, Virginia, even with history harking back to Washington and 100 years before, there was little sign of nobility now. It presently seemed to be the muck pushed to the end of a hog house. Yet it was to get worse.

Ned finally made his way back to the hat shop after an hour of walking the streets with Jake in tow. Upon entering the hat shop, he spied a man holding a cane with grey hair and beard, kindly face, and quite plump.

The man spoke up, "How may I serve you young man? Welcome to Porter's Hattery, finest establishment in the South."

"Mr. Porter?" Ned asked.

"Why yes, I am owner and operator, and sometimes clerk. A man of many hats." Mr. Porter chuckled at his own pun.

"Mr. Porter, sir," Ned cut to the chase. "I was wondering when the next train leaves north."

The portly old man's face became gravened. He looked around instinctively and slowly replied, "How many passengers, and destination?"

Ned quickly replied, "One to Buffalo."

Instantly, Mr. Porter said, "Right this way young man."

They disappeared behind a counter and then through a curtain that led to a back office leaving the clerk still as he was over an hour ago, with his head buried in his ledger.

Mr. Porter shut the door to his office and looked at Ned. "Who has sent you, sir?"

"My name is Ned McDonald. I am from down Gloucester way. As to who has sent me, that would be Elsa Wildermuth."

Instantly, Mr. Porter smiled with the whitest of teeth Ned had ever seen and said, "Ah! Elsa! And how fairs the Fraulein? You know if she was not married..." and at that Mr. Porter stopped short, smiled and said, "I was most fond of the dear woman."

Ned told him of Elsa losing her husband in death.

"I am sorry to hear of this," responded Mr. Porter.

Ned continued, "But she is well!" He then broke into how Lizza and he had happened upon Elsa, which turned into a rather lengthy story.

Mr. Porter understood the situation and asked, "Well, Mr. McDonald, how is it I can help you where Elsa cannot?"

Ned inquired about the possibility of securing papers for Lizza. Mr. Porter paused to think for a moment. Then smiled. "It's been some time since I've done such a thing, but I may still have contacts at the State House. It will take several weeks."

Ned nodded as Mr. Porter continued. "You know, Ned, Richmond already has over 2000 freed slaves. So, she will have to secure work, and with a bounty on her, she will have to have an employer who is a sympathizer. This will be necessary in order to help conceal her identity. I have someone in mind at this very moment. This will all take some time, perhaps, as I said, a fortnight or so."

Ned nodded and asked, "Then shall I come to you or will you reach out to us at Elsa's if all or in part can be had?"

Mr. Porter responded, "No! You come to me in two weeks' time and bring Lizza with you."

Ned eagerly replied, "I will be here, sir!"

Mr. Porter told Ned, "I'm not 100% sure, but I believe I can pull everything together. Now go tell Lizza and I'll see you here, two weeks from today."

Ned stuck out his hand and firmly shook Mr. Porter's hand and said, "Thank you, sir, thank you!"

As Ned turned to leave, Mr. Porter said, "Please give my warm regards to Elsa."

"I shall," Ned said as he went through the door.

Chapter 5

Working for the Next Opportunity

Ned mounted Jake and headed toward the recruitment station. He had seen it earlier as he walked the Richmond streets. As he tied Jake off in front of the office and started in, he paused and stepped back to think a moment, then sat on the street curb next to Jake. He knew he and Jake had an original purpose, but his new purpose now had to include Lizza.

In walking and talking with wounded soldiers earlier, he spoke with a man who was a scout separately attached to a brigade, and after much thought realized this could serve both ends. It would leave him flexibility to get to Lizza if necessary and not be charged with desertion. His superb horsemanship and Jake's speed and stamina could serve the post well. Ok, he thought. I can do this! Ned got up and went inside.

As he came out of the recruitment office, after much finagling and diplomacy, he had secured a letter of introduction as to his use as a scout at the discretion of General J.E.B. Stuart. Ned now needed to secure gear before heading back to the Clarkston area, including a pistol, carbine rifle, short saber, a new saddle, a saddle blanket, bit with headstall, saddlebags, an oil cloth and a coat. The money from the farm was most handy. Well spent, he thought to himself.

After a great deal of trouble, he found a place to stay and livery to keep Jake for the night.

At daybreak, Ned mounted Jake, all regaled in his new tack, and headed toward Clarkston and his love.

It felt good to get out of the city into the fresh air and countryside, away from the heaviness of Richmond and masses of people. He was not use to so many people.

He passed again through Mechanicsville, and after a mile outside the town, he came upon two riders who hailed him to stop. He quickly sized up the strangers as of questionable character. The toothless one asked Ned if he had seen a slave girl that fit the description he gave and told him that she might even be riding on a horse with someone else.

"Not on my travels," said Ned. As Ned was speaking, he noticed that the one man kept looking at him strangely.

Finally, the toothless one said, "Sir, aren't you Clark McDonald's boy from Gloucester?"

"Proudly, I can say that I am," replied Ned.

"Then why are you in these parts, McDonald," the man asked.

Ned quickly, with lie and truth, told the pair, "I've joined the army and am headed to see my Auntie before reporting to my regiment." Now he turned the tables and asked, "What are you boys going to do, join up also? Every man is needed you know."

One responded, "Nah, we have a cause of our own, slavin's our job."

"Well, boys, I'm off," Ned said. "Good luck to you." Over his shoulder, he said, "If you're going into Richmond, it's filled on every street.

"We are going anyway," they said. Ned headed towards Gloucester now and sealed his dupe with, "Hope you find the nigger girl." He squeezed Jake's flanks and headed out, never looking back as to create suspicion. Ned thought that they would whore and drink in Richmond, then in a stupor, head back to Gloucester. After believing he was out of site of the slaver's, he headed back toward Clarkston.

When Ned arrived, Elsa had company, Lynn Brown of Clarkston. She had come to see Elsa, and spent the day visiting and telling of the two slave hunters asking folk in the area about Lizza. They were bandying a sizable amount for Lizza's return or information about her whereabouts. After getting nowhere, they headed out toward Richmond.

Lizza had quickly taken to Lynn, and she to Lizza. The three spent the day talking about slavery and the future for white and black folk alike. They agreed that it should go, but how without bloodshed? The southern states didn't want to be told by the North how they should behave and plant their crops and for what price. To the three, it was all so convoluted.

The two weeks at Elsa's went quickly. Ned and Lizza prepared to leave. During those 14 days, Ned had taught Lizza some basic riding skills, so she could ride Belle to Richmond. She took to it like a natural. Belle, although a draft horse, was sure footed with a smooth gait no matter the pace. She was the horse that Ned's mom preferred to ride.

The day was a warm one for fall. Elsa had packed some food for them, her new close friends. "Now," Elsa said, "Don't forget an old woman, you two."

"Oh, Elsa!" said Lizza. "How could I ever forget you? I could not, and we will see each other again. I'm sure of it."

Ned followed up with, "Most likely sooner than we all think," not knowing what that meant. He felt compelled to say it, but why?

Elsa was there to see them off. "Okay children, now go! God speed! You know how to get letters to me," she said.

"We will Elsa," Ned came back. He then gave Lizza a leg up on Belle and swung up on Jake.

"Go," said Elsa, "before I rain tears."

Ned and Lizza trotted off.

The next afternoon, the two came into Richmond. The trip was uneventful so far. They had passed a few rebel soldiers, but nothing of any account.

Ned walked in the Hattery followed by Lizza. Since leaving Elsa's, the two had acted as if Lizza belonged to Ned. Mr. Porter was behind the counter. His clerk, still with his head in the ledger of two weeks ago had, again, never looked up.

Mr. Porter quickly recognized Ned and, the store being empty of patrons, immediately spoke, "Ah! Ned, my boy! I was hoping to see you very soon. Then, turning toward Lizza, said, "and you must be the one who this lad is smitten with."

Quietly, Lizza said, "Yes, sir!"

"Well," responded Mr. Porter, "You are everything Ned said you were. Now! Come into the back so we can talk, so I can tell you what I have gotten accomplished."

Mr. Porter shut the door to his office, sat at his desk and said, "Sit; sit, please."

Ned and Lizza sat down and watched Porter open the sack next to his desk. He pulled out what looked to Ned as documents. Mr. Porter straightened the papers and went over each one. When he seemed satisfied, he looked at Lizza. and commented, "My dear lady, these here documents declare you a free Negro! Now, they are as good as any free Negro's, unless challenged by the previous owner. If anyone besides that should challenge you on the matter, they will be more than satisfied. Do you understand?"

"Yes, sir!" Lizza said smiling.

Mr. Porter cautioned, "You still must be careful."

Then, Mr. Porter looked at Ned. "I have also secured an employer for Lizza."

Switching his gaze back to Lizza. "My dear, your employer will be Elizabeth Van Lew. She is a very prominent woman and has a family that has been long in Richmond. She is a hardline Yankee sympathizer," he explained to Ned.

"Lizza, she wishes you to be a housekeeper. You will have your own room and time to yourself," Mr. Porter said. She listened as Porter continued, all the while, her eyes were filling with tears of joy. "Now Lizza, Mrs. Van Lew is a kindly woman. She does want to meet and talk with you, and I related to her that if you were as Ned described to me, I was sure there would be no hitch. She will discuss your duties and pay with you. Now, Lizza, remember, if at any time you don't feel comfortable with anything about the arrangement, you can decline the job. However, I feel after you meet Elizabeth you will take to her very quickly."

Ned spoke up first, "Mr. Porter may we go see Mrs. Van Lew today?"

Mr. Porter responded, "But of course! The three of us will leave for her mansion immediately. It is a beautiful place, towering shade trees, gardens and a pillared portico. It sits on Church Hill and is quite possibly the finest home in Virginia."

Mr. Porter handed the documents to Lizza. She touched them carefully, lifting each page as if they were fragile relics of centuries past. Ned leaned over and gazed at them. He reached out to touch Lizza's arm and she turned to look at him, her lip quivering.

Ned smiled and lovingly said, "A new life begins."

With tears tracing her cheeks, she nodded her head, all the while trying not to burst into full tears.

Mr. Porter urgently said, "Let's go, no time to waste!"

In less than twenty minutes, Mr. Porter, with Ned and Lizza in tow, knocked at the large oak doors of the Church Hill mansion.

As the door opened, a tall thin black man in, at least, his sixties said, "Yes, Mr. Porter, good day. I will announce you to Mrs. Van Lew. Please come in; it will be but a few minutes."

Little time had passed when a willow of a wisp of a woman came floating, as it seemed, down the wide sweeping staircase. She had fine, almost edgy, features to her face. Halfway down the stairs she smiled, "Ah! Mr. Porter. How good it is to see you again." She walked directly up to Lizza. "I surmise you are Lizza," she said, grasping her hands in hers. "You, my dear, are more precious than described." She then looked directly at Ned. "And you are Ned McDonald. Welcome to my home."

She took a few steps back, still standing almost too erect and proper, and said, "Now, shall we get down to why we are here?" She looked to Ned and Mr. Porter. "If you two will follow Tom here and make yourselves comfortable, young Lizza and I will go and have a chat to get acquainted. Come, my dear"" she said reaching for Lizza's hand. The two disappeared down a long hallway.

After almost two hours, Elizabeth and Lizza returned. Ned began immediately searching Lizza's eyes for some hint of revelation of their long talk. Elizabeth, with her arm around Lizza's waist smiled and announced, "I am satisfied with all things in and about Lizza. She has accepted my terms of employment." Lizza was beaming. Mrs. Van Lew looked at Ned. "I am adamantly against what you believe young Ned, however, I am making concessions for one reason and only one. I can see most clearly the love between the two of you. I do hope that your choice, Ned, does not thwart that which your heart desires in Lizza and her in you."

At that Ned boldly told Elizabeth, and perhaps for the first time, voiced his convictions. "I love Lizza dearly and I do what I am compelled to do not only for my father and his memory, but for Virginia and the choice it has made. It is my home I know no other. Where Virginia goes, I go. If it were different here, I would go. The lunacy of these days is not to be reckoned, at least not now. Each man must choose. I have chosen, right or wrong. Yes, I found my love in Lizza. It would seem to many, how could both be had? I know not if this is even possible, but as sure as I stand before you, Mrs. Van Lew, I will try!"

The staunch Federalist looked upon the young man before her, and although in complete opposition, she saw one thing, a most salient conviction in this man on both fronts.

Mrs. Van Lew said, "I pray, Ned, you may stand the rigors of that bode in the years to come."

The last night together, Ned and Lizza walked the Van Lew's grounds. The morning would see Ned off to a future that no one could predict. The South's struggles had just begun. The lovers had, with Elizabeth's help, arranged correspondence protocol, set up to not only protect Ned and Lizza, but also Elizabeth. For a known Federalist protecting a runaway slave and allowing a Confederate combatant to write her residence, all took intrigue no one needed to see or turn ugly.

Lizza showed Ned her own room, a first in her life, and told him of her duties. There were so many first-times for Lizza, she felt pleasantly overwhelmed. That night the two voiced their love and commitment to one another, and, although Lizza harbored doom for her lover, she voiced not a word to her knight.

Ned stayed the night at the Van Lew's. That night brought him the anxiety of leaving Lizza for who knew how long. It was painful to think of. Letters would have to suffice; they would have to quell the longing he would feel for her.

The morn had come; the long hugs and kisses were over. Ned took Lizza's hand. "I must go, Lizza," he said. She spoke not a word; just nodded her head in agreement. Ned said, "Look for my first letter and then write to me." There were no words. She could only nod her head in response.

Ned swung up on to Jake and adjusted his wide brimmed hat, looked at Lizza, winked, and said, "I love you! Don't ever doubt it," and reined Jake down the lane back to Richmond's craziness.

Only after Ned and Jake had disappeared out of sight, did Lizza begin to sob uncontrollably and fell to her knees with her hands in her face. Even in all the trials and tribulations of her years before, she had never felt worse. Her heart was breaking.

Elizabeth came down the steps of the portico, "Now, now, child, you must trust God that He will return him to you. God will sustain, you shall see."

Chapter 6

A New Adventure Begins

Ned headed for Mr. Porter's. He had paid for Ned, along with Jake, to take a train to get north as soon as possible. The destination was Centreville, Virginia. There was no promise in the letter; it was just an introduction. General J.E.B. Stuart would have to decide for himself if Ned would suit his needs for a scout. As he headed north he reasoned, a good horse with speed, stamina and horsemanship, such as Ned had, surely could be used. Mostly, though, his thoughts were of Lizza.

His thoughts also replayed what Mrs. Van Lew, a Virginian just like him, had said and how they could think so differently. What he did not know was that Mrs. Van Lew would become a prolific spy for the North, while in no way endangering the two lovers. Elizabeth would be personally thanked by U.S. Grant, General of all northern forces by the end of the war.

During the last few miles to Centreville, Ned pulled out his letter of introduction to Brigadier General Stuart. He knew he had to somehow impress Stuart straight away. He might not get another chance. He also realized there was no guarantee to be used in this capacity, so he prepared himself to be used as they saw fit.

Ned's train pulled into Centreville and he went to Jake on the double. He quickly and thoroughly went over Jake, checking for injuries he may have sustained on the train ride. Ned's stud was as sound as ever.

After tacking Jake, he asked about finding the General's headquarters. Around Centerville, there were buildings going up everywhere, storages for food, fodder, ammo, cannons, and equipment of all kinds. After getting directions, Ned left to find General Stuart's headquarters with the letter of introduction in hand in case his intent was challenged. He approached a guard outside the headquarters and presented his letter. The Sergeant disappeared inside the tent and in a few minutes emerged with a captain who said he was the assistant to the General, Captain Bryan.

Captain Bryan said, "This letter says here that you are a possible scout?" Even as he questioned Ned, he was sizing Ned's 6'2", 200-pound frame.

"Yes, sir", Ned replied in his best marshal voice.

"And that chestnut stud is yours?" the Captain asked.

"Yes, sir, he is," said Ned.

"He looks to be well-bred and looks fast," the Captain responded.

Ned said proudly, "Never been beaten!"

The Captain then challenged Ned, "Well now, suppose, you show me some of the skills you and your stud have."

At that very moment, from down the lane leading to headquarters, came the flashiest officer on either side of the war. From the ostrich feather in his hat to his bright yellow shirt, knee high leather boots and his bright red beard, General Stuart played the part he believed he was born for to the hilt. He was, perhaps, the finest cavalry officer to ever mount a horse in the history of the United States. The General dismounted.

The Captain said, "Good afternoon, General, you are just in time. This possible scout sent from Richmond was just about to show his skills."

The General looked at Ned inquisitively and said, "Well, son, by all means continue. My interest is piqued."

Ned mounted Jake, leaned toward to his ear and spoke in soft tones. Jake's ear instinctively turned to the side to take in Ned's words. Ned had said, "Jake, steady big man. We're on stage. Give me your best." Jake seemed to understand.

Then Ned ever so slightly pulled on the reins while lifting, not an inch, upward. Up Jake went on to his hind legs, striking out in the air with his front legs, then down came the fourteen-hundred-pound stud. Ned cued Jake once more and Jake crossed his legs one over the other and then side passed for twenty feet and back. Jake didn't miss a beat. Then after heading into a lope from standing still, they broke into a full gallop, headed toward a four-rail fence and cleared it easily. Then they turned around and came back for a second go. Once again, they cleared it easily.

By now the entire headquarters of staff officers was watching. Ned and Jake raced down a sandy section of road. By using only cues, Ned asked for Jake to drop on his hocks and slide for twenty-five feet before coming to a stop. The duo was not through yet, though. Jake stood while Ned spun in place, pivoting off Jake's hindquarters, three hundred sixty degrees. Then he snap-turned back the other direction, three hundred and sixty degrees, thus finishing their skills.

"Down big man," Ned said. Jake stretched one leg fully out and bent the other as if to bow. Ned tipped his hat and dismounted, patted Jake's neck simply saying, "Up boy!" Up the big stud came. Jake coolly chewed on and rolled around the bit in his mouth as if nothing had just happened.

Above the hoots and cheers, the General could be heard saying, "Bravo!" clapping wildly.

Then the Captain handed the General the letter of introduction. After giving the letter a quick once over, he looked up and said to Ned, "Young man, I dare say, I have not seen a more skillful display of a horse and horsemanship." He motioned to the Captain and said sternly, "Captain, find suitable lodging for our new scout and his fine stud, and see that they get settled. He will dine in my tent tonight. Do you understand, Captain?"

"Yes sir, General, sir," snapped the Captain.

"He and I will discuss horses and his future with this brigade." The General then turned to Ned and smiled, and then at Jake, before snapping around and disappearing with a strut into headquarters.

In the weeks and months that followed, all seemed to melt into a blur. Ned and Jake took quickly to a marshal lifestyle and the life a scout lived. He wrote letter-after-letter to Lizza, who replied as soon as one arrived. They wrote of their love and concern for one another.

Lizza spoke often of the kindness of her benefactor and the books she enjoyed on limitless subjects from Mrs. Van Lew's vast library. The new world she had stepped into had opened her eyes to so many ideas and subjects. She truly appreciated the time to herself to care about nothing at all if she so chose and, of course, the time to think about her love, falling asleep each night with Ned on her mind. She spoke of long conversations with Elizabeth, which opened her mind further. She was as happy as she could be without Ned beside her.

After some time, Ned had found a four-day period and made the trip to Richmond to see Lizza. It was fleeting, to be sure, but the visit reaffirmed the love and commitment they carried in their hearts. Their bond was stronger than ever. This time ended much too quickly for the two and, once again, the scene of leaving played out as before as Ned left Mrs. Van Lew to console a sobbing Lizza.

Chapter 7

Ned and Jake in War

The months passed by, it seemed, so fast. Ned had been to Richmond, joined in service, found himself attached to the 1st Virginia Cavalry under General Stuart and, from October 1861 to the spring of 1862, Ned and Jake had come to meticulously hone their skills.

Ned was mostly assigned to vedette duty as a lone rider or in pairs scouting out further than the picket lines. He had come to love the dangerous duty and thrived on its intrigue; it suited his growing restless nature. In a year, Ned and Jake's skills and abilities quickly became legendary within the Cavalry and the army. His daring, boldness and audacity in gaining information and assessing correctly what he had observed were very advantageous.

The summer of 1862 saw the Battle of Seven Pines, Battle of Mechanicsville, Battle of Gainesville, and the slaughter of Malvern Hill. Ned had seen action in all the battles around Richmond, which saw the Union leave the area with its tail between its legs. The action did not stop at this. The following September of 1862 found Ned in the bloodiest day of the Civil War, Antietam or Sharpsburg.

Robert E. Lee had seen fit, while being outmanned and with the peninsula so ravaged, to take the war north and into Union territory. So, into Maryland, the rebel army crossed the Potomac River. After three-days of struggles, standoffs and draws, with both sides claiming some measure of victory, General Lee pulled the rebel army back down into Virginia, shoring up defenses behind Fredericksburg on the south side of the Rappahannock River.

Then, by December 1, 1862, Lee found good ground and his entire army, entrenched, was waiting for the northern General Burnside to make a move. And so it came on December 13. The battle reached its full crescendo with absolute slaughter, seven thousand Union casualties. Union men were simply murdered even though Lee was out-numbered two-to-one. Lee, ever so wily, continued to deduce his counterparts' thoughts. So, he claimed victory and both armies went into shut down mode for the winter, all the while staring at each other through freezing weather, snow sleet and rain.

With spring, both armies would begin again, but, neither side could ever imagine the ferocity only hell could unleash.

Ned had been battle-tested many times while mounted on Jake, who never flinched no matter the heat of rifle fire or cannons booming. Sometimes it seemed like the heavens were falling. Jake had always carried Ned to safety. It appeared at times that they were absolutely as one, thinking and anticipating together.

January of 1863, however, brought into the war an era of fighting the likes that the Civil War had not seen before. There existed in the rank and file of the 1st Cavalry a man even more skilled in the art of scouting than Ned McDonald. His name was John Singleton Mosby, also a Virginian, and before the war, a lawyer in western Virginia. Ned and Mosby had gone on countless vedettes together and complimented each other perfectly.

Mosby was held in high regard by General Stuart. So, when he, also a restless spirit, approached Stuart of forming an independent squad to harass and gather information in, around and behind the Union army. General Stuart, with his great audacity, saw huge merit in such a plan and allowed Mosby to hand pick his own squad. He chose nine men, all from Virginia and the 1st Cavalry. Ned was selected first.

Mosby could count on Ned for cool resolve for a mission, and no matter how hot or uncomfortable it might get, Ned and Jake would go on. In a fortnight, the squad had grown to 15 men, all Virginians, except three, who were from Maryland. Ned's journey, his real role in all this madness, would become clear now. The time had come that

Ned was to be tested, above all, of who he had thought he was and the way he was raised by his mom and dad.

Around mid-January, the small band of horseman left the main body of the Confederate army and operated independently. They entered into guerrilla warfare. On to Fauquier County they headed, the northern neck of Virginia to Rector's Crossroads, nestled in the Piedmont in the shadow of the Blue Ridge Mountains. It would be in this area that the band of rangers would be based and search out Federal companies and regiments. The small band of men, Mosby's Rangers, found shelter and lay low between raids in the homes of sympathizers from Upperville to Middleburg, an area of about ten square miles. It is here that they waited until Mosby reached out to them, in part or all of them at once.

One important family of sympathizers was the Taylors. Winston, his wife, Jean, and two daughters, Molly and Sarah. Winston was confined to a wheel chair. His sixty years showed terribly on his face and body. Jean, 50 years old, was energetic and ran the household, and the two daughters, Molly, 21, and Sarah, 14, helped take care of the father. The family was secure in money from past generations.

Ned liked the Taylors. They took to him. They had lived in this area of Virginia for over 100 years. Blakely Grove was east of their house and only five miles from the crest of the Blue Ridge Mountains, the land rich in bounty.

When not on raids, Ned found his down time filled with helping the Taylors in work repairing fencing, barn chores, and whatever else that was necessary. Ned took care of it for keeping him in room and board. Money Ned gained on spoils, as the Rangers called it, was given to the Taylors. The Taylors' had left to fight and, in a short time of their leaving, were killed.

Molly was quickly attracted to Ned. She was a typical southern belle in speech and mannerism. At 5'5" tall and 125 pounds, she was used to getting what she wanted. Molly had come home recently to live. Her husband had died at Bull Run, the same battle as Ned's father. She was the mirror image of her mother, with her beautiful face and red hair. She used all the gifts God gave her to get what she wanted. As beautiful as Molly was, Ned was not swayed or tempted. His love was in Richmond. Molly, however, had thoughts of a different kind. And that was that.

Chapter 8

Success and Disaster

As spring came on, Mosby and the Rangers were most active in raids, not only on the east side of the Blue Ridge Mountains, but over the mountains into the Blue Valley. The Blue Valley had become the major artery for moving men and supplies for both the North and the South alike. The area was ripe for food, for men, and horses. It was ebbing and flowing in control of both armies.

Ned and Jake were returning from one such raid. The band of seven had been south on the border of Fauquier and Rappahannock Counties. There they had harassed a regiment for two days that had encamped and were rousting residents of their food and horses, and gaining information. Finally, Mosby's band left with a small booty of five horses and $5,000 of Union money, a nice reward for only seven on this raid.

The band headed north and had slipped between the Thumb River and Rattlesnake Mountain. They passed the most northern tip of Rattlesnake and the south end of Cobbler Mountain, and then picked up the pace to reach Salem before dark. Then the seven split up to go to their individual hideaways until the next time.

Just outside Salem, on the way to the Taylors, Ned had come to an elbow in the road, passing a copse of trees. He could see the road stretching before him and some 100 yards away, a dozen or so Yankee horsemen coming his direction. As he looked at them, he could tell they had seen him also. There would be no getting past them with a contrived ploy. His identity had been ousted over a month ago. He had to run. Thankfully, he had come to believe that with Jake under him, he could get out of trouble faster than he got into it. This was truly a test of that theory!

Ned swung Jake around 180 degrees, gigged his stud's sides, and yelled, "NOW JAKE!" The horse dropped into the earth tearing at it with his hooves, pulling the ground behind him. He unfurled his long legs as the men gave chase. Ned headed down a turn in the road to a bridge over the Cromwell's Run and headed toward the small mountains that stretched north and south for about 10 miles.

Ned remembered a narrow logging road over the mountain. Its entrance was somewhat hidden. He headed to it. If they still were coming, he would continue toward the Bull Run Mountains. He flattened against Jake's neck.

He was covering 28 feet with each stride as Ned was urging his friend, "Fly big man."

Jake's ears pinned back flat showing Ned he was all about business. Ned's stirrups were thrust to the rear and his head was rising and falling with the motion of the mighty animal beneath him. By then Ned had given him every inch of the reins so he could run flat out. This horse was born to run! His nose was inhaling huge volumes of air and after one mile Jake had not slackened on stride or hoof turnovers.

Ned could see a lone horseman about 1/4 mile behind who had not quit hunting him. He slowed Jake down, so as not to pass the hidden entrance to the old timber road. And he said to himself, "There it is, Jake, let's go!"

Up the winding steep road Jake hauled Ned. Even after such a supreme effort already given in this chase, Jake still pulled the two up the mountain. As they neared the crest, Ned pulled Jake to a stop and dismounted. He strained to see through the dark to catch a glimpse of the other horse and rider. He listened carefully to hear the oncoming horse, but could not quite make out any sounds. Jake's heavy breathing was masking any other sound. Finally, there it was; the sounds of the rider urging his mount up the steep road. Somehow the solider had found Ned's path. He decided to end the chase right here and now. After all, it was but one rider. He ran to Jake and rode further to the crest, where he pulled Jake some distance off the road into a clump of trees and climbed the boulder. It was from here he would ambush his pursuer.

Ned sat low on his haunches straining to hear. It seemed much too long. He almost stood to see where they were. Maybe the solider had called off the chase, but once again he heard the heavy breathing of the horse coming with a great deal of effort. He tensed every fiber in his legs.

The moment he saw the horse's head, he sprang fully laid out, smashing into the rider. They fell into a heap on the ground. Ned began slamming his fists into either side of the soldier's head. Each swing landed true and with power. He realized after five or six blows that the man went limp. He pulled his revolver out and stood up. The solider was not moving, so he leaned down to turn him over in order to see his face, all the while keeping the gun pointed at him.

The epaulets on the soldier's coat told Ned that he was an officer, a captain. Ned started to lean down low to tell if the man was alive or not. He couldn't make out the face in darkness. He started to feel for a pulse when the Captain reached up with both hands and grabbed for his neck. Before he had fully realized what had happened, the pistol flashed. The captain fell back now dead.

Ned had shot many men over the past months, but not this up close and personal. It shook him for several moments. He stood with the pistol loosely at his side staring at the lifeless body with a face he still could not make out. After a few minutes, he gathered himself and knelt to go through the man's pockets. He found a watch and a letter with a picture in it in the coat pocket. In the other pockets, he found tobacco, rolling papers, a cross and chain. He then rose and went to find the Captain's horse.

After some searching, Ned returned and loaded the solider and secured him to his horse. He mounted Jake, and leading the other horse, started down the eastern face of the low mountain. He could not leave this solider to bleach-his-bones on this ridge. Although an enemy, this captain was someone's son. Perhaps even a husband and father. They would want to know what happened to him.

They were headed toward the Bull Run Mountains and Hopeville, which sat on the western base. Ned had recalled an undertaker who lived there.

He pulled up Jake in front of the undertaker's business and saw a light on the second story. He knocked sharply a few times and waited. Soon, the door opened and a tall man asked, "Yes, can I help you, young man? It's getting late."

Ned responded, "Yes, I know, sir, but I have nowhere to take this dead captain. I thought it best to bring him here. I could not leave him up on the mountain," Ned said still reeling from the previous events.

The proprietor had learned not to ask too many questions. Although a dyed-in-the-wool Virginian, he had always played it down the middle. Ned offered the man money to help take care of his services.

The man answered, "Yes, that would help, young man. Now if you will help me bring in the body, so I can place him on the table."

The two struggled to get the body inside and placed it on the embalming table. Up to this point, Ned had not gotten a good look at the man's face and he didn't really want to now, but he felt compelled by some strange force. He stepped from the foot of the table and fully took in the Captain's face. He stared in disbelief. It couldn't be.

"It just can't be," Ned said aloud.

The undertaker was taken aback. "Excuse me, son?"

"No, it can't be," Ned repeated as he stepped away from the table, all the while becoming more ashen by the second.

"Do you know him, son," the undertaker asked.

"Yes sir," Ned stammered, "He's my cousin." The Captain was Ned's father's brother's oldest boy. He started to tremble. "Oh! God what have I done? Dear God, what have I done!" Hot tears coursed Ned's cheeks. He stumbled out the door to fresh air. He felt faint and sick to his stomach. He sat on the steps, trying to pull himself together.

After a great deal of time, he reached for the letter and picture he had found on his cousin. Since it was pitch dark save for the light at the window, he walked to it to see the picture more clearly. Ned saw himself from several years ago with Roger, who now lay dead inside the very window that lit the picture. In the pictures were also Ned's father and Uncle Dave. The pictures were taken when they had gone to the funeral for Ned's grandmother in Staunton. Roger was six years older than Ned. During that time, he had come to look up to his cousin. The two weeks in Staunton were a sweet memory, since he had come to know his extended family for the first time.

He was confused as to what he should do now. On one hand, Ned fully knew, that as an identified ranger and not recognized as army, if caught he could be outright killed even without a trial, especially for killing a Union solider, an officer. If he left straight away, no one would be the wiser, for he believed the undertaker would give no information. With his head reeling, Ned sat back down on the stoop, quietly praying and thinking as to what he should do.

The undertaker finally came outside and said, "I don't envy your position and I feel for your loss young man, but did you say you could help with expenses?"

Ned now knew what he should do. "Yes. Yes, sir." He reached into the saddlebags hanging from Jake, pulled out a wad of bills and handed it to the undertaker, saying, "Here, this should cover everything."

"I should think so," said the man.

Ned quietly said, "Please do your best work. I am taking him home to rest."

Ned had an unpleasant task before him, but one he could not walk away from. He must face, no matter how awful, the family of his father. Roger must be taken home. Ned's pains were etched across his face.

The man, feeling sorry for Ned, said, "Young man, I'm not a religious man, but I'll pray for you."

"Yes sir, thank you. I'm going to need all the help I can get," replied Ned gravely.

It came to Ned that he needed to write Lizza and tell her briefly of the terrible events and that she should expect him in Richmond shortly. He quickly penned the letter and asked the man if he could get it mailed. The man agreed to do it, stating that he had good connections. Satisfied, Ned said goodbye after telling him he would return in approximately three days.

Ned rode out into the dark, deep in thought, regarding the peril of getting his Union officer cousin through Union infested country. He would have to secure, along with his personal items back at the Taylors, a buckboard to carry the coffin. It was an extra-long ride to Blakely Grove, for the thoughts and anxiety that Ned felt were the most painful he had ever experienced, even greater than the loss of this mother and father.

Back in Blakely Grove and in the Taylor's home, Ned and his host family had gathered in the parlor to hear him tell them of the terrible events of the previous day. The entire family was struck with pain for what he was experiencing, for Ned had become endeared to all the family, especially to Molly, who came to Ned and wrapped her arms around him. She kissed his cheek. "My dearest Ned, I am quite sure God does not hold you in any way but love and forgiveness." The words rang hollow with Ned. The last 24 hours had numbed him.

Ned asked for and received from Molly's father the buckboard. He offered to pay him for its use, but was refused. He also wrote a short letter to Mosby, briefly telling him what had happened and that he would return if all went well. And if he should not return, that he felt honored to have known and served with him.

Ned said his goodbyes to the family as a whole in the parlor. It was only Molly who followed him out to personally see him off. Jake was already harnessed to the buckboard and was awaiting Ned.

Molly lovingly said, "Now Ned, you must write to me and keep me advised of your movements and plans. I shall worry on the verge of insaneness if you do not. You are aware of my great affection for you and although you do not feel the same for me yet, you will in time. Even dear father has hopes privately that you will someday be part of this family."

Ned could not believe what he was hearing from her, especially at a time like this. But, he had come to know Molly's forthright ways.

Ned calmly looked at her and said, "Molly you are a beautiful woman to be sure, and you deserve a good man. One will come your way one day, I am sure of it. However, I am not he."

At that Molly smiled and confidently said, "Oh Ned, one day you will come to know my words are the truth and we will make father a very happy and proud man."

Ned shook his head in disbelief. She had not heard one word he had said. He politely smiled and agreed to write the family as he could find time, for he knew his new-found friends would worry.

"Molly, I must go. I have a long way to travel." He hugged her, and she took this time to give him a passionate kiss on the cheek. Ned pushed her away strongly, yet gently, and climbed up onto the wagon seat. He released the wheel brake, snapped the reigns and urged Jake down the road.

Molly ran after them for a short way yelling out, "I'll wait for you Ned. I'll be here when you return!" She slowed to a walk and stood there in the farm road until Ned and Jake were out of sight. Molly's last words drifted in the morning wind, "You'll come back, Ned!" She turned and walked back to the house.

Ned trotted Jake along the road headed back to Hopeville. Although a saddle horse, Jake had also been schooled in a harness. His father had often used Belle and Jake in tandem in farming and Jake took to his new job with his usual level of enthusiasm. Jake had always had a perfect temperament and a good mind to please.

Ned knew he just needed to get to Richmond. He sought solace and comfort in Lizza. It had even crossed his mind in the last two days to get Lizza and go as far west as they needed to escape the madness of these later days, possibly even farther than the newly created West Virginia that had succeeded from Virginia to join the Union. So many things clouded his thinking. He needed Lizza to talk with, which he was sure of above all else.

Ned reached Hopeville without incident and loaded his cousin's coffin and fastened it down securely, as the undertaker had done with the body within the pine box. They both understood the trek before them.

Richmond, from Hopeville as the crow flies, was a 90-mile distance. However, Ned would head toward the Blue Ridge Mountains to travel south under its shadow before heading southeast. With this path, Richmond was 150-mile distance.

He could catch the central railroad at Gordonsville and go west to Staunton, but he needed to see Lizza before going there. He was undecided if he would move on west after taking his cousin home. Ned and Jake were to travel through Rappahannock, Madison, Greene counties before turning to the southeast going through Orange, Louisa, and Hanover counties before entering Richmond's Henrico County.

Ned was dressed in nondescript clothing, as was the body of Roger. The hilly country in the Piedmont of the Blue Ridge tested Jake's stamina. Ned paced him, all the while covering as much distance as he could during daylight. Each day they covered some 40 miles. On the morning of the second day, just after covering 5 miles, Ned had to lay low. He had come upon a Union regiment. By nightfall, the regiment moved out, northwest, away from Ned's path to Richmond.

The demands on Jake were heavy, although he never showed fatigue. Ned had decided to rest Jake every ten miles or so, making sure he was watered. They came upon Richmond's outer defenses almost 4 days after leaving Hopeville. The time had given Ned plenty of opportunity to think about a great many things. He mostly thought about the meaning of this war and how he was to confront the family with the truth. He thought of Lizza, and his need to see her, and how, maybe, everything would be okay when he saw her.

Lizza had received Ned's letter a full day before he reached Richmond. She was shaken by the news and went to Elizabeth for solace and counsel. The months together had formed a close bond between the two women.

After reading the letter, Elizabeth confided, "Oh! My dear. These are the very events I feared, the confrontation and death of brother vs. brother, father vs. son, and now cousin vs. cousin. How terrible are the times in which we live and the horrors that are played out each day on battlefields. Your Ned will need strength from you, all the support and understanding you can muster when he gets here. This event will take much fortitude. And in this act, hopefully, forgiveness and understanding will be forth coming. You my dear, Lizza, will be instrumental in his healing."

Ned had come into some resistance in getting through Richmond's outer defenses, but good fortune walked by at the right time. A previous ranger, who had decided the life of a ranger was not for him, had joined the regular army and had been posted as guard at the pass-thru. As Ned was being questioned as to his business in Richmond, the now Private spoke up as to the person Ned claimed he was. He graciously thanked an old comrade and continued the last few miles to Richmond and on to Lizza.

Chapter 9

Lizza's Struggles

It was a sunny day and Sunday mid-morning when Ned drove down the street to the Van Lew's mansion. As he pulled up, Elizabeth was there to meet him. She greeted him with excitement and said, "Well, you're here safe! I'm sure you're anxious to see Lizza. She will be home shortly. She and Tom have gone to church and if all remains as each Sunday, they will be in sight soon."

Tom had dropped off Lizza at the African Baptist Church on 1st and Byrd Streets across town next to the penitentiary. Tom attended the First African Church on Broad and 14th Streets back toward the Van Lew's. As customary, he would pick up Lizza after services. They had followed this routine for months.

It was almost 1:00 p.m., the time they usually arrived back home. Ned had barely had time to put the wagon and coffin in the carriage house out back and brush off road dust in preparation to seeing Lizza. He had decided as he crossed the central rail tracks that he would take his cousin home on the train instead of enduring the ordeal of crossing the Blue Ridge Mountains in a wagon. Passing through Rock Fish Gap was easy enough, but speed was of the essence in the matter.

As Ned rounded the end of the mansion, Elizabeth was calling to him, "Tom's here, Ned, come quickly!" Ned caught sight of the carriage, but saw no Lizza.

As Elizabeth and Ned walked up to Tom, still seated in the carriage, he had a furrowed look across his face. "Tom, speak to me! Where is Lizza," Elizabeth asked? Ned repeated the exact words.

Tom did not raise his eyes; then he mustered the strength and began. "She was not there! I went to the corner where Lizza awaits me, and she was not there! I waited, and then began to drive up and down Byrd Street and Canal Street, then 1st and 2nd Streets. I saw no sign of her. Finally, I saw a friend and asked if he had seen Lizza after church. He told me Lizza was anxious to get home and started walking alone down Byrd Street near 5th Street." 5th Street was where Tom came down the hill every Sunday.

"I did not see her, Ned," he said, as he looked at him sadly, "I thought to myself that loony girl. She's so much in a hurry to see Ned. After I passed back up and down 5th Street once more, Broad Street to Byrd Street, I stopped and questioned all I could who were walking in the area."

"Then, I saw another woman friend. She told me that not twenty minutes before, three policemen and two other men had put a woman kicking and screaming into a carriage and headed toward the tobacco warehouse on 7th Street, and then they turned up the hill. She said she could not tell who the woman was; they had her covered with a blanket. The story she told me chilled me all the way down my spine."

As Tom finished the story, tears filled his eyes. "Honestly, I was on time as usual and I didn't see her, Mr. Ned. I fear for her, if she was the one! I don't know, I just don't know," he said with his voice beginning to crack.

"Stop it, Tom! Stop it right now!" Elizabeth said to Tom sternly. "Take us back to town to Byrd Street, and hurry. We have precious time to lose and can waste not a minute!"

The three approached 7th Street and headed down toward the river. All three scanned each side alley, doorway, and street as they went. Ned instructed Tom to let him out at 7th and Byrd. He began asking about Lizza, as the other two began trolling up and down the surrounding streets. Elizabeth had told Ned that Lizza was wearing a flowered dress when she left earlier that morning. After twenty minutes on foot, a clearly agitated man and drunkard waved Ned down and asked, "Are you the one looking for the Negro flowered woman?" The man was shaking terribly as he spoke.

"Yes, I am. What is it you know? Tell me quick old man!"

The man stammered, "Well, sir, I saw it all. The flowered woman walked down Byrd and turned up 7th right over there." Ned hung on every word. "A wagon followed slow, like behind her, for some distance. When she got to the tobacco warehouse, the drunk pointed his shaking finger at a wagon from which five men jumped out and grabbed the woman. They seemed to ask her questions and, as she tried to pull away, they threw a blanket over her and put her screaming into a carriage, and then disappeared up the hill. She was screaming the whole way." Ned's heart sank and he lowered his head into his chest. "I heard her screaming all the way up the hill in a shrill voice," the old man said.

Ned cried out, "Oh God, Oh God, no!" He turned and ran as fast as he could back down Byrd Street to find Elizabeth and Tom. He saw the carriage as it turned onto Byrd Street. The carriage rushed to him as Tom could tell he was very anxious. Ned climbed in and frantically began telling what he had learned only minutes before.

Elizabeth prayed out loud, "Oh my God, hold her safe!" She knew immediately what they needed to do. "They have taken her to the slave pen, the auction jail! Somehow they found her identity. Tom! Get us to 15th and Wall Streets," Elizabeth said with great urgency.

The slave pen was also a holding jail for owners for a small fee. For only 30 to 50 cents a day, they could secure them. Elizabeth explained that they would most likely have to sort out the situation before a judge, and that it wouldn't happen until tomorrow. Lizza could not be released to anyone until then. Elizabeth quickly went over in her mind how? How had she been found out? They had been so careful. It had to be happenstance.

The trio pulled up in front of the jail. Elizabeth told Ned and Tom that it would be better if they stayed in the carriage. She had hoped to manipulate the guard, as was a skill of hers. She used it most successfully in visiting Union soldiers in the prison. Elizabeth pushed the door open. The stale air of alcohol, tobacco and sweat filled Elizabeth's nostrils. It gave her to reflexive gags. She had to compose herself.

Seeing a man sitting behind a raised desk, almost nodding off to sleep, she approached him. "My dear man," Elizabeth began, "I wonder if you might impart some information. I believe that a Negro woman in a flowered dress was recently brought here for temporary holding. Do you know of such a woman?"

The jailer replied, "Madame, I have many darkies back in the pen, both men and women. I am at liberty to give information about not a one, at least if I am to keep my job. Times being what they are, you will get nothing from me!"

Elizabeth decided this was not the man she needed to be talking with. They would have to wait until tomorrow morning to be at the owner's office at 17th and Broad Street. The owner of the jail was Silas Omohundro. Elizabeth knew of him. Although in a revolting business, Silas was known for honesty.

Elizabeth went back outside to Tom and Ned, but was not able to tell them what they wanted to hear so badly. She said, "We have no choice, Ned. This matter will have to be handled tomorrow. We will be at Silas' office first thing. I detest this man, but he's honest and we will bring Lizza's papers in hopes that they will carry enough for her release." So, with great reluctance, the trio headed home.

Chapter 10

The Forceful Freeing

At daybreak, Ned mounted Jake and headed toward the middle of town and the holding pen. Before leaving, he told Elizabeth he would meet her there after she had seen Silas. He could not wait; he had to get to where Lizza was and, if possible, let her know that he was near.

Ned got down off Jake in front of the pen entrance. A big, husky man sat propped against the brick wall smoking a large cigar. He introduced himself, as he admired Jake. Ned began with confidence in an assuming and unattached manner. "How is the woman they brought in last night, the one in the flower dress?"

The man responded, "Ah! Yes! Now that is a special darkie. I'd like to have a go with that one, but she belongs to Mr. Foster of Gloucester. You work for Foster, do you?"

"No," Ned said, "But I do know she is a free Negro and works for the Van Lew family."

"Is that so?" the man replied. "Well, I guess there is some settlement to be worked out, eh?"

"Yea, I guess so," Ned casually commented, trying hard not to show his anxiousness.

"You been here all night," Ned asked?

The man said, "Nah, I left at midnight. I just got here. Things will get moving this morning, a lot of business." At that the door opened and a thin sickly old man came out and half smiled.

"Well, at least we got rid of one last night," he told the cigar smoker.

"What you talking about you, old coot," he asked as he took another puff on his cigar.

"You know, the Foster darkie; they got a release last night by going to Judge Nixon's house. He signed her release to Foster. Guess he was anxious to get home."

Stunned, Ned asked, "Are you sure old man?"

"As sure as I'm standing here," he replied.

Ned asked again for clarity, "The girl in the flower dress?"

"Yep! That's the one alright. They left at 2:00, early this morning." the man replied.

Ned spun around, mounted Jake, and headed back to the house to catch Elizabeth. Maybe she hadn't left yet. His thoughts raced. Jake tore through the streets and soon reined up in front of the mansion. He ran up the steps, pushed the great doors open, and yelled for Elizabeth. She came, half running at the sound of her name being called in such urgency.

"Whatever is it, Ned?" she asked with a quizzical expression.

"Lizza's headed back with Mr. Foster himself; they left around 2:00 am," Ned said, as he paced back and forth in front of her, holding his head in his hands.

Astounded, Elizabeth shrieked, "Oh God! Dear Lord! Ned, how did they secure her?"

Ned cut her short, "It doesn't matter now. I have to run them down, Elizabeth! I have to leave right now! They have over a 7-hour head start. If I don't leave now, I will never catch them!"

"Whatever will you do when you catch them?" she asked.

"I don't rightly know. I'll have to figure that out when and if I do catch up with them," he told her. "I have to go, though, time's a wasting! One more thing, Elizabeth, will you send my cousin's casket on to Staunton? I'll have to take care of that problem later."

At that Ned and Jake flew down the drive and on to Mechanicsville. He figured Foster would prefer the Gloucester Peninsula route. Most folks down in Gloucester did when going and coming to Richmond. He also knew, even as fleet of foot as Jake was, there was no way they could overcome a 7-hour head start. They would need divine providence to intercede if they were to even have a chance. He set Jake at a pace so he could cover much ground and distance.

After passing through Mechanicsville, Ned slowed as he neared Crumps Creek. Ten miles gone, Jake needed to cool down some before drinking 3-5 gallons of water. He threw water on Jake's flanks and back and over his neck. Ned decided to change into his ranger garb before going on.

After a time, he led Jake up the steep bank of the creek. As they came to the road's edge, Ned spied a carriage in the distance heading his way toward Aylett. It appeared to be pulled by two grays, but it was hard to tell at this distance.

Ned's thoughts raced. Foster always preferred the grays. His heart began to race. If them, they must have stayed in Richmond last night. He strongly wished it so.

He led Jake back down under the bridge and ground tied him, then scrambled back up the bank and found a vantage point where he could observe and not easily be seen. From that spot, he had a 200-foot distance to access the carriage and its contents. Ned's heart was still pounding, what if? Now what, his mind asked? His ranger days were about to come in handy.

As the gray horses and carriages closed quickly, he caught sight of the driver. He didn't know him. Then, there it was! He had but a glimpse of the inside of the carriage; the flowery dress! It was Lizza!

Ned slid down the small rise and reached for Jake. Half stumbling, he fell into the creek. He scrambled back up onto the road and onto his steed. Moving forward, Jake lengthened his stride to the hilt, fully opened up. Ned had his revolver at his side. As he and Jake were screaming along, he felt as if he was in a raid. Adrenaline coursed his veins. Jake was hunting down the carriage and he seemed to know instinctively the goal.

As he came up on the carriage undetected, he swung to the opposite side as Lizza. He reined Jake out to the very edge of the road. Still the driver was clueless of the duo. Ned saw the small step alongside the vehicle as his goal. He had to time his leap from Jake. Jake's ears pricked to the side as he listened to Ned steady him. Once the two were in tandem, Ned leapt off Jake and perfectly landed with one foot on the step, while grabbing the doorframe with one hand. Balanced, he shoved his revolver into the side of Foster's head.

Ned yelled, "Stop this carriage now, Foster!" Foster yelled even louder for the driver to stop. As the carriage pulled to a stop, the driver still didn't understand exactly what was happening. As soon as he did, he leapt off the other side and left for parts unknown.

Foster's eyes were frantic as Ned directed him to get out of the carriage. "Now Foster, make a wrong move and lose the side of your head!" Ned yelled.

Ned soon had Foster sprawl face down on the ground. Then, Lizza, hand cuffed and shackled, stepped out of the coach. Even so, she was still the most beautiful sight Ned had ever seen.

"Quick Foster, the keys to the chains," Ned demanded.

With anger in his voice, Foster told Ned that they were located in the trunk on the seat. Ned reached in, got the keys and quickly released the chains. Lizza immediately grabbed hold of her man. Although she had just undergone a terrifying 24 hours, she was so beautiful. He couldn't believe she was once again in his arms.

"Get up you dog!" Ned said, as he pulled Foster back to his feet.

Foster had a quizzical look on his face. "I know you, don't I?" he asked.

"That you do, I am a McDonald," Ned said.

"Yes! What are you doing, McDonald, robbing me of my property?"

At that Ned backhanded him, knocking the slaver to the ground bleeding from his nose and mouth. He again pointed his revolver at him and said, "I ought to kill you right now. She is not property, you slug!"

Foster covered his head with his hands, as if to receive the inevitable.

"No, Ned! Please don't!" Lizza pleaded, as she pulled her torn dress back over her breast as best she could.

At that, Ned leveled the pistol once again and asked, "Did he do that to you Lizza?"

Ned shoved the barrel hard against Foster's forehead and firmly increased the pressure on the trigger. He then fired three shots. Foster fell back as Ned screamed a primal sound. The bullets buried in the ground; he had lifted the gun as he fired.

"Please, Ned, let's go and leave him! Please, my love! Look at me, Ned!" she pleaded.

Ned looked at Lizza and saw the truth in her words.

He grabbed Foster up and threatened, "You leave her alone and forget you ever knew her! You understand me?" he yelled staring unblinkingly at Foster.

Foster saw hell in Ned's eyes.

Ned, loudly spoke to Foster, "I will kill you if I so much as smell you or in any way catch your putrid wind, I will hunt you down!"

Ned then shoved Foster so hard that he hit the ground and tumbled over.

Then, he unharnessed the grays, fired his pistol and screamed. The two horses disappeared around the turn. He handcuffed Foster to the carriage wheel, shackled his ankles and whistled for Jake, who had been quietly munching some scrub grass.

Foster saw a glimpse of future. "You can't leave me here like this! I could be here all night," he whined.

"Exactly!" Ned came back. Consider yourself lucky you are even alive!"

Ned swung up on Jake and put out his hand to Lizza. She swung up behind Ned, not forgetting a previous lesson. The two left Foster and headed the way they had been traveling. Several miles later, Ned swung back south and headed back to Richmond to give the impression that Richmond was no longer for them.

Chapter 11
Facing Up to Unpleasant Realities

Lizza and Ned spoke very little as they rocked in motion with Jake, who had been heavily ridden these last twenty-four hours, as well as a few days before. Jake was asked much, but as always, responded. The trio got back to Elizabeth's and all were ecstatic at seeing Lizza. She had become like a daughter since coming to Church Hill. After the excitement died down, reality set back in.

Elizabeth agreed with Ned; they couldn't stay in Richmond. Foster was a man not to be deterred. With threats hanging over their heads, Ned and Lizza knew that they must leave soon. Their plan would include taking Roger back to Staunton and deal with that unpleasantness.

Preparations began for the morrow. Ned got Belle and Jake ready and the coffin loaded on the wagon. Lizza and Elizabeth put her things into trunks and loaded the wagon. Elizabeth offered to pay the train fare for Belle, Jake, the coffin and the lovers. They were in a hurry because Ned was afraid that Elizabeth's home would be one of the first places that would be searched when and if they decided to look for Lizza because of what happened at the pen. Ned was also concerned for Elizabeth's welfare because of her involvement.

Elizabeth said, "I can handle these types; my concern is for the two of you." And she then asked, "Where will you go after Staunton?"

"I am not sure right now," Ned replied. "All I know is that I have to face kin and then move on to safe country as soon as possible."

That night Lizza came to Ned's room. The circumstances seem to compress time and, too often, lost chances needed for physical affirmation. They needed one another, the expression of a long reined-in passion. That night, unknown to them, a seed was sown. The two had conceived out of love; a love not looked upon kindly by some.

The next morning, Elizabeth stood with Ned and Lizza upon the station platform at the Central Railroad station at 17th and Broad Street, which sat in the Shockoe Valley. Jake and Belle had been loaded along with the casket.

Elizabeth hugged both of them and bid farewell goodbyes. "Well, get word to me," Elizabeth insisted.

Ned agreed he would. He had said the same to Elsa, and at least, while Lizza had been in Richmond she had written her. Ned also had not written the Taylors. Ned had a pain of guilt for not fulfilling a promise to ones he cared for and who had cared for him. Those who had shown so much kindness, and now in this diminutive woman with a heart of a lion, he saw a crack in her as her lip quivered ever so slightly. He stepped to her and kissed her forehead.

"We owe you a debt never to be paid. You are, and always will be, in our hearts," and with that, the two lovers climbed aboard the train, found a seat, and Elizabeth disappeared on the platform. She was not about to lose her composure in front of anyone.

Lizza instinctively sat across from Ned, but he motioned her to sit next to him and he held her hand. He cared not what others might think or say. And hoped someone would say something, any voice of displeasure of their pairing.

Soon they were out of Richmond. By nightfall the two would be over the Blue Ridge Mountains and in Staunton. The unknown of this trek, Ned could never prepare for.

With the train rocking and swaying, Lizza, laying her head on Ned's shoulder, fell asleep. There were looks of disgust and shame, but not a word was voiced. All Ned cared about was Lizza being by his side once again.

The run of 50 miles to Louisa Courthouse Station, Virginia, got quickly behind them. The short stopover allowed the train to take on water for steam. Ned gently rested Lizza's head against the window. She was still tired from her ordeal.

Ned went back to check on Jake and Belle and his cousin. He found all well. As he climbed back in the passenger car, he saw half way down the aisle where Lizza awaited. She had a terrified look on her face as a man was screaming and shaking his fist at her. Ned walked fast and with purpose and said nothing as he slammed his fist to the side of the tormenter's head. The man reeled down the aisle. Lizza jumped to stop Ned from a follow-up smash. The man fell into an empty seat five rows to the rear.

As he got to his feet once again, Ned said to him, "Mister, you are about to lose your life if you want to try me or my lady again. What will it be?"

The man said not a word and staggered to the rear and out of the car, then disappeared. Ned looked Lizza over for any sign of injury. She said, "I am fine Ned. He just came up and woke me screaming 'Nigger, who do you think you are? You and that whitey ought to be hanged. You need to be taught a lesson and put in your rightful place.' "

Ned pulled her to him and embraced her, as he looked over her head. He saw nothing but disapproving eyes and, as he made eye contact, each one looked away in disgust. They sat back down as the train steamed up and pulled slowly out of the station. He thought to himself, are these my fellow Virginians that act in such a way and display contempt for other humans? He thought about what his father and mother would think about their pairing.

"Ned," Lizza asked, "Will we always face this? This hate is instilled in them and distilled to a purity."

He told her, "We will find a place someday, Lizza, trust in that, a place where we will not have to deal with this hatred, so we can raise a family."

Her eyes followed each word his mouth formed. After a time, she finished his last words with, "I love you, too," and laid her head once again on his shoulder as passengers looked upon them with disgust.

The train pulled into the Staunton Station. Ned's stomach felt taut and sick. The task before him was the most terrible thing he could conceive. They searched and found several hotels, but were turned away. None would allow Lizza to stay. The last place suggested a small hotel on the edge of town owned by a black family.

They both went into the quaint looking hotel, which was actually more like a boarding house. They found it very inviting and nicely furnished. The warm smell of food was enticing. The hotel was run and owned by Jim Smith and his daughter, Bessie. The place had only six rooms, but it was almost never filled to capacity.

Bessie greeted the two as they stepped inside, "Hello. Can I help you?"

"Yes," Ned said. "Lizza and I need a place to stay at least for one night, but maybe longer depending on what tomorrow brings."

Bessie asked, "So, you will need two rooms then?"

Ned quickly responded, "No ma'am, one will be just fine."

With that Lizza squeezed his arm and looked up at him and smiled, and then seconded Ned's words, "We will need only one room, thank you."

The hotel had a small livery stable. Ned asked about keeping Belle and Jake and the cost of using a wagon. He was told that the livery was a self-tending one. They only had help to clean stalls, not feed and groom horses, but that they had a wagon to use for a small fee.

Ned told her that he had his own horse to hitch up with. He settled the total bill in advance, signed the ledger and picked up the saddlebags he carried on the train.

Bessie said, "I will now show you your room. I think you will find all satisfactory."

She opened the door to the room. Both Ned and Lizza were pleasantly surprised. It was as nice as any in Richmond.

Bessie politely inquired, "Will this be acceptable?"

"Oh yes," Lizza told Bessie, "more than enough."

Ned settled Lizza and then left with Belle hitched to the wagon to get Roger and Lizza's trunks.

Lizza and Bessie quickly got into conversation just like old friends.

Bessie asked, "He your man, Lizza?"

"Yes, Bessie, he is my love to be sure," Lizza answered.

Bessie offered, "He is a strapping man. He good to you, Lizza?"

Lizza said, "How do I explain Ned's devotion to me? His actions and thoughts are always for me and our future. He would lay down his life for me without as much as a blink of the eye."

Lizza went on to tell the story of their by-chance meeting and their trials and good times. An hour had quickly passed by when they heard a wagon pull up and go around the hotel to the livery stable.

Ned had also found out on his trip to the station that his kinfolk still lived in the same house outside of town.

The morning would come all too quickly. Ned would have to face his aunt and uncle. Roger would finally rest on the land he was born to.

After bringing in the trunks, Lizza went to bathe. Ned and Bessie now got to be acquainted. He learned that Bessie's dad was born into freedom unlike Lizza.

Ned asked, "Where is your father, Bessie?"

Bessie responded, "He is with a northern regiment working as a wheel right. I get a letter once a month or so. I fear for him, Ned. They will surely kill him if they capture him, a black man aiding a Federal army. I keep this place going the best I can and I pray for business to keep it afloat. Somehow I manage. Lizza tells me you two are to be married."

Ned positively answered, "You bet. In Lizza, I have found what my father did in my mother."

Bessie seconded him. "She truly loves you, that is to be sure. She has told me about your torments and that everywhere you turn you find bigots. Does that surprise you, Ned?"

Ned responded, "I suppose not. My belief in Virginians has been torn down, but we will find a place, maybe out west, where we can raise our family."

Ned and Bessie spent a good hour talking until Lizza returned and walked in behind Ned, who was seated at the table. She put her hands on his broad shoulders. She bent around and kissed his cheek. She smelled fresh with rose oil from the bath. Ned left to clean up and the two new friends continued from their previous talk.

Later that night Ned lay in his bed unable to sleep thinking of tomorrow. The morning came. Ned dressed and said good-bye to Lizza and reminded her to rest. He hitched Belle and headed into the damp warm morning. He wished for the happier times here, as those he remembered earlier in Gloucester. He headed east out of town and covered eight miles, five of which wound through hills with roads heavily rutted by the torrential rains of the spring. The McDonald land and house came into view. Ned reined back on Belle and stared at the house as if it to be the enemy.

Guilt and shame enveloped Ned and with it came empathy for what those in the household would soon have unloaded on them. After ten minutes, Ned knocked on the slightly chipping painted door. He again knocked more strongly. He kept telling himself what must be done. After several more minutes and when no answer came, Ned descended the four steps and walked to the rear of the house to see if he could find someone.

As he reached the west corner, he somehow noticed the out of control azalea bushes. His mother loved azaleas. He saw Auntie Bev shucking corn on the porch.

"Auntie," he called to her trying to sound happy. It took a few seconds for her to realize it was her nephew, Ned.

"Yes, Auntie, it is me," he said.

"But how? When? Where's your mom and dad," she asked. As she stood she dropped the corn and continued, "I had not heard you were coming. I would have prepared properly. Where are your mom and dad? Are they with you?"

Ned answered, "No, Auntie, it is just me." He hugged her with underlying tenderness. Auntie Bev had always had a soft spot for Ned ever since their visit for Grandma's funeral. Ned then added, "Aunt Bev, daddy died at the Bull Run Battle."

"Oh dear God, No Ned. I had not heard. Oh! My dear boy. How is your mother?"

Ned sadly responded, "She also has died. She got the fever and passed not but a short time later."

Aghast at the news, she stepped to him and embraced him tightly. She looked at him and said, "Ned, you always have a place here with us." She gave him as much comfort as she got from the words. He, however, felt the guilt building even stronger at the words of comfort.

"Auntie, where is Uncle Dave?" Ned asked.

She said, "He is with the Federal Army camped outside Fredericksburg, or at least was at his last letter."

In response, Ned asked, "Uncle Dave joined in with the Federals?"

She answered, "Oh! Yes, Ned, and your father?"

Ned replied, "He joined the Confederacy."

She said, "Oh no, they fought each other at Bull Run. How very awful to think of."

Ned thought of what Lizza had told him about Elizabeth's comments, brother against brother.

She added, "And Roger left West Point to serve the Federals. He is a Captain with a group fighting against the Mosby Raiders. I should hear from him soon; his letter is overdue."

Ned almost fell out at her words. He summoned all his strength to stay upright and calm, but in his mind he was screaming with pain. This can't be happening, he thought.

Ned, with his hands in hers, began to tremble and said, "Auntie I have come with the gravest of news."

She shivered and spoke, "My Roger? My Dave?" like it mattered which one.

Ned responded, "Yes, Auntie, it's Roger."

She closed her eyes and let go of his hands and covered her mouth, as tears flowed out of her tightly closed eyes.

Ned couldn't speak. He could not seem to form the words.

Auntie Bev fell to her knees and sobbed with deep primal guttural sounds; sounds that tore at Ned's being.

He found himself reaching out hesitantly to touch her head, but she reached out and wrapped her arms around his legs while still kneeling. Ned placed his hands on her head and looked skyward, tears streaming down his face. The blue sky and warmth could be another place, another time, for this was surely hell.

They stayed like that until she cried herself out and slowly arose with his help. She asked, "Where is my son?"

"Auntie, I have brought your son home. He is on the wagon," Ned responded.

Anxiously she said, "Take me to him."

With her arm in his, they came out in front of the house and stood silently looking at the casket.

Struggling, Auntie said, "Ned, I want to look upon my son."

Ned helped her into the wagon. He pried up the temporary nails in the lid and released it from the bottom.

As he did this, she stood stoically staring straight ahead and very erect. For a full two minutes, she stared like that and then very slowly cast her eyes downward. A serene look covered her face, then a slight smile, and she uttered, "His hair has grown measurably."

She fell to her knees and stroked his hair and traced his face. Before she arose she kissed his lips. "Rest my son, rest well," she said lovingly. She climbed down and disappeared into the house.

Ned followed her inside and found her sitting in the parlor mending some clothes. Without looking up, she said "Tell me nephew, just how did you come upon Roger, my son?"

Slowly Ned's words formed, "Auntie, I fought with Mosby's Rangers." Her eyes lifted and flashed with fire as she stared at Ned. Her eyes were vibrating wildly.

"Tell me more. I am listening," Auntie said accusingly.

Her countenance unnerved Ned and he stammered, "Auntie, it was I. I...I killed Roger, your son, my cousin."

Just as unnerving, she blinked several times and cast her eyes back to her sewing.

"Auntie, I didn't know it was Roger," Ned said, beginning to sob. "If only it was I instead."

"Yes, nephew if only it was you," she said coldly without lifting her eyes. She looked at him and he at her before she once again became stoic. Ned stood awhile and then turned to go outside.

She spoke, "We will bury him next to his grandmother and you will begin now. It is the least you can do before you go, and the sooner the better."

"But, Auntie..." Ned started.

Auntie stopped him, "I need no explanations. I have heard all I need to hear. I expect him to be properly buried before nightfall and you to be gone as soon as you finish."

Ned had been digging for about two hours. After climbing out of the grave, he stood up and looked down the hill toward the house. Not fifty yards away Auntie stood there looking out the window with her hand holding back the heavy curtain. They both stood looking at one another and then, finally, the curtain swung closed.

After another 20 minutes, Ned closed the grave and patted the last bit of dirt smooth with his shovel. He pulled out his kerchief and wiped away the dirt and sweat from his neck. The day had got quite hot and humid even for July.

Ned went to the house and entered. He peered around for Auntie. She startled him, as she was standing in the shadows. Once again she was rigid and unblinking. She slightly turned her head as if to see what she thought she saw. She spoke, "Roger, where have you been? You have been gone so long." Ned stood not knowing what to do. "Come son, give your mother a hug."

"Auntie, it is me, Ned."

"Come now, son," she said again. Ned slowly stepped to her. She reached and hugged Ned as only a mother can hug her only son. She laid her head on his chest and slowly started sobbing. Ned's heart was breaking at her pain. He was now feeling how much she had endured. Is this what this war means, Ned asked himself?

Ned did stay the night and to him it seemed, at least to Auntie, that he was Roger. As Ned was half waking up at daybreak, he felt a presence. He opened his eyes and there stood Auntie. He was half startled trying to clear the fog of sleep.

She said, "Tell me Ned, tell me the events that led up to Roger's death."

Ned and Aunt Bev sat on the edge of the bed together as he told her of the circumstances that led to this travesty and pain. After much struggling to get through this ordeal, he told her, "And that is how it happened, Auntie."

Stillness came over her. She reached around him and held him tightly. "You will always have a home here, Ned. How could you have known? I know this to be true. I feel it to be true." She stood and grabbed his hand. "Now come and help me prepare breakfast."

With calm silence, they prepared the meal and sat quietly and yet not uncomfortably. At last she said, "It took immense courage, dear Ned. I am more than ever endeared to you. Tell me you will stay a spell before you leave."

Ned softly answered, "Auntie, I have someone else who has come with me, a woman."

"Your wife, Ned?" she asked.

"No, Auntie, hopefully soon though. I have left her in town at Smith's Hotel."

"Yes, I know the place. A nice Negro man owns it," she said.

"Yes, that is it," Ned said.

"Why did you stay there and not one of the others?" she asked quizzically. Then her eyes opened wide and she stared. Ned was prepared for the icy stare of the previous day, but not this. "She is a Negro, Ned?"

"Yes, Auntie, her name is Lizza," Ned bravely answered.

"Well, I've never, nephew. Isn't that a hoot?" Aunt Bev grinned.

Ned looked unsure of how to take her response.

"Well, when do I get to meet her, this future McDonald?" she asked.

Taken back, Ned said, "I guess today, I will have to fetch her."

She responded with excitement, "You must go and bring her today. I so want to meet her! And be in time for supper. We will have a service for Roger. I will call the family together. We will celebrate his life and the beginning of you two joining in life together. Now go bring her. You will stay with family, not in a hotel. I will not hear of it. Not a word, and go now!"

In town Ned loaded the wagon with Lizza's trunks and tethered Jake to the wagon. Lizza said her goodbyes to Bessie, as she wished her good luck, and then offered a prayer of blessing over them. They hugged and then Ned helped Lizza into the wagon. They waved and smiled as they headed out of town.

As they pulled up in front of the house, Lizza said, " Ned, I am nervous, what if she doesn't like me?"

"Trust me, she will adore you," Ned said positively.

As he helped her down, the door to the house opened. Auntie was dressed in what had to be her finest black dress. It was trimmed in crimson, fully pleated, and had sheer puffy sleeves. Her hair was immaculately combed and parted in the middle, and pulled back in an intricate bun held there by a crimson net. She was striking to look at.

She openly greeted them, "Ned and Lizza, you are home at last. I have been frantic with anticipation of your arrival."

Like Elizabeth months before, Auntie seemed to glide down the steps of the porch. Lizza looked at Ned for assurance. Ned smiled and told Lizza to go to her.

Lizza walked hesitantly to meet her as Auntie walked with her hands out to welcome her, just as Elizabeth had done.

"My dear Lizza, welcome," she said.

They stood holding each other's hand and Auntie spread her arms as if to get a better look at her. She offered, "Oh Ned, she is lovelier than you let on." Lizza smiled sheepishly.

She went on, "Now child don't be shy. We are family now and I am privileged to be the first to welcome you."

Lizza was overwhelmed at such a reception. She liked Auntie immediately. She radiated warmth and truth.

Auntie added, "Now you must get ready. The family will arrive soon. Reverend McElroy along with his family will be here shortly, even on such a short notice. We will have a service for my son's brave service to his country and then celebrate his life and your lives together. Roger would want it so."

The family all lived within two miles of each other. The first of them soon arrived along with the Reverend. Before long all were gathered in a solemn service at Roger's grave. The tears flowed and continued as they, en masse, walked to the house to console each other. They began to remember and celebrate his life, as they all ate together at the rear of the house.

As the day wore on, Lizza seemed to move easily among his relatives. She captivated each and every one of them. She glowed, as Ned had never seen her before. Ned just sat amongst them, all in the shade of the elms, in conversations with cousins and aunts, all the while watching Lizza with pride. They were all there except 15 of the men folk, who were serving with the Federal Army somewhere in Virginia.

Ned found his way into a long conversation with his Papa McDonald. He was almost seventy years old. They mostly talked of obligations and his beliefs not only of the war, but of Lizza. Papa had fought with Colonel Jackson against the British down New Orleans way in 1814, while Ned's great grandpapa had fought with George Washington in the Revolutionary War. Papa urged Ned to follow his beliefs no matter how unpopular they might be.

"Believe first in yourself and then the rest will be taken care of," insisted Papa.

Papa was a large man in his day and was still imposing although somewhat infirmed. Ned had fallen close to that tree, as it were. His all gray hair and long beard gave him a sage appearance. His large forearms and hands could still seemingly handle a musket and bayonet.

Papa spoke adoringly of Andrew Jackson, as the finest leader in battle and as President. He told Ned, "Your father was so very proud of you. I tell you this now for you know he was a man of few words. He would be happy for you and Lizza, as I am. Also, you need to know, as you have probably reckoned, your Auntie Bev has told, and will only tell, me the events of your cousin's death. I find no fault, only pride in you, Ned, for the task that was laid before you and how you handled yourself in this matter. It was that of a true McDonald. Your ancestors smile upon you, as does your cousin Roger. Yes, even he, Ned. I believe in this as you should, too."

Chapter 12

The Family and the Wedding

The long dark shadows came on quickly and all pitched in cleaning up the day's doings. As everyone said their goodbyes, Auntie and Lizza were at the center of attention. Each stood patiently to embrace them. Once more, and once again, they welcomed Lizza to the family. After everyone had left, Auntie walked alone to sit and talk with Roger. Ned and Lizza sat with Papa, who had stayed over for the night.

    Ned was to take Papa back to cousin Dean's, where he lived with their family. Dean, along with the other men folk of the family, was fighting with fervor while attached to Hooker's Army. They were camped on the north side of the Rappahannock River, facing down the Confederates and General Robert E. Lee on the south side.

    Since Ned had left Mosby's Rangers, he had heard piecemeal that Lee would be making a grand move. Of what though, no one knew. Lee epitomized audacity, so anything was possible.

    The next morning, Ned dropped Papa off at cousin Dean's and assured him he would see him again before leaving the Staunton area. He had thought he had finally decided to leave with Lizza for the further reaches of Virginia, but exactly when he was not sure.

Western Virginia had succeeded from Virginia to become known as West Virginia and a State of Union North. The western part of Virginia had no plantation owners and the farther west you went, the slave ratio to whites was less. In fact, Hancock County, in the most northern part of West Virginia had not a single slave in the last census. It was situated above the town of Wheeling, which sat nestled like a finger between Pennsylvania and Ohio. Ned thought that would be a good state to begin with. Maybe, just maybe, they could leave the slavery behind at last and begin to raise a family.

They would have to go through the Blue Valley's full length, headed north under the shadow of the Blue Ridge Mountains. Finally, the railroad that traced the Virginia and Maryland border could take them west, then north to Hancock County.

While riding back to Auntie's, Ned thought he would go by the Confederate Armory that Papa pointed out to him upon going to Deans. He would try to get some actual updates of the war first hand.

The Staunton Armory was the principal supplier to Lee for all ordinances. At the Armory, he had talked his way into speaking with a major and was surprised by the news. Lee had stolen a key end run north, passed by the Federal Army, and had gotten into Pennsylvania to a place called Gettysburg. A major battle took place with frightening losses of life. The Major had received dispatches as to the feasibility of getting ordinances north before a confrontation of the two forces, but it was found that Lee had outrun his supply chain.

Today, July 13, Lee was preparing to cross back into Virginia, by way of the Potomac, as once he did for the battle in Maryland at Antietam Creek. Normally, Ned's emotions rose and fell on news of the Confederate in battle and its outcomes. Now he was ambivalent. His feelings had changed, as had his allegiance to Virginia. It was no longer his battle cry. It was the United States that he now stood behind. Ned felt drawn more than ever to the Federals, as had his family in Staunton; even though it was a hotbed of the Confederacy, especially at this particular time.

Ned headed back toward Auntie's and Lizza. All the way there he had been hounded by the desire to do his duty for the side that was just and for a cause that fit the United States' original ideal and one that the forefathers had fought for. On this ride, things became clear to him. Ned's epiphany was made known. It grabbed a hold of him with the power of a tornado. Why had he not realized these things before? The family was right on their choice. Ned, at that moment, became a Federal solider.

Ned sat with Auntie and Lizza in the parlor and started into a long, well thought-out, lucid speech about where he believed this war was going and the need to affirm his place in this war. He needed to feel he had played an instrumental part in the eventual reuniting of the Union, the Union his Papa and ancestors had so unselfishly given their lives for.

Lizza understood and even silently agreed as she listened intently while an hour went by. Ned spoke with such a passion, yet her heart sank with despair and sorrow. She understood that he once again would leave and once again she would not know if he would return to her. It was more than she could bear.

As Ned finished, Auntie could see that Lizza and Ned needed time to talk privately. After Auntie left the parlor, Lizza and Ned just sat and looked at each other, each one seemingly trying to memorize the other's every line.

The love that they exchanged during this quietude was one of intense endearment and great sensuality. A full two minutes passed during which they etched into their minds their lover's face.

Lizza slowly stood, took two steps and stopped only inches from her love. He wrapped his arms around her narrow waist. While still sitting on the edge of the settee, he laid his head against her stomach as she slowly stroked his long hair. Neither knew that at that very moment a child was being born. The child of a slave girl and a white boy conceived out of love.

"Ned," she spoke first, "I am your woman and you are my man. I believe above all else we are to grow gray together. I fear, though, a terrible thing, while I know not what, that something will harm you or me. I fear you leaving me. I know no words that could convince you not to go. I also would not try. You have brought the gift of love and trust to me. I give the same in return. If it is to be tested once again, then God wills it, and I will trust in him once again."

His heart filled to the brim with love at her words. Her strength he so admired. No other woman could stand in her stead.

"Lizza," Ned said, "If you were to say let's go right now, I would not hesitate."

"I could never say that, my love. You must fulfill your destiny. You would never forgive me if you walked away," she said, all the while looking down at him. "Our time will come, Ned. You must go."

As he looked up into her soft iridescent, mullata green eyes, tears traced his cheeks. "God has surely blessed me with you in my life, Lizza."

At this she realized that no more should be spoken on the inevitable. "Come Ned, we must go tell Auntie," she uttered.

That night, the three decided that Lizza would remain in Staunton with Auntie and Ned would leave to find his place in this war.

Ned needed to leave soon. He felt that something glorious and settling was in the wind, perhaps a final push to end it all. That night the lovers sat on the edge of Lizza's bed.

Ned told Lizza, "If I should lose contact with you and you must leave here, I will find you." At his words, Lizza felt a coldness, the likes of the north wind, go up her spine.

Out of propriety, Ned had asked Auntie if he and Lizza could share the same room and bed this night. She did not hesitate and gave a knowing nod as she headed to bed.

It was a night of intense passion between lovers, filled with crying and ecstasy. It filled their need for each other and ended with them lying exhausted in each other's arms.

Before week's end, the family had gathered at Auntie's once again and a wedding of the first order was to take place. Ned had asked Lizza in a most acceptable manner for her hand in marriage, and without hesitation she accepted.

The morning of the wedding was cool as Auntie and several women-folk helped Lizza on with her dress. It was light beige, a fully belted hooped dress, with double buttons down the front and white collar and white cuffs. Lizza made the dress even more beautiful with her dark skin. Cousin Sharon had made a head wreath of flowers to crown Lizza's head and when Ned caught sight of her, his emotions overwhelmed him.

All in attendance understood the meaning of such a union in such a unique time.

Ned and Lizza both said yes to the question that committed them to each other heart and soul until death. The future was yet to be written for these two, but to have gotten this far was something of a miracle, and it was not lost on anyone.

All in attendance agreed in the beauty of this day. The afternoon was left to feasting and celebration.

Auntie exclaimed, "Isn't it poetic, a black and white union in the Confederacy's backyard!"

And Sharon exclaimed, "Hallelujah!" and everyone responded together, "Hallelujah!"

Chapter 13

The Taylors and a New Allegiance

The next day, reality set in. Ned returned Bessie's wagon and bought some extra tack for Belle. Jake was once again regaled in his ranger tack, breast strap, tack stay, double rigging, girth, and double reined. Ned was in his new red shirt. Lizza thought he cut a handsome image.

Ned was getting a late start. He headed through the Shenandoah Valley toward Cross Keys, 15 miles or so north. Then he headed east and through Swift Run Gap, which was almost due west of Fredericksburg. Ned figured Lee would settle his badly battered army somewhere south of the Rapidan, or perhaps back behind Fredericksburg once again.

The news from the Major at the armory spoke of decimation in ranks. There would be great losses in prisoners, desertions, and the like, and it would be some time until both armies would be prepared to pursue further campaigning.

Ned was heading to the Taylors once again. He had planned to rejoin Mosby, yet this time he was planning to plant himself as a spy to glean plans in all aspects of raiding and pass it to the Federals. He thought he would then move to the main body of what was now General Meade's army that he took over from Hooker.

Meade had acquitted himself in a stellar manner at Gettysburg. President Lincoln, however, had found fault with Meade's perceived idea and a fatal blow was lost.

Meade, though, did cross the Potomac River and so once again the President was looking for a real general for the 7th time. Lincoln wanted someone who understood the ugly truth of war and how to implement steps to its end in what now had become a death lock for opposing forces.

As Ned passed thru Swift Run Gap, every fiber in his being was screaming out to return to Lizza. The urge to return was so powerful that he had to yell at himself, "Keep going, keep going, you need to keep going." He kept repeating this out loud and soon he and Jake made great time and there was nothing to impede their progress.

The roads were good as was the weather. Ned made the Taylors without incidence and pulled up at the entrance. He wondered if they would be able to tell if he had changed his allegiance. He hated to lie to them.

Ned urged Jake up the lane. Molly was there and first to catch sight of Ned. "Oh Mother, come quick it is Ned. He has returned. Everyone come quickly. It is Ned. He has come back for me. Oh, glory be!"

Molly hiked up the front of her dress and sat out hell-bound running to meet him. By now all the family had gathered out in front of the house. She grabbed for the reins and guided the two back as if they were conquering heroes returning after a great victory.

Ned dismounted and was smothered with hugs and kisses. Molly put her arm in his as if to say, my man has returned. Her smile spoke silently, "I told you so, I told you so. I told you he would come for me."

Ned greeted everyone and was overwhelmed with the love they had shown. Jean, the matriarch, was openly overwhelmed at his return. She said, "We thought you were lost or dead, Ned, when we heard nothing from you. We prayed daily for your safe return."

At that Molly said, "Amen," and gripped his arm tighter. Ned looked down at Molly. He had forgotten just how beautiful she was.

Winston asked, "Ned, are you back to continue with Mosby?"

"Yes, Mr. Taylor, I am." Ned gave only a partial truth. This was his first lie to the Taylors and it did not sit well with him.

"Ned," Mr. Taylor continued, "The Federals have been busy all over the county trying to catch Mosby but have found no sign."

Ned felt that, probably, Mosby had moved to assist in shielding the army when it moved down the valley to harass the Federals as they moved into Maryland and Pennsylvania.

He also was told that there had been some torching of farms and feed crops by those they thought were assisting Mosby's men and that folks were rounded up and sent north to be imprisoned.

"The Federals have been here three times in two weeks, Ned. They have left us alone because of my condition and suspect us of nothing," Winston added.

That evening, with the entire family in attendance, Ned gave the story of his travels, less any doings with Lizza. The latter was not information they could fathom, especially not Molly. Ned also asked further about the searches and who the soldiers were attached to. He gleaned knowledge to be used for Federal intelligence. He knew that when he rejoined Mosby, he had to be perfect in his acting. Mosby had a sixth sense in his survival as a leader, and for his men. He had ferreted out others who had betrayed him earlier, since it could affect their mission.

Mosby, while a small wiry man of only about 130 pounds, had an intenseness that could intimidate one when he wanted to. His eyes could look straight through a man. He was a leader of the first order, a leader who led by example, and he expected no less than his own actions in others. Mosby could ride all day in the saddle and show no fatigue. His bravery was unquestioned.

That night before going to bed, Ned went to the barn to check on Jake. He thought he had felt a hot spot on his left front leg. He could not afford to have Jake come up lame. As he ran his fingers down the backside of his leg, he felt the tendons, but felt no heat or swelling. Perhaps he was wrong on the earlier check. He continued to give Jake a good once over. He never looked better.

Ned spoke to Jake, "You need maybe another 25 pounds Jake, but, boy you are looking good, big man." He was so proud of his steed. He hung Jake another bucket of fresh water and then mucked the stall once more before turning in for the night.

He shut the stall door and turned to find Molly standing right in front of him. She smelled so good. He thought her hair was oh, so fine!

Ned said, "I just need to take care of my friend. He is part of me I guess. We have been through a lot, he and I."

Molly responded, "Yes, I suppose devotion is key to a good relationship. Ned, you know that I am very devoted to those things I am passionate about." She then moved closer to him, put both of her hands upon each of his shoulders and started to clasp her hands around behind his neck. Her voice had grown slow and sultry. "Ned, why do you not kiss me?"

Ned was surely stirred, and who would not have been at such a woman. She was desirous in every way, a belle any Virginian man would want to pursue and petition to marriage. But instead, he grabbed her firmly by the wrists and put her arms down to her side, releasing them.

Ned said, "Molly, how do I tell you? Your offer is most flattering. I would normally be drawn to your offer, but you see, I cannot entertain that which you offer me."

"But why ever not?" she pleaded in her sweetest southern belle voice. "I have much to give a man."

Ned responded, "That is true, Molly, but Molly, I love another woman. I have since before I came here the first time. I don't want to hurt you, but I have also married her just days ago."

Aghast, Molly, unbelievingly said, "You what?"

Ned continued his explanation. "I married a girl after going to Staunton."

To which Molly stammered, "You are married?"

Ned said, "Yes, Molly."

At his answer, Molly began striking Ned on the chest repeatedly with her balled up fists, then slapped his face. Before storming out of the barn she screamed at him, "And to think I entertained the idea of marrying you and raising a family! And so did mother and father! Now you embarrass me like this! You led me on Ned McDonald!"

At that point Ned calmly responded, "Molly, I never led you on. You created this in your own mind."

Molly retorted, "No Ned, you have disgraced me. How will I ever heal? I hope you will be leaving soon." She spun on her heels and huffed out of the barn.

Ned muttered to himself, "Well, that went well," and sadly hung his head and followed Molly into the house.

As he started up the stairs, Molly's sister, Sara, asked, "Is it true Ned, what Molly says? Are you married?"

Ned forthrightly said, "Yes, Sara, it is true." To which Sara surprisingly responded, "Well, I guess that I should forget about you looking my way. I was hoping you would notice me."

In response, Ned smiled at her and said, "Oh young Sara, I am touched by your words. He leaned to kiss the top of her head.

Sara kindly said, "I am happy for you Ned, even if sister is not."

Sara was on the cusp of being every bit as beautiful as Molly. She was as charming as Molly, but not as disingenuous. "Sara," he said, "If I had another life to give, I believe it would be given to you in a few years."

Sara smiled and blushed, and said, "Ned, sister will calm down by morning and she will soon set her sights on yet another man."

Ned added, "Oh, I am quite sure of that, Sara. Now you and I need to get some sleep. Sara, thank you again for the sweet words." They both headed for their bedrooms.

In the dark, Molly lay in bed steaming hot at her perceived slight by Ned. She thought, I will show him! Embarrass me, will he? Ned will rue the day he treated me in such a manner.

Molly's conniving side was at full stride and morning light would find her at the temperature of full revenge.

Ned, on the other hand, was falling asleep in his room with Lizza fully in his thoughts. He kept bringing up the face he loved so dearly and had etched so indelibly in his mind.

That night, on the settee, before getting in bed, he had written a letter to Lizza and left it on the desk to continue it in the morning.

A fortnight passed with Molly holding up the icy treatment toward Ned.

Ned was now waiting for the great armies to settle down in their camps and lick their wounds. He had just put word out to Mosby that he was back at the Taylors. Awaiting his call, Ned filled his days during these last few weeks by making repairs around the farm.

He also got to know Sara a lot better, but only at the expense of leers and sneers from Molly.

Sara had told Ned, "I don't care what she thinks, I like talking with you. I don't care what she says."

Ned liked Sara. She was down to earth and put on no airs. Ned thought, she and I are a lot alike.

One night after everyone had been asleep for several hours, Ned was awakened to a fuss downstairs. He opened the bedroom door and walked down the hall and peered down the stairs. There stood Mosby and several rangers, who he immediately recognized. Also, there stood Mrs. Taylor and Molly.

Ned descended the staircase and asked Mosby what this late-night disturbance was about.

Mosby came back in his all business voice. "It is time we have a talk. What say you, Ned?"

Mrs. Taylor looked confused and concerned. Molly looked contentedly smug. Ned knew this was no social call. They all walked into the parlor.

Once there, Mosby cut to the chase, as was his style. "I hear that you have married a Negro girl."

Ned immediately shot a stare at Molly. He knew what this was about now. Molly stood with her arms across her chest with an evil smirk on her face. Sweat began to bead heavily upon his brow. Everyone waited in anticipation for Ned's reply.

"Yes," he said proudly. "Yes, I have." Ned was staring now at Molly.

Mosby then said, "Well, then, in and of itself, I have no problem with this. What say you, then, to your setting yourself up as a spy for the Federal army?"

Mosby's steely gray eyes glared at Ned and seemed to dare him to affirm the barrages leveled at him by Molly.

With conviction in his voice, albeit a lie, Ned said loudly, "No, I have not." He turned to Mrs. Taylor as he spoke.

If he had said, "Yes," Mosby would have hanged him no matter their history together.

Molly yelled with a shiver, "Liar, liar!" and looked to Mosby to continue his questioning.

Mosby said, "I have a copy here, Ned."

Ned took it from his hands and tilted it toward the light. The letter was a direct copy of the one he had sent to Lizza. It was the one that he had carelessly left on the desk that night until the next afternoon when he had finished it to send.

Ned thought, how could I have been so careless.

Molly, again with great venom said, "Deny it, try to if you can! You can't! Nigger lover!"

Ned stared directly at Molly and summoned some great acting as he said, "Is this my reward for scorning your advances and petitions for seductions, Molly?"

Molly shot back, "You flatter yourself, Ned McDonald."

Mrs. Taylor looked at Molly and said, "Is this a contrivance of yours for his not looking your way, for surely you did hope for all those things."

Mosby shifted his gaze from Ned to Molly trying to discern the truth.

Molly pled, "It is word for word. I swear on Ma Ma's grave. It is all true. He has duped all of us. Most of all you, Major Mosby!"

Ned quickly came back with, "I have but my reputation Major, and as you well know it goes unblemished. In action, you have seen first-hand countless times my devotion to each mission and disregard for my own life. Would such a man be a traitor?"

Frustrated, Mosby told them all, "I have neither time nor inclination to ferret out this maze. For now, you will be taken to the Provost Marshall behind the Rapidan River. He will decide this matter. I have much to do! If it is deemed as such Ned, you may return to us with no further action or show of contempt from me or the men."

Molly, unable to contain herself yelled, "Traitor! You are a Benedict Arnold, that is what you are Ned McDonald."

"Molly, that will be enough," said Mrs. Taylor.

Ned extended his wrists to be bound. "That will not be necessary," Mosby said, "at least not now."

As Ned was being led to the door, Sara, who had come down the stairs and had been listening in the hall, quickly caught on to the seriousness of the meeting.

Molly once again yelled, "Leave us, traitor!"

This time it was Sarah who said, "Shut up, Molly! Just shut up!"

Molly looked shocked at Sara's words.

Sara ran and hugged Ned's waist.

"It's okay, Sara," Ned said as he bent to kiss the top of her head. "I have to leave for but a little while to straighten all this out."

"Sara dear, come to mother now, it is as Ned says. It will have to be sorted out, then he will return."

Ned responded, "I will come back, Sara."

Molly again yelled, "Like hell, they will hang you, Nigger Lover!"

This time Mrs. Taylor and Sara in unison said, "Shut up, Molly!"

Into the darkness, Ned left the Taylors, with all but Mr. Taylor, who was still asleep, seeing him go. They all held much different feelings at seeing him go away, in custody, and with his life in the balance.

Chapter 14

The Meanness of Prison

Ned was taken to Lee's Army behind the south side of the Rapidan, but was soon sent to Richmond to be imprisoned at Libby Prison. He knew Libby's reputation. Elizabeth had been visiting Federal prisons since the Bull Run battle. The overcrowding and other conditions were deplorable at the very least. Elizabeth had convinced General Winder, who oversaw Richmond and its prisons, to let her bring some comfort to the men.

Libby was a ship-chandlers loft at 12th and Canal and, as of late, routinely held 5,000 prisoners, men of all ranks. The overflow was put on Belle Island, which sat in the middle of the James River at the foot of Richmond. It, too, soon would be overflowing.

The day that Ned was brought to Libby, General Winder had been inspecting the prison and its condition. He met Ned and his guards on the way out and questioned the escorts as to the charges against Ned.

After their response, the General abruptly responded, "Ah! Perhaps a hanging will be in order. We need to make examples of such men. Would you agree young man?" pointing his question to Ned.

Ned said nothing. He just stared straight ahead. He was still angry at not being able to present his case to anyone yet and was bound and paraded through Richmond.

"Is this his horse?" Winder asked, admiring Jake.

The response was, "Yes, General."

The General barked directions, "We'll first take him to Castle Thunder with the other spies and traitors, not here with these soldiers who fought bravely. Then, bring his horse to me."

Ned bristled at the General's orders. To even think of another owning Jake angered him to the core, but, at least for now, he could do nothing. At that Ned was led away to a converted tobacco warehouse now known as Castle Thunder.

The solders and Ned pulled up to the entrance of Castle Thunder, one of the most notorious prisons in the Confederacy. This prison held all manner of suspected spies and traitors, civilian and military, it mattered not. It was unlike Libby's, which, because of overcrowding, men were thrown into large rooms to fend for themselves in eating and sleeping. Since space was at a premium, men mostly just sat or laid down where space was available.

Castle Thunder had cells to separate and isolate the men to try to mentally break down the spirits of those held there. Before even entering the building, Ned could smell the urine, the sweat-laden air wafting about. The smell was nauseating. It was into this unknown environment that Ned was led through the dark entryway.

Ned's first night overwhelmed his senses with sounds, yells, heat, and rats. The cells held a straw-filled mattress that was thrown into one corner. It was blood stained and the sweat odors wreaked off it. It was surely infested with lice, he thought. There was a bucket filled with water to drink and bathe with and another for relieving himself. Each filled and emptied once each day. The only light available filtered through cracks on the walls from the hall. He slid down the wall in the corner and felt hopeless for the first time in his life. It was a state that he didn't like at all.

Late that first night Ned's door creaked open and in stepped a man by the name of John Caphart, his hands holding a 4-foot long club. Tapping the wooded floor with his club, he offered an evil sneer. Ned saw four other men come in behind Caphart and then move to stand with two on each side.

Ned knew that this was no reception party. He quickly decided to go for one man and try to kill him instead of trying to fend off all five. He thought, I'll kill one before they try to kill me. Ned chose the man on his left as they stepped toward him. He made his move at the singled-out thug. He slammed into him, knocking him backward and then landed on top of the man.

The others, surprised at Ned's aggression, hesitated long enough for Ned to slide off to the side and get a headlock around the man's neck so he could pull even tighter.

Caphart saw a brief opening and smashed the club into the side of Ned's head. Ned felt as if all the lightening in the heavens went off in his head at once. That was immediately followed by a heel into the groin. He groaned heavily and instantly there followed a kick that landed across Ned's face splitting his lip and nose. Blood began pouring from his wounds. The kick threw Ned back off his victim, who crawled away coughing and gagging for breath. Now, free from protection, Ned received the full fury of four men. All he could do was curl up and receive each damaging blow. He finally fell unconscious from the load of blows.

Ned awoke later, alone, with every nerve in his body on high alert from pain. A pain level he had never experienced before. He strained to see, but his eyes were all but swollen shut. The lacerations all over his face had distorted it. He had a metallic taste in his mouth. He spit blood out over and over. His gums were traumatized from a series of blows. Luckily, he still had his teeth. He groaned as he tried to move toward the drinking bucket. His hair was matted to his face from the blood and his thighs ached horribly. Finally, he got some water down his throat, albeit with great effort, and then he collapsed into a fitful sleep.

As the morning came Ned awoke to his pain once again. Now, the pain was even more intense than earlier. Caphart had thrown a bucket of water on him. As his silhouette stood in the doorway, he threw some clean clothes down and ordered, "Get dressed, now! You have someone here to see you. " He could barely stand, much less get the clothes on.

Caphart bellowed, "I'll be back in two minutes, be ready."

Ned changed and stayed standing. He felt that if he sat down, he would never get up again.

Caphart returned with two of the men who had beaten him the night before. Ned was led down the hall and descended the steps with great effort. Each step caused him to feel as if he would fall. One man led the way and the other followed Ned, with Caphart in tow.

Ned could barely walk. Each step made him relive the blows from last night. Finally, they stopped, unlocked a door, and shoved Ned in a room. As he stumbled into a heap on the floor, he winched in agony. He gathered himself and pulled himself into one of two chairs.

In the dimly lit 12x12 room, he almost drifted to sleep in the chair until the door opened. He looked to the door but could not make out the personage as it was heavily backlit from the hall.

The guard told the visitor, "Ten minutes! That's all!" and slammed the door.

The voice he knew immediately. It was Elizabeth. "Dear God, Ned, what have they done to you? Praise God you are still alive."

Elizabeth had many contacts within General Winder's office and was notified with each Thunder prisoner that came in. She could barely make out Ned's face from the beating he had received.

"I wish I were dead the way I hurt," Ned said. As he peered through the slits of his swollen eyes, Elizabeth smiled. Her eyes were filling with tears.

"Have you heard from Lizza," he asked her.

She replied, "Yes, in fact, several times Ned. I was heartened to hear you got married."

"Please tell Lizza," he struggled to say.

"I already have, Ned," she stopped him. "I sent a message to her as soon as I heard you were brought here. I will send another when I leave you and let her know I've been to see you."

Ned struggled to speak, "Tell her I love her, Elizabeth. Tell her to try not to worry and please don't tell her what you've seen here."

"I will not tell her about this, Ned," she confided.

Ned said, "Tell her my every thought is with her."

"I will Ned," she responded, and added, "Now Ned, you must not do anything to antagonize this vile Caphart. Do not give him reason to beat you for surely he will kill you. I know this man. Tell me you will not."

"I promise, Elizabeth," he uttered.

Chapter 15
Preparing for Escape

Elizabeth now confided, "I already have a plan in the works for your escape. It began before I came here today. Get your strength up the best you can for you will need it in a few days. I have petitioned General Winder to see you on my demands, of which he granted. I will put Caphart on notice. If he beats you again, I will go straight to Jeff Davis. The President will not stand for it. He's done this before, but continues with no compunction. He knows I am a woman of my word."

She had brought medicine with her as she had learned it was needed with any visit to Castle Thunder. She quickly dressed Ned's wounds and gave him a shot of whiskey, although it was going anywhere from $115-$160 a gallon. It was a pain soother, so Elizabeth used it as a medicinal healer.

The door opened and a voice called out, "Times up, Miss Van Lew, you know the rules."

She spoke quickly and sharply rebuked the voice, "Yes, I do, but I'm not quite sure you animals do! You touch this man again and Jeff Davis will hear of it. You know I'm a woman of my word."

"Yeah! Yeah! Times up," the man said.

Elizabeth bent and kissed Ned's head and quickly whispered in his ear, "Get strong! Be strong, Lizza awaits you!"

Those words brought tears to his eyes, yet great resolve.

"Look at me, Ned," Elizabeth said.

He looked up at the frail woman with the heart of a lion.

"I will not let you be here long, believe in me. Do you believe me, Ned?" Ned nodded his head wearily.

She stopped briefly at the doorway on the way out. "You will not touch him again. Remember what I said."

Ned was taken back to his cell and thrown headlong back into his cell. He collapsed into a heap in agony onto the wooden floor and fell asleep.

Two days after Elizabeth had come to see Ned at Thunder, Lizza received the message that she had gone to see Ned. It said, "He misses you very much, his every thought is with you, and his great love for you remains ever strong."

After reading the message, Lizza clutched the paper to her chest and over her heart. She prayed for her man as she continued to read. The message also told her of the pending charges that he faced and of Elizabeth's plans to find relief for him. She told Lizza that under no circumstances should she come to Richmond. And that Elizabeth would quickly handle the matter to a satisfactory result. Lizza thought she understood the unstated sense that Elizabeth alluded to.

The morning Lizza received the letter was yet another that she was sick and losing her stomach.

Auntie sat and talked with Lizza. "My dear, I think you are with child."

Lizza smiled and said, "I dared not believe it, Auntie," as she beamed a broad smile, "Yes, this is so wonderful, Auntie." As they hugged each other, Lizza said softly, "Thank you, Lord Jesus." She touched her stomach and caressed it.

Auntie stood back and knowingly smiled, understanding exactly what Lizza was feeling at that very moment, but she also stifled the pain she felt for the loss of her son at the same time. And putting her personal feelings aside, she added, "We must get word to Elizabeth to tell her the great news and to let Ned know. It will bring him great strength. It will gird and sustain him through the days he faces in that place."

Lizza wanted desperately to get to Ned, but heeded Elizabeth's writings. She did, however, go immediately that day to share the news with her friend, Bessie, who she was sure would be as happy as she. Lizza found out that she was correct as Bessie shrieked with happiness and excitedly hugged her good friend.

Bessie had always wanted to be a mother. At the same time, to remember her own mother was painful. The two friends would soon realize just how close they really were. So, Auntie, Lizza, and Bessie started preparing for the new McDonald.

The days passed quickly for Elizabeth and soon, once again, Ned and Elizabeth sat in the 12x12 room as she explained that all was in place. The bribe money to the guard was half paid. The remainder was to be paid at Ned's delivery and the guards escape north. In three days time, after the nightly changing of the guard, the plan would be set in motion.

Ned told Elizabeth that General Winder had taken Jake for his own. "Well then," she said, I'll have to pay General Winder a visit won't I. Don't pay it any mind Ned. Jake will be waiting at the appointed place and time. You'll ride Jake to safety."

She then quickly laid down the events that would take place for the escape. She was glad to see that Ned looked stronger and better than on her last visit.

"Now Ned," Elizabeth said, "Are you ready for news from Lizza?"

He excitedly responded, "Yes, tell me!"

"Well, Ned, it seems that another McDonald will be coming into the world."

Ned for a moment didn't grasp Elizabeth's meaning, then his eyes opened wide as he could manage and Elizabeth smiled. "Yes, Ned, Lizza is with child, your child!"

"How glorious is this," he yelled. He grabbed Elizabeth's hands and brought them to his forehead and bowed his head, saying "Thank you, Jesus. Thank you."

Ned was soaring with excitement as he was led back to his cell. He cared not about his still quite evident pain and the conditions he lived in. He stopped counting the rats he had killed that the guards threw into his cell. Ned sat against the wall and closed his eyes and carried his thoughts away to Lizza, oblivious to the smells and sounds that hounded him.

Chapter 16

Serious Trouble for Lizza

That very day in Staunton, Auntie prepared to go to town leaving Lizza to do some knitting that Elizabeth had showed her how to do.

Auntie told Lizza "The woodman is going to deliver a cord of wood sometime today, so keep an eye out for him. We are in need of the good hardwood logs he always brings."

Lizza agreed, "Yes, of course, Auntie. I'll be on the back porch. I just plan to sit and knit, and enjoy the cool morning. Shall I leave him instructions for him to come by again?"

Auntie responded, "No, that will be alright. I'll reach out to him later."

Lizza sat all that morning knitting her coming child's clothes. She hummed some tunes her mother had taught her as a young girl. She drifted in thought as noon came around, as did J.T. Sigel, the woodman.

Thirty-year-old JT was a powerfully built man from the constant chopping that was his job. Where he came from, no one was quite sure, he just seemed to have shown up some 12 years ago. He was heavy browed with a thick, full. long beard and a German accent. JT always seemed to have a musty smell to him as if he bathed very seldom. The price he charged for wood was very reasonable and he was always prompt in his deliveries. He talked only when asked questions. He seemed to care little for small talk.

JT pulled up alongside of the house as Lizza was knitting under the shade of the elms, the sun streaming through the canopy. He stopped, off to the side of the porch, and asked Lizza if he should stack a cord of wood in the usual place.

She responded, "Yes, I guess."

Auntie had left no special directions. JT jumped down and got to work stacking the 4x4x8 cord of wood.

Lizza had an uneasy feeling that he was watching her. Each turn of her head caught him staring with a noticeable lust on his face. She asked, "Are you done JT. I can pay you and you can be on your way."

He uttered, "Not yet, missy, I'm in no hurry."

At that she got out of her chair and went into the house and shut the door. She felt very uneasy now. She went to the window and peered out to see JT staring directly at her, smiling with bad intent. She ran to lock the door only to have the door come flying back at her as she reached for the lock. She spun on her heels to run for the front door and felt herself slip and began falling forward. As she fell, she cried out. "Auntie, come help, help!" as if her words would stop what he had in mind.

With hate in his voice, he yelled, "It's too late! She is not here. I've had you on my mind for a while."

Lizza tried to push herself forward and up, when his full weight crashed down on top her slamming her chest and face into the floor. She cried out in anguish, "Oh! God, no please, I am with child. Please have mercy. No. No. No. You can't, my baby!"

JT was not about to grant her pleas for relief.

He began frantically reaching around to the front of her dress and, at the same time, he was hiking up the back of her dress above her buttock. Lizza was helpless. She was trapped. His strength and weight were too much for her.

She could smell his musty stench and his foul breath breathing on her neck. As a young girl, this had happened before and she had learned to lie still to get it over with. She sobbed while calling out Ned's name over and over.

JT's deed was done. He stood up and pulled up his trousers as she pulled at her dress to cover her backside, all the while keeping her face down to the floor. She could still hear his heavy breathing as he told her, "If you don't want me to do this again, you will not say a word. You hear me, Lizza?"

She nodded yes to get him to leave. She heard his brogans on the floor go across and in front of her and out the door. He was gone, but anger was welling up inside her, a hatred for his taking her and those in her past who had done the same thing.

Lizza stood and began to shake uncontrollably with such anger as she had never felt before. She looked to the pantry where the pistol hung. She grabbed it and made sure all was well with the piece. Ned had showed her how to use it for emergencies. She walked to the door and calmly opened it, stepped through and proceeded across the short porch to its edge and the steps.

A calm resolve of revenge overtook her, even with her dress ripped down the front and still half hiked over her buttocks. Tears filled her eyes.

She calmly called to him, "JT." He was pouring a bucket of water down his front and down his pants. She called again, "JT."

He slowly looked back over his shoulder and saw the revolver leveled at him. He turned fully to face her. The scared look was gone from her face. It unsettled him for a second, but then he said, "You want more?"

He had barely said the last word when she put a bullet into his forehead. His head violently snapped back and there was a fan-like spray of blood, lit by the rays of light that came streaming through the elms. He fell back and hit the ground, fully laid out with vacant eyes open and staring at the sky.

Lizza sat down on the porch and the revolver fell slowly from her fingers and bounced down the last step. She began humming, all the while rocking back and forth slowly, looking at the dead body before her. For an hour Lizza rocked.

Finally, Aunt Bev came around the back of the house driving Belle and stopped to see Lizza's rocking and starring. JT's wagon blocked her view of him. Bev got down and walked the length of JT's wagon and horse before she saw JT starring up at her with a hole in his head, blood pooled in one eye. There was a rivulet of blood running down his cheek and across his ear.

"My dear God! What happened here, Lizza?" She did not respond. Lizza had unresponsive eyes. Then, her eyes began tracing the ground to Auntie's feet and then her body until her eyes met Auntie's.

Lizza simply said, "He shouldn't have done it."

"Done what, Lizza?" Auntie asked frantically.

Lizza blinked slowly twice and said frankly and matter-of-fact, "He took me."

A shocked Auntie said, "Oh! Lizza! Oh! Dear Girl! Dear Lord in heaven, no!"

Auntie started to cry as she made her way to hold Lizza. They embraced as they both sobbed. Bev held her with great love and compassion, as Lizza buried her head in Bev's shoulder.

Suddenly, Auntie realized the need to act quickly in disposing of JT and his property. "We need to get rid of everything, Lizza, and now! The authorities must never find out. Do you understand?"

Lizza nodded without saying a word.

Auntie quickly remembered a cave that Roger had found as a young boy. It was far up the rise behind the house in amongst some boulders and brush. The cave was an ancient site with animal bones, arrowheads and such. It was about 1/4 mile up the hill.

Auntie ran to the barn for a tarp to wrap JT's body in, then took Belle and put her harness on the wood sled. She tried to pull JT on to it then said, "Lizza, I need your help. I cannot do this myself."

Lizza snapped out of another trance, and then helped, but not before kicking the corpse in the head.

Auntie set the driving reins over one shoulder, around her back and under the other arm. She snapped the reins and yelled, "Haw, Belle."

Belle stepped out pulling the sled and the body. Auntie guided Belle with calls of haw and gee, or left and right, as Belle did as she had done many times in Gloucester pulling a load, except this one was a first.

Soon, the women and Belle were below the shale scree and boulders.

Now came the hard work. The two women had to pull the body up the remainder of the way. It took some 30 minutes to get JT up the steep grade. They dragged the body into the cave and pulled it in as far as they could until the roof of the cave lowered such that the body could go no further.

They both emerged into the afternoon sun covered with dirt and dust, sweat beading on them from the great effort. Auntie, with Lizza, began to cover the entrance with rocks and scree to entomb JT. Hopefully, to never be found. Finally, this part was complete.

As the two went back to the house, a thunderstorm raced in from the west drenching them and covering the sled tracks. The storm abated and the hot sun beat down once more on the valley.

"Lizza, we must get rid of the wagon," said Auntie.

Again, Belle was hitched to his wagon. Auntie drove the wagon to a secluded grove of trees, unhitched Belle, and torched the wagon with several gallons of kerosene, which reduced it to remnants and metal.

She headed back to complete the last phase, a most unpleasant act, but one that had to be done.

JT"'s horse was unique in that it was missing one ear, lopped half off in an accident. The duo led the horse into a valley with a deep gully that traversed the length and was covered with deep grass. Auntie led the mare into the gully and with one well-placed shot from the pistol that had killed JT, she killed his horse and left the body to be scavenged. In no time at all, it would become unrecognizable bones.

Auntie knew full well that no one would really miss JT. He had no friends. Folks would figure he had probably just moved on. So, Lizza and Auntie would never be suspected.

That night her biggest concern was not the web of deceit that had been woven. Instead, it was Lizza and her state of mind. At bedtime, Auntie had Lizza sleep in the same bed to keep close tabs on her and be there for immediate comforting if she should relive the horror of the day.

The morning came with yet another thunderstorm that crashed for several hours, as the two busied themselves with daily chores. Auntie knew Lizza needed to keep busy to somehow forget, knowing full well she would not.

Chapter 17

The Escape

In Richmond, the day came quickly for Ned's escape. He was becoming anxious to leave this hellhole that he had found himself in. The heat of the day became more stifling. The smells seemed to worsen, never to be gotten used to. His sanity steeled with the thoughts of Lizza and their child she carried. The screams and pain of others around him, those he could not see, began to take its toll. All day long cries for food or water rang out. Beatings Ned could hear made him angry.

Finally, the escape day gave way to the night and he readied himself, stretching his legs that still were painful from the clubbing he had sustained. At least Ned could now see. His swollen eyes had abated, although they were still black and blue. All in all, he was now capable of moving quickly. He wished he could go to Staunton and Lizza. But, the authorities would go there first to search for him, thanks to the letter that had brought him here in the first place.

Ned could hardly wait to be riding fast and far, and to freedom. Elizabeth's plan was for him to go to Clarkston; Elsa's would be his hide out for a few days. Then, heading north to join the Federals with information they could use along with his experience.

The change of the duty guard came off as usual, as Ned had seen since being here. It was now 10:00 p.m. He listened closely for the guard that would help facilitate and initiate the escape. Soon he could hear him coming down the hall for the first pass of rounds.

Ned's door latch opened and the guard asked "Ned, are you ready?"

Ned nodded, "Yes." He barely heard the click of the lock. The first phase was complete. The door was unlocked.

Ned was to wait until the next cell check, 15 minutes later, then quietly slide out of the cell and go quickly down the hall as the guard continued his cell checks at the opposite end. He was to descend the stairs and drop into a small alcove to wait until the guard returned. He would lead Ned through the maze of halls to the back of the converted factory and the alley to freedom.

The other guards were on the roof at each side of the factory and in the front. The back was free and clear of anyone. A fence cornered off two adjacent alleys, but a breach had been made for the escape. It all seemed too easy to Ned. Jake was to be in the adjacent alley waiting. The guard would lead Ned out of town to a house, where Elizabeth was waiting with the remainder of the money for the accomplishment.

Ned kept thinking, the guard was going to blow the whistle on the whole affair and keep what money he had already. On the other hand, he figured that the man could not explain all the events satisfactorily, so he was all in with the escape. So, Ned stayed with the plan.

Ned, from his hiding spot, could hear the boots of his guide coming down the stairs. He heard a door open with a key. On the other side sat a sergeant at a desk smoking and drinking, and becoming drunker by the minute.

Ned's guide said, "All is well, Sergeant," then closed the door and locked it once again.

He went quickly to the hiding spot and motioned to Ned, "Let's go, and hurry! I have to report to the Sergeant again in 15 minutes to make another round report. If we're lucky, we will have maybe 30 minutes head start before they suspect anything."

The two ran along the hallways each step reminding Ned of his beating, but the adrenaline helped to subdue it. They quickly reached the back door and unlocked three locks then entered the alley. At first they looked up to the roof, but saw no one there. Ned's eyes adjusted.

He then saw a young boy in the alley holding two horses. At seeing the two men, the boy said, "I'm done here, good luck," and disappeared into the breach in the fence.

It was Jake who acknowledged Ned after scenting his old friend. He had to shush the big stud. "It's alright, big man. It's me. I'm okay. You missed me, huh?"

Jake sniffed Ned's hand as he patted his body. The guard mounted his small bay mare and walked his horse through the breach. Ned walked Jake through and, with great effort due to the pain, he mounted Jake despite it.

It was good to once again be with Jake in the saddle and slapping his neck. Jake's ears perked with pleasure at the soothing sound of Ned's voice. The guard led the way down the alley and soon they were at a full gallop going southeast down Court Street.

Ned had to check-up Jake, since his speed was much more than that of the mare. The two turned up 20th Street, which turned into Mechanicsville Turnpike Road. Up the hill they tore. Their destination was about a mile and a half outside of town and off the Turnpike another 1/4 mile, where a non-descript house was and Elizabeth awaited her friend.

The escapees encountered no delays or problems. It seemed so easy. Someone was going to pay heavy for Ned's escape. Hopefully, it would be the Commandant. If so, Ned would feel that he had gotten some revenge.

The two horses reined up in front of the house. The mare was fully lathered and breathing heavy. Jake was breathing hard but not nearly as much.

Elizabeth heard the horses and directly came out to meet the two. She was beaming as she gave Ned a big hug and kissed his cheek. "God's been good," she told him. She paid the remainder of the money to the guard.

The guard responded, "I need to step into the wind and leave."

Elizabeth suggested he wait until closer to morning before going on. To attempt the outer defenses this time of night would be very dangerous. All people would be heavily checked and questioned, and possibly be detained. To go at an early hour would find most asleep even at their posts.

The guard thanked her for the advice, but said, "I believe I'll take my chances and cover as much ground as I can before first light." He wished Ned good luck and thanked Elizabeth for doing business with her. He doffed his hat, gigged his mare's flanks with his spurs and headed out into the moonless night.

Ned and Elizabeth went back into the small house. "Ned, you must try to get a few hours sleep. We will take care of Jake for you. Your next leg of travel will begin soon. When I wake you, I will give you instructions."

Ned agreed to the need for sleep. He was out almost as soon as he hit the pillow.

Days before, Elizabeth had laid out the route that Ned would follow and the hour to pass through Richmond's outer defenses. She had sympathizers posted along his route to assist him on the confusing roads of the White Oak Swamp. Several hours had passed and as Ned slept, Jake was fed, watered, cleaned and brushed.

"Ned! It's time to get ready," Elizabeth said, jostling him softly.

"Yes, yes, I must go," he replied. He was half awake and half asleep. The injuries he sustained at the Castle also reawakened. "Oh, am I sore, Elizabeth."

She responded, "Yes, and I'm surprised you can still move as you do. Here is a map. It's simple to follow until you get outside the defenses. Then you will have sympathizers to the Union who will be at the ready with a lantern at each turn. They will direct you as to which way. You should try to reach Mrs. Baker's, your final destination, before first light. Mrs. Baker is but a short distance from Bottom Bridge, which you will cross tomorrow night. From there you will go to Elsa's. She will expect you no later than two night's time. There you will move north to Union lines and safety."

"How can I ever thank you," Ned said as he kissed her cheek.

They hugged and then she showed Ned the points of interest on the map that would help him escape Richmond reaches. After the briefing, Elizabeth told him it was time for him to go, for the appointed hour had arrived. They went into the warm damp night air. Jake greeted his friend with the usual low rumbles and air blowing through his soft nose.

"Well, Jake, we're off." Once again, they would be riding into the night just like with Mosby. Jake shook his head up and down as if to agree. Ned swung up into the saddle as Elizabeth stood back. "I'm not sure when I'll see you, again Elizabeth."

Elizabeth positively answered, "Ned, you can be sure we will. I'll get word to Lizza, when it is confirmed you're safe at Elsa's."

Ned motioned with a nod as he swung Jake around and headed out to the main road. He had some thirty miles to go to Mrs. Bakers. The most direct route was on the main road, Seven Mile Road, but Ned needed to be secluded, cloaked in the night on little used roads.

His first leg was back toward Richmond, skirting the south of the city to get on Central Road and slip the outer defenses. The late night would help his passage also. Sleeping guards and Jake's speed were key to his secrecy. Twenty minutes after leaving Elizabeth, Ned could make out the outline of the berms and redoubts of the defense line. He moved ahead then stopped, awaiting a response.

After waiting and hearing no halts or calls, he called to Jake, "Let's go big man, now or never." Jake broke into his stride.

It had been some time since Jake had unfolded his long legs. He was all in for the run. Ned's night vision saw the path he needed to take. He laid low against Jake's rising and falling neck. They were covering over 28 feet with each stride. His ears were pinned back and his attention was fully on the task at hand.

Ned expected at any time to hear a commotion of halts or rifle fire but strangely none came even as he approached and passed the line of redoubts. However, just as he felt free and clear, he heard no rifle report, but he did feel the sting in the back of his arm. It jerked his arm forward. At first he was unsure of the pain, but quickly realized that a minie ball had found its target. Ned felt around with the other hand as Jake continued his blistering pace. The warm sensation and thick fluid between his fingers confirmed a wound. He let Jake run for another 1/4 mile and then slowed him up and stopped.

The wound was bleeding heavily. He ripped his shirt and tied, as best he could, a knot to slow the bleeding, and then continued on his mission

Finally, he saw the first lantern. It was Mr. Johnson leading him off on a small road headed north. Another mile went and there was the second lantern. Mrs. Evans showed him east. And yet another turned him onto a one-horse path no more than a logging road.

Ned could smell the heavy air of the White Oak Swamp. As he moved along, he kept adjusting the cinch around his upper arm, which was becoming numb from lack of circulation.

He now crossed City Road and the Fletcher's pointed him northeast to a wide road that connected with Seven Mile Road and City Road.

He was feeling weaker as he rode on in the night. Blood soaked his side and began to ooze onto the flanks of Jake. The two came to a rise in the road, and then up and over a mound some 60 feet tall that rose out of the swamp and across its summit for some 100 feet and down the other side.

At the bottom a lantern shone brightly. Ned blinked, his eyesight was fading. He slumped in the saddle. It was Mrs. Baker; however, as Ned approached the light, he could not make out the personage. The light went dim and then out. He collapsed onto Jake's neck. Jake immediately came to a stop. He knew Ned was not right and turned his neck to look back at Ned. Mrs. Baker was quickly at the two travelers' sides. She lifted her light and saw a very pale, blood soaked man. She secured him to the saddle and quickly led Jake down the last 1-1/2 miles to her house.

A widow for one year, Holly Baker had tried to keep the small farm going since her husband of two years had died at Second Bull Run. Holly had never seen the Rebel's view or her husband's. Now she did a small part, even though her view was that this war made no sense to her.

With great effort Holly got Ned off the saddle and mostly dragged him into her modest home; Ned came to briefly, but wasn't much help. She deftly attended to his wound and dressed it. She cleaned him up and laid him in her bed just as he went unconscious again. She would have to watch, hope and pray he would awake.

It was then that she really looked upon him. He was easy to look at, she thought. He must be about my age. She couldn't help but admire his physique and also see the heavy bruises he had sustained while at Thunder. It was as she was told. He was beaten. A tear ran down her face.

Holly went to fetch Jake and tend to his needs. She closely checked him over, watered him and rinsed the lather from his sides and chest. She had to admire this fine animal. She bedded Jake into the barn with her mare, who she called Mrs. Lincoln.

Holly sat in a chair next to Ned's bed with cool compresses to hopefully awaken her new house guest. She dozed off.

Finally, Ned's whispers awoke her, "My horse, is he safe?"

"Yes, Ned, he is with mine in the barn and you are safe here with me. You fainted just as you got to me. You made it, Ned! You made it! Barely, but you did!"

Ned tried to get up on his elbows, but fell back. "No, Ned, you must rest. You lost a lot of blood."

Ned realized that she was right, but forced out, "Ok," and closed his eyes.

Holly squeezed his hand. "I'm here, you hear me, Ned? If you do, squeeze my hand twice." Ned squeezed weakly. "Good, Ned, now sleep. I'll be here."

Later in the morning, before first light, Mrs. Cartwright and her daughter, Linda, came to see if the nightrider had made it. She was to start the message back to Elizabeth as to his success or failure. They both decided to wait before sending word back.

Mrs. Cartwright said, "Let's see what the next hours bring, Linda." Linda would be the one to go to Richmond with the news.

Chapter 18
A Surprising Family Relationship

The morning that Ned awoke after his late-night ride, in Staunton Lizza arose to a promising day. She felt strangely optimistic. She felt, on this morning, that no one or nothing was going to take away a moment of the joy of carrying her man's baby.

Lizza walked into the kitchen and said, "Auntie, I'd like to go see Bessie. I feel she needs to see me and I need to see her."

Auntie measured a look at Lizza to which Lizza said, "Really, Auntie I am fine."

Auntie offered, "Not a word, child," to which Lizza responded, "Yes, dear Auntie." Auntie lifted a finger vertically against her lips and raised her eyebrows.

Then, Auntie Bev broke into a wide grin and said, "Go, enjoy Bessie and this day God has given us."

Auntie looked out the window twenty minutes later to see Lizza riding Belle down to the main road. She watched until Lizza crested the hill, then her eyes went up toward the rise to where no one must find who lay there. She had to shake herself from that which her eyes stared up at, and then she got back to work.

"Come in, Lizza," Bessie shouted with glee. I've had you on my mind for days. I was going to come see you tomorrow."

Lizza said, "I know Bessie, but I felt forced to come see you."

Welcoming her, Bessie responded, "Come in and sit. I have much to tell you, Lizza."

As they sat at the table on the side porch and sipped freshly brewed coffee, Bessie told her, "Lizza, since you came to Staunton and with the last time we saw each other, I've been knowing something. We are closer than just friends."

Lizza immediately agreed, "Yes, yes, I have felt it too, Bessie."

"Sit right there, Lizza. I'll be right back."

In less than a minute, Bessie returned with a cloth tied pouch. She sat and looked at Lizza with the most loving eyes. She handed the pouch to Lizza.

Lizza took it, all the while looking right into the eyes of Bessie. She opened it and carefully pulled from the pouch an old picture. In the picture stood a black woman with a plaid button down dress and a white apron, a kerchief around her neck and her hair wrapped by the same plaid pattern in her dress. She had a white baby in her arms and, on either side of her, there were two black teen girls dressed very similarly. They had two infant black babies. Lizza had to look twice and then looked up at Bessie with a questioning gesture.

"Bessie, that is my momma, how did you get this?"

Bessie's eyes were swollen with tears by now and she said, "It was sent by my momma and your momma. That is you and me in the girls arms, Lizza. We were twins."

Lizza covered her mouth as tears fell heavily. She looked at Bessie and questioned, "We are what?"

"Yes, Lizza, sisters! Didn't you feel it somehow? You must have."

Lizza said, "Maybe. Yes, but we are, aren't we?"

"Yes, dear sister!" Bessie said with outstretched arms. Holding each other, they cried with joy.

As they sat holding hands, Bessie related in detail how their mother was told she had to give up one of the twins.

Lizza questioned, "How could she have chosen Bessie?"

Bessie then said, "I am not sure how, but she had to and I was chosen, Lizza."

Lizza said, "Bessie, momma never told me she had twins."

"I did not know until Papa Smith told me either, Lizza," Bessie confided. Bessie continued, "When I got older, Papa Smith gave the picture to me, as he was asked to by momma, when I was old enough.

You know, Lizza, when you told me of the county you were raised in and all, I began to question, and I was right." Bessie raised her hand in a fist and exclaimed, "Praise be to God!"

"Amen, Bessie," replied Lizza. They both laughed and cried holding hands and dancing in a circle like girls half their age.

Through the rest of the day, they did odd chores around the hotel together, laughing and thinking about momma. Bessie had a thousand questions. They talked of Lizza's coming baby and of even someday soon, perhaps together, going to see momma.

"Wouldn't she be a surprised girl," Lizza said. "Hopefully, this war will allow us and the outcome will be soon."

The day closed fast; too fast for the sisters. Lizza told Bessie she had to be getting home or Auntie would worry. Especially since she promised her she would be back before dark.

Bessie responded, "Lizza, then you must come back tomorrow to stay for a few days."

Lizza agreed, "I will, I promise. Tomorrow morning." Lizza waved and blew a kiss to her newfound sister as Belle carried her back home. Both Bessie and Lizza were feeling completeness in the knowledge of having one another.

On her way to Auntie, Lizza had to pass by Mrs. Whitcomb's, whose husband was the sheriff's deputy.

Mrs. Whitcomb called to her, "Oh! Lizza dear, just a moment," so Lizza reined in on Belle. Mrs. Whitcomb then added, "Lizza dear, tell Auntie that Fred will be out tomorrow to ask questions about the disappearance of JT. Have you heard anything of him?"

"No! No!" Lizza said as convincingly as she could.

Mrs. Whitcomb then said, "Well at any rate, please pass on the news, will you?"

Lizza answered, "I will. I will, Mrs. Whitcomb."

Then Mrs. Whitcomb commented. "Oh, come here please, I have this freshly baked zucchini bread. Please give it to Auntie."

Relieved, Lizza said, "Yes ma'am. I'm sure she will enjoy it, Mrs. Whitcomb."

Lizza was outwardly shaking as she got on the road to Auntie's. She spoke out loudly to herself, "Oh dear Belle, it is going to be okay. You needn't be scared." She patted Belle's neck as if Belle knew or even cared. Somehow it did calm Lizza down, and at the end of the ride, she had another one-way conversation with Belle as she left her in the barn and went to the house.

Chapter 19

Another Family Relationship

As Ned awoke, Holly was right there and said, "You look a lot better, Ned."

Slowly Ned formed words. First was, "How is Jake, was he shot?"

Holly offered, "No, I've checked him closely. He is fine, eating and wooing my horse, Mrs. Lincoln. They've quickly become friends."

He smiled weakly and said, "A real lady's man he is."

Holly smiled and said, "Now Ned, I've sent word to Elizabeth. Just this last hour your color came back to your face. I've taken good care of the wound. It was a clean wound and hit no bone. We must keep it clean."

Previously, as Ned began to learn, Holly had been forced into service in the Seven Days Battles. She had learned a lot from Phoebe Pembroke who befriended her. Phoebe was still in Richmond wearing herself out in the hospital on Chimborazo Hill. The hospital was the largest that the confederate had in the south. Phoebe was basically in charge of a unit in the hospital. Her presence was surely felt and needed. She was to be there even until the war's very end.

Now Holly fed Ned some milk bread, for even in his condition he was famished.

She asked, "Where are you from, Ned?"

In between bites, he told her of his life in Gloucester and that his father and mother had come from Staunton, Virginia. He related that, "My mother was orphaned with her sister when she was thirteen. Her sister was but seven years old and they went to live with a great uncle."

As he said these words, Holly said, "Stop, Ned, stop!" Holly paused carefully to choose her next words and said, "Ned, my mother had the same experience as yours. Did your mother leave home at 15 years old and leave a sister behind?"

Ned blinked his eyes looking on Holly. Softly he said, "Yes, Holly."

And she responded, "Ned, would your mother's name be Helene?"

Again, slowly came, "Yes."

Holly continued, "My mother's name was JoLynn."

Ned knew the name. His mother had told him the story of having to leave because of torment. The family hated Helene but doted on JoLynn. In the following years, JoLynn also left for they turned on her as well. She moved to Richmond and Holly was born out of wedlock. JoLynn did every kind of job she could to earn a living for herself and her baby. She died shortly after Holly's wedding a couple years ago, still wondering about her long-lost sister, Helene.

Holly then said, "Ned, we are family, cousins! I've never known family, only momma!"

Ned reached for her hand, as she did his, and almost silently she sobbed with Ned's hand to her face.

Ned in a hushed tone said, "You are not alone now, dear cousin."

Holly was a beautiful woman who married below her potential, but she loved her man who now was gone. Dead for a lost cause, at least it seemed so to her. Even the hard life on the farm had not diminished her beauty. She, like Ned, was also a good horseman. She loved horses for more than her obvious need of transportation.

Holly went on, "Well, cousin Ned, I guess I cannot lose you as a patient or I will also lose my only family member." She gave him a kiss on the forehead.

"Now rest. It will be a few days before you can travel and head to Elsa's. You will be safe here. I will be told if we have snoopers about looking for you. But, no one really wants to come into the White Oak Swamp area."

The days passed and Ned healed up, at least to the point that he could ride. They decided to leave on the 4th day after Ned had arrived.

The newfound cousins found out about each other's lives, or at least mostly. Ned's mother spoke only seldom of her sister, JoLynn. It seemed to cause her much pain even after all those years. It was the same with JoLynn. They were in such close proximity, but might as well have been across the ocean.

Holly told Ned, "I'm going with you to Elsa's."

Ned responded, "Not no how… No way!"

Holly reminded him, "Ned, you need someone to ride as good as any man, and I know that country. Besides, if you get shot, I'll be there," and she smiled sheepishly.

Ned added, "Not funny, Jo, not funny."

And Holly responded, "You know, Ned, momma called me Jo. I like it."

Ned quipped, "Then, Jo, you will be called."

Chapter 20

Healing and Moving On

Holly felt that the farm was readied to be left behind and would be overseen by the Cartwrights. As they left, the night was cloudy and dark which was good for night riding so as not to be detected. They would pass into three counties, Henrico, New Kent, and King William and finally crossing the Mattaponi River to Clarkston and the safety of Elsa's.

Holly, now called, Jo, in the remembrance of her mother, took the lead and she didn't miss a turn. They wound north, then east and then seemingly south.

Ned asked, "Jo, are you sure you know where you are going?"

"Ned," she came back irritated, "Up ahead in less than a furlong is the Richmond and York railways."

Sure enough, there in 220 yards was the railway. They crossed over the rail tracks and proceeded north.

She told Ned, "The Black Creek empties into the Pamunkey River and there is a little used ferry. Hopefully, it is still there."

And it was. Relieved, the duo ferried the river and continued on.

Jo asked, "How do you feel, Ned?"

He answered, "Sore, well, but sore! My strength is good. I will tell you if I cannot keep going."

Now into King William County they followed the Pamunkey north-northwest. All rivers east of the Blue Ridge traversed the Virginia landscape in a southeast flow. Their next goal was to skirt Brandywine, which lies 5 miles from the Mattaponi River.

Ned remembered that Elsa had told him years ago about a ford that could be found if the river was low enough. It was due south of Dunkirk at a stand of trees behind the river. If only they could locate it and the river was low enough. Upon reaching the river they had to split up, one of them went up river and other down trying to find the ford in the pitch early morn.

Ned also remembered that Elsa had said that a two-story log cabin sat right at the river's edge on the Clarkston side. He told Jo to look for that cabin. If it was still there it might be hard to see. They had two hours tops till first light. Elsa's was only 5 miles on the other side of the ford.

The two went in opposite directions agreeing to go only two miles or so then backtrack to each other with their results. Ned had not gone but a quarter of a mile when he found the unique cabin. He whistled as loud as he could and listened. Then it came, a responsive whistle down river. Soon Jo came into his sights.

Ned said, "Well, I guess I know where I'm going."

Jo responded, "Yep, I'd have to agree. Is it fordable, Ned?"

Ned uttered, "I'm not sure. Let's go swimming, eh?"

Ned urged Jake down the grassy bank and he stepped into the black, slow moving water. Jake placed his feet carefully as the water flowed quickly at his flanks. Jake had to lift his head and much more.

Ned yelled back to Jo, "Looks like we will be swimming for it, but the water depth remained constant and soon Jake leaped up on the steep bank.

Jo and Mrs. Lincoln had a tougher time. Unlike Jake, Mrs. Lincoln had not the experience of a cavalry horse. The mare balked several times and, being a full hand shorter than Jake, started to try to swim. Fortunately, she persevered and, with great relief, half stumbled out of the river.

Jo said, "I had my doubts, Ned!"

Ned added, "Me, too, but next time she'll do better."

Ned took the lead and headed almost due east. He should hit the road that he and Lizza had come north on from Gloucester a year ago. Sure enough there it was. Elsa's house was dead ahead. They rode down through the pines that led to Elsa's.

The travelers checked up as Ned called out to the house, "Elsa, Elsa!"

"Who is calling," came back a voice of an old woman.

Ned instantly remembered her German accent, and answered, "It's Jake."

He used his mounts name for security. Surely Elsa would catch on. "Yes, come on Jake, but only if Ned is with you."

Ned smiled and the two rode up to the small house and the old woman. Elsa started clapping her hands with glee just as she had done many times before. It tickled Ned to see her this way.

"Hug, hug! Ned, I need a hug." She was engulfed by Ned's bear hug. She patted his back, "Oh my, Ned, you cannot imagine how happy I am to see you. I worried so very much when you didn't arrive on the appointed day."

"Yes, well we had a bit of a setback. I was shot coming through the defenses and barely made it to Holly's house, which was the final stop."

Elsa looked at Holly, "Oh! my dear. How are you? Forgive my manners. It's just that my excitement at seeing Ned clouded my thoughts. Come, come into the house."

Inside, Elsa looked at Holly. "My, my Ned, you always bring beautiful women to my home."

Sheepishly, Holly said, "Thank you, Elsa."

"Elsa," Ned spoke up, "Holly is my cousin. I never knew her and as fate would have it Mrs. Baker here is family. We both knew not of one another. Our mothers were sisters."

Once again Elsa clapped with glee. "Oh! Happy times. It is, even in these terrible times."

Ned said "She likes to be called, Jo, which is a nickname. Her mother was named, JoLynn."

Elsa responded, "Alright then, Jo. Welcome to my home. Any family of Ned's is also my family. Sit. Sit please. You must be hungry."

"Yes we are, or at least I am," said Jo.

"Me too," piped Ned.

As usual the house was filed with the smell of good cooking. Even in these times of great shortages all throughout the south, Elsa found an opportunity to continue on with her ways as she had done for decades.

Elsa added, "Tomorrow, Ned, I will go to Clarkston to send notice to Elizabeth that you are here safe and secure with me. I know she will worry till she hears. Now, let me see that wound."

Elsa looked at it closely. "Well, I must say, you've had good attention."

Ned motioned to Jo. "It's her work. She saved my life. I fell faint from lack of blood just as I reached her. She got me back safely to her house and tended to my needs and nursed me. I would have died, I presume, had she not been there."

Elsa offered, "Very fine work, Jo. You can tell that you kept it clean and dressed often."

Jo smiled. "I couldn't let my only known relative die," she said, as she winked at Ned.

Elsa cut to the chase. "Ned what are the plans? Do you plan to go north soon?"

Ned responded, "Elsa, I'm not sure."

"If I may, Ned," Elsa continued, "I have sent a letter of introduction to a man who has solid connections in Washington. From there you should find safety and, if you choose to, find a place in the Union army. I have laid out the events to him as I know them of you. I should receive, in a week or two, his thoughts and results in this matter. Now what are your thoughts on this?"

Ned finished chewing and swallowed down some milk, nodding his head up and down before swallowing the last bite. "Yes, Elsa, as like before, your years of station master on the underground railway has me covered and leading me in the right direction."

Elsa beamed with pride and said, "Well, it's what God has decided to do with me, Ned. I just obey."

Jo smiled and said, "Ned your description of Elsa was exactly as you indicated. Elsa, you are a saint."

Elsa retorted, "No, No. I'm just a servant. That's all. No more no less." Jo smiled, stood up, put her hands on the old woman's shoulder and leaned to kiss the top of her head.

"Now, Ned," Elsa said, as she took command once more, "Tell me of Lizza. What is the latest news?"

Jo looked questioning toward Ned. She had not really grasped that Ned had a woman or so she thought.

Ned immediately said, "Lizza is carrying our child."

And, as before, Elsa stood quickly and began to clap giving praise to God. She raised her hands to the ceiling saying, "Praise God, Praise God. Oh, happy day, Ned!"

"Yes, Elsa it is good," he said, as his eyes filled with tears.

Jo looked happy but confused.

Ned saw the look on Jo's face and added, "Jo, I never really had the time to give the whole story of my life. Since the first time I came here to Elsa's... "

After the next two hours of Elsa and Ned relating the past years, Jo was all in. She listened closely, at times wiping tears and smiling and laughing.

As the tale finished, Jo said, "Ned, my dear cousin. I feel so very close to you in this short time. You are my family and anything I can do, I will. You have but to ask."

Ned looked at Jo and nodded slightly as he closed his eyes knowing that in Jo he had not only a cousin but also a good friend.

Elsa chimed in, "This is a great day, but now we must follow the routine I've prepared in case there are those who may seek you out as they did Lizza. Ned, you will have to follow this routine until you leave for the northern lands."

The next several weeks found the threesome into a routine. Ned mostly took it easy in order to heal up and rest from Castle Thunder and his gunshot wound, while Jo and Elsa tended the canning of vegetables and drying and salting pork. The two women also made Ned a new pair of pants and a shirt.

Poor Jake was becoming barn sour, he wanted to run. His restless nature was most evident to Ned when he would come out of the house into the safety of the night to visit him in the barn and walk him around for a couple of hours each night.

Winter was coming early this year. The evenings came on chilly with frost on the ground most mornings.

Chapter 21
Becoming a Union Captain

In Staunton, after weeks of searching and hundreds of questions asked about the where-a-bouts of JT, the interest waned and folks soon forgot. JT's competition in wood delivery happily took over and JT was all but forgotten.

Auntie Bev realized this in a week after the deputy sheriff came to ask questions. All settled into a normalcy and on alternating nights, Lizza and Bessie visited. The two sisters were an amusement for Auntie. She loved to watch them act like little girls, a time lost together, but played out now as grown women.

Ned and Lizza were able to get letters to each other and continued to profess their love. Lizza continued to show more and more as the weeks passed in her pregnancy.

At last, after many months had passed and with winter still having a grip on Virginia, a letter came from Washington wanting Ned to be presented to Brigadier General Cokas. In the letter's briefness, it only stated that his services could be used to their fullest and amnesty was given for prior exploits. Please come as soon as possible. Ned was excited, wondering if he would get to fulfill his destiny as he believed it to be. At last, this may be the opportunity!

Ned sat to write a letter to Lizza as to his moving North and to be ready to move herself. He was going to try to get her to Maryland if possible.

Elsa thought differently. She believed Lizza was safe enough with Auntie Bev. "Ned you must trust us in this. Your Lizza is good and safe."

He was anxious to see his wife, but with much convincing by Jo, Ned agreed to keep her in Staunton unless dictated by serious changes in the valley.

"Ned," Jo asked, "I would like to go to Staunton when you head north. I might be of great help at sometime or another. What do you think? You yourself said that Auntie indicated in her last letter that she looked forward to meeting me."

Ned responded, "Yeah! I like that idea, Jo. I really do."

Elsa seconded the thought.

Jo explained that she would still like to stay with Elsa until the first of April. "You might need me if a late snow comes on."

"Sweetie," Elsa said, "I will be fine, but I would love the company."

"Then it is settled," Jo rang out.

Ned smiled his broadest smile and said, "There are so many things to be grateful for in these times. We forget to appreciate what we do have. We have good friends and family. It's the tie that binds."

Elsa commented, "Where have I heard that before?"

Ned kissed Elsa. "Old woman," he said, "I Love you dearly. Someday you will hold my child in your arms."

"Ned," she said, "If I live to feel your and Lizza's child in my arms, I will feel my life's work is complete."

Ned added, "If not for you, Elsa, Lizza and I might not have made it."

Thoughtfully Elsa said, "Possibly, Ned, but all things happen for a reason. Trust in God, Ned, always trust in Him. Now you need to leave tomorrow and we have many preparations to make."

At nightfall the very next day, Ned and Jake were on the move. Goodbyes, along with hugs and kisses from Jo and Elsa, were over and, at the same time, Ned's letter to Lizza traveled overland to Staunton.

In two days' time, Ned was across the Rappahannock River into Federal territory, moving into King George County and then Stafford

County, all along the way his letter from General Cokas was his pass to move further North.

Ned and Jake got into the Stafford Court House about 4 p.m. the second day. Jake finally had eased up from his anxiousness. The two days of moving fast and thru the night had calmed him down.

Ned was halted and asked his business and destination, and for his credentials. The Captain looked the letter over and said, "Stay here while I go see the Provost's Office." As he departed, the Captain left two guards to make sure Ned stayed put.

After two hours, a Major with Ned's letter in hand walked up and said, "Well, it seems you are to remain here until advised otherwise. I have wired Washington with a message to General Cokas and until that reply comes back you are to remain in these parts. You are not to leave here. Am I understood?"

Ned replied, "Yes, I comprehend Major. Where may I put up for the night?"

"That is for you to secure," the Major scoffed.

Ned figured a night on the ground was to be his lot.

The Captain came back and, after overhearing the exchange of words, said graciously, "He can share my tent, Major."

"Very well, Captain," the Major responded and added, "He is under your charge."

The Captain turned to leave and said "Come, Ned, I have some coffee and biscuits. You look like you could use some vittles."

"My horse, Captain," Ned added, "He comes first."

The Captain responded, "Bring him along. He can picket with my two horses; we have plenty of hay and fresh water."

For over an hour Jake enjoyed Ned's calming attention.

Ned entered the Captain's tent and thought, Nice! It had pennants, a canon slung back chair, pictures, two cots, one recently added just for Ned, fresh biscuits and the smell of boiled coffee, butter and apple butter.

Ned commented, "Very comfortable, I see Captain."

"Yes," the Captain said, "Being attached to this Provost Office has its amenities. That's some letter, Ned."

Ned then briefly gave a rundown of his past three years.

The Captain responded, "Ned you have had quite an exciting time to say the least. Mine has been boring for the most part of this war."

"Each to his duty I guess, Captain," Ned quipped. "Your Major seemed doubtful of my letter, Captain."

The Captain responded, "Never mind him, Ned. The Major is a pompous ass."

Ned laughed, "Yes, I can see that."

Early the next morning as the tent mates awoke, the Major came to see Ned. "Well, I have a reply. You are to stay put. General Cokas will be here in two days' time to meet with you. You are now under our flag. You have an appointment to the rank of Captain. Any and all questions from here on out must wait and be directed to the General. Do you understand, Captain?"

"Yes, Major," said Ned in his best martial voice. "I comprehend completely."

The Major continued, "Very well, Captain Dokken will help you become acquainted with such military matters pertaining to your rank. Am I understood, Captain Dokken?"

And, as to ape Ned to the pompous Major, Captain Dokken replied, "Yes, I comprehend, Major."

"Very well! Carry on," and once again the Major strutted off.

The regiment that held the Stafford Courthouse and its surrounding area quickly came to see Ned, after hearing of the new Captain among them. Everyone seemed to seek a look at this ex-confederate who now held the rank of Captain.

Everyone there was also impressed by Jake. Not a horse had any seen before was to compare. Be that as it may, Ned and Jake still were challenged to a race, which Ned respectfully declined. He could not risk an injury on a frivolous bet.

Captain Dokken and Ned formed a quick bond. Both came from humble lifestyles and both had lost their parents since the war began. Captain Dokken, as Ned, had a wife with a child to come. He also shared, as quickly as he could, the expectations of a Captain.

Ned already knew most by just being around military matters, even though still a civilian. He was rustled up some semblance of a uniform, which would be satisfactory until one could be bought.

The Major was correct in that General Cokas arrived at the courthouse in two days' time. Ned was summoned to meet with the General within the hour of his arrival. "Come in, Captain. I hope the appointment pleases you."

"Yes sir, General," Ned responded, "It is more than I deserve."

The General went on, "Not as I can tell, Captain. Your skills can be exploited to a great advantage. I must apologize that a return letter took so long. We did some investigation into you and your reputation. It is well known, not only with the Rebels, but with this Union Army. Yes sir!"

Continuing, the General explained, "Now as formality only, as you can understand, I will need an Oath of Allegiance to the United States Army and to your country to which you were born."

At the request of the General, and with the Major and Captain Dokken present, Ned was repatriated and officially commissioned.

The General excused the other two officers and said to Ned, "Sit, Captain."

For three hours, General Cokas outlined his duties as he saw them without divulging all. "Captain in several weeks, these duties I outlined will be put to the test with a new Commanding General in whom you will be attached. And to his staff, suffice it to say, you will not speak of this to anyone." The general drew his eyes seriously at Ned.

Ned quickly responded, "Yes sir! But of course!"

The General continued, "Until the commander is announced, you shall not know either. The President has some minor obstacles to get through, but it will surely happen. I will tell you that this new General has heard of you and pointedly asked for you on his staff. So you see, it was imperative that we investigate even unto finding your wife, a Negro, who is living in Staunton."

Ned bristled at the knowledge. His demeanor changed.

The General went on. "The Provost called, Ned. It's not a problem, Captain. I have only to ask one question."

"Yes sir," Ned came back tentatively.

Going on, the General said, "Would you feel more assured if we brought her behind Union lines?"

"Well sir, as for now," Ned sighed in relief, "I believe her to be safe with my Aunt."

The General interjected, "You mean Aunt Bev!"

"Yes sir." Boy, Ned thought to himself. They did search me out.

"Well, Captain," the General added, "If at any time you should change your mind, we will move her to a place of your choosing."

Ned positively responded, "Thank you, General."

The General commented, "Not at all, Captain. I, too, have a wife I brought out of New Orleans after the war started."

The General brought the meeting to an end with, "Now, Captain, have you any other questions?"

"No sir, you have been most thorough," Ned answered.

"Captain, I have one more order, or rather a strong request," the General said.

"Yes sir?" Ned said questioningly.

"Captain," the General added, "I would like you to be my aide at a formal affair to come soon. You might enjoy it."

Ned said, "Why of course, sir! I'd be happy to attend."

Finally, the General added, "Very well. I'll give you the particulars in due course. You are dismissed, Captain."

"Yes sir," Ned answered and gave his best salute.

Up to now Ned had never saluted anyone. The General smiled and walked Ned out of the tent to see the Major and Captain Dokken awaiting them.

The General said, "Major, you may use the new Captain for a short while. Soon, he will be called by me to be on reassignment. Do not use him but for duties light in nature. He must report for his assignment in the best of health and that goes for his famous horse as well."

Ned smiled and the General asked, "Jake, isn't it, Captain?"

"Yes, General," Ned said, "He is right over there."

The General glared at Jake and said, "Fine, fine animal. A blind man could see that," and added, "Well, gentlemen, I must be off and back to Washington. Oh! Major, attire the new Captain with a formal uniform and an appropriate field uniform."

"Yes sir, immediately," the Major responded.

"Good," added the General.

The three saluted the General.

Chapter 22

Molly at the Ball

In the preparation for the winter ball no expense was spared. The structure was prepared specifically for this affair. Buntings and flags lavished the walls, ceiling and rafters. It was as if this was a last hurrah before the spring brought more death and destruction.

Socialites from Washington and various field officers and their escorts were in attendance. The fare was beef and oysters, confectionary creations of many kinds and alcohol of all sorts. It was an event to surpass all since 1860.

Captain Dokken helped Ned in the nuances of this affair and in looking natty in his formal uniform. He was a sight to behold.

The General and his escort were complimentary of his appearance. Ned drove the carriage that took the threesome to Warrenton for the ball. He knew the area well. This was the operating area of Mosby. There was extra security all around. In fact, four regiments posted the countryside.

General Cokas surely was pleased. He was attended this night with a beautiful escort, a handsome aide, and the finest horse to pull them.

The attendants assisted the General and his escort off the carriage upon their arrival. Ned could hear the music and talking while he sat on the carriage. He was then instructed to find the carriage a place and come inside.

The General added, "All aides will be seated to the right as you enter. They have your name and rank at your seat. Remember, keep an eye out for any need we may have."

"Yes, General," Ned responded.

Ned entered the 150' x 80' building. It was magnificent. Never had he seen such decorations and fineries or beautiful women wearing dresses in colors of every hue, and Union officers smartly attired. It was a sight to behold. He tried to take it all in, the band, the rows of tables of food that never seemed to end, and to find General Cokas.

Finally, he caught sight of him with the help of his escort's bright canary yellow dress. He made eye contact with the General and he nodded as to his location.

Ned began to gaze around the large room. A woman, of shapely form on the dance floor in a waltz with a Colonel, caught his eye. He moved around to get a better view of her face. Immediately he ducked behind a Lieutenant.

"It can't be!" he actually said out loud. He took another look, and then realized that it was Molly and knew that he had no reason to hide.

Almost embarrassed he looked around to see if anyone had observed his actions. He stepped closer in hopes that Molly would see him all decked out in a Union Captain's uniform.

There, she saw him! She looked dead at him as the couple danced passed. She took a double take and then moved out of sight on purpose before the second look.

Molly turned ashen faced. He could see her looking frantically as they danced away. She was so alarmed that her Colonel escort kept asking her if she was okay.

Ned observed her request to quit dancing and they found their way to the table with none other than General Cokas and his escort. Ned just stared at her from his hidden spot among other aides.

Molly continued to scan the group of attendees. She lowered herself in the chair, which was surprising for a woman who sat perfectly at all times.

Ned moved at once to a spot not to be seen by her, but General Cokas spied him.

The Colonel with Molly continued to notice her agitation. She tried to dismiss it but after an hour she excused herself to go to the ladies' parlor.

As she moved along, Ned shadowed her until she disappeared into an alcove which led to a women's powder room. He made haste to get the General's attention.

With contact being made, the General excused himself from the table.

The General asked Ned, "What is it, Captain? You seem concerned."

Ned replied, "I am sir. The woman, the escort of the Colonel at your table, I know her very well. She is from these parts. She is the daughter of the family I holed up with while I rode with Mosby all that time. Her name is Molly and she is a fervent Confederate!"

Inquisitive, the General said, "Is that so? You are sure it is her, Captain?"

Ned responded, "As sure as I ever can be about anything."

"Very well, Captain," the General said. "Post back out of sight and I will question the good Colonel."

General Cokas pulled the Colonel aside as Ned watched from afar.

The Colonel was clearly taken aback and then took his seat once more while trying to settle himself.

General Cokas sought Ned and they went outside.

The General said to Ned, "Well, it seems this Molly, as you call her, is Kate Winstern of Rockville, Maryland. I have no doubt as to the veracity of your charge Captain, so you and I will stay here. The Colonel, on the pretense of getting some air from the heat inside, will bring Molly out here. I'm not sure what her intentions would be other than to be spying, if it is she. You shall come up and surprise her from behind and call her name out as you approach. We will observe her reaction."

In not five minutes the Colonel and Molly stepped outside as many were getting some fresh air.

Ned called out quickly, "Molly, how are you?"

Molly unconsciously responded, "Oh, I'm ..." and then she caught herself and saw Ned at the same time.

Ned continued, "So, Molly, how have you been?"

Molly didn't even try to foster an alibi or story. With venom, she spewed, "I see not as good as you, Captain."

Ned replied, "It seems the tables are turned. What do you say, Molly, wouldn't you agree?"

She spit at Ned's feet. The Colonel called out to a guard, "Sergeant, please detain and put a detail on this woman for safe keeping. She is under arrest."

"Yes, Sir!" the Sergeant responded.

"Molly, now it is your turn," Ned said.

"You're hog muck, Ned, nothing more!" she shot back.

The Sergeant and the detail took Molly away to be taken back to Washington and held for possible spy charges.

Ned felt sadness, not gleeful redemption, for what he endured because of her. He had liked Molly and, if not for Lizza, he possibly would have courted her in the end.

Molly was taken by train to Warrenton Junction and held until she could be questioned in greater detail.

"Captain," the Colonel said, "you will be needed for questioning tomorrow as well. This woman duped many to get here tonight, including the Provost and the Pinkerton. The Colonel then excused himself from the evening.

General Cokas, of course, granted his excuse under the circumstances. The General and Ned went back to the evening affairs.

The next morning Ned showed up at the makeshift jail in Warrenton Junction. After some questions pertaining to his knowledge of Molly and her family, Ned was excused, while the Colonel was also questioned as to how he had come to know her and who did the introductions.

After about three hours of waiting, Ned was called back for further questioning. Molly had stonewalled all interrogation so far. Ned thought about it briefly and asked if he might speak with her.

The Pinkerton man said, "I don't see what good that will do since she has such a hate for you."

"Perhaps, just perhaps," Ned said, "that's what's needed for her to spew in anger those answers you might seek."

"That might just work," said the Pinkerton as he thought, looking off and rubbing his whiskered face. "I suppose it's worth a try. We will bring her to you and I'll have my man standing in the closet. You must engage her immediately to keep her from being alert to her surroundings."

So, with all things in place, the guard brought her through the door of Ned's room.

"Oh no, I'm not going in there with that scoundrel," she yelled.

"What's the matter, Molly," Ned said quickly, afraid I might move your emotions of love for me again?"

Molly bit on the hook once again. "You flatter yourself, McDonald," she started to say to him with a raised finger, shaking it furiously. "I'll tell you something, McDonald, there are finer men than you all throughout the south. You are a no-good Northerner who pretended to be of good southern pride. You northern men are so gullible to a southern belle's charm. It was so easy to dupe those to get with all the brass. Five men in succession fell to me, five, McDonald, all spoke freely of many a secret with the thought they might have a chance to bed me."

Ned came back, "So, all five bedded you, Molly? Whatever would your family say?"

"No, McDonald, I said they thought that they might!" Molly paused and caught herself. Her venom had ebbed enough as to catch that she had been caught saying too much.

"Take me from this man's sight," she said to the Pinkerton.

As the agent in the closet stepped out, Molly's shoulders dropped. Immediately, she said, "My family knows nothing of my goings on. I left without even saying good-bye. Please, my family is innocent!"

"Come ma'am," the Pinkerton said.

Molly's eyes filled with tears as she was led away.

Ned called out to her. She turned to look at him with the most sorrowful eyes. They looked at one another. In a dramatic heartfelt tone, she said, "I'm sorry for what I did to you, Ned. I loved you! You knew that."

Ned nodded a little as the Pinkerton escorted her away.

Ned talked briefly with the lead Pinkerton. He said, "I can tell you that she is correct. Her family are fine southern folks and only wanted to keep isolated, to ride out the war and get back to normalcy."

The Pinkerton shot back quickly, "Is that why they kept you safe in their home while you ran with Mosby and his Raiders, because they wanted to be isolated?"

Ned had no answer. He only said, "Please, they are good people. Go easy on them."

"Pending all findings, they will be treated accordingly," was the reply.

Ned was distraught. He even thought of going to Molly's home, but he decided better of it. He had so much more to do. He had to push this all from his mind. He mounted Jake and headed back to the Stafford Court House.

Later, he sat and wrote Lizza a long letter lamenting his missing her and how he wanted to feel her and put his hands on her stomach as she grew with their child. It had been seven months since he had seen her. By now he knew she was probably beginning to waddle as she walked. He smiled at the thought of watching her get in and out of chairs. Ned's one solace was that Auntie Bev was with her and Jo would soon be there also.

Chapter 23

Meeting with General Grant

March came in with ease in '64. It was looking like an early spring, or at least it seemed so. Ned was contacted the second week of March to go to Morgansburg, due east of the Courthouse. Morgansburg sat north-northwest, ten miles from the confluence of the Rapidan and the Hedgeman Rivers to make up the Rappahanock River. Ned was given no other information, only that he was to report to Adjutant General Rawlins. He was anxious and nervous. He knew that this was what General Cokas had, in a roundabout fashion, imparted to him about his duties.

Arriving in Morgansburg, Ned wondered who this General was that had requested a recent repatriated civilian and had given him Captain's bars. Ned found the Colonel's tent and climbed off Jake.

A Corporal took the reins and said, "He will be taken good care of, Captain." The Corporal stood at attention waiting to be saluted off.

Ned replied, "Yes, thank you, Corporal."

Captain Logan approached, "Captain McDonald, I surmise," he said.

Ned responded, "Yes, Captain, I am."

"Very good then," Captain Logan said. "I will show you to Colonel Rawlins. You are quite prompt. That is good. Colonel Rawlins is a stickler for carrying out orders and promptness."

Ned stepped through the canvas flap.

Colonel Rawlins looked up and said, "Captain, I see you have one attribute to be coveted!"

Ned responded, "Sir?"

"Promptness, Captain, I tolerate nothing less. I'm understood, I take it?"

Ned responded, "Yes sir, men die at the lack of promptness!"

Rawlins hesitated, "Why yes! Very well. Sit Captain." Rawlins then wore out Ned's ears for two hours about the command, its expectations, and the anticipation of every man on the staff.

After all of this, Ned asked, "Colonel, sir, if I may?"

"You may, Captain."

"Sir, who might our General be?"

"Why, Captain, of course. Lt. General U.S. Grant."

Ned had heard the name and understood that he was the Commander who never let go once engaged with the enemy. He remembered overhearing General Longstreet speak with rebel J.E.B. Stuart, as follows: "I know this man Stuart, he is my cousins husband. He will go through a brick wall instead of around it. He never covers the same ground twice. God forbid we in Virginia should ever face him."

Ned said, "Pardon, Colonel, you said Lt. General?"

"Yes, Captain, over all Union forces," the Colonel replied. "Not since George Washington has one been bestowed the rank. Now, Captain, the General will be here on or about the 24th. Captain Logan will introduce the staff to you and your duties before General Grant's arrival. Captain Logan," the Colonel summoned thru the flap.

"Yes sir, Colonel?"

"Captain Logan, you know what I want, see it gets done."

"Yes Sir! Colonel, Sir," snapped Captain Logan. Turning to Ned, he said, "Come, Captain McDonald."

The two stepped into the warm day. Ned noticed that early leaf buds appeared on the trees, a sign of new life. He couldn't help correlate that with Lizza, budding with life within her. A pang hit him. He said a silent prayer for her and the child.

Ned was involved in paper work assisting Colonel Rawlins and riding up and down the Rapidan, clear down to Falmouth opposite Fredricksburg, bringing orders to Commanders from General Grant until he arrived.

All along the union front, the question was asked of each commander, hadn't we had enough? It became a joke in the ranks, new general, then we fight, then retreat. It was a sore spot with the enlisted men, blood spilled, nothing gained.

Finally, Grant rode into camp.

Ned was waiting at the Potomac; he knew all was quite different. He could feel the electricity in the air. He then returned to the headquarter tent with the usual protocol of bringing a response from his last destination.

Ned was running Jake long distances less and less each day. More and more wire was strung for Morse code communication.

Colonel Rawlins informed Ned that at 4:00 p.m. sharp, General Grant had asked to speak with him at his tent.

It was now only 2:00 p.m. and he had time to tend to Jake and clean road dust from his uniform, which he still did not enjoy. His uniform was uncomfortable compared to his scouting clothes.

Ned arrived at General Grant's tent at exactly 4:00 p.m.

"How may I help you, Captain," the Sergeant asked.

"Yes, Sergeant, I have an appointment with General Grant."

"He expects you, Captain. He asked to send you right in."

Ned poked his head through the tent flap tentatively. "General, Sir," he announced himself.

The General responded, "Captain McDonald?"

"Yes sir," Ned replied.

"Come in please. Brandy?" asked Grant.

Ned said, "No sir, I do not drink."

"Fine. Sit, sit please."

Ned sat at the table.

The General offered, "I expected a ghost to come through the flap. Your reputation of appearing and disappearing is well known in your scouting exploits."

Pleased, Ned replied, "Yes sir. Thank you."

The General went on, "Not at all, Captain. It is for this reason that when I heard of your repatriation I requested you upon my appointment to head this army of ours."

"Yes sir," Ned answered.

"I need a skillful rider with an exceptional horse. Jake is his name?"

Ned positively responded, "Yes sir, Jake."

"Well, in the course of which I intend to move, I need communication and observation skills that can be counted on. I intend to hammer Lee into submission. When we begin in the weeks to come, we will not retreat. You know what I mean, Captain?"

"Yes sir, you do not retreat," Ned replied.

The General spoke back, "No, I do not!"

Ned looked at the General. He was under 6 feet and maybe 150 pounds, cropped beard, intense eyes and cigar chewing. He loved the cigar. He looked like a field Colonel. His dress was not sloppy but careless. His hands were like a farmer's, rough and strong. Ned thought maybe this unlikely looking General had what it took to end this war.

The General continued, "Can I count on you, Captain?"

Ned strongly replied, "Yes sir, yes you can!"

The General went on, "Good, you are acquainted with many of the corps commanders by now?"

"Yes sir," Ned answered.

The General then said, "I am keeping General Meade in his position. He will dictate orders. On the other hand, you, Captain, answer to me and me alone. You will be my eyes and ears for first-hand observation of the front and battle. Forgive me, but sometimes my deputy commanders are clouded on what they see so as to enhance their own accolades. I will tolerate no milk toast commanders!"

Ned proudly responded, "Yes sir, I understand!" He liked Grant more and more.

"Come, Captain. I want to be introduced to Jake."

" Sir, yes sir! "

As they left the tent, Ned followed Grant and they saw three black horses. The first was a 14.2-hand black pony named Jeff Davis, a horse captured at President Davis' brother's plantation near Vicksburg. The second was a shiny, well-proportioned horse who was 15.1 or so. He was named Egypt. The third was Cincinnati. He was a magnificent powerful 17-hand black beauty, a real match for Jake.

The General told Ned, "Cincinnati was a gift from a businessman from out west." Grant used all three horses.

Ned said, "Such a strong stable, General!"

"Thank you, Captain," the General replied.

Ned said, "Not at all, General," and added, "Cincinnati is a rare piece of horse flesh."

"Yes, I'm most proud of him," the General responded.

Ned was soon to find out that General Grant, although unassuming in stature, was a master horseman. He was rated the best horseman of his class at West Point. The two men made their way casually to Ned's tent and where Jake was picketed.

Many along the way didn't even recognize the General in his appearance. Most just stared and half saluted. The salutes were not a concern to Grant.

"There he is, General," Ned said proudly.

"Yes," the General replied as he paused and kneeled down studying Jake. "Yes, Captain. He is what all have said. Yes, indeed."

The General then approached Jake with an extended hand. "Well, Jake, I'm your new General."

Jake turned to observe the man before him. In Jake's schooling, Ned had taught him tricks to honor.

Ned commanded, "Salute, Jake!"

Jake raised his right leg bent at the knee as high as possible.

Grant smiled. "At ease, solider Jake."

Ned told Jake, "Down," and he resumed chewing some hay.

The General said, "It would be a good race between our horses, eh, Captain?"

The General picked up a stick, broke off the offshoots and started to whittle as he walked.

Grant was clearly taken with Ned. Back at the General's tent, Grant asked Ned, "I would like you to have dinner with me tonight, Captain. I want to talk horses. There are so few men who know horses. Shall we say 7:00 p.m.? I won't keep you late Captain. I have a meeting with General Meade after dinner."

Ned quickly accepted, "Yes sir, General, 7:00 p.m."

"You are dismissed, Captain McDonald. Oh, and Captain, please be not on ceremony with your attire."

Ned answered, "Yes sir!"

The dinner that evening was brief. Ned did notice that Grant liked his meat almost char burnt. After dinner, the talk of horses was filled with techniques and even saddle and tack preferences.

After all the conversation, Ned knew he really liked Grant and that the General thought the same of him.

Chapter 24

The First Battle Under General Grant

General Meade came in the tent before Ned had been excused. Ned, of course, had heard of Meade. Meade was in the long line of Generals to head the Union Army. Meade was the savior of Gettysburg, but as the rest had faltered in pressing the reels when an advantage was gained. Meade, however, would be retained in his previous command, General-in-Chief. Grant would oversee him closely in the field.

General Grant greeted General Meade, "How good to see you! Come in." Meade was ramrod straight, a sour puss and mercurial in attitude, his wrath was meted equally to subordinates.

General Grant said, "I believe you know Captain McDonald, now with my staff."

Meade looked Ned over top to bottom and offered, "Rather slack on your appearance, Captain."

"Yes sir," Ned replied.

Grant spoke up for Ned, "At my request, General."

"I see. Yes, I am aware of the Captain and his past," Meade stressed. "I hope your usefulness outweighs your rebel exploits."

Ned Responded, "Yes sir, General Meade."

General Grant then said, "Captain, you are excused till morrows light." Ned replied, "Yes sir, General Grant."

The meeting of Meade and Grant was to assure Meade of his retention and not demotion to the western theatre as others in the past had been. Meade left the meeting consoled and relieved, but a tight rein was kept on Meade's actions.

Grant was to exert great effort with Sherman, his long-time friend in the South, and Butler on the Virginia peninsula coming north to Richmond. As Grant pressed south, he wanted no reprieve for the rebels.

Sherman, as he said, would make the Deep South howl! And he would. He said, "War is hell! The uglier the better, the sooner this war will end!"

Since early March in 1864, Ned had gotten a letter once a week, the latest saying that Jo had arrived in Staunton and that she was good to have around, she was always tending to Lizza's needs. Lizza was a few weeks, by calculation, overdue, at least they all thought. Lizza told Ned that she was ready to pop. Auntie had her laid up in bed awaiting their child.

As Ned was thinking of Lizza while making his way back to his tent, he heard, "Captain McDonald!" Ned swung Jake around as the Sergeant ran to him. "This came for you this morning."

Ned turned it to the fireside light. It was from Lizza! He said, "Thank you, Sergeant."

The aide smiled. "Hope it's good news, Captain."

"I, too, Sergeant," Ned responded, and then unsaddled and told Jake, "Stay here, old man." Ned sat next to the fire. He fumbled in opening the letter in anticipation of hearing from his love.

"My dearest husband and love, I have given birth to your most beautiful daughter!"

Oh! God! Tears flowed heavily for Ned. He had to compose himself before he could continue. It took a while.

"She did not want to see the world yet, but with urging from me and much coaxing, pushing and with the great help of Auntie and Jo, she opened her mouth to try out her lungs. I can say her lungs are most healthy. She suckles with much enthusiasm. Auntie says she is as healthy a baby she has seen. She wants to hold her whenever I sleep. Jo is greatly taken with her! Her full head of hair is more than I expected. Oh, and how beautiful is your daughter!"

"I would like to name her, Ned. Since we did not discuss names for her, I prefer to use a name I once read in a book with the main woman in the story, called Christiana. If it be alright with you, so shall we call her?"

Ned nodded his head and said aloud, even though he was by himself, "Yes, Lizza, Christiana she shall be."

Lizza, in other letters, had told him of Bessie and of their good times being together. "But my Bessie became weak in the knees as I was giving birth and had to await Christiana's entrance outside. Bessie, while most taken with our child, attends and dotes over me constantly. I fear her thoughts as she thinks I will pass on. I tell her momma brought two of us, Bessie, I believe I can manage one. Still she dotes. I do love her for it, though. I miss you so terribly and pray diligently for your safety and speedy return. I hope for a letter soon. Love Always, Dear Husband, Lizza."

Ned stared into the firelight, tears dropping on to the dusty ground below him. If only momma and daddy could have seen their grandchild, he thought. Then, it came to him. Maybe they already knew her!

Ned wanted to go see Lizza and his new daughter. He thought about requesting a leave, but his sense was otherwise. Grant knew the moment when the spring campaign would begin. And that he needed Ned. So, he thought better and entrusted Lizza to his Aunt and cousin.

Ned was on the move for weeks living up to General Grant's expectations. On May 3rd, Ned was gathered with Grant and Meade's staffs. It was then given all intents for the push south. At the same time, Sherman and Butler would begin. The Blue and Grey would very soon become so engaged that it would be a death lock of survival, the likes and scale heretofore had neither side known.

The Union had some 118,000 men with five corps, one being cavalry. The Confederate had nearly 61,000 with three corps, one being cavalry. The opposing armies sat on the Rapidan River on opposite banks. Grant wished to surprise and flank General Robert E. Lee and the rebels, but Meade's dalliance and lack of coordination forced the Union surprise to be stopped. Meade's timidity came to light before the first skirmisher fired a shot.

Ned was following along, noting progress and failures for General Grant. Ned moved over the Rapidan in the Van Guard Corps. Almost immediately the wilderness, as it was known, began to show that no battle could be played out here with success, as many had seen in the Chancellorsville Battle, where now bleached bones and skulls sat amongst the entangled forest floor.

Ned heard rifle fire, sporadic in nature, growing then ebbing. He traced and retraced the long armies strung out for miles and miles, coming down the Old Orange Turnpike to Locust Grove. He heard musket fire in a din the likes he had never heard; a few cannons, but musketry in a constant crescendo.

Ned found General Warren's 4th Corps stranded on the old Orange Turnpike. For over five miles, the rebel's Brigadier General Gordon was making a regrouped push to plug a gap in General Warren's line. It was successful and the fragmented Union line fell back.

Ned saw men running hell bent with total fear and screaming, "We've lost the line! They're coming from everywhere!"

As Ned pushed forward, he and Jake moved along a deer-track logging path in order to get a grip on the prevailing circumstances. Thousands of muskets filled the forest with thick smoke. Ned found it hard to keep his bearings. All along the way, he found men lost from their regiments. Fighting in small pockets of men.

Ned pulled out and inserted himself further northwest. He found a stable front, but men firing into what they could not see, only at sounds. Fires were increasing along the whole front. Smoke choking and blinding both armies. Ned heard whistling or errant bullets go by him repeatedly. He pushed on in his assessment. Not good! There were many men lying all over the forest floor. Some were unable to move from wounds and many being burned alive. The pungent smell of burnt flesh and burnt powder permeated his nose. Ned had never witnessed such scenes. Jake flinched at times but was there to respond to every cue.

A voice rang out, "Help! For all that is Holy, help me!"

Ned looked around and saw a man clawing his way from a fire that had caught him afire. His pant legs and skin were burnt, and his screams pierced Ned's ears.

He dismounted Jake and knelt to see if he could help. The Private was in absolute agony, one of the cannons fired had found its mark and had torn chunks of flesh from his legs and broken both.

"God, help me," the man yelled.

Ned, for the first time in this war knew not what to do. He looked around frantically to find someone to help the soldier. No one was close enough to help. Minie balls were filling the air, tearing at tree trunks and tree limbs were falling all around.

As Ned looked back at the man, his eyes were lifeless. Out loud Ned yelled, "Dear God, save this soul."

Ned grabbed at his clothing to find something personal to contact his family. He found a letter! He shoved it in his shirt. Laid the soldier's head on the forest floor to stare up through the smoke into the blue sky above this maelstrom.

Ned put his hand on the soldier's head and said, "Dear God, save his soul. May he see the gates of heaven."

Ned stood and swung into the saddle. He had seen enough, and headed back out the way he had come. Darkness came and he needed to report to General Grant. As quickly as he could, he returned to headquarters. He got off Jake and without giving him his normal attention, looked for General Grant.

Ned saw Grant on a stump bent over whittling a twig and said, "General Grant, sir! Captain McDonald reporting."

Grant looked up slowly, his eyes revealed already that he knew what Ned was to say.

The General said, "My dear Captain, I have hope you have news better than my preliminary ones," and continued to whittle.

Ned reported, "General, it is not what we wanted to achieve. The fighting in these battles is severe and battle lines and groups are impossible. We cannot sustain many days as this. I fear the tally possibly 7,000 to 8,000, with the rebels much less." Ned waited for a response.

"Yes," Grant finally came back. "I impressed on Meade the magnitude of his harm and the urgency to strike, and turn his flank. That loss, my God, the men lost."

Ned, for an hour, detailed his day and observations, while Grant listened and continued whittling.

Ned finally said, "That's all I have, sir."

The General then said, "Captain McDonald, what would be your next move if you were I?"

Ned uncomfortably responded, "Oh! Sir I don't know." He paused and then added, "I suppose I would reengage tomorrow in hopes of pushing Lee, somehow, out of this morass of wilderness."

The General came back with, "Precisely, Captain, that is exactly what I will do. Lee will soon know who I am firsthand."

Grant stood, raised his hand and rested it on Ned's shoulder, and said, "Fine work, Captain. I am most grateful. Get some sleep and resume your duties tomorrow. I will see you tomorrow evening."

Ned replied, "Yes sir, General."

Ned started to leave, paused and said, "General sir, if I might add."

"Yes, Captain?" the General responded.

"Well, General," Ned replied, "the army, while at first was bullied, they came to regroup and stand. It was something to see the change of faces as new resolve came upon them."

The General responded, "Yes, Captain, these fresh troops are like a new bird dog, gun shy at first and a need to find their place."

Ned said, "Yes sir, Goodnight General."

"Good night, Captain," the General replied.

Ned awoke on May 6 and pushed open the flap to his tent. The dense fog did not bode well with the day to come. He could feel the wetness in the air on his face as he made his way to tend to Jake. Ned had not slept well at all since the previous day's events replayed in his head, especially relative to the private he had gone to aid.

Later that evening he penned a quick letter to the address that was on the letter he had taken off the Union Solider. Even with his first-hand knowledge of the death, Ned was easy with his message, stating only that the solider died a brave and valiant death holding his assignment to the end. After penning the letter, Ned quickly put tack on Jake and dropped by Grant's tent in hopes of seeing Meade. When Meade wasn't available, he headed back to the front.

As Ned and Jake went down the Germanna Plank Road to intersect Old Orange Turnpike, he spied the road he had exited out of the battle yesterday. It was just after Mrs. Spotwood's land. She was, in fact, out on the road watching the movements as Ned stopped. "Dear woman," Ned said, "You need to move north of the Rapidan."

She forthrightly responded, "Dear young man, I shall never leave!" Her conviction was strong and Ned had neither the time nor the words to convince such a woman.

After responding, "God be with you, dear lady," Ned headed west-southwest on the one-wagon wide road.

After riding awhile, Ned heard the pop of muskets immediately ahead. As he got to the Union forces, he found himself in the midst of General Sedgwick's 6th Corps.

Over the night, a semblance of order had been attained with both armies. The Union army was laid out in a lazy S-shape, mostly north of the Orange Turnpike. General Warren's corps abutted General Sedgwick's and extended for a half mile over the Turnpike. Makeshift beams were trees felled and stacked hastily, giving protection. Ned found the 6th Corps and first division commander, a man named Wright.

Wright recognized Ned. And asked, "Captain, have you news from Grant? We are in a bit of a pickle amongst this forest."

Ned answered, "General, no not this morning. Grant was with Meade. However, I am sure direction is forthcoming. I only observe and report as for now."

"Very well, Captain," Wright said.

Then Ned asked, "General Wright, is your right flank well protected?"

The General reported, "Yes, as far as I can tell. You are welcome to see Captain, but my scout affirmed that this morning."

Ned responded, "Thank you, General, I will."

Ned made his way behind the Union line through the heaviest undergrowth he had ever seen.

Minutes after Ned and Jake had left Wright, a courier brought orders to Sedgwick and Warren. They were to stay put in order to keep General Early and his rebels in check while the Union forces posted south with General Hancock's 2nd Corps that was going against General A.D. Hill and his corps of rebels.

Ned made his way to the end of the Union lines and pushed farther on. At last he was out of the thickness of the brush. He came to a creek called Flat Run. Moving slowly and carefully along its bank, he pushed ahead hoping to find Confederate skirmishers or, if lucky, look to the south to see signs of the tail of the Confederate's left flank. After careful searching, he caught sight of soldiers ahead.

Quietly tying up Jake, Ned sidled north for over 1/4 mile and, finally, he spotted no rebels.

"This is not good," Ned whispered to himself. "The rebels have overrun our right flank."

With secrecy and stealth, Ned quickly returned to Jake, who still had not moved, and said to him, "That's my man, Jake. Good boy." The two carefully picked their way back for Ned to find General Wright.

Ned reported his findings of his scouting to Wright, who did not seem receptive to Ned's assessment.

As the halo of musket balls had now begun for a second day, Ned uncomfortably said, "General Sir, I am most concerned."

The general shot back, "Captain, I have said thank-you to you once too many! You are dismissed!"

Keeping in mind the tail of the Confederacy that overlapped the Union was under the direction of Brigade Commander Golden, a most capable Commander, Ned had to try once more, and said, "General Sir, I must stress…"

"Good day, Captain," Wright yelled and shot Ned a strong look of disgust.

"Very well, General," Ned said, and then left.

Chapter 25

Ned's Report and Grant's New Maneuver

Ned headed around the Lazy S of the battle line to Warren's corps. He was happy to discover that the Union overlapped considerably the Confederate's right flank. Ned hoped that the denseness of the forest would keep any flank-turning action from being tried. But, Ned recalled General Stonewall Jackson who had done just that years ago right in these parts at Chancellorsville. He had rolled up the Union's right side and sent thousands of men running.

 The battle that morning became as bad or worse than the day before. For hours upon hours men were moving up, falling back, thousands being killed and others maimed, as that private, being burned terribly. Some of the fires still burned from yesterday. Musket smoke, burning brushes and trees. It was almost impossible to see and breathe.

 Unknown to Ned, during this day, General Longstreet, Grant's wife Julia's cousin, was seriously wounded and taken eventually to Staunton to be on the mend. He had turned the Union's flank of General Hancock once again, successfully flanking in morass. But after Longstreet's injury, the rebels faltered.

 Lee then ordered General Ewell to press the advantage at the very place Ned had warned General Wright about that day. Gordon pressed and collapsed in the Union's right flank, as Ned had said could be done.

At around 6:00 p.m., Gordon and the rebels, with relative ease, captured two brigadier commanders and around 500 men. Finally, with a reinforced effort, the successful flanking was stopped.

As Ned got back to where his day had begun, the furious fever of battle still raged. Men were being rushed to secure the right flank, others rushing to the rear after being wounded or just plain scared at the onrush of rebels with their bone chilling screams as they assaulted the Union lines.

At last the second day's muskets subsided, the forest crackled with fires and smoke blanketed for miles. Hurt men, by scores, were being carried to the rear on blankets in agony. Screams for help were heard everywhere, as were pleas for mercy. Men committed suicide instead of being burned alive because they could not move fast enough or move at all.

The wilderness battle ended. Over 17,000 Union soldiers dead or maimed, while General Robert E. Lee's rebels suffered only half the number.

Ned found himself terribly upset, sad and mad at the day's events and unnecessary losses. He rode alongside of the Germanna Road while wagons carried men north across the Rapidan River. Many men were hurt, but some not badly enough to be put on wagons. Some struggled on makeshift crutches and some with heads wrapped and covered with blood. Ned could smell the unforgettable odor of blood and it in abundance.

Ned reined up at headquarters, dismounted and was told that Grant expected him, but that he was with Meade and two division commanders. Ned heard heated words exchanged. So, he moved to a respectable distance and waited till he could report to General Grant.

Ned sat against a tree and closed his eyes. He thought to himself, is this war, is this what General Sherman wants all to see and experience? As the scenes he had laid eyes on these last two days replayed in his mind, he became nauseated and vomited. He stood to breathe deeply and put his mind elsewhere. He went to Jake to check him over and sooth his own spirit. It came to Ned, God's been with us! Not a scratch on either of us, Jake and me, after all this in two days and over the years.

Ned put his arms around Jake and laid his head along Jake's neck. The smell of a horse was always soothing to him. Jake held still and made small muffled noises in response to Ned's affection. The two were aware of what they meant to each other. His heavy snuffles of Ned were bonding for Jake.

Ned was then hailed to Grant's tent. Ned said, "I'll be back, big man, and I'll clean you up and brush you." Jake shook his head up and down.

General Grant said, "Come in, Captain. I have assessments complete from my divisions. Now I want your observations and assessments."

Ned responded, "General Grant, Sir, respectfully to what I saw was Sedgwick's 6th Corps, which is all I got to be with today. And as I was learned later, per your orders, was to keep Ewell checked. That was done as well as could be expected, General, with one crucial exception. I learned that the first division of Sedgwick's corps was over extended a measurable distance by rebel forces. My scouting determined that a possible turning move might be had if so pressed. I quickly informed Division Commander Wright of my findings. I was dismissed after repeatedly and earnestly seeking recognition of my findings."

Grant chewed at his cigar in the corner of his mouth while playing with a fork on the table, and asked, "Captain, did you reveal this to General Warren of 5th Corps?"

Ned answered, "No General. At the time, I was with Warren's Corps, he had engaged a stymied Ewell's corps of rebel General Rodes."

Grant then said, "Captain, in the future, if you come upon a similar situation, you will impart it to an adjacent division commander so he, at least, knows of his flanks possible situation."

To which Ned responded, "Yes, General, I sincerely apologize."

Grant continued, "Not necessary, Captain. You could not have done a better job today. It seems to me, this may be a draw at this place, a stalemate as if it were. Captain, once again I ask you, if you were I, what would you do tomorrow?"

Ned thought for a moment and then said, "Well, sir, I would not continue the futile fight here, and I would not fall back in retreat."

Grant pulled his cigar from his mouth and pointed it at Ned. "Very good, Captain." Then he reinserted the cigar into the corner of his mouth and, once again, began to chew on it. "Continue, Captain."

Ned went on, "Well, sir, I suppose I would move into the open country."

Ned stopped and went to the map on the large table. He gazed at it for a minute, as Grant looked at Ned's finger tracing the map. "There, General Grant, Sir, I would move as quickly as possible and circle southeast to here at Spotsylvania Courthouse."

Grant said, "Move over 100,000 men over 20 miles with an end run on the likes of Robert E. Lee?"

Ned promptly answered, "Yes sir."

Grant said, "Excellent, Captain. In my previous meeting, I wrote orders to that same conclusion."

Ned stood up straight and was smiling like a cat that had just eaten the songbird.

Grant then added, "Well, Captain, you may be a Corps Commander one day."

"Yes sir, General," Ned said smartly.

Grant told Ned, "The move south will take place immediately. If we can steal this march on Lee, we will be between Lee and Richmond. I pray that Meade will not fail as with our last move."

Ned offered, "Yes, General, I can say the soldiers will be satisfied that they will not be retreating."

And so it was! All had known that the rebels had got the best of the engagement of two days, and in the past, when whipped or stalemated, the Union fell back to lick the their wounds.

When Commanders that night ordered to pack it up on the night of the 7th and move out, all figured here it goes again, retreat. But, soon the northern track became a constant southern track. All up and down the road there were wagons and trudging tired men, all became excited and elated they were not retreating. It raised spirits and cheers for Grant, which had to be stifled because this trek was only miles from the rebel's right flank. A testament to drilling and training and battle-tested men was to pull out of a deadly two-day battle without reprieve and attempt a silent march. Grant was being true to his reputation, lockup and never let go or give respite to the enemy. It's what old Abe Lincoln had been searching for since the onset of this war.

Grant said, "Move out, Captain. There will be no sleeping this night."

"Well, Jake," Ned said as he got back to Jake, "the General said no sleep tonight."

Grant's orderlies had attended to Jake and watered him while he was with the General.

VIRGINIA WINDS

Ned's thoughts drifted to Lizza and his infant Christiana. He bowed his head after mounting Jake and said a prayer for them. And he asked God to see him safely through his duties.

"Amen," Ned said aloud. "Now I have to go! Focus, Ned, focus," he told himself. He and Jake tore down the road and spent time weaving in and out of men, wagons and columns trying to reach the lead division.

All along the way men trudged, but they were light hearted. They embraced this new trek that no other general thus far had taken.

All the while Ned kept asking at intervals, "Whose division? Whose regiment?" to gauge how far he was getting. Jake saved Ned several times by side stepping troops, as Ned couldn't help but daydream of his family.

"Sorry, Old boy! I missed that one. That is why I need you," he said as he patted Jake.

Robert E. Lee did catch on to this attempt at stealing a march around his right flank, but Grant had the most direct route. Lee, as always, figured out where Grant would try to go. The sly grey fox had done it too many times to be lucky. Lee sent Ned's old Confederate General J.E.B. Stuart's Cavalry Corps to head off Grant and delay them until the Rebel Army could make the long way around and take the Spotsylvania Court House.

Stuart could only delay such a force, but finally had to pull out. Sure enough, Lee got there and dug in sufficient enough to stop Grant. Once again, the two great giants walked up for battle.

Grant tried to dislodge the rebels, on his arrival, but without success. On the 10th, Grant was to hit the center with a hard blow, led by an energetic young colonel, Colonel Upton. Upton broached an idea, but even with some success, they were repulsed. This loss, and the loss of Core Commander General Sedgwick, saddened Grant terribly.

Yesterday, the 9th, Ned had been surveying the lines along with General's Sedgwick, Wright, Getty, and Rickets, Grant's Division Generals. Ned was to take some observations of his own and those of General Sedgwick to Grant over two miles away.

Some rebel sharpshooters, up along a skirmish line, were firing at the five of them. Wright advised that they move to a safer location.

In response, Sedgwick laughed in disdain, "They, gentlemen, could not hit an elephant at that distance."

135

Ned was only half a step behind Sedgwick when, at the end of the last word, a minie ball slammed into Sedgwick's face below his eye and killed him instantly. Ned actually caught him before he hit the ground.

Grant later said in the loss of Sedgwick, "I could not replace him with an entire corps of soldiers."

Ned sat at Grant's tent and watched him chew his cigar and lament the loss of such a beloved leader of men. He had to find a replacement.

Ned thought that Hancock, the hero of Gettysburg, would be a good choice.

Grant asked Ned, "Captain, if you were I, would you have assaulted the rebel line?"

Ned responded, "General, even though beaten up and tired, I believe in the Hancock Corps."

Grant then added, "Yes, I thought of that, too, but I'm pulling them back for rest. I believe in Warren, although he's still green. I must battle test his Corps more."

Ned gently reminded Grant of his failure to tend to flanks days earlier and he got rolled up.

Grant quietly answered, "Yes, I know Captain, but I have to put him in again in hopes that he's learned."

Ned agreed, "Yes, sir."

Grant continued, "General Warren and Colonel Upton assaulted and fell back. However, the assault proved that if the numbers were great enough, the assault would prove productive."

For this, then, Grant used Hancock's men as Ned suggested. The silent center, known as the Mule Shoe, was assaulted by 20,000 of Grant's men. The Mule Shoe was a meat grinder. Lee had pulled cannon's back too soon. Consequently, as the assault began again and when Lee finally brought back cannons forward to the line, it was too late for effectiveness.

Grant's men poured up and over. Rifle fire and bayonets were hardly ever used. Now, rifles were used as clubs. It was war at its most basic element. Men fell on top of men half-dead, pushed down into the mud to die of no air; three to four deep laid dead on one another. It went on so long that men fell back to rest and fell asleep in the midst of the din and dying. They awoke to once again engage in battle. The slippery hills were wet and muddy, and blood ran freely and pooled everywhere. This area became known as the Bloody Angle.

Ned had commandeered a cannon and ordered a few men to man the artillery piece. They got out seven rounds before their cannon was disabled and the two men that helped him were lying dead.

Ned had shrapnel crease his head slightly and the explosion threw him three feet back in the air. Jake was 30 yards back when Ned got to him. Ned's whole side was bloody, head to boots. He found medical help at Grant's tent.

Grant's surgeon said he would live and added, "It creased the skull good."

Ned was dizzy for days. His ability to walk was impaired. It was worse when he got on Jake, but he pushed on.

Grant came short of insisting that he take to the cot. Ned would have none of it.

Later in May, an assault took place that brought no results; however, there were 20,000 casualties on each side. Grant saw the futile attempt at this spot as he did in the morass of the Wilderness Battle.

Ned attended the staff counsel that night and in attendance was Meade. It was a tense affair.

Back on 10 May, Cavalry Commander Sheridan had accused Meade of timidity and lack of generalship in not taking General J.E.B. Stuart.

Grant had, once again, trusted Meade and he had failed. Grant now wanted details from Meade as to why he had failed.

Ned sat off to the side wondering how such a General, who was the victor at Gettysburg, could perform so miserably.

The proud Meade sat ramrod straight the whole time, pragmatically trying to convince Grant his worth in the face of his shortcomings.

Finally, Grant said, "Gentleman, that is all," as he rose from his chair.

Everyone stood and shook Grant's hand. Meade was clearly dejected despite his false front.

Grant then said to Ned, "Captain, please remain behind."

Ned responded, "Yes, General Grant."

Meade cut a look at Ned and then left.

Grant searchingly asked, "My generals, what will I do with them, Captain? Sit, please sit. I am going to have a shot."

Ned, obliging the general, said, "Sir, I believe it might help me if I had a good shot also."

Grant chuckled, "That's my boy." Grant grinned as he handed the bottle and a glass to Ned and chewed his smoking cigar. He then asked, "How's the head, Captain?"

Ned answered, "Headaches, but I'm fine. Time will heal."

Ned watched Grant slam back his glass of whiskey, and then copied Grant, as if to show he knew how. It choked and burned, and it caught his breath.

Grant slapped the table in a roar of laughter and said, "I remember my first time, Captain. You are alright, Captain! Yes, you are alright! Have another."

Ned sipped the rest and Grant laughed even louder. Grant settled down and wanted to get Ned's thoughts.

Ned began, "General Grant, I still believe it was the right tactic to pursue, contingencies affected the taking at Spotsylvania. The missteps in wrong roads added to the confusion and, as such, in being timely. Our maps of this area are totally inadequate. I had been in this area years ago, but, even so, I know not every turn that could give an advantage."

Grant nodded while listening. He whittled all the while, and said, "Captain, I have to bait Lee into an open battle. No assaults of secured lines."

Ned quickly responded, "Yes, General. But in the observing I've done, I don't believe Lee will take that bait. Not now, not after the losses these last eight or nine days. He cannot afford such a confrontation."

Grant responded, "Yes, that may well be, Captain. Captain?"

Ned said, "Yes, General."

Grant continued, "If you were I, what would be your next move?"

Ned once again thought long while Grant whittled. Grant said, "Take your time, Captain."

Ned went to a map of Virginia. "General, I believe I would make haste for Hanover Junction."

"That's some 25 miles, Captain," Grant said as he came to the table.

Ned added, "Yes sir. Lee will surely shadow us from the East. If we sidle south-southeast, it's a footrace, General. We'll move General Warren and Wright in one column to the west, Burnside east of him

VIRGINIA WINDS

in a column and Hancock to sprint on the outside shielded by the others. Lee will shadow what he sees of the other two."

Grant then asked, "Okay, Captain. And what of the North Anna River?"

Ned said, "Sir?"

Grant asked, "Captain, after passing over the river, if Lee does engage, what then? We are locked in by the river."

Ned answered, "Yes sir. We approach not as an entire army, but stair-stepped so to speak; in echelon, in three crossings. Lee is too depleted to address four corps at three crossings. Lee only has General A. P. Hill, General Ewell and General Anderson. He is greatly outgunned."

Grant retorted, "Captain, you underestimate Lee. But for sure we will move south-southwest and try to force his hand into a major deciding battle."

"Yes, General," Ned agreed.

Grant quipped, "I do like your boldness, Captain. Never lose that as a leader."

Ned smiled and said, "Yes Sir, General."

Grant, in good spirits, asked, "Now can I interest you in a cigar, Captain McDonald?"

Ned said, "No sir, I believe I've honored you enough tonight."

Grant slapped his young Captain on the back and chuckled. "See you at daybreak Captain. Much to do. We must move soon."

Feeling better, Ned said, "Yes, General. Good night."

Grant, being well pleased with his new Captain, said, "Good night, Captain."

Ned spent extra time with Jake, trimmed his hooves, brushed him, and pulled his mane and tail. Made him look like a new coin. Jake ate up the attention. It had been some time since Ned could dote on his companion. Jake had been steadfast and true in the terrible weeks passed. "Old man, I don't know what I would do without you!" Jake shook his mane. It now was even length and shiny. Ned studied his legs for soundness and his hooves.

"Let me see your teeth," Ned said as he pulled back Jake's lips. He checked for ticks and cuts and abrasions. "My friend you're in good shape. It is as if you were only a pleasure horse!" Once again Jake shook his mane and shivered front to back. His shiny coat glistened in the firelight.

Chapter 26

Finding Family

The next morning at Massaponax Baptist Church, with pews set outside, top Generals met. Meade was still retained as Grant's number-one Lieutenant. Grant sat while others conversed and read newspapers. Grant wrote general orders for the next moves south and specific goals to be attained.

On 21 May, Grant's Grand Army moved to the south. Lee was now hampered because on May 11, he had lost General Stuart in a battle with General Sheridan. Stuart was shot by a Union foot soldier with a revolver. Stuart was dead, the dashing bold cavalry officer, perhaps the finest of either Union or Confederate. Lee would be willing to give up an entire corps to have Stuart back.

In Washington D.C., they called Grant a butcher.

Ned moved as usual, unimpeded by any group. The latitude he was given allowed his observing all manner of a 100,000 plus men. He took the time to observe men's horses, wagons and anything that one could imagine in a moving city as large and as long as the war train was. It took over one day to pass any one point.

He had stopped at Milford Bridge, as it crossed South River where it emptied into the Mattaponi River. Ned let Jake linger in the cool water as he climbed the bank to sit at the bridge's edge. As Jake

VIRGINIA WINDS

was below, he watched regiment after regiment go by. Men of all shapes, sizes and ages; boys unable to shave to grandfathers, some of them.

At first glance he wasn't sure he saw what he saw. Yes, it was. Ned shouted, "Uncle Dave, Uncle Dave, I'm Ned!"

The soldier looked with a questioning face, and then lit up ear-to-ear and smiled. "Ned! I'll be a possum's behind!"

Ned jumped off his perch and ran to his uncle and they gave each other big hugs and slapped one another on the back.

Uncle Dave said, "Let me look at you, Ned." He pushed Ned back as he clasped his shoulders. "My you're my brother's spitting image. All grown up, and look at that, a Captain no less. Bev told me you had repatriated and you had been attached here in Virginia, but she'd left it at that."

Ned responded, "Yes Uncle, I'm a forward observer. I report solely to General Grant."

Uncle Dave answered, "Well, I'll be! Grant no less! Your cousins and two uncles are with Hancock's 2nd Corps also. They all are with 2nd division. I'm with Hancock's 3rd division. We all have gotten through somehow."

They talked amidst all the dust and noise of the war machines going by.

Uncle Dave added, "Ned, your dad was a brave man. He fought for his beliefs and his choice of the rebels. Caused not us to love him any less."

Ned then said, "Uncle, I thought the same as he until Staunton."

Uncle Dave answered, "Yes, I know! Well my boy, I hear we have a new McDonald! Happy, we all are! The others also heard the news. I guess you carry on where my dear son left off."

Panic gripped Ned. Guilt washed across his face.

Uncle Dave continued, "Yes! Ned, he gave his all as you do now."

"Yes, Uncle, I, I try," Ned stammered.

Uncle Dave said, "McDonalds have given, even with George Washington."

Ned nodded then changed the subject. "Uncle, I'll come to see you tonight for a while. I have to see the rest of the family also."

Uncle Dave smiled. "Ned, God keep you son! Your daddy looks down and smiles."

141

Ned, somewhat relieved, said, "I hope so, Uncle. You'd better go. I'll see you later?"

Uncle Dave responded, "Yes, later tonight."

Ned slid down the bank quickly after Jake and headed to find his family in all this mess of a war machine. He headed to find the 2nd Division.

Ned finally found 2nd Division and rode along asking for the McDonalds. Did anyone know any McDonalds? Nothing anywhere. Just as he was going to give up for now he heard behind him, "Captain! Captain, I'm a McDonald."

Ned wheeled Jake around and asked, "Where is the man that said he's a McDonald?"

A soldier said, "Me, sir!"

Ned said, "Soldier, step out!"

The young man came to Ned. He did not recognize the young boy, maybe 15 at best. He looked seasoned albeit his age.

"Your name, soldier?" Ned asked.

The young man answered, "Cameron McDonald."

Ned almost gasped, and said, "Cameron!"

He was called Little Cam when Ned saw him last, he was but what, five years old then? Cameron was Uncle Jesse's youngest son. He was Ned's dad's youngest brother's son.

Cameron look puzzled. "Captain, sir, may I help you?"

Ned dismounted. "Cameron. I am Ned McDonald."

Cameron responded, "Ned, Sir, yes, oh! My cousin, sir, Ned! Yes, Captain, I mean Ned."

Ned embraced his young cousin.

Cameron added, "Father is with Owen's Brigade, Ned. He should be coming up soon."

Ned said, "Stay with me, Cameron. I'll see you are covered with your sergeant."

Cameron joyfully responded, "Yes sir, I mean, Ned."

For a bit, Cameron looked as the line went by. "There, that's father's regiment."

They strained to pick him out. Finally, Cameron pointed. Ned's uncle was talking to the man at his side. He wore sergeant stripes.

Ned yelled, "You there, Sergeant McDonald!"

Cameron's father looked to the voice calling him. A captain mounted and his son, Cameron?

Uncle Jess became concerned and broke ranks. He came to his son, all the while looking at Cameron, and said, "Captain, what is the problem?"

"No problem, Uncle Jess," said Ned.

Jess looked up at his name being called and immediately knew the Captain, and excitedly responded, "Ned! Well, I'll be. Your daddy's image!"

Ned and his uncle embraced.

Ned said, "Uncle Jess, it's good to see you."

Uncle Jess responded, "And you, a captain! Look at those bars!"

Ned smiled.

Uncle Jess continued, "We heard of your change of mind."

Ned answered, "Yes, it finally hit me."

"Ned, I'm sorry for your mama and daddy," Uncle Jess continued.

Ned responded, "They stay with me, Uncle."

Uncle inquired, "Who are you attached to, Ned?"

Ned said, "I am on General Grant's staff. I am a forward observer and report to him alone."

Uncle Jess commented, "Well, I'll be! Is he what they say, Ned?"

Ned replied, "Well, he's a fine man to start, but he is a bulldog, Uncle. He will win this war for us all. He sees war as terrible and all must give their time to end it."

Uncle Jess responded, "Good, its been a long time coming for his kind."

Ned went on, "Uncle, this will end. It would be over now if we had him years ago. Well, listen, Uncle and Cameron, I have to get going."

"Yes, of course," Uncle Jess responded.

Ned then said, "Uncle, I'm going to take Cameron up to his unit and I'll see you all again soon! I'll be checking up on all of you."

Ned mounted and gave Cameron a leg up on Jake.

"Father, see you!" Cameron yelled.

"Uncle, keep your head down," Ned added.

Jess smiled and tipped his hat.

As Jake turned, Jess yelled, "Looks like one of your dad's horses."

"It is! It is!" Ned confirmed as he rode off.

Cameron was dropped back with his unit and Ned rode up to the front of the army.

Family, Ned thought more and more of it as the months wore on. How important is family? Perhaps it takes a life lived as intensely as war for men and women to see how important their family is.

Days later Grant had to pull out of the North Anna area and Hanover Junction. Robert E. Lee had lured Grant into a trap so quickly that Grant had to extricate his army, once more not engaging in open-field battle.

Once again, Ned found himself with Grant giving his assessments in his tent. The scene was always the same, talk of horses, tactics and the question, "Captain, if you were I, what would be your next move?"

Ned, as always, stood and went to the map on the table, which was there in the same spot in the tent. Grant sat chewing on a smoking cigar and whittled away at a stick while sitting in the same chair, legs crossed, and seemingly quite content.

Ned saw it instantly. "Cold Harbor, sir."

Grant responded, "Exactly, Captain. And you can bet Lee sees exactly the same place. We'll get there first."

Cold Harbor was an inn. From English definitions, Cold Harbor is any inn that gives shelter for sleep from the elements, but serves no meals, only drinks and some sandwiches.

That's it! The race was on. Grant pulled out and went South. Lee did the same. Grant banked on Hancock getting there first, or at least shortly after, to engage in battle before Lee could entrench the area. With its back to Richmond, only five miles away, the stakes were getting higher as Richmond loomed ahead for the Federals and in the rear for the Confederates.

As so often happens, Lee got there and was entrenched before Hancock could get there. Once again, it's to Hancock's detriment.

On June 1st, darkness found Hancock floundering blindly. Ned arrived to the vanguard and kept them from a swampy area around Owens Hill. They skirted to the east and found Lee directly in front with an intricate, but temporary defense.

Consequently, on June 2nd, Grant had to put off the attack until June 3rd to regroup and plan his approach, once again finding himself in a siege type of attack. Lee, again, dictated the day.

Grant said to Ned, "Captain, this is not what I want, but it seems it's all my generals are capable of presenting me with. So, if it is, how do I respond? It would seem my commanders are in collusion with Lee. Captain, you are my echo. If you were I, what would you do?"

VIRGINIA WINDS

Ned came to like these games, as it were. At the map, he looked long. He had, earlier that day, surveyed the miles of front and the ground.

Ned responded, "General, Sir, I don't like this ground and I believe it to be worse than the wilderness. Lee has dug in here a formidable front, like never I've seen before, and in quick time. If we go with him, I believe that a calamity will occur in the swampy area ahead, the uneven terrain, even not knowing what lies beyond our eyes. I fear this piece of ground, General."

As Grant whittled, Ned turned to look at the General, who arose and joined him at the map.

In mid-stroke of a whittle, Grant spoke quietly, "I fear it more than any I've faced, Captain."

Ned responded, "Yes, sir."

Grant then continued, "Yes, yes, but I fear I must do this thing. Lee wants us to come. He's never been more ready. He thinks I will quit upon not succeeding here on this ground. I have to move on him to set his mind on that fact. Do you see, Captain?"

Ned doubtingly responded, "No sir, I don't. I don't see that."

Grant then offered, "I have not been planning far enough ahead for this fox in the last month, but I have to now. If I could do it differently, I would. War is hell, Captain, for both sides. It must be played out so that he will abhor it later and hopefully learn. I pray God forgives me for the orders I have written."

Ned looked at the General.

Grant's steely eyes had saddened. He started to whittle again. "After tomorrow," he continued, "They will be after Lincoln in droves to relieve me. Then, I'll reveal my hole card."

Ned could not keep his eyes off Grant. This man, he thought, how does he do what he does?

Ned rubbed his eyes and said, "General, if it means anything to you, I believe in you."

Grant firmly answered, "Yes, it does immensely, Captain."

Grant was just as his friend General Sherman had described him. All of his life he had shrugged off setbacks and defeat and tried again and again.

"We are much alike, but different," Sherman once told a newspaperman. "I plan for what might be over the hill, and Grant, he worries about what-if after he goes over the hill. Always moving never letting up."

145

And so the orders were written. Attack along the front in the morning of June 3rd.

Ned thought of the last weeks, as he sweat, lying on his cot. There had been no rain for a long time and dust was on everything. Men had not even had time to bathe. Some had not in a month. No rest for Lee meant no rest for the Union. Some even wished for retreat weeks ago. They couldn't have foreseen what Grant had in store. They sang his praises then. Would they after the morning to come?

The lines of battle were so close at points that taunting was being slung about. Ned tossed and turned. He could sense all too strongly that annihilation was coming. He could not sleep. The heat forced him out of the tent. He went to Jake and fiddled with him and then walked out near the men lying about waiting for morning.

It was strangely different than the last month in meetings like this. These men were writing letters and sewing them into their shirts with addresses and such, even into multiple pieces of clothing. The bode of death was so strong. They wanted to assure their identification in order to notify loved ones at home.

Ned left to find Cameron. He had to find him. He could not allow a 15-year-old boy to kill himself. It was only a mere 1-1/2 hours till daylight. Ned got Jake and rode off to Hancock's Corps. Upon reaching Hancock, he found the General in preparation. Ned wanted to pull out every one of his family members from the slaughter.

General Hancock knew Ned well and thought a lot of his bravery, both as a Rebel and now. Hancock cherished his attributes.

"General, Sir, I must ask for a favor you might not look upon kindly, but I am compelled."

Hancock had a voice that boomed. "What is it, Captain McDonald?"

"Sir, I have a 15-year-old cousin in one of your divisions and I would like to pull him out of the battle. I have four others in this battle, cousins and uncles. As I believe Sir, I may lose all of them. My cousin, sir, has been with you since 13 years of age. He has shown bravery and devotion beyond his years General. Please, sir!"

The normal flashing eyes of the real savior of Gettysburg were subdued because of a still nagging injury the General incurred from Gettysburg. One that still was kept open because of infection. It sapped his normal fire, however, he rallied when it counted.

The General responded, "Captain, you find your cousin, and you drag him if you must. It's by my order; he is relieved. Go, Captain."

Ned elatedly said, "Yes sir," and yelled as he ran out of the tent. He had no time to waste. Ned asked about to find Cameron. At last at the early light, he found him, rifle in hand staring into the distance.

"Cameron," Ned said.

It startled his cousin. "Captain, I mean Ned!" Cameron was surprised. "What? Why are you here?"

"Cousin you are to come with me," Ned said.

Cameron answered, "I can't Ned. We go into battle soon."

Ned said, "Not you, Cameron. You are to come with me!" Ned's voice was firm and direct.

Cameron responded, "I can't Ned. They need me!"

By now a dozen soldiers around Ned and Cameron had become interested in the banter.

Ned became firm, "Cameron, you're not going this time!"

Again, Cameron said, "I always go, Ned!"

Ned repeated, "Not this time! Do you understand me?"

"No!" Cameron resisted.

Ned sternly said, "I have orders from General Hancock, you are to pull out now, Private!"

Everyone realized, even before Cameron, what was taking place, and they said, "Cameron, go with the Captain! Cameron go with Ned!" All got vocal. "Leave Cameron. We've got this one. We will see you later."

Soon his whole company was telling him to fall back. All realized this battle was different. Most would not return. Cameron just looked around and then his Sergeant came to him. He had seen the boy's bravery many times and his unwillingness to leave this time. The Sergeant grasped both shoulders and looked at Cameron with understanding and said, "Private, go son! Go with the good Captain. Go now!"

Slowly Cameron looked around at all his much older comrades of so long.

They nodded, each one mouthed, "Go, it's okay." So, he left with his cousin.

Cameron looked back after mounting up behind Ned. The whole regiment got wind of the goings-on. As Cameron looked back, all members of his regiment were saluting him. He broke into tears

147

saluting them while sobbing for he knew their fate. They knew theirs also and would not have it be his fate, at least not here.

Ned and Cameron dismounted at Hancock's command. Hancock approached the two cousins and said, "Captain, so this is your cousin."

Ned proudly answered, "Yes sir, General."

"Yes I am, General sir," seconded Cameron.

The General offered, "Well, I have heard fine things about you."

Cameron proudly said, "Thank you, sir."

"That being so," the General said, "I am assigning you as my orderly while you are here at my headquarters, and for services rendered over the years, you are now Sergeant MacDonald."

Cameron responded, "Yes, sir."

Ned smiled with relief and also for the General allowing Cameron to save face by this last-minute move.

"You begin immediately," the General said.

Cameron immediately answered, "Yes, sir!"

Ned walked to Jake, while Hancock followed along. Ned said, "General, how can I thank you?"

Hancock replied, "Captain, years ago I may have cussed you." The General patted Ned's back. "Now, let's go do our duty."

Pleased, Ned responded, "Yes sir, General."

Chapter 27

A Deadly Battle

Ned was off and away on Jake to find his uncles. The time was so very close for the Union army to push forward over the six-mile-long line that would cross at places only 100 yards or less. The Union cannons began to roar and belch great plumes of smoke. Standard procedure was to try to soften up the opposing line before charging forward with the infantry. The men were kneeling and at the ready in their formations. The great wave of men to cross no man's land was at the ready.

As Jake and Ned came to a halt, Ned decided to observe from a distance. Ward's Brigade was directly in front of him. Astride Jake, Ned fished out his binoculars, given to him by Grant. They were the finest, French made. He scanned back and forth looking for a glimpse of family. He caught a profile of Uncle Dave's unique nose. He had broken it as a child and it remained the same all his life. He kept the glasses on him and he watched Uncle Dave patting men beside him. He looked to be consoling those about him. His arm was around the soldier next to him, while talking in his ear over the din of cannon fire. It was as if he could not release the glasses from his uncle. Dave stood. Now all were standing. Ned scanned ahead. There stood the Colonel urging them to rise, waving his sword over his head rallying the regiment.

Ned saw the Colonel yelling, but could not hear him. However, he, for sure, was calling on each man to give his best. Ned scanned left and right all along northwest and southeast. Men stood up with their colonels, rallying to duty.

Ned shivered. His body related to the scene now being played before him. Quickly, Ned found Dave again. He would follow him as far as he could. Dave's regiment, with all others, stepped off walking at first in perfect alignment. Rebel cannons began to fire faster now. Grapeshot and solid shot for now, but soon they would fire canisters and men would fall, 10-20 at a time.

Musket fire of Rebels soon came with the speed of the Gatling gun now used in some places. Dave began to quickstep with the rest of his regiment. Then, the double quick, it was a full out run to overcome the enemy beyond their temporary defense and silence their cannons and muskets.

Men fell quickly, some writhing on the ground, some thrown in the air minus a limb, even two, and bodies landing in a heap. Ned saw one man clearly hit with dust marking the spot. He was hit three to five times before he hit the dirt.

Dave fell! Oh, God! But he got up. He tripped. Yes, he's going on. Dave never ducked into a swale in the ground as some did. By now the hellish hot lead was seemingly covering every inch of space in the air. Dave's Colonel was decapitated by a solid shot. The ball continued on to kill four more men. Never has a brigade sustained such annihilation. Dave led maybe 22 men who stayed with him.

Ned yelled, "For God's sake, Uncle get down!" He was screaming as loud as his lungs would allow, "Get down!"

Dave, and the now ten with him, hit the bottom of the breastwork, the defense area. They were slightly covered for a moment. Then, as if in concert, 50 to 60 Rebels climbed over on top of the breastwork and fired point-blank at the lonely 11 soldiers, who, with no support behind and none to come, fell.

Ned yelled," No!" His voice fading in the sounds of battle, a deafening constant din as if a volcano blew with its lava killing everything in its path.

Ned sank in the saddle, his eyepiece to his side. Dave was hit three to five maybe six to seven times. Almost at once he fell back and spun to face Ned. He saw the agony, even as mini balls pierced and took life from his Uncle. Ned continued to force a look out over the uneven terrain and focused on Uncle Dave. He moved not at all. Flashes from cannons and muskets crossed his eyepiece.

Slowly, he moved from the scene to scan up and down the battlefield. Men were broken in two and slaughtered. Some were hit 30 to 40 times after they were dead, mutilating the corpse. The carnage in these 8 to 12 minutes had never been seen before in this war or any war. In less than one hour's time, 7,000 Union men died. Lee had lost less than half of that. The destruction was unparalleled. Men crawled back for help, many wounded, only to be killed as they went on.

Veteran Colonel Oates of the 15th Alabama, who also lead the assault on Little Round Top at Gettysburg, which was a bloodbath, had said later, "Union dead covered a full 5 acres laid as thick as 3 to 5 deep. Murder it was. Nothing less."

It was after the first wave and dismal failure that Grant was prepared to send another. At this, a General, just promoted after Spotsylvania and the charge of Mule Shoe, had said "Our men are brave but cannot achieve impossibilities."

Also, Captain Barker of the 12th New Hampshire said, "Our losses are to no purpose." Colonels soon, all along the line, refused to lead men into another blood fest. Grant's losses of over 50,000 men over the last month proved staggering.

The hot summer sun beat unmercifully on dead and living alike; the screams and pleas echoed over the battlefield. Both sides clearly heard every plea. Pleas for water, for help, some shot themselves as in the wilderness. Rebels took potshots at those still living out in front of them.

Ned could not move. Then, eventually, in a methodical walk, Jake took Ned to Grant's headquarters. The smell of bloodied bodies began to waft over the 6-mile front towards the York River, behind the Union army.

An orderly sergeant told Ned that Grant was not to be disturbed by anyone this night unless Lee himself stood outside.

Ned hung his head for a moment. "Very well, Sergeant," Ned said.

As he turned to go, he heard sobbing coming from inside the General's tent. Clearly, it was a man.

Ned looked at the Sergeant, who said, "Come back tomorrow, Captain. He will see you then."

Grant, the rock, the bulldog, the butcher as they now called him, was sobbing uncontrollably at his men's death. He clearly grasped his orders and what they had wrought during the last 30 days. This is what he had to do. He knew it all too well before he did it. And now he suffered the reality of what he knew. The grand plan had a painful ugly side; this was war-ugly.

Ned grabbed Jake's reins and walked back to his tent and, after witnessing what he saw today, he began to cry. He didn't care who saw. He had lost at least one family member. He could not help but think that's how daddy died giving his all to the last effort in his last breath, and for what?

"For what!" he screamed. Jake jerked at his friend's scream. "Is this what all of this comes down to? This is not honor! This is murder!" Ned was mentally gone.

He moved Jake to seek out his family's regiment. He knew Dave was dead. Were the others? In the late night, Ned found the remaining regiment of the McDonald clan.

There were 1,079 men in total in Uncle Dave's regiment who went into battle that morning and now only 350 were fit for service, nearly 70% casualties. Ned asked about the McDonalds. The tired men he spoke to were still shell shocked from the beating they took. These men had been battle tested and yet still shocked at the day's battle.

The answer Ned got was not good. The McDonalds were not at roll call that determined casualties. He was told, "Captain, Sir, I believe all of them went down before we stepped out. They had gotten together. I guess they knew, as we all knew, and if they should die they would die together. I saw them hold hands and pray before we stepped off."

Ned knew! He wished differently, but he knew. He went to his tent quickly and tended to Jake. Jake could feel no sorrow.

Ned said, "I'm sorry old man. I have to lie down."

Ned fell asleep amongst the sniper shots and small mutual fire that was used to harass. He wished at that moment that one shell would land on his tent, because once again he would have to tell Auntie. Now it was her love, her husband, and Ned had witnessed both her men die. Why had they all come this far from the beginning to die now!

Ned was up early to see Grant. The day was stifling hot. The surrounding area all around Richmond was a swampy area. Malaria and sickness began to sweep the ranks. All on both sides began to succumb to heat and sickness.

Grant asked Ned into his tent. Ned now looked at a man with resolve, not at all like the man who sobbed for his loss of men. Grant was like this, sob and weep for his losses, then regroup and act as if he never dropped a tear.

Grant said, "Come, Captain."

Ned responded, "Yes, General".

"Well, Captain," the General said, "I believe I need no briefing from you. It is all self-evident. I fear Washington will descend on me as the vultures to carnage."

Ned said soberly, "Most likely, sir."

The General responded forthrightly, "Yes, well I have a little something for them and Lee in the days to come."

Ned looked quizzically, waiting for a rundown on the surprise, but none was forthcoming.

The General's response was, "You shall know in due course, Captain, but as for now, I will keep it close to the vest."

Ned replied, "Yes sir, General. General, I will be with Hancock's men if you have no objection. I have family, as I have come to know, and I wish to find if they survived yesterday."

Grant offered, "I have none, Captain, proceed. You're excused. I will call for you when I need you."

Ned responded, "Yes sir, General." As Ned left the tent and mounted Jake, all corps commanders and their deputy commanders were arriving for a sit down with Grant.

Ned was distressed as he found the McDonald's regiment. None of his family had been a straggler to find his way back, as so often happened. The number now was 400.

Ned went to a breastwork with his binoculars and looked out over the ground where they had entered into battle. With his eyepiece, he saw bodies strewn everywhere. Some clearly dead, others clinging to life, some 24 hours injured, with no help. Many covered themselves with dirt and anything available to not have pot shots taken at them as they lay critically hurt with no help to reach them. Or worse, they could end up dead. Some men dug holes in the ground with their hands and bayonets to lie in. It tugged at his heart; cries for water were constant.

Chapter 28

Cleaning Up the Mess

Ned went back to Jake, then had found the Colonel of the regiment, who was sitting doing absolutely nothing.

Ned said, "Colonel. I'd like to get some men to help get some of your men back to safety."

The Colonel responded, "If you're crazy enough to try or there are men crazy enough to go with you, good riddance."

Ned could not believe this man was a colonel. "Yes sir," Ned said, and left to find someone, anyone to try with him.

As night fell, he had a dozen volunteers and they got off in the hot night, each man crawling as flat as possible and dragging five canteens around his shoulders and neck.

The men followed Ned's instructions. "Even if it takes all night, use slow movements, stop and wait, then move again."

The cloudy night helped cloak the 13 men. After some 30 minutes of crawling flat to the ground, Ned found his first man alive. He had been there 36 hours with a broken leg and two mangled feet. Ned slid into a low area where the man laid asleep until Ned awoke him.

The soldier was beyond surprised. He simply asked, "Where have you been?" Ned told him to drink slowly, even though he was hungry for water. He did as he was told.

Ned asked, "Is there anyone else close to you here that is still alive?"

The response was, "Yes, 25 foot ahead! A boy dug a hole and he was alive at least when dark came."

Ned said again, "Drink slowly!" Then Ned left the soldier and canteen, then continued to move closer to the Confederate line.

The air was filled with death and rotting corpses. Burnt bodies sweetened the foulness with a sickly putrid stench. Ned found the boy. He was dead. He said a prayer for him, and then he heard a cry for water to his right. He started after that voice.

Quietly, Ned said, "I'm coming."

Even in this inky-black night rebels still fired shots from rifles hoping to hear agony as their minie balls found a body.

The Union soldier was a company commander, his shoulder shattered, one foot was blown off and somehow the man had not died.

Ned said, "Here, take it, get some water. Easy, easy, not too fast."

Through the next four hours, Ned zigzagged across the battlefield to hand out all five canteens. At one point, he was only 100 feet from the Rebel line. Almost every man he found had died. All the others with Ned who had volunteered did the same with varied success. The last man Ned found he felt would die soon without medical attention. The man was 150 pounds or so. Ned had him lie on top of his back as he crawled flat to the ground pulling both along, the man helping as he could. Ned's great strength and stamina were now surely being tested. He was full of sweat and the dirt turned to mud on him. He crawled for 45 minutes like this. At last they found safety. There they found medical attention for the man and his life was saved.

Ned made return trips and saved several others. Other solders saw Ned's approach and began the same torturous ordeal to retrieve men and help them to safety. All total that night they saved 48 men. Others along the line of battle, in turn, began to take Ned's venture to heart. Several rescuers died helping that night, but hundreds were saved and assured life.

The following day more died. As night fell, once again, rescuers volunteered with their reliefs to take over as the venture was very exhausting work, and again hundreds were recovered to live.

Ned was cut all over; his legs, stomach and hands were raw, as all were who engaged in this rescue effort.

Finally, came the white flag and a truce for the Union to retrieve corpses to be buried. Rotting bodies would be a health hazard to both armies. Ned took part in this grizzly work. He was in hopes of finding some of his family members, although at this point they were probably dead.

Many who volunteered to retrieve friends were sickened by the work. This was new to battle hardened soldiers. Most times the infantry moved on or retreated and the bodies were left to be captured or retrieved by special details of Negro contrabands.

Ned went from corpse to corpse, lifting and turning heads with lifeless eyes. Some faces were not to be recognized by anyone. There were bloated bodies, swollen and distended stomachs all around. Ned wondered, is this what glory and bravery are about? Are these men more gallant because they lie here?

Someone said to Ned, "Captain Sir, come here. I think you might want to look at this soldier."

Ned saw him from 20 feet away. It was his uncle, Russ McDonald. His body riddled with bullet holes. Maybe 25 to 30 hit his torso alone. Three to his head and one leg was blown off.

"Oh God, dear Uncle!" Ned fell to his knees sobbing.

The soldier who had called Ned over said softly, "Come, Captain Sir. He's crossed over the river. He feels none of these holes."

Ned looked up at the Sergeant. Tears stained a grimy tired face. Ned's face was blank from expression. He said, "Really, I suppose, Sergeant. Yes." Ned laid his hand on his uncle's head and said a prayer. He took his knife and cut a lock of his hair. He found the letter that Uncle Russ had penned to Jenny, his wife, and put the lock of hair inside. He rose up and went to look for Uncle Dave.

As Ned neared the spot where Uncle Dave had fallen, rebels with rifles in hand were there and silent along the line. They had no jibes or taunts. The solemnness of the scene-of-horror before them spoke to a special understanding.

Ned looked at his Uncle, then knelt and stroked his head. His body was greatly distorted and decaying.

Ned then looked up at the rebels. He glanced slowly both ways then spoke, "This man was my uncle, my father's brother. He is gone, as my uncle back there a piece." Ned was losing it. "Is this what we want? Is it?"

No one spoke. Everyone on the berm knew the answer.

Ned searched for the letter Dave wrote the night before. There, about half written, was the letter. He took a lock of hair and put it inside for Auntie Bev. He stood up, looked once again and turned to find any other members of family.

After one step, Ned heard, "No, Captain! None of us understand!"

He turned to see a scrawny boy of maybe Cameron's age saluting him. Ned returned the salute. He then left for the Union lines. He was not able to find the other family members that day. However, two letters were brought to Ned from their mutilated corpses. That evening Ned sat to pen his family members and send the fallen families their letters penned the night before the battle.

He wrote only a brief letter to Auntie, telling her that he was positioned to see her husband's brave actions as he led his men into hell itself without flinching. He was a testament to the last effort with the last breath. Ned knew no more was needed for her right now. She would want only the basic facts of her husband's death.

Chapter 29

Preparation for Grant's Next Adventure

That night, Ned sat with Grant's council of generals. The somberness was heavily felt.

Grant said, "Generals, this paper calls me the butcher of men. I regret the actions I had to take. The sacrifice that was made was, to me, unavoidable. It is a commander's nightmare for orders like I made. I had hoped for lesser deaths, but we are soldiers. Are we not? My engagement of Lee here was to set up a grander movement that he will not expect, especially after such a result of this battle. He will believe us to lick our wounds and retreat. He is known for audacity! Yes?"

Some responded, "Yes, General Grant."

Grant went on, "Well, gentlemen, watch my audacity, now listen up. When it begins, we will move around Lee's right to the James River, cross the James River and take Petersburg, which lies due south of Richmond. Take the railroads from all directions and choke Petersburg and Richmond at the same time."

Someone offered, "General Sir, Lee will not allow such a move. He will anticipate your move and cut it off."

With a slam of the fist on the table, Grant roared, "He will not! Do you hear me? This March is as good as stolen and a man has not moved yet. I need no general who does not believe in this!"

No one spoke.

Grant went to the table and said, "All of you come here! Here's how it will be made." All leaned into the table as Grant went step by step. He looked up at everyone after he was done and said, "No mistakes or errors! No excuses, none, or you will be at an outpost in the Oregon territory! Am I clear gentlemen?"

Ned sat with his back to the tent taking in each man's facial expressions. The urgency of Grant's words was clearly showing on their faces.

And Grant continued, "I will lay out clear orders for each of you with quite specific goals that will be met. Tomorrow at 8:00 a.m., be here gentleman! Now attend to your men. As for now, they are to believe that we will stay in this forsaken piece of ground. See that all are fed and your wounded are moved north. We wait for nothing when the hour arrives."

After the others left, Ned, as usual, stayed behind. Grant was chewing his cigar, as usual, studying the map. Ned looked at the map and began to study it. Before Ned was a man that he had come to admire. A man who had ordered his family members to their deaths, or did he? Yes, he did! If not him, then who might have? Ned's mind raced upon a great many things over these last 50 hours.

Grant spoke, "Captain?"

Ned responded, "Sir."

Grant continued, "It seems you're off somewhere else."

Ned replied, "Yes, General Grant. Guess I'm lost in thought about losses of my family."

Grant understood and said, "Yes, but at such times, we must find the strength to push ahead and end this whole mess, mustn't we?"

Answering, Ned said, "Yes, General Grant."

Having Ned's attention, Grant said, "Ned, come here."

Ned looked surprised at being called on in such a personal way. Grant, at that moment, did it to ease the strain and be human. Grant genuinely felt the strain his Captain had on his shoulders.

Grant continued, "Ned, as soldiers in the Federal Army, we're weary and apprehensive with the events that the last month have brought us." Then Grant spoke in a surprisingly personal manner, saying, "Sit, Ned, sit. Tell me about your father."

Ned, feeling a little more comfortable, responded, "Well, sir, he was a man I look to be like. He knew about horses and farming. He loved his God and my mother."

Ned went on ceaselessly for an hour as Grant listened and smiled and nodded his head at the appropriate times, all the while chewing his cigar and sipping some whiskey. As Ned continued to speak, Grant filled a small cup with whiskey and pushed it toward Ned. Ned sipped it like an old drinker.

When Ned finished talking about his father and mother, Grant said, "I like them, Ned. I believe your father and mother and I would have been good friends."

Ned felt better, and replied, "Yes sir, General." He also realized that Grant had allowed him the time needed to vent, and offered, "Thank you General for letting me talk."

Grant said, "Not at all. Not at all. We all need a way to unload. Julia, my lovely, dear wife, allows me that most often. If not for her, this war would be unbearable for me, Ned."

Ned replied, "Yes, General."

Grant then added, "Well, let's get some rest, shall we?"

Ned happily said, "Yes sir."

"Good night Captain," Grant said, as he smiled at Ned.

"Good night, General," Ned responded.

Ned left with a much lighter load, than when he came to Grant's tent that night. He found Jake, the old man, as he was endearingly called.

Ned showed affection and appreciation for Jake as he said, "I need a hug, how about you?" Jake was sniffing Ned's hands as he stroked Jake's soft nose, an arm around his neck. "We've come far, haven't we?" There they stood, friends understanding one another. Ned rubbed Jake's shoulder in small circles, as a mare would do to its young colt or filly. Ned felt the impact of Jake in his life. Jake was that last link to his father. He whispered to Jake, "Well, old man, I need to get some sleep, as do you. Tomorrow I feel we move out."

Ned slept soundly that night dreaming about Lizza, their daughter, Christiana, and life after all this is over. His heart carried him into his prayers for family and for all whose lives this war has taken.

Chapter 30

Family Members' Growing Concern

In Staunton, Auntie Bev became greatly disturbed by the paper reporting large losses of men. She also felt that the feelings of Staunton residents, who were the majority for the Rebels, were becoming more and more vindictive and confrontational in town over the last few months. Up to now it was an understood difference between the small contingent of Federal sympathizers and the Rebel sympathizers. But, things seem to have changed, as Grant applied new tactics to pushing Lee back, sending General Sherman to do the likes in Tennessee, then Georgia.

General Siegel's Germans were pushing into the Valley from Staunton to Maryland. The screws were tightening down. Supplies for soldiers and civilians alike were sorely lacking, and with it came a shortage of understanding and tolerance.

Bev began, "Girls, I don't like the hostilities we are now feeling around these parts, and the rest of the McDonald clan feels the same. I think that shortly we may have to find a safer place to be if it continues."

Lizza asked, "Where could we go.?"

Jo quickly said, "West of the mountains into West Virginia, where we could be with Union folks."

Auntie said, "But, for sure, if it be Rebels coming through this valley, as things have gotten to be lately, I will not stay to see their intentions."

"I think you are right," said Jo.

Lizza was visibly shaken. "They wouldn't take my baby, Auntie?"

"No, dear Lizza," said Auntie, "But I won't be caught in a crossfire of wills of these two armies. I know humankind. If things get terrible, retribution is not a far jump, and people lose good sense in times like that. They look for the closest to them to lash out at, and I will not have that be at any of us or our family."

Lizza brought Christiana to her bosom from her lap, as if to protect her from what Bev had just told them.

Auntie continued, "I believe I heard that Wheeling, West Virginia, is a place where we could go and yet still not go too far west. I heard that almost no slaves were there, even before the war in that county. I believe it's in an Ohio county. It sits in a sliver of land between Pennsylvania and Ohio."

Jo said, "It sounds safe. Union on either side."

"Yes, it does sound nice, Auntie," said Lizza, "But how about my sister?"

"Bessie can come too, of course," answered Auntie, "And I should think that she would want to if it gets to the point that we should leave, Lizza."

Lizza responded, "I have to let her know of what we're talking of here, Auntie."

"Lizza, of course," said Auntie, "We can tell her in the morning. She is still coming tomorrow, isn't she?

Lizza responded, "Bessie wouldn't be late, Auntie."

"No, I guess you're right, Lizza," replied Auntie.

Jo smiled and put her arms around Lizza, and added, "I would die rather than let anything happen to you and this young McDonald, Lizza."

"I love you too, Jo," said Lizza.

Chapter 31

Something in Common

Ned awoke. The morning was still dark and all were moving out. General Smith and the 18th Corps were sent back where they came from when the battle began days ago to White House Landing, a supply depot for the Union. It sat on the Pamunkey River that led into the York River then the Chesapeake Bay. Smith and his corps sailed down around the Virginia Peninsula and up the other side toward Richmond and Petersburg. He wanted to secure that area before the entire Union army got there. It was a slight retrograde and swing around Lee's right flank. To pull out an engaged army is tough enough, but to do it without bringing about an assault was more difficult.

Grant managed to move out and pull around behind and across the York River, below and before Petersburg, before Lee even knew where he was. Lee discovered him gone, but where? Grant's audacity even outshined Lee's, the master of audacity.

During the trek across the Virginia Peninsula, Ned was with his family's old regiment. It had been filled with some green recruits. Ned found solace among these men, who shared the experience of saving men after that awful day and that long and gruesome horrible night.

Ned reined Jake up. There was a teamster driving a wagon of supplies. A normal army wagon could hold supplies for days, thousands of pounds worth. It was to the side of the road, but was slowing things moving along. Grant wanted no such things, no excuses. The black man was struggling with his young black boy to exchange for a fresh wheel. Several others jumped in to help. Ned asked the team master about how long he had been broken down.

"Just a few minutes, sir. It just happened," the man responded.

Ned replied, "Very well. What is your name?"

The man answered, "My name is Smith. I'm a wheelwright when we're not on the move, sir."

Ned pressed for some reason, even though he needed to move farther forward.

The man continued, "Sir, I'm from Staunton over the mountain."

Ned inquired, "Staunton, you say?"

In response, the man said, "Yes sir, I own a small six room hotel on the edge of town."

Ned, surprised, asked, "Smith, would you have a daughter named Bess or Bessie?"

Smith smiled and said. "Yes sir. I adopted her from her slave mother to save the child."

Ned, half to himself, said, "I'll be, isn't that something!"

Smith quickly responded, "No sir, it was my duty!"

Ned added, "No, Smith, I mean I stayed at your hotel several months ago."

Feeling pleased, Smith said, "You did, sir?"

Ned responded, "Yes, I did. I met your lovely Bessie. I stayed with my wife Lizza."

Surprised, Smith responded, "Lizza, sir, yes."

An understanding came to both Smith and Ned at the same time.

Smith said, "Your wife is my daughter's long-lost sister! Bess told me in her letters."

Ned responded, "That's right, Smith!"

Smith then asked, "How do you like that, sir. Isn't that something? I hear your Lizza had a little girl."

"Yes, her name is Christiana," Ned replied,

Smith, feeling positive, said, "How wonderful, sir."

"Yes," Ned replied, grinning from ear to ear.

"And to meet you here of all places, sir," Smith added.

Ned went on, "Yes, how fortuitous it is. Bess worries a lot about you, Smith."

As I do for her," Smith responded.

Ned replied, "She does very well in keeping your business going. I have never stayed in a nicer place."

Smith replied, "Thank you, sir."

Ned answered, "Not at all, Smith. However, I now must move forward."

Understanding, Smith said, "Yes sir."

Ned extended his hand and Smith took it and said, "Thank you, sir."

Ned's response was, "For what, Smith?"

Smith replied, "If not for you, I never would see Bess find her sister."

"Yes, well, Smith, or Lizza," Ned added. "I'll see you again, Smith."

Pleased, Smith said, "Yes sir, have a good day."

Chapter 32

Military Moves, Family Moves

The bold move that Grant had pulled off was so complete that Lee hadn't figured out that Grant had left, was across the James River behind him and south of Richmond, with Petersburg squarely in front of the Union army. It wasn't until the 17th of June that Lee knew where Grant's army even was. It was a piece of tactical brilliance.

Ned was fairly close to Elsa's and thought briefly of seeing her, but it was just too far. He saw for the first time what can be accomplished if all is well coordinated; and this time it was. Ned thought to himself, as he watched the army snake by, could this be the last move?

Then, General Lee pulled around to Richmond and sent more troops to shore up Petersburg. He also sent Early and his corps, which only had 8,000 men. As well, Lee felt that he could march down the Shenandoah Valley and push out the Federals that were causing a ruckus. Doing this would keep the valley open and clear for Rebel use. This, he thought, would keep the Federals from coming down and getting behind his men at Petersburg.

General Early left on or about the 14th of June and went to Charlottesville and then dropped down south-southwest to Lynchburg. On the 17th of June, Early pushed over the Blue Ridge

Mountains and was poised to push down the valley in a clearing movement.

On June 22, General Early was camped at Pink Castle in the Shenandoah Valley. The town sat between two mountain ridges low in stature, named Purgatory Mountain to the northeast and Craig's Mountain to the southwest; Catawba Mountain was to the South.

News traveled fast through the valley north to Staunton. At last, General Early would clear out these Yankee interlopers. At the same time, Mosby's Raiders and Rebels hit. They had run all over the Valley causing headaches for the Union.

Auntie heard this news and knew it was not good. She had heard of Early from many and that he cared not what any thought of him. A most austere man and caustic nature, and these were his good traits. He would burn Chambersburg in Maryland after crossing the Potomac to scare Washington, D.C. residents. The Chambersburg torching was in retaliation for General Hunter's burning and looting in the valley. Early would also torch VMI, Virginia Military Institute, a beloved school attended by dozens of generals and officers in the war.

Auntie talked to the McDonalds, who were scattered around Staunton. To her disbelief, they all had decided to weather the storm in hopes of the good graces of General Early or that he would be held in check below Staunton.

Auntie sat with Lizza and Bessie as Jo fixed some dinner. "I believe we should move on up to West Virginia to Wheeling, as we talked about," Auntie said strongly. "It is no telling what they intend as they come here. What is to say a battle would not take place right out our front door."

"I agree," Jo said. "The safe way is the right way. Besides, we need to protect that little one at all costs."

Lizza hugged Christiana tighter.

Bessie had a concerned look. She had a hotel to consider. She said, "If these rebels get the notion they might burn down a black man's business just for spite."

"It's a big decision, ladies," Bev said somberly.

They all nodded their heads in agreement, then just looked at one another waiting for one of them to decide for all.

A long spell passed and then Lizza said, "Ned would not want me here with the baby. This is a different war than it was two years ago. The heat is turned up. The stakes are greater. The rebels are desperate and will do anything now."

Jo seconded Lizza's thoughts.

"Yes, we leave as soon as possible," Auntie said. "I agree, we leave tomorrow."

Bessie said nothing. They all looked at her for a sign of agreement in the move northwest.

"Bessie," said Lizza to her sister, "Yes?" And waited for her to agree.

Bessie responded, "Lizza, dear sister, I cannot leave. I cannot leave Poppa Smith's and my hotel to those who will sack it."

Lizza was now unhappy, and retorted, "And what will you do to stop them, Bessie? Tell me what?"

"I don't know, Lizza," Bessie came back calmly. "I don't know. I know that I can't leave. Maybe, if I'm just here, they will have mercy."

"Mercy, Bessie?" asked Lizza.

Now came Jo, "Mercy, if you're white or Union blue, but you, girl, are not safe."

"Stop," said Auntie. "Bessie, you think on this. And no matter your choice, we leave. Do you understand? We leave tomorrow!"

"Yes ma'am," said Bessie.

Lizza was now crying. She was so upset at Bessie for even considering to stay behind.

"We prepare now, ladies," Auntie added.

Lizza offered the saddest goodbye as Bessie left for Staunton and her hotel.

Bessie said, "If I am to go, Lizza, I will be here before daybreak. If I am not, I will be staying. I would hope you can understand, Lizza."

Lizza spoke back, with Christiana in her arms, "Well, sister, I don't. I don't get your thinking in this matter."

They both hugged a tentative goodbye as Bessie kissed Christiana.

Bessie responded, "God be with you both, Lizza."

"Bessie please!" said Lizza, breaking into sobs.

Bessie replied, "Sweet sister, Lizza, God will provide. He always does. Now I must go."

Bessie rode off in her carriage as Lizza, holding Christiana tightly, watched her go over the rise in the hill.

Lizza, in hushed tones, said, "Bessie, please come with us." and then kissed Christiana.

The three began to pack what they could. The two wagons held family furniture from generations ago, valued pictures, bedding, and kitchenware.

Lizza and Jo followed behind their General, as Auntie gave out orders. It stays, it goes, and we burn this. We bury this. It stays. All through the night they packed and loaded the two wagons. Auntie had two draft mules to haul the bigger, heavier wagon. Belle would pull the smaller, lighter one herself. Auntie Bev would drive the team of mules and Jo would drive Belle. Lizza and Christiana would ride along with Jo.

The house had considerable things left, but Auntie deemed them to be not missed upon a return if they were gone. Uncle Russ' wife, Jenny, and her young sons and 12-year-old daughter would come to check on the house from time to time. She lived the closest.

When Bev had gone to talk to Jenny about leaving, she was asked, "Auntie, have you heard from Dave for I have not heard from Russ for some time?"

Bev responded, "No, I haven't, but we need not worry. You know they always write. A letter will come soon, I'm sure."

Ned's letter to Auntie still had not made it, but was to be delivered soon. The same was true for those to Russ and Jesse's wives, with their last words written and locks of their hair. The war had effected the McDonald's with crushing blows, and was still to bring more devastation.

Auntie made one last walk up to her son's grave, laid a wildflower upon it, knelt, prayed and told him, "I'll be back, son. We must go away for a while. Soon everyone will return home, of that I am sure." She kissed her fingers and touched his grave.

Lizza and Jo watched in the starlit night as she said her goodbyes. Lizza hurt for her. He was her only son and she had had the strength to forgive Ned. This had made an impression on Lizza. This was the moment that Auntie had to do what she felt was right and that was to leave her home of 19 years. Lizza also realized that she was doing it for her.

All was ready. Both wagons were filled and Auntie made one last pass throughout the house. She grabbed the pistol from the pantry. It was almost left behind. Both wagons had a shotgun at the ready if needed.

VIRGINIA WINDS

Lizza looked down the road toward Staunton, no Bessie. Her heart sank, but she knew last night that Bessie would not be making the trek north.

They climbed into the wagons and Auntie said, "Well let's get started. We have a distance to go. I trust in God that there will be someplace in Wheeling, West Virginia for us to stay until all this is over."

Auntie yelled, "Hie!" and the two mules started off. Jo spoke at Belle and the small train of refugees started north through the valley towards Maryland. Lizza told herself not to look back for Bessie."

"Lizza," Jo said, "She will be fine. She did what she had to do."

Responding, Lizza said, "I know, Jo, it's hard to leave when I just found her. She is the world to me!"

"I know, Lizza," answered Jo, "But it is best to take Christiana out of any possible harm's way. You'll see Bessie soon. I feel this war is now short-lived. Grant is on the Rebels like a hound on a raccoon's scent. Soon he will have them bayed up like an all but dead coon."

Lizza added, "I hope so, Jo. I hope you're right!"

Bev kept thinking as she drove her draft mules down the valley. My word, we have to cross river after river, mountain ridges of untold numbers, the Alleghenies and their treacherous roads. As Bev kept this line of thinking, she decided to take the wagon straight through the valley and cross only a couple of rivers, the North Fork of the Shenandoah and the Potomac River, only small ridges to negotiate that way, and then into Maryland. They would then push into Pennsylvania and on to Chambersburg, where Auntie had a great aunt and uncle living. Surely, there, safety could be found.

"That is it," she said, reined up the mules and went to talk with Jo and Lizza, who were behind her.

Bev suggested, "I believe that for safety all around, we should head for my great aunt's home in Pennsylvania. It's a place we can find shelter."

The women agreed that this sounded like a much better idea.

"Well, it's settled! We shall move due north," Bev responded, and off they set.

Auntie's caravan, of sorts, made it 20 miles to Harrisburg the first night. They stayed at an inn there for the night.

The next day General Early and his Corps of 17,000 camped at Staunton.

The three women and the baby were at a point north of Front Royal, Virginia, 80 miles north of Early, and they maintained the distance between his army and them as they crossed the Potomac. However, before crossing the river, the travelers were stopped by none other than Mosby, the infamous Raiders of the Confederacy. This was his war in these parts. He had 50 men with him as they came up to stop Auntie.

"Madame," an officer said, "I'm sorry for stopping you and these wagons, but I must take a quick look as to your contents. I am quite sure you have no Union contraband, but I need to satisfy my men. You understand!"

"Yes, I am sorry," Auntie said. "Your name, kind sir?"

"I am Colonel Mosby," the officer responded.

All three noticeably caught their breath!

"So you've heard of me," Mosby said.

Jo, Auntie and Lizza, of course, knew him from Ned's Confederacy days. He had, in fact, sent Ned away to imprisonment in Castle Thunder.

Auntie replied, "Yes, Colonel, we have!"

"Well, Madame, you know then I am not about harming women."

"Of course you are not Colonel, for that would make you at least a rascal, or worse, a beast," Auntie answered.

Mosby was visibly taken aback at Auntie's words.

"Please, Colonel, inspect our wagons."

After 20 minutes, they set aside their concerns.

"If I might say, Madame, your load seems to indicate a hasty retreat!"

"No, Colonel," Auntie said, "We are tired of the hostility up and down this Valley and we leave for quieter land to the north. We will certainly return upon resolution of this conflict."

"So, you were a good Southerner?"

Auntie answered, "I am, Colonel, as are they, but as you can see, a small child and young women still full of life should not be a casualty of the conflict as should anyone not embattled in service. Wouldn't you agree, Colonel?"

Mosby replied, "I would, Madame. I would."

Lizza thought, so, this is Colonel Mosby, the man that Ned had so admired. He was intense with his eyes, really quite small of a man, but he spoke gentlemanly and courteously."

Mosby then said, "Ladies, I bid you ado. Please have a safe journey."

"We will," Auntie said.

Colonel Mosby tipped his hat, and with a motion to his men. all dashingly dressed, thundered up the Valley the way they had just come. Mosby was off to cause as much discontent as possible and make the Federals as ill at ease as he could.

All sighed relief, especially Lizza, for she had all of Ned's letters wrapped in her cloth bag and strapped to her waist underneath her dress. She knew Mosby was aware of Ned's escape and repatriation. Lizza thought what might have happened if Mosby had discovered Ned's wife and child. Possibly it would be a ransom to get Ned to surrender to the Rebels. Well, thank God for protection.

The rest of the trip north was uneventful and, as Auntie hoped, they found safe harbor with Auntie's great aunt in the quiet town of Chambersburg, far north of all the war machines and 20 miles inside the Pennsylvania border.

The letters came to Staunton. They hit hard and caused a terrible grief amongst the McDonalds. Auntie's letter was with them. She would not know of her husband's death for some time, nor would Ned realize where the women in his life were, when they had left, or when they would return.

Chapter 33

A New Siege Begins

Petersburg was under siege by the Union Army. It looked as if another Vicksburg was at hand. Grant did not want such a tactic, but realized it was all Lee could put together. The defenses were most formidable. And so, it began.

General Early had gone clear down the Shenandoah Valley, over the Potomac, and, on July 5, set upon Washington, D.C. It was Lee's hope that Early could force Grant's hand and deploy a good part of his men to shore up Early's assault.

Grant deployed General Horatio Wright's 6th Corps to Washington. With some trouble, General Early did reach the outer defenses on July 11th. Amazing as it was, since June 12 or so, Early's men marched 20 miles per day and over half his men had no shoes. These Rebels were of the toughest sort, hardened by battle and with only the barest of food and supplies.

Grant summoned Ned to his headquarters. Ned entered the room that Grant took for his office. The house was nicely appointed. It was the best headquarters Grant had had all during this war.

"Come in, Captain, sit," welcomed Grant.

Ned sat.

Grant then remarked, "Captain, Early is moving on Washington. It is a plot of Lee's to force my hand to relieve us of our numbers here and at Richmond."

"Yes, sir," Ned replied.

Grant continued, "If you were I, Captain …?"

Ned smiled and finished Grants standard question: "What would I do?"

"Yes, Captain," as Grant gave a grin and lit a new cigar.

"Well, sir, Early, with his numbers, could not take and hold Washington. All he could do would be to raise holy terror." Ned thought before continuing.

"Yes, Captain?" asked Grant.

Ned responded, "Well, sir, it would prove to be harmful for the President if they did do just that. The November election might bring a new President if it should show that Lincoln allowed such a thing." Ned paused again and then added, "A new President might, after Lincoln's failure, want to come to terms with the Confederacy."

Grant pulled his cigar and pointed at Ned, and said, "On the barrel head, Captain. You see the desperation in Lee and Jefferson Davis?"

Ned replied, "I do, sir."

Grant retorted, "I will bite at his feint, Captain. And to ensure that Early cannot raise too much hell, as you put it, I am sending the 6th Corps to help bolster Washington and I am sending you along, Captain, for my eyes. Telegraph me to apprise me of your observations. This siege here in Petersburg will surely break the Rebels and will bring us Richmond at the same time, but it may take all winter and then some. You will serve me better along for the ride to Washington."

Ned quickly responded, "Yes, General."

Ned rode north up the Potomac to Washington.

The 6th Corps arrived and was closely followed by the 19th Corps that Grant had sent from Louisiana. Washington now had three full Corps, the 6th, 8th and 19th to confront General Early's Rebels.

Ned rode Jake down 7th Street to Fort Stevens, the northern most point where Early was headed. Washington was like a city Ned had not seen. Women in their finery turned out and thousands and thousands lined the street to see these Union soldiers come to defend the nation's Capital.

Ned was out past Fort Stevens behind the skirmish on July 11th. He rode west along the Union lines, which went clear to the Potomac River and beyond. So, when General Early, with General Breckenridge, arrived, Ned then rode east and found General D.H. Hill, whose men spread from Rock Creek to Bitter Branch Creek.

Early's 12,000 to 15,000 men were spread thinly.

Ned found the Union front well prepared for an assault. Six major forts were linked together with roads behind to move men freely and unhampered.

Ned sent a wire on the 11th to Grant stating, "The preparedness and the added troops with battle experience, unlike the 8th Corps stationed in Washington, were assured of a repulse of any attack Early might present." Ned also said "General Wright did put Washington's 8th Corps in reserve behind the 19th Corps on the far west Forts, and Wright's 6th Corps on the far east, with assorted other regiments and civilians armed in reserve as well."

That day, Ned set up on the highest point he could find and scanned to watch movements of General Early. He knew Early would test the Union line tomorrow, searching for a weak point but not knowing the reinforcement that the Union had in place.

Before turning in, Ned sent a wire to General Grant: "I've spent all day, and as per the last message, I still believe Washington safe. Early with his movements will strive for a breakthrough in the morning. His movements betray his intentions. I believe he thinks he faces untested soldiers. We shall show him otherwise. Your faithful servant, Captain McDonald."

The morning of July 12th brought some softening-up fire from Early's batteries, but soon it subsided, unforceful feints by the Rebels were tried all day.

Ned finally found the 6th Corps, which would detach several divisions to force Early's hand with an attack at both ends. The Union batteries belched smoke and fire as they began.

Ned caught sight of him. It was Abe Lincoln. He was but 25 feet from him. He was taken with his appearance. Lincoln was very tall, at least 6'4" to 6'6". He thought he walked gangly. His arms swung quite freely. His clothes didn't seem to fit quite well. His face seemed gaunt. He was quite pale. All this taken into account, he seemed quite in charge. His eyes were constantly in motion, taking in all the movement with a knowing and inquisitive sense at the same time.

As the Rebels began to return fire, Abe moved toward the action; he climbed upon a fortification in order to see, as if being unafraid of near-flying lead. Ned forgot all about watching the 6th Corps and their maneuvers to report to Grant.

Finally, with great urging, Lincoln removed himself from harm's way. As he looked around, Ned and Lincoln caught eyes. Lincoln half saluted to Ned with two fingers. Ned returned his best salute. Lincoln gave a nod as he then continued to take in the beehive-like activity of battle.

The 6th Corps pushed out beyond the skirmish line and attacked on the two parallel fronts. It was soon apparent to Early that he might come to know God here. So, after setting ablaze many houses outside of Washington, Early pulled out. It could only be to his detriment if he tried here further.

Ned sent his report to Grant, and from his point of view, Washington seemed safe. Early's posts pushed back the way he had come; They headed to the Valley and ascended to Staunton.

Ned left the 6th Corps since he expected that they would follow after Early's Rebels.

After tailing the last of Early, Ned found a contingent brigade that had headed north. He couldn't figure why. He decided to follow Brigade Commander McCausland as he headed north. General Early had, earlier on July 9, held Fredericksburg for a ransom of $200,000 or he would torch the town. They came up with that amount and he moved on. Ned followed McCausland out of Maryland. They went into Pennsylvania. Why? To him it seemed that they had not enough to do except mischief.

The brigade went right on through Greencastle. Ned stopped to ask what towns lie ahead. The brigade did nothing to Greencastle, but took on food and other provisions, some horses and any shoes they could find to shod their shoeless Rebels.

An old woman, who lived north of Greencastle, told Ned that they had taken her 10 sheep and she heard they were headed toward Gettysburg. She said, "Yes, Captain. I chided these vermin ridden men after taking my sheep. They laughed, and said, 'be glad we have skipped your town dear old lady, for we will avenge VMI and the loss at Gettysburg.' "

Ned responded, "VMI has been torched, dear woman," and then asked, "Did they say they would torch Gettysburg?"

She replied, "No, they said only that they would avenge."

"I hear you, dear lady. I fear they will torch Gettysburg," Ned said.

The woman added, "Captain, if they are, they've headed in the wrong direction. On further is Chambersburg."

Ned had not gotten any letters from Lizza since June 9. He had no idea that Auntie, Lizza, and Jo had cleared out of Virginia for safety and gone to Chambersburg, Pennsylvania. The war was headed right to the very place the trio had sought safety, all this unbeknownst to Ned.

Grant was angry at the goings on northward, so he ordered General Sheridan to go after Early and clean the Valley. Grant wanted it stripped of all potentially useful army needs, food sources, shelter, everything.

By August, Sheridan would put his forces together, some 30,000 men, twice those of Early's, and set out after him to scour the Valley of all Rebels for good.

Ned saw the smoke on ahead, rising over the foothills beyond him. The Cumberland Valley was lush as the Shenandoah Valley and Virginia. Ned would then cross the Conococheague Creek, which lay six miles south of Chambersburg. The smoke was rising higher and higher. Ned thought to himself, dear God, they have torched the town.

Ned asked Jake for some of his speed and off they went. "I hope they did not go to Gettysburg next," he said to Jake.

Ned caught sight of Chambersburg and the flames licking upward after the smoke, and yelled, "It's an inferno, Jake. That's all this is. Damn them!" Ned quickly realized that he could do nothing, so he headed around the outskirts to the east of town.

As he came upon a rise in the small road, he saw the Confederates heading south back towards Greencastle. He then decided to head towards Chambersburg. He went towards a church at the center of town, where the steeple and roof seemed to be on fire.

Ned left Jake under an elm tree. At the center of town everyone had stopped trying to douse the flames. It was running its course now. Homes, businesses, stables, everything burning except the large church. It had embers trying to ignite its roof, but men were quickly attending to those lit pieces.

Women were wailing as children clung to their clothes. Men tried to gather valuables into the street, the winds fanning the flames hotter. Smoke swirled throughout the streets as ashes fell on everything.

Ned thought to himself, how senseless. He knew that Lee had been through here in '63, into Maryland and Pennsylvania going to Gettysburg. At that time, Lee had issued a general order that no civilian property was to be harmed. It was to be paid for, albeit, with Confederate currency. Now this, a school being burned.

Ned needed to report to Grant through Washington. But how, all the telegraph wires have been torn down, so no one could get the word out.

A man addressed Ned. "Captain, I'm the Mayor."

Ned asked, "Mayor, how far to Gettysburg?"

The Mayor replied, "Over 20 miles, Captain, east-southeast from here."

Ned responded, "Mayor, I'm going to Gettysburg to report what I've seen here. I report directly to General Grant. Then, I will return back before I head south to keep tabs on the Rebels."

The Mayor made a request, "Captain, please ask the Mayor in Gettysburg to help us, as best he can, by sending wagons with food, clothes, tents and anything that would help, even lumber."

Arriving in Gettysburg, Ned got his message off to Grant. After waiting some time for a response, Ned decided to return to Chambersburg. Along the way back, he was told by some men, as he passed through Cashtown, that more help would be coming to Chambersburg. He thanked them and went on.

Arriving back in Chambersburg, Ned found the burnt city already busy trying to rebuild. He stood watching with the Mayor and Sheriff. Wagons were coming and going, taking burnt things from houses to the outside of town. Burnt homes and houses were already being torn down and the trash loaded into wagon after wagon.

Ned said, "Well, Mayor, it looks as if your city is on the road to recovery." The Mayor replied, "Yes, Captain, we can't let mere ruffians dictate our lives. We are lucky though, Captain. War still moves in and over towns and cities more than once in the South."

"I guess you might look at it like that, Mayor," Ned responded.

Chapter 34

An Unexpected Reunion

Ned looked at the wagons in line to be filled. He saw a draft horse from the side and behind, and said, "Boy, Mayor, I swear that's my Belgian draft in line over there. If I were in Virginia, I'd say it was."

The Mayor looked to where Ned was speaking, and offered, "In fact, Captain, the owner is from Virginia. They arrived only weeks ago."

Ned glanced at the Mayor with a serious look and uttered, "You said Virginia?"

The Mayor answered, "Yes, Captain, three ladies from Staunton, here to stay with the McBride family. It's their grandniece."

Surprised, Ned said, "McBride? Are you sure that's the name?"

"I'm sure, Captain. Why do you ask?" the Mayor replied.

Ned responded, "Mayor, come with me, will you?"

Ned walked on a beeline towards the horse and the wagon. He asked himself, "Was McBride Auntie's maiden name?" He wasn't sure, but he thought it was something like that.

Ned knew it was his Belle before he got to the side of the horse. He excitedly shouted, "Belle, Belle girl!"

Belle turned to look at Ned and, knowing him instantly, gave out a loud nicker after nicker. "It is you, Belle girl," he said, as he stroked his second favorite horse. "What are you...?" Before he finished the words, came a voice.

"You there! Captain! Please leave the horse!" Jo screamed.

Then, being surprised, Jo yelled, "Ned! Ooh sweet, Jesus! Ned." She covered the 25 feet between them in three bounds, it seemed, and jumped into his arms.

Jo exclaimed, "Oh dear, God, what are you doing here, Ned?"

Ned, having trouble containing his excitement, said, "It's a long story, Jo. But why are you here and where is Lizza and Auntie?"

Jo replied, "Auntie has the mules hitched to a wagon. She just left to dump a load outside of town."

Anxious, Ned asked, "Where is Lizza, Jo, where is she?"

"She's safe, Ned," Jo responded. She's at Auntie's family 2-1/2 miles north of town with Christiana. They are fine and safe, Ned! Oh! Your little girl, Ned, she is so beautiful and precious!

"Tell me how to get there, Jo, please quickly, Ned begged.

"Relax Ned. I'll take you," Jo said.

Ned quickly responded, "Okay, let's go."

Jo pulled the wagon out of line and mounted Belle bareback, as Ned got Jake.

The two rode north at a gallop but soon Belle tired.

Knowing how anxious Ned was, Jo said, "Go ahead, Ned. Take the next right. It's the only house, two stories, well-kept grounds and a large elm tree shading the premises.

Ned entered the road off the main road and started yelling, "Lizza! Lizza!" It echoed around the secluded acreage and into the house where Lizza sat sewing with great auntie Myrtle. Both perked up at the hollering, not really hearing anything but a man yelling.

As Jake slid to a stop, Ned was already off and walking fast towards the house. Lizza made the door first, and Ned had stopped dead in his tracks as Myrtle came up beside the stunned Lizza.

Then Lizza screamed, "Ned!" At that the sleeping Christiana awoke and began to cry. Myrtle went to fetch the child.

"Lizza," Ned said softly, as she jumped into his arms and sobbed heavy tears of joy. "Oh, my love," he said in her ear.

Lizza said, "I love you, Ned. I've been so worried."

"Look at me, Lizza," Ned whispered.

She pushed back as he wiped her tears, taking in every line of her face, as he did the night they were together before leaving so long ago. They sank to their knees and then Ned sat on the grass with her on his lap, her arms around him professing their undying love.

Jo came up finally, reined Belle up, and stopped to witness the beautiful reunion of two people she had come to love dearly.

By then, Myrtle came through the door with Christiana on her shoulder. She had quickly calmed the child. "Lizza," she said, "I think Christiana wants to meet her father."

"Oh! Ned, come," Lizza said, as she jumped up and grabbed his hand. Lizza took Christiana and cradled her in her arms. "Here she is," she said as she folded back the linen cloth from around her head.

Christiana blinked at the bright sunlight.

Ned was in awe. "Can I touch her?"

Lizza understood his tentativeness. She took his hand in hers and placed it on the child's head.

Ned beamed and just looked at Lizza lovingly.

All four were in tears on the grass in front of the green house in Pennsylvania, it seemed far from the horrors of war. Ned traced Christiana's fingers and put his finger in her palm, as Christiana squeezed around it.

"She is beautiful, Lizza. Just as you said," Ned said adoringly.

"Yes, and she's strong and healthy," Lizza uttered.

After much fawning, Ned sat on the porch holding Christiana with Lizza sitting in front of him, leaning with her hands on Ned's knees.

Jo sat with Myrtle on the porch swing, as Jo told Ned of their reasons for leaving and their trek north. She related Mosby stopping them, which at the mention of his name caused Ned to become on the alert at her words. For an hour they sat on the porch.

Then down the lane came Auntie driving the mules and yelling something over and over. She stopped and set the wagons brakes and jumped down, and said, "Well, I'll be. I don't believe it. When the Mayor caught up with me and told me of this surprise, I could not believe it. Come over here and give your Auntie a big hug."

Ned gave up Christiana to Lizza, as Auntie kissed both of Ned's cheeks and said, "How did you ever?"

"I don't know," Ned answered. "Fate, I guess?"

Auntie replied, "Fate? Nope! God, dear nephew!" She continued, "We've been nonstop, Jo and I, helping in town, but I now need some rest. After resting, Jo and I need to go back," she said.

"Auntie, you were right to come here," Ned said.

"Yes! For more than one reason, but Lizza pushed us over to leave when she said, 'Ned would not want me here with the Rebels coming.' "

Ned agreed, "You're right, Auntie, I would not."

At that, a rider came into the clearing and asked, "Are you Ned McDonald."

Ned responded, "Yes, I am."

The man responded, "Sir, I've ridden hard and long to find you. This message is for you."

Ned opened it and read:

From: General Grant
To: Captain. McDonald.
Your message received and acknowledged. Please give my regards and regrets to Chambersburg and its residents. You are to move south and join General Sheridan in the Valley at great haste, Major. Job well done!

Lizza looked for some indication from Ned about the message.

Ned said, "I've been promoted." He beamed as he handed the message to Lizza, and she handed Christiana to Ned to hold. Her eyes scanned over the message.

"When?" Lizza questioned, "Tomorrow?"

Ned replied, "Lizza, I need time with you and Jake needs rest." He told the rider, "Thank you, young man, for finding me."

The man responded, "Not at all, sir. Well, I'm off back to Gettysburg."

That same night Ned began to give Jake a going over. His left front leg was heated on the backside. Ned felt again. Yes, it was hot, and Ned said, "Hold, Jake." Ned lifted the lantern to check the spot. No swelling. Not yet. The hair was laying smooth. "Is it sore, Jake?" Ned asked.

Jake lazily looked at Ned as he spoke.

Ned added, "We will have to look at that in the morning, big man." He was not too worried, since for countless times Jake had a similar ailment that amounted to nothing. Ned then tended to Belle. It had been some time since he had attended her. She loved the attention.

Ned, caringly said, "Well, girl, they have taken good care of you. That's for sure."

Belle responded positively to Ned's words.

Ned then said, "Well, you two, I'll see you in the morning."

As Ned turned to leave the barn, he saw Auntie Bev. She had been standing against the barn door watching him. She half smiled and said, "Ned, while you were with Grant, did you see my man or any of the family?"

Ned's eyes narrowed and he did not hesitate. "Yes, Auntie, all of them. I saw them before we got to Cold Harbor."

Ned's eyes could not hide the truth. Auntie's eyes filled with tears as she said, "He is dead, isn't he?"

And again, without hesitation, Ned responded, "Yes, Auntie, all of them except Cameron!"

"All of them?" she stammered.

"Yes all, Auntie," Ned replied.

Their eyes fell from one another.

Auntie continued, "I knew Ned! I knew! He came to me in my sleep. He called to me. I awoke and went to the window. He stood at the road, Ned, waiting with a smile. He spoke to me. He did not yell from that distance and I heard him as clearly as if he was in the room. He said go on about. I am here with our son. We wait for you, and he smiled and next to him my son became clear to see. I cleared the sleep from my eyes and as I looked back they were gone. I knew then, Ned. So, your words confirm what I saw that night was real."

Ned choked up and said, "Auntie, he was a brave man to the last. He helped others be brave at the moment of danger. You must have left for here before the letters I sent to the family arrived. Each was the letter they had written home to all of you the night before the suicide battle the next day. I put a lock of their hair in every envelope. I saw them step off to battle and watched them die, Auntie."

Ned began to sob at remembering the site that day. "I could save only Cameron. I pulled him from his regiment moments before the battle. I couldn't save the others! Honestly, I could not!"

Ned became uncontrollable and collapsed to the straw floor. Straining, he said, "I watched them die. Yet, I sat at the back safe. Oh, God! Why I watched it I don't know. They all were cut down. All the men! All of them."

Auntie knelt and covered his body with hers, feeling the sobs and his body wracked with pain. She felt his guilt at not being with them, yet safe. "Ned, it's okay."

"No, it's not," he cried.

Finally, he stopped, totally wrought from exhaustion at the letting of emotions.

Auntie tried to help as she said, "Ned, you saved one. I tell you, Ned, the others would not have given to pulling out of battle. This I'm sure of! You saved our Cameron. You saved him to come home to his mother. Don't you see?"

Ned looked at his aunt as she continued, "Your assignment called for another duty and you did it. If you had been with them, all of you would be dead! Do you see, dearest nephew?"

Ned nodded his head, yes.

Auntie said, "Now stand up and give me a hug. Compose yourself now. You must! We all rejoice in your return and safety, and you to revel in Lizza's and Christiana's love. Do you understand me?"

"Yes, Auntie, let's go. Let's go to the house."

The next morning, Ned arose and went to the barn to check on Jake. The swelling had gone down. "Good," he said, but he decided to wait one more day before leaving his family.

As the baby slept, Lizza and Ned, hand in hand, walked the property down to the road talking and enjoying that which they really had never done before. Their lives had been chaos at every turn.

Then, as they sat, Lizza said, "Ned, what will we do after this is over? Will we raise our little girl?"

"Of course, Lizza," Ned responded.

"No, Ned, where will we go to live?" Lizza continued, "I want to see beyond the western mountains. Ned, I hear of the land that you can see forever, mighty rivers, mountains bigger than the Blue Ridge. Maybe we could have a big farm and have more children."

Ned gazed off while listening as Lizza spoke. The soft wind blowing and the songbirds chirping made it all seem possible.

Softly, Ned said, "That would be nice, my love. If it's what you want, then we will do it. I, too, have thought of going west to start anew, a new place away from the land I have loved, so torn to pieces."

Lizza laid her head on his, as they stood holding one another.

Ned added, "Lizza, at times I felt I would never see you again and that I wouldn't want to live if I lost you."

"I, too," said Lizza. "You know, Ned, we've been so blessed all these years. Think about the adversity we have had from our first meeting that day outside Gloucester." She went on, "Do you think people will ever accept our marriage and seeing you and I together with our children?"

Ned answered, "I'm not sure, Lizza. Not everyone, anyway. It might be too much to expect from some."

"I think you're right, but maybe in Christiana's life it will change completely or maybe in her children's time," she proposed, and added, "Ned, I am worried about Bessie back in Staunton. If you get near there, please check on her and let me be assured of her safety."

The night brought the two to yet another, not so often, experience and that was to sleep beside each other. Holding one another and hearing each other breathe. They cherished this night, but too soon morning came.

Ned left after painful goodbyes to his four women, Lizza, Auntie, Jo and Christiana. He knew now that he would receive all of their letters and his letters would be received. And that this is where the four of them would wait out the war. He felt some secureness in that. He felt relieved.

Chapter 35

A New Maneuver

Since his foray to Washington, D.C., Early had entered the Shenandoah Valley and ceaselessly marched his men back and forth, to and fro through the whole Valley. Every General that Grant had sent was an attempt to put away, once and for all, Early. As well, his Rebels and Mosby, and his hit and run tactics, but they would return beaten and bruised.

General Sheridan was still getting his men in fighting trim. When he pushed up the Valley from the Potomac River, the two Generals sparked, retreating and advancing back and forth, afraid to fully engage. Each looking for their ideal place and time to strike that would be a knockout blow to the other.

Ned had caught up with Sheridan. The General had asked Ned to keep an eye on his old Rebel Commander, Mosby. It was a dangerous assignment, for if he was caught, they surely would hang him on the spot. However, it was a mission that was necessary. Mosby was hitting supply wagons and causing great disruptions.

Early and Mosby often did not act in concert. General Early looked upon Mosby and his men as undisciplined ruffians. The truth be told, Mosby's Raiders were quite disciplined and greatly causing problems to Sheridan. He was seriously helping Early whether the General would admit it or not.

Ned knew their tactics and what they looked for in information to use to their advantage. So, Ned shadowed. He lay in wait at gaps they frequently used to pass into the Valley over the Blue Ridge Mountains. He knew their lairs in Loudoun and Fauquier Counties, or as they called it, the Land of Mosby's War.

One day, following Mosby's men, less Mosby himself, Ned came upon General Early and his corps amassed around Winchester. This town had changed hands many times with two battles already fought in and around its limits. It was mid-September now and the weather of cold rain and snow was but a short time away.

Ned knew Sheridan was 25 miles to the north and headed south of the Valley looking for a good shot at Early. So, across the Opequon Creek, Ned headed down the Valley to warn Sheridan of Early and the Rebels who were dug in at Winchester.

Ned crossed at the railroad crossing after Stephenson's depot. He followed the Winchester and Potomac railway towards Harpers Ferry. There, just outside Harpers Ferry, he found Sheridan.

Ned reported to Sheridan, "General, I happened upon Early and he is no longer on the move as in the past. He is dug in tight at Winchester. He looks to make you assert yourself there. He maintains the same number of men."

Sheridan responded, "Very good, Major. Good work. If it's in Winchester he wants a fight, by God, I shall oblige him. I will crush his men and his spirit and rid this scourge."

Sheridan was met half way in route to meet Early by Grant. Grant came to discuss this matter of Early and his still quite evident presence in the Valley, giving Lincoln and Washington D.C. fits. Sheridan advised Grant that he now had Early where he preferred to fight him, and the plan was in action at that very moment. He assured Grant he would punish Early and lay to waste the Valley in a maneuver of Grants ideas of waging war.

Ned rode up with Sheridan to Winchester. Sheridan imparted to him his expectations of information. "We cannot and will not fail here, Major. It's imperative that we drive them ahead of us like cattle to slaughter."

Ned replied, "Yes sir, General."

Sheridan added, "I need all your eyes can take in. You and Jake need to be from one end to the other. I want the whole picture. Do you see what I'm getting at?"

"Yes, General," Ned answered.

Sheridan continued, "Now move on up ahead and begin. I want an assessment to gauge any changes I may need to take."

Ned and Jake went on ahead and crossed at Mill Ford, about 5 miles northeast of town. He angled southwest and came upon Redbud Creek. Two creeks emptied into Opequon Creek. Winchester was five miles west. The town sat between the creeks.

Sheridan's plan was to send the Federals due west between the creeks for a frontal assault with strength and, at the same time, to put it hard in with the Federals left. From Opequon Creek to Winchester, there is a big ravine that moved uphill to the town with heavy timber on either side. So, with a frontal assault, it was hoped that the Federals right could turn the rebels left and roll them up.

It was September 19. The morning was bright, not a cloud in the sky, not even a breath of wind. Ned couldn't get the advantage he needed to view the rebels. So, he rode off on a road going north, then the road ended. It went nowhere. He looked to the West. There was just what he needed over a half a mile away. A rise of land stuck out like a monument of sorts. It was rocky with crags on both sides.

At one point, leaving Jake, he grabbed his binoculars and ran over the rough ground, falling over and then down a ravine through the thick overgrowth. At the bottom looking up the escarpment, he traced the path to the top. He would work his way up the heavy rocky slope, clinging, grabbing and pulling himself up and up.

Finally, at the top, Ned was completely soaked with sweat. He then moved to the south edge, climbing along carefully. A fall here meant that he could tumble some 100 feet before hitting rock below, and then fall again on down another 60 feet. Ned caught his breath and looked out toward Winchester. His view was complete. He was northeast of town about 3 miles.

Ned put the glasses to his eyes and could see directly down the rebel trenches and their line of defense. Ned also saw Sheridan's men deploying to create their lines of attack. Behind the town, Ned saw the old Milroy forts on a hill with cannons pointed east. The three forts looked to have two batteries each at the ready. It looked to Ned that Early held nothing in reserve. All of his men were spread thinly between the creeks that Winchester was between. Early's only advantage, that Ned could see, was the Winchester Turnpike that went north and south through the center of town. It gave a quick passage of movement if Early needed to shore up his left or right.

Ned had seen enough. Off he went, almost falling several times in getting back down this rocky outcrop. He swung into the saddle and headed to find Sheridan. He was on the south side of town. Sheridan was now aligning his front.

Arriving at Sheridan's headquarters, the General welcomed him, "Major I've been expecting you. What have you!"

Ned reported, "Sir, Early is all in on the front across yours. He holds nothing in reserve, albeit, several batteries west of town. He is well fronted."

Sheridan replied, "As I expected, Major. He's tired of running up and down the Valley from us. He's going to settle it here and now."

So, with more information that Ned gave Sheridan, it took the better part of the day to assign positions and giving those in reserve and the cavalry their assignments. Sheridan seemed to be always prepared.

The assault didn't step off till late in the day. The battle then raged back and forth with each gaining ground then falling back. The withering fire rivaled any battle before. Musket pops became as one. The fire of muskets was so hot that the 114th New York Regiment lost 185 men. They fell almost at the same time, dead, lined in a row, as they fell forward.

Regiment after regiment was sent forward. Slowly, after overwhelming numbers prevailed, the Union lines turned the flanks and drove the rebels pell-mell towards Winchester, seeking relief and shelter.

After roll call on both sides, the Federals lost over 5,000 men to the 4,000 that the Rebels lost. As always, the rebels seemed to have fared better in losses, but they could not play the game of attrition. The North had yet an untestable reserve that was bottomless.

Ned followed movements closely. The escaping rebels were looking for a place to lick their wounds, as it were, and they found it 20 miles south in the Valley between Little North Mountain and Massanutten Mountain or Three Top Mountain at a place called Fishers Hill in the Valley. At this point, the area is only 4 miles wide. Early had spread his entire army corps across the gap and faced north to receive Sheridan's attack that was sure to come.

Ned had shadowed Early's retreating army to the Valley. He slipped behind North Mountain in hopes of moving out in front of them to assess their strength as they passed by. From the mountaintop, Ned saw no sign of Early in the narrow valley below, so he moved back north across its ridge.

Finally, Ned saw them. They had rallied up at the narrow valley entrance. Ned could see that their numbers had been sadly reduced and yet these ragamuffins were still game. Ned knew first-hand these Rebels operated short on everything except bravery and encouragement.

Ned caught up with Sheridan as they came upon Early's land. He gave his information of strength of numbers and then headed back to the ridge to observe.

Later, Ned crossed over to Massanutten Mountain and picked out a shimmering of light. He saw lookouts doing just as he, but for Early on the opposite side of the valley

Sheridan had sent men behind North Mountain to see if they can do as Ned had done and get behind Early as they trekked away from Sheridan. Ned was sure the lookouts on the other side of the valley were watching and gave Early warning of the movements.

Ned kept an eye on Early's army, but hour after hour no response came at the flanking movement of the Federals. After all day, there still was no adjustment for the flanking. Could the lookouts not have seen? But how could they not, if it was in the bright light of day.

Ned fell back south along the ridge to scout the progress of General Crook's Brigade and to warn him if a counter move was to be sent his way.

So far, Grant's initial movements were successful, up, over and down the east side, as General Sheridan kept Early's front busy with feints and even encroaching to several hundred yards.

The Rebels soon saw their fate. They had been boxed in and so once again battle resumed as they fought through Crook's Brigade with their gut and tenacity. It was a costly escape.

General Early, finally continued south and the Rebels came to stop at Brown's gap just northeast of Staunton. Sheridan stopped 20 miles northwest of Early at Harrisburg near the south tip of Massanutten Mountain.

Finally, Early received his reinforcements sent from Robert E. Lee. So, it became, at these two spots, two armies just eying one another for some time. Sheridan, however, was having a hard time maintaining his supply lines, in part due to Mosby's Rangers. So, he needed to decide soon what he should do for his next move, because surely Grant would want one without delay.

During this lull, Ned had scouted in and around Early's position at Brown's Gap on the Blue Ridge Mountains. Early's forces had been heavily reinforced in the last three months because he had taken a heavy loss in men. Sheridan had come to appreciate the quick information and accuracy of Ned's reports.

Chapter 36

Helping Bessie

After reporting to Sheridan, Ned decided to swing west and south to Staunton just to check on Bessie for Lizza. He rode through town at 2:00 a.m. He had put away his uniform and wore his civilian clothes.

He knocked several times at the door. Then on the other side of the door he heard Bessie say, "Yes! What is it? We are full up. There are no rooms available."

Ned responded, "Bessie, it's Ned. Open up." Ned heard her excitement.

She said, "Oh! Quick come inside!"

Ned remembered the smells of the first time he and Lizza had come here. It was the same enticing aroma. He hugged Bessie tightly and said, "Lizza is very worried about you!"

She replied, "Yes, I know Ned, but it was the right decision for me to stay as it was for her to go. But how did you find her, Ned? Did they write you?"

"No," Ned said, "I happened upon them, Bessie, in Pennsylvania!"

"In Pennsylvania?" she questioned.

"Yes siree," Ned responded. "In my travels, I was led to Chambersburg, Pennsylvania. The Rebels had gone to burn it for the

Federal's burning of the VMI, and I, by chance and luck, found them. They had decided to go to her great aunt's instead of West Virginia."

"I'll be," said Bessie. "So, you've seen Christiana."

Ned, beaming, said, "I have! And how beautiful she is!"

"Yes, she is," Bessie agreed and excitedly added, "Oh! Poppa Smith!"

Ned, surprised, said, "Yes, but how did you know?"

Bessie continued, "Well, Ned, I finally got a letter and he had told me of your by-chance meeting. He was impressed with you, Ned."

Ned responded, "Well, the same goes for him."

After an hour of catching up, Ned was falling asleep. Bessie gave him their best guest room and he fell fast to slumber.

Bessie woke him at 11:00 a.m. that same day. It was his first good night's sleep since Chambersburg. Bessie and Ned continued their talk after he had eaten a hearty breakfast.

Ned asked, "How are the folks here in town taking this valley tension?"

Bessie replied, "Ned, it's getting worse than ever before. There are very few here in Staunton that will even talk to me now. I've been refused service at shops that I've used for years and they've known me since before I could walk."

Concerned, Ned asked, "Have they threatened you, Bessie?"

Bessie said, "Only slightly, Ned. But I see it getting worse if this war stays here around Staunton. Everyone is worried with both armies only 20 miles north of here. The Rebel sympathizers are worried that the Union army will flee and take the slaves here in Augusta County." Augusta County, where Staunton was, had 20.5 slaves per 100 whites. It was among the highest in the Valley.

Ned expressed his concern for her and she responded, "Ned, when the Rebels came through here at the beginning of the summer, although sneered at as they passed here, I was not harmed or threatened. Nor did the mostly shoeless, unwashed, hungry man who tried to steal from me. Most just asked for water, which I gave them freely from our well. But that's all. As I said before, it's those I've known all my life that I see becoming hostile. I did go to your aunt's house to check on it after the Rebels moved north out of here. Not a fence rail or board on the house was touched. Not even a window broken."

Ned nodded, "I guess Southern manners still prevail."

Bessie said, "Yet, I'm glad that they went north. Did a battle take place?"

"Yes," Ned replied.

In a reminiscing mood, Bessie said, "And you and Lizza both have had adversity thrown up at you, although differently. Ned, your mom and dad died within months of each other. Lizza, a slave all her life, was torn from her roots and sent away, leaving and running several times. Yet, the last time she happened on a lonely road to find you to take her away at last. This is not a per chance meeting or pairing."

Ned listened.

Bessie continued, "God brought you two together, Ned. It's the only way I see it. Your love for each other, for sure, was born out of desperation. But it was in that desperation that the seed was planted. The rest was left to her being a woman and you a man. Not a black woman and a white man. I believe you two were born to love each other and pass on your love to generations to come, and to look back with pride in your great grandparents. We were different in rearing, but there it ends."

Ned finally said, "Thank you, Bessie. For I believe as you, as does Lizza. But whites and blacks alike don't see that."

Bessie said, "Ned, I could not have picked a better man for my sister even if I looked into God's cupboard to select him myself."

Ned laughed as they both took the other's hands. "Thank you, Bessie."

She responded, "Not at all, brother-in-law," and she put her arms around him and kissed his cheek.

Bessie then fetched the picture she had shown Lizza. Ned was greatly moved by the picture. To him, Lizza more than Bessie looked like her mother. Ned could see the firm resolute look on her face, a woman who always did as she was told, that her life was not her own.

Ned couldn't help but think, at least now, one generation removed from her and her daughters, now free, not set to a life of control and subservience and to degrading of their very existence.

Bessie broke his thought, and said, "Ned, someday soon, Lizza and I will go find her."

Ned, without even thinking about what he was saying, said boldly, "I promise to you before God, Bessie, I will find and bring your mother to you and Lizza." Ned had stood as he said these words and looked with commitment at Bessie.

She replied, "Ned, I doubt you not at all!"

Ned nodded his head in agreement.

Bessie looked at Ned and said softly, "I see why Lizza loves you so very much, Ned! I pray that I may find a love like that."

Ned then told her, "Someday, Bessie, I know someday you will have a fine man!"

In their hours together, the two grew to understand one another and formed a close bond. It was a bond of family. Ned could not help but think that those closest to and that know him the best are all women, Bev, Lizza, Jo, Christiana, Elizabeth, Elsa and now Bessie. It amused him, but it was true!

A knock came at the door and Bessie answered. It was the Sheriff's wife, Pearle. Bessie welcomed her, "Yes, Miss Pearle?"

The lady said, "Bessie, I've come and I shouldn't have. If some find out I've come to see you, it wouldn't look good for my husband." Pearle was clearly upset looking back over her shoulder as she spoke.

"Pearle, please come in," said Bessie.

Pearle responded, "Oh no! No, I can't."

"Then what is it?" Bessie asked.

Pearle continued, "Bessie, we've heard the Yanks have hung Rebels in retaliation for an outright murder of a Lieutenant. Two Bessie, two! They were from Staunton."

Ned moved near the door to listen, but not be seen.

Pearl continued, "Johnson's boy and the Dixon boy. Both families are all up in arms at any northern sympathizers. It is well known your daddy aids the Yanks. The Johnson's and Dixon's are at this very minute in the center of town inciting and fanning the flames of anger and reprisal. If I were you, I would stay locked tight in there until it goes away, and I tell you this, Bessie, out of respect for you and your Poppa Smith."

At that she ran off and down the street. Bessie watched her go, still holding the door handle. "Oh! Sweet Jesus, Ned!" she called.

"Yes, Bessie, I heard. Please shut the door."

As she did, she laid her head on the door and offered, "Ned, I don't believe this, it is always something."

Ned responded, "I'm afraid it is, Bessie." He put his arms around her as she leaned back to his body.

Bessie then said, "Hold me, Ned, as I say a prayer." Out loud Bessie gave thanks for the gifts of God's love and asked for Ned's and her family's safety and for a quick resolution to the war. "Amen," she concluded.

Ned responded, "Amen!"

Bessie turned to Ned and said, "Must you go right away, as you said? Must you today?"

Ned answered, "No, not now, Bessie. I will stay or take you with me, whatever it calls for. We will wait and see how they act first. I trust they will calm down once they have time to sleep on it."

Comforted, Bessie said, "I hope you're right, Ned. I hope you're right."

Ned got his rifle and pistol, secured all the doors and windows, and then they waited. It was all they could do.

Two days went by and nothing happened. No stirrings, no fires, no gun popping sounds.

Finally, Ned said, "Bessie, I think you should leave town. I can only believe this could get bad at any time for Union people. All it's going to take is one more thing like this and there could be mobs ramming and looking for retaliation."

Unhappy, Bessie commented, "I know Ned, but Poppa's business?"

Being serious, Ned said, "Bessie, Poppa can somehow replace this, but not you. He would not want you to die trying to fruitlessly save the hotel."

Bessie replied, "I know, Ned. I know, but where will I go?"

Ned told her, "To Pennsylvania or Richmond. Elizabeth would gladly have you."

In turmoil, Bessie said, "I don't know, Ned. I don't know what I should do now."

All day they discussed Bessie and her future. She finally decided Staunton was too dangerous of a town to stay in as a northern sympathizer. Richmond it was going to be. She would go to Elizabeth's. The two packed trunk after trunk and took them to the dressmaker next to the Smith hotel. She would and could be entrusted to the items that Bessie needed to save. All that was left behind could possibly be lost for good.

At 9:00 p.m., Bessie, behind Ned on Jake, set off and traced the railway tracks through Rockfish gap towards Charlottesville some 48 miles away. It was there that she could ride the train to Richmond. It was the very path Lizza and Ned used to come to Staunton.

Bessie kissed Ned and clung to him for an extended hug.

Ned offered, "Bessie here is your introduction letter. It's not too revealing, but Elizabeth will understand it's from me and keep you safe as long as need be. You will fall in love with this little woman."

Bessie, positively responded, "I'm sure Ned, Lizza has told me so much about her."

Ned asked, "Please update her on all of us."

Bessie said in appreciation, "I will, Ned," as tears fell from her eyes.

Ned consoled her and reassured Bessie, "You will be safe with Elizabeth."

She answered, "I know, Ned, but I'm worried I'll never see you again." Her words were with a deeper love than she wanted to share. For even though he was her sister's man, she, too, loved Ned, or at least she had come to believe it. The words only fell on Ned's ears as concern. He did not understand her deeper meaning.

Bess arrived safe and sound and quickly fell into a routine and did love Elizabeth. Soon regular letters passed back and forth between she and Lizza in Pennsylvania.

After leaving Bessie, Ned headed towards the Blue Ridge and found safe passage by following the Rapidan River to its headwaters and then down the Western slope, while picking his way, slowly at times, over very precarious ground, but surefooted Jake prevailed.

He caught back up with Sheridan, after a jaunt to Brown's gap to assess any changes to Early's position. Early was quite content to let Sheridan make the next move.

Chapter 37

Continuing the Battle

After much posturing by each army, on October 5 Sheridan got the final approval from Grant to lay waste to the Valley of food and shelter. So, Sheridan spread the Corps across the width of the Valley, which was, for the most part, from Harrisburg, 20 miles north to Staunton, 20 miles wide all the way to Marilyn and Harpers Ferry. They set ablaze food storehouses, barns, and homes until the Valley was completely razed. Valley residents pleaded and cried to be spared, but rare was it to be granted. Cattle, sheep, and horses were driven down the Valley to be used by only the Union army.

The Valley filled with smoke, as a reminder to folks left behind and to those ahead of the army as an omen of the same treatment to come. Folks tried to move quickly to not suffer the same fate, but only a pittance of property was saved. In the end, 70 miles of the Valley were destroyed, 3000 barns filled with grain and farming implements. There were 5,000 head of cattle and 4,000 sheep taken down the Valley. It was the approach that war is hell. Hell for all.

Finally, the corridor which had been used so successfully by the Rebels for tactical movements and sustenance, was squeezed tight, never to be used again.

Sheridan instructed Ned to ride ahead to help flush out locations and activity by the, thus far, successful Mosby and his Raiders, who had made his supply lines so precarious.

Jake and Ned rode in the west shadows along the base of the Blue Ridge Mountain ridges in search of any potential raid on Sheridan's men, who were now spread out thinly across the Shenandoah Valley.

At full numbers, Mosby was well past battalion in strength. He could, if necessary, bring to bear 750 men. But, those 750 riders were almost like a brigade with their cunning, bold strikes that were swift and complete.

Ned carefully picked his line of travel, for he needed to see and not to be seen. He knew these parts well, for he had crossed over these mountains and back so many times while with Mosby. Ned chose small round mountains close to the gaps through the Blue Ridge. He carefully watched the gaps before moving north farther and farther.

At last, after scanning the gaps and surrounding country at Buck Mountain looking West, Ned watched Manassas Gap and Chester Gap south of it. The gaps sit in Fauquier County, a hotbed for the Raiders. From the North, along the base of the Blue Ridge, Ned counted 100 riders. They stopped short of Manassas Gap. Ned thought they're waiting for others to rendezvous before crossing into the Valley.

The two gaps sat due east, almost, from the northern tip of Three Top Mountain and the confluence of the north and south fork of the mighty Shenandoah River. Ned figured about 20 or so miles, possibly only 10 miles per day would be covered by Sheridan. They were close to the same distance down the Valley. Had Mosby seen them coming and planned a large assault on the ranks? He must have, because Mosby liked much smaller attack groups. It appeared that he had something bigger in mind.

Ned found his way off Buck Mountain and set off for Chester Gap, about 5 miles south of Manassas Gap. Jake's feet pounded hard on the road. Jake and Ned loved this hell-bent like running. It was Jake's birthright to run. They covered 5 miles to Chester Gap, and up and over the pass to the Valley up ahead, in no time before descending into the Valley.

Then, Ned saw the southern fork of the river and Three Top Mountain on the Lieutenant Massanutten Mountain. Ned saw no

Federals this side of the mountain. The bulk of Sheridan's forces could come north, up the other side of the mountain that ran north and south, directly into the Valley. The mountain was 15 miles away, Ned reckoned, so off he went across the southern fork of the river. He skirted the north tip of Three Top Mountain in hopes of warning Sheridan or one of his generals.

It was October 18th. Ned had finally made it to the top of Three Top Mountain to look west for Sheridan and then back east for Mosby and his men. Then, as he looked out north, spread out before him was Sheridan's men, gathered in the center of the Valley at the tip of Three Top Mountain. They covered miles and were encamped for the night. Unbeknownst to Ned, Sheridan had gone to Washington, D.C. to see the Secretary of War, Stanton, and was on his return to his army that very day.

Ned scanned for more of the Union army back south, whence the union had just come. He gasped. There they were. Early's men closing in from behind. Ned realized that the Union had not a clue of this action. Lieutenant General Longstreet, Lee's old warhorse, as he was affectionately called, was also in route with his men to crush Sheridan. Ned sat atop Three Top Mountain to gather as much information as he could get before descending into Belle Grove or around Cedar Creek.

Before dark, Ned saw that Early's men were not going for a frontal attack but a blindside assault. The men took off all but their rifle, pistols and ammo. They dropped bedrolls, tin cups, pans, and canteens. They were moving silently around the base of the west face of Three Top Mountain, north to the tip just across the North Fork of the Shenandoah. The Federals had no idea of them, at least not now.

Finally, after seeing the planned movements, Ned found a quick dissent to the Valley opposite the Federals. He then located a ford in the river, but the rebels were hidden all around making it impossible to cross over the river. Ned spun Jake around and eventually followed the Manassas railroad tracks back east crossing under the Trestle at another ford. He almost ran smack into Mosby's men camped for the night. Peering from a safe distance, he found far less than the numbers he observed before. That meant, at this minute, Mosby was probably probing Sheridan's men; he was one to ride on when others rested.

Quickly, Ned headed west to Belle Grove where, from atop Three Top Mountain, he had observed Sheridan's large contingent camp.

As Ned approached the camp and finally made his way past guards and skirmishers, he found General Wright; the same General who had ignored his last observation in the wilderness battle.

Ned said, "General Wright, I wish to speak with General Sheridan. Do you know his whereabouts?"

Wright answered, "Major, yes I do. What is it? I have command until he returns, which he is doing at this very moment. We have intercepted a message that Longstreet and Early will team up to attack us here. Sheridan has been notified and should be here soon."

Ned quickly replied, "Yes, it is true, General Wright, for I have observed not only Mosby and all his battalion, but Early just over the North Fork, not 2 miles from here at Bowman Ford. They are poised to surprise us. I watched from 2 p.m. this afternoon of their build up in preparation, until I could not see them for the darkness of night."

The General responded, "I see, I see, Major. Well, I'll send someone to verify. I'm sure you won't mind."

Ned answered, "General Wright, of course not, but you, Sir, quite respectfully, are to lose. General, I saw a large buildup of men. Mosby prefers not to assemble. I assume he will hold himself in reserve in case Early needs it. However, they often work independently, but Mosby hits like a brigade, Sir. He also knows where to be most effective in such a battle."

Wright sternly responded, "Well, Major, you have been most complete, I dare say! So, you would have me believe that I have been so fooled and outfoxed."

Ned answered, "No Sir, General."

Ned saw now, as once before, Wright was to ignore him. Ned excused himself, bent on finding a general who would listen. A short time later, Ned found General Crook, who told him that was Wright's business, dismissing him with a wave. Ned left him to find another general.

He soon found General George Armstrong Custer, the dashing Boy General. He was all decked out in his blue velvet uniform fringed with gold and his flowing golden curly hair. It was a sight to behold!

After going over the Rebel movements with him, Custer said, "Dammit man, are you sure?"

Ned firmly replied, "Yes, I am, General Custer."

Custer responded, "By God, this is an army of inept generals. Ride with me, Major."

Off they went to see General Wright. But, before they could get to him, there came musket pops, increasing in volume, and screams were clearly heard from men charging and those retreating.

In a commanding voice, Custer said, "Major, Sheridan is close to here by now. Go down the Valley and search him out at all cost. You hear me, man?"

Understanding the seriousness of the request, Ned replied, "Yes, General."

Custer added, "Tell Sheridan to come with great haste. I fear, too, Mosby hangs in the balance."

"Yes, sir," Ned answered, as he turned and headed toward Wide Turnpike Road.

Ned did not know it at this moment, but Sheridan had already left Winchester and was only 18 miles away. The General had heard the cannon's roar and he, astride his horse Reinzi, was in a full gallop to command his army.

Ned could hear the increasing sounds of battle. Early's main force had now crossed by way of the Turnpike; the Union forces were greatly surprised. Men ran in retreat, leaving horses, cannons and tents, and running barefooted, some only in long johns. A complete surprise! It was a thorough rout of the Union by the Rebels. Early proved again, by a show of force, that he was not going away as Sheridan had surmised. A costly underestimation by Sheridan!

Ned rode Jake at full gallop. He urged Jake for more speed and he responded. Ned was aware that Jake was running to parts unknown, but he had never seen him give so much effort. Perhaps Jake knew the urgency.

Ned looked at a horseman running at top speed coming down a rise in the road. He could just make out Sheridan on his black charger, Rienzi. Ned shut down Jake and spun him around, going back the way he came in a trot all the while looking back to gauge Sheridan and Renzi's speed.

"Now, Jake!" as he let Jake run once more. Perfect! Now Jake and Renzi were running neck and neck. Ned didn't want to stop Sheridan. Time was of the essence. Ned yelled the situation and information he had about the front, as the two stallions rode stride for stride, their necks rising and falling together.

Closing in on Belle Grove, coming down the Valley Pike, men were running as if Satan himself was on their heels.

Sheridan commanded, "Major, help me get control of this shameful retreat!"

Sheridan began with inspiring and threatening commands. He actually got the fear shaken in the men, just by his very presence.

Ned was inspired and attempted to emulate his General with only some success. Ned astride Jake, hollered for bravery and duty. Jake reared as Ned queued for him to do so. The mere sight of Ned and Jake did more good than Ned's actual words.

Slowly the men gathered themselves in, regaining some courage and duty to their country. Ned ran drag, encouraging their haste, as they began to trot back to Belle Grove, some men in their underwear only. Ned thought to himself, if the situation wasn't so dire, it would be a humorous sight to see.

Sheridan continued barking orders and the men responded. At one point Sheridan was all over the field inserting regiments and divisions and giving orders. He rode by Ned and yelled, "Major, find Custer as soon as you can! Tell him to let no one to the east of him or to let anyone down the eastern side of the mountain. We will harry them down the west side of Three Top Mountain!"

Loudly, Ned answered, "Yes, sir!"

Ned then headed east to the eastern flank, or right flank of Early's morning raiders. He found Custer putting his men into position and repositioning his cannons. Ned gave the information to Custer and started to leave to find Sheridan for further orders.

Custer ordered Ned, "Major, I need you to direct the company at the farthest end. They have not a capable commander as the two senior officers are dead."

"Yes, sir," Ned replied and took off. He had not led so many men in a direct battle. He said loud enough to be heard over the din of cannons, "Did you hear the General, Jake? He wants me to lead a company. We'll give it a go, old boy!"

Ned felt adrenaline coursing through his body and building up to an excitement he had not felt before. He wondered if this is what my uncles and daddy felt as they waded into battle. He found the company of cavalry and the Lieutenant, who had taken command until he was to be relieved. It was apparent the Lieutenant was all too ready to cede command. Ned rode forward to see the landscape and the alignment of infantry in front of him.

Ned's new company would support the infantry and try to turn the flank of the Rebels if necessary. But more importantly, try to keep Rebels from escaping down the Luray Valley south, should a Rebel rout take place. He sat on Jake scanning with his binoculars. There at the rear of the Union infantry, off to the East set apart from the rest of the Union army, were horsemen. They were clad not in traditional cavalry garb. Each man was dressed differently, unique, albeit, cavalry boots. It was Mosby's men! He picked Mosby out clearly. He wore his white trousers and a large feather jutting out of his hat. They all sat in formation. Ned knew they would only engage if the battle called for reserves. Mosby could not afford losses in an all-out frontal engagement. His tactics were to hit fast and leave faster.

Ned called on the artillery for the rifled cannon to fire at Mosby to create an untenable position for him. The young Lieutenant was most skilled and put the first round directly on target. Ned watched with his glasses. Four men and their horses went down immediately, as the whole lot of them went into disarray. Another shot was dropped into the Raiders. Soon, all headed back over the knoll out of sight. Ned yelled, "There, that ought to suit them, eh?"

"Yes sir, Major," the Lieutenant said.

All at once, at about 3:00 p.m., the push south began by the Federals. They waded into the Rebels with great resolve. The morning's routing that they were given was forgotten. They now had Sheridan back in command. The infantry in front of Ned handily took on the regiments in front of them.

Ned was looking at the tip of Three Top Mountain in front of him. As the Federals began to take control, Ned began to wave and rally his men. They then rumbled down the hill as one wave. Ned and his company overlapped the Rebels and drove them to the center of the valley. With the escape down Luray Valley impossible, Ned's men were firing their carbines and pistols, some swinging their sabers at the Rebels. In less than two hours, all the remnants of Early's army were across the north Fork River.

As this was all heated up, Ned remembered Mosby. He whirled Jake around to see no trace of him or his men. Mosby left Early to his own devices. True to form, Mosby was not to risk his ranks to be thinned unnecessarily.

All the Federal cavalry pushed and harried the Rebels once more south, through the valley for the final time. General Early eventually regrouped and headed toward Petersburg to help Lee in the defense of Richmond.

This had been a costly battle. The Federals lost almost 6,000 men; the majority of these happened during that morning's battles. The Rebels lost 3,000 men and 1,500 became prisoners and were sent to the North.

The next morning, Ned went to find Sheridan, but not before reinstating the Lieutenant to his post until another replacement could be found. Also, before leaving, almost all the men came to Ned to show gratitude for his display of leadership. All of them knew of his history with the Rebels. Ned's name had become well-known by this time in the war.

As he stopped to water Jake, he eyed the seriously injured Confederates being attended to. He heard his name called, "Ned!" It was a faint call, but he heard it. He looked around and saw no one he knew. A Confederate, attending a man on his back, said "Major, this man wants to speak with you; he's hurt bad!"

Ned walked over with Jake in tow. Ned saw him and knew him immediately. He only knew him as Patton.

"I thought it was you," Patton said weakly. "Before you all stepped off, I saw you out beyond us. I said to my mate, there's only one man with a horse like that."

Ned knelt down. "Patton, how are you?"

"I'm to die, of that I am sure," he gasped.

Ned grasped his hand. They had met during Ned's Rebel days while at a party during the winter before he joined Mosby. Patton had been invited to General J.E.B. Stuarts tent. His family was a prestigious family going back to George Washington. The Patton's had lost many family and kin in wars. Patton's grandson would become, perhaps, the finest battle general of all time.

Ned asked, "Can I tell your family anything?"

Blood was now seeping out of the corner of his mouth, as he coughed and gasped for breath. With great difficulty, he told Ned to tell his family, "I did my duty as expected of a Patton."

Ned nodded and blinked, yes.

Patton continued, "And that I loved my wife and children."

Again, the same, Ned motioned.

Patton squeezed Ned's hand tighter, as if trying to hold on to life a bit longer. Then, he relaxed and left his body. Ned still clasped his hand and said, "God, please save this soul and bless his family."

Ned stood and looked around at the remnants of battle: the dead bodies, some mangled, equipment everywhere of every description, dead horses. He shook his head in sorrow.

Another man spoke to Ned, "Major, Patton here told me, as he looked across at you upon the hill, 'You see that man upon the fine charger, Guffy?' I'm Guffy, Major," he said. "He wished that he had had the guts to do what was right and not what was expected of him as a Virginian, like you did! Patton admired you, Major."

"Thank you, Guffy," Ned responded.

The man answered, "Yes sir, Major."

Ned then said, "Guffy, I will give his words to his family at my first chance. You can be assured of that."

Guffy, in appreciation, said, "Yes sir, Major."

Ned mounted Jake and continued on to find Sheridan. He found the General, who told him that he was a credit to his country, this army, and his family. Sheridan told Ned that he was to return to Grant and that he hoped he could avail of his services in the future.

Ned positively responded that, "It would be my pleasure, General. Any time I can be used. Jake and I are at ready!"

Sheridan answered, "Ah, Major, that reminds me, today as we were racing back to Belle Grove."

"Yes sir," Ned responded.

The General said, "I am interested to know, was Jake at full stride or top speed, for my horse Reinzi still had more speed to give?

Ned knew Jake was not even close to top speed, but gave way to his General. "I believe so, Sir. I believe you would have left me behind had you put the spurs to your mount!"

Sheridan responded, "I thought so, Major, but Jake is a fine stud, indeed."

Ned answered, "Thank you, General. He and I appreciate the observation."

"Yes, well have you any other needs or requests?" the General asked.

"Yes, in fact I do, General. I would like to have a few weeks to see my wife and child if it's viable."

"Well, I can't see why not Major. I will give you four weeks before reporting to the siege in Petersburg. I will also inform General Grant. I believe he will find allowance for your service rendered. Okay, Major?"

Ned answered, "Yes sir, General Sheridan!"

"And Major, ..." the General started to say.

Ned said, "Yes, General?"

The General continued, "Even before today's battle, I have requested that you be given the rank of Lt. Colonel and with Grants assured approval, I believe it's only a matter of weeks before confirmation."

Ned joyously responded, "Yes sir, General!"

The General concluded their meeting, "You're excused at this time, Colonel."

Ned was grinning so big he thought his face would crack. "Yes sir, General, sir!" He saluted and rode away on Jake.

"Yes sir, Colonel," the General added.

"Jake what do you think? How does that sound to you?"

He spent the rest of the day saying farewells to men whom he had come to know these last few months. As he laid trying to sleep that night, he felt proud of his accomplishments with the Union. While back in Staunton he had so wanted to be useful in this struggle, for he had changed so much as far as his thinking. But, in the pride, he also felt the shame of being a participant in all this killing and horror that a battlefield leaves behind. Is there honor in that? He wasn't sure as he fell asleep that night, finally thinking of Lizza and Christiana.

Chapter 38

A Renewal with the Taylors

On his fourth day of leave, Ned headed northwest from Fredericksburg. He eventually had found Patton's mother to impart his heart felt sorrow for the loss of her son. He gave her Patton's last words that later would be given to his wife.

Ned was going by the Taylors. He needed to tie up loose ends with them over Molly's arrest. This was in some ways tougher than giving the Patton's the bad news. Ned, in those early days, was as much a part of the family as if he were the Taylors' son.

Ned stopped at the road before going up to their pathway. He thought of leaving. He also thought that Mosby could be nearby or even they may now have another living here as he did.

"Come on Jake, let's go."

He only put Jake at a slow walk. He wished not to hurry the inevitable. No one came rushing to him like the last time he was here; no Molly to scream his arrival. Ned looked around behind him before knocking at the door. Still no one. As Ned hit the door for the second rap, open it came. It was Sarah. She screamed a shriek that almost hurt his ears.

"It's Ned!" She jumped into his arms and excitedly kissed him all over his face. Before he calmed her down, Ned saw Jean. He wasn't sure of her feelings. She just stood watching Sarah fawn over him.

Excited, Sarah said, "Mama, look! It's Ned!"

"I see, Sarah," she answered. Then a big smile broke over her face, and she said, "God has answered my prayers, Ned. You have been watched over and are safe and you came back."

Ned held Sarah's hand as she got as close to him as she could.

Jean came to him and kissed his cheek, as she laid her hand softly on his other cheek, and said, "Come in and sit. We have much to catch up on."

Ned asked, "Sarah, where's your father?" Jean interjected, "He passed away two weeks after you left Ned."

"I'm sorry, very sorry," Ned responded, and then pulled Sarah close.

Jean left briefly and returned with some tea. There was some silence, and then she began, "Ned, I know all about Molly."

"She deserves it, mother," Sarah said and looked disgusted.

Jean then shared more fully about the circumstances, "Ned, Molly began acting very eerie in many different ways after you were taken away. Her talk of the Union was beyond Confederate good sense. As I will put it, to be delicate, she would disappear for days at a time and she would not tell us where she went. We, at times, didn't even know she had left. She talked of paying the Union back in spades for their invasion of Virginia and stripping the countryside of everything. She would not talk to me about it. She looked angry all the time. Ned, it was scaring me. She even knocked Sarah to the ground!"

Sarah said quickly to Ned, "It didn't hurt."

Ned smiled and kissed her head and said, "You know the circumstances of her arrest then, Jean."

"Yes," Jean replied, "We were visited by Provost's and Pinkerton's men for some weeks after her arrest. Our house was gone over several times. They were courteous, I will say that, though, Ned. On the first visit, however, they accused all of us of spying, but soon they dismissed it."

Ned said, "Jean, I did tell them that you were good, kind people."

"Yes," Jean responded, "They said that you had asked them to be easy with us."

Ned said, "Yes, I did. I was worried for all of you, even as I pointed Molly out to them."

Jean replied, "It's probably a good thing, Ned. She might have gotten herself killed."

Ned asked, "Jean, I've heard nothing about her since. What have you heard? What do they intend to do?"

Jean answered, "If we're lucky, Ned, nothing at all, except keep her locked up in Washington D.C. They have nothing other than her word about secrets. They have no papers or letters, no one saw her with Rebel spies or in Richmond, only her promiscuous activity. I care not even to talk about that."

Ned told Jean, "She was almost violent as they found her out that night at the ball in Warrenton."

"Ned," Jean responded tearfully, "I went to see her in D.C. and she would not even agree to see me. It broke my heart."

Sarah then said, "Mama cried all the way home, Ned."

"Well, I plan to go see her after I leave here," Ned said. "I don't know if she will see me. But I'm going to try, Jean."

Jean then added, "Ned, there's something else. I don't know if I should tell you, but I trust you implicitly. After her arrest, after it was in all the papers, and a few months later, we had a visit from a woman. Her name is Rose O'Neal Greenhow. I don't know if you know of her or not."

Ned immediately recognized her name, and said, "Yes, of course I do. She was held for spying at the start of the war, for sending information about the impending attack at Bull Run. Her information led to the victory by the Confederacy."

"Yes," Jean said, "She's the one. Well she has been to England and France trying to secure support but found none. On her return, they thought she had drowned as their blockade runner was stopped and she attempted to escape."

Ned said, "They found her body, Jean!"

"No Ned, it wasn't her," Jean quipped. "And she has preferred to keep it a secret so as to do more rebel spying if she can. So far she hasn't. She is with a family not a mile from here. You know them, it's the Brewster's."

"Yes, of course," Ned replied.

Jean continued, "Rose came to see me when she heard of Molly's incarceration. She came by to try to console me from her experience in the same prison. Rose was a socialite in Washington before the war and still has contacts for the Rebel cause." Jean then added, "As for me, Ned, all I want is for all this to end. It's been too long. Who cares, anymore? I want my life back again. Do you think for one minute every lowly soldier really gives a possum's behind about why he fights? He fights because he's told to."

Ned had to agree to the point. "Yes, you're right, Jean."

As Sarah sat on Ned's knee, Jean noticed the officer's insignia on Ned's shoulder, and asked, "Well, Ned, you've been moving up I see."

Ned halfheartedly said, "Yes, I do what I feel my duty is, Jean. I work at what I feel is necessary to make the Union whole again."

"I guess I can't find fault with that, Ned," Jean said.

Ned had just begun to warn Jean to limit her contact with such a woman as Rose when a knock at the door was heard. The door opened and a voice called out. "Jean, it's me."

They all stood up as around the corner entered no other than Rose O'Neal Greenhow.

"Oh, my!" Rose said quickly, seeing Ned was a Union officer. Then she said very calmly, "Now, isn't this awkward!"

Ned wasn't sure at first, then Jean said, "Yes, isn't it! Ned, I would like to introduce you to Rose O'Neill Greenhow. Rose, this is Major Ned McDonald of whom I have spoken to you many times and so affectionately."

Then, just as smoothly, Rose stuck out her hand for Ned to take.

Ned said, "It's a pleasure, Miss Greenhow."

She responded, "Charmed, I'm sure, Major."

Ned followed up quickly with, "Miss Greenhow, I suppose I should ease everyone's mind here. I have come here to see my friends and nothing more. What is said here, and what is seen here, is left here, unless I hear words that might be detrimental to the Union. I have no other matter of this day."

Jean said, "Thank you, Ned."

Sarah giggled. It seemed even she grasped the gravity of the moment.

Rose then said, "My, my, Major, you are as Jean and little Sarah described you to be, a most handsome man and with good taste and manners. Again, Major I am most charmed."

Ned was taken with Rose, even though her manner of speech belied her guile and cunning. She was most attractive to look at and, even at mid-life, she gave off an aura of great attraction. He quickly saw how she could gather information in those early days of the war.

Rose once had said, "My spying employed every capacity with which God has endowed me."

And Ned saw that it was a lot. She had looks, curves and intelligence. Her black hair and dark eyes flashed. And these made for a man's worst trap. Her most charming manner could disarm a man at the drop of a hat.

"Come sit, Rose," Jean urged.

Rose said, "Oh, Jean, I just thought I'd see how you were faring and if you have heard any of Molly."

"No not a word, Rose," Jean answered.

Ned said charmingly, "Please, Rose, sit."

Rose replied, "Well, well, how can I refuse such a handsome man's request."

Sarah was seeing the sexual tension of Rose in her manner and she rolled her eyes, then asked, "Mother, may I be excused."

"Yes, Sarah, of course," Jean responded.

Sarah looked at Rose and then leaned over and kissed Ned right on the mouth. It caught Ned and everyone off guard.

But Rose, not one to be unnerved said, "Well, Major, even the young women find you charming."

Sarah humphed and left the room.

"Excuse me, if you will while I see to my daughter's manners," Jean said.

Rose spoke first. "Well, Major, it's just you and me. I have so much wanted to meet you after Jean talked about you as she has. I also have heard much of you over the years in your Rebel exploits. Now, even the papers speak of you and your famous horse."

Ned replied, "Well, thank you, Rose. May I call you Rose?"

Rose responded, "Why, yes, of course. I could not think of being anything but on a first name basis with you, Ned," as she seductively gazed at him.

"Well, Rose, I must confess, I had heard of you before I even joined the Rebels. At that time, of course, I wanted to meet you, a lady spy. It was then, for me, most attractive to think about."

Rose quickly responded, "And now that you have met me, are your expectations sadly shortchanged?"

Ned knew the trap of words that she was laying before him, and replied, "Well, Rose, I will say this, if I were not married to the world's most beautiful woman and so very much in love with her, I must say I could not find a woman more perfect to pursue more intently than you."

She laughed. "Ned, that was a very good answer! I like it, and I like you. Well then, if ever the world's most beautiful woman finds you not suitable any longer, I, in fact, do most heartedly accept your pursuit. And that Major is a standing invitation."

"Thank you," Ned said, as Jean reentered the room.

"Well, I see you two found conversation," Jean said.

"Yes, Jean, most stimulating, wouldn't you say, Major?"

Ned blushingly agreed.

"Well, I really must be going home."

Ned stood and said, "Rose, my words of earlier are my bond."

"I'm sure, Major," she said, as she put her hand out.

Ned graciously took it and kissed it.

And Rose added, "Jean, I might need escorting back for surely I will swoon at such a kiss as that!"

"Oh! Rose!" Jean said teasingly.

"Well, I'm off," Rose said.

Ned walked her to her carriage and helped her up, as Jean waited at the house on the porch.

Rose told Ned, "I wish only to find quiet, Ned. My days of secret operations are over. I'm no longer useful for such a cause. I tried, but I'm too well known. Now, if this war will come to an end, I may be able to find a man to grow old with."

Ned said, "I believe that will not be a problem, Rose."

She touched his cheek and said, "Ned, if only I was younger, married or not, I would steal you away for my own."

Ned obligingly said, "Rose, I have no doubt."

Then off she went.

Ned thought, you know she's right, I probably would follow her.

"She's something, isn't she?" Jean said, as Ned climbed the stairs to the porch.

"That she is, Jean."

Jean then added, "She always comes to check in about Molly. I feel sorry for her, though. She wants to do what she feels strongly about, but her time is over."

Ned said, "As for the Union, Jean, it's a good thing that it has all passed her by."

Goodbyes were said and Ned headed north.

Chapter 39

A Journey of Sadness

Ned would go ahead to Chambersburg first. Then try to see Molly. Ned felt an urgency nagging at him to get to Lizza. Jake and Ned made good time. He could see Chambersburg in the distance, then only a short run to Lizza.

Through Chambersburg, Ned could see a dramatic difference from the last time he left, buildings rebuilt, businesses up and running. It was good to see. It was clear to him that the whole town had rebounded.

Finally, at the house where Lizza was, Ned dismounted Jake. It seemed no one was about. He knocked at the door.

Jo answered her face distraught and ashen. She said, "Ned, it's you! You got our…, but how…, we just sent it?"

Surprised, Ned asked, "Sent what, Jo?"

She replied, "That Lizza was very sick."

Frightened, Ned asked, "Where is she?" He pushed into the house, and yelled, "Lizza!"

Auntie grabbed Ned and said, "My boy, Lizza is in a bad way. We have a doctor from Gettysburg on the way."

Ned asked, "What is wrong with her?"

Auntie responded, "We don't know yet. She has stomach cramps that have her wracked with pain, even into her lower back."

Ned reacted, "I must see her."

"Go quietly, Ned. She has been given some laudanum. She is quieted some."

Ned entered the room and saw Lizza lying still, but with pain written on her face. He softly said, "Lizza, my love, I'm here."

As he knelt next to her bed, her skin warm and sweaty, she tilted her head to see her love, "Ned," she struggled to say, "You are here."

Quietly he said, "Yes, Lizza, I'm here. Oh, love, we have a doctor coming."

She nodded, but pain filled her body. She stiffened to brace for the waves that shot through her. He grabbed her hand and she squeezed it as tightly as she could. Ned winched at seeing her in such a state.

For a full five minutes, it kept after her. Then it subsided. He wiped the sweat from her brow.

She opened her eyes slowly and spoke ever slower. "I've missed you, my love."

Ned responded, "I've missed you, too! Don't try to speak, Lizza. I'm not leaving you."

In came Jo and Auntie, who said, "She got like this after we arose this morning. She complained at first of her stomach and it got worse as the morning went by. Before 11 o'clock, she was winching with great agony. She lost her stomach and we thought it would soon get better. Instead, she got worse."

Ned never took his eyes off her as they related her day. "She's very hot to the touch, Auntie."

Auntie replied, "I know, it worries me. We keep cold rags on her, but it does no good. I have not an idea, Ned, what is ailing her. We finally called for a good doctor in Gettysburg to come. It was four hours ago that a rider left to fetch him."

Lizza then screamed, as she bent up onto her side grabbing her stomach, and begged, "Oh, Ned, make it stop. It hurts so bad."

Ned was frantic.

Jo and Auntie got on either side of the bed as Ned sat up close to her head.

Lizza was in sheer agony and was starting to thrash about.

Ned's eyes filled with tears at seeing her in such pain.

"God, help her please," Ned said out loud, "Help Lizza, dear Jesus!"

Ned had just said the last word out loud when Lizza sank back and closed her eyes completely relaxed.

Ned looked at Jo and Auntie in surprise, and uttered, "It worked! God listened!"

Auntie slowly took Lizza's hand and felt above it at the wrist. She reached for and lifted her eyelid as Ned watched intently. Auntie then lifted her arm and laid it across her stomach. Without looking up, she said, "Ned, she's gone!"

The words hit Ned like nothing ever before. "Auntie," he said, "What are you saying?"

"Ned, she's gone home to Jesus."

Ned screamed so loud that Jo put her hands to her ears.

Auntie instantly began to sob.

Ned yelled, "No, no! Lizza, wake up!" He put his head to hers. "Please, darlin', wake up. You can't leave me! Please, please! Wake up." He kissed her face over and over and moaned, "Come on, I'm here now. It's okay, Lizza, it's okay."

Auntie laid her hands on his arm, "Ned, my son, Lizza is gone."

"No! No, she's not gone!" Ned yelled. "Don't you understand, Auntie, she can't be. She just can't be." He cried as he collapsed to his knees sobbing. "She can't be," he repeated over and over.

Jo had come to him as Auntie had and they both hugged him. No words were spoken now and Auntie's aunt and uncle gathered at the door of the bedroom to witness the scene of loss.

Ned arose finally, with Jo and Auntie's hands still touching him. He gently said, "Please, I need time with my wife."

They nodded and shut the door slowly behind them.

Ned pulled the chair close to the bed next to Lizza's head and whispered, "Lizza, can you hear me? I love you." He then laid his head on her chest and his arm across her waist, and softly asked, "What am I to do now, Lizza? We were going to go out west. You said you wanted to see forever, see mighty rivers and mountains, bigger than the Blue Ridge Mountains. We were just getting ready to live our lives, Lizza. Where do I go now, my love? How do I raise Christiana? How do I tell her how beautiful you were, how wonderful you were, Lizza? Now life is nothing if you are not with me. Don't you see that?"

Ned looked at her peaceful face as if he expected her to answer his questions. He traced the lines of her face with his finger as if not to forget each line, as he once did before in Staunton. Ned gently kissed her lips and lay his head once again on her chest.

After quite some time, in a sleep-like state, Ned faintly heard, "Ned, you will be fine. You will be a good father! You will tell Christiana about me and she will know me with her here with you. I am with you. You still have much to do here. Doubt not my love for you. We will meet again."

Ned then awoke. He was confused. He remembered each word she had just said. He heard her voice. He looked at Lizza. Her calm face was still unmoving, yet he had heard the words clear as a bell. He then realized, she had come to him. It was Lizza.

Ned told her, "I will love you always. Wait for me."

The door opened. It was Auntie and Jo looking confused. Auntie said, "Ned, are you okay?"

Ned quietly replied, "Yes, I am now, Auntie. He said, "Like uncle came to you, Lizza spoke to me, Auntie. She really did."

Auntie lovingly responded, "I know, Ned, I do believe she did."

Ned then asked, "Where is Christiana, Jo? I need to hold her.

Jo got her and gave Ned's daughter to him. He sat on the porch rocking as she fell asleep again. For two hours as she slept, he held his daughter, an everlasting link to Lizza.

Ned went back and forth for days with great sorrow, but always to feel soothed by holding his daughter.

Lizza's burial and service was on the property. She was temporarily buried; later to be permanently placed in the ground back at Auntie's in the family plot. It was hard for Ned to grasp her passing away. The future was so close. The war wasn't far from ending. He knew that. He could feel it.

That morning Ned knelt while holding Christiana at Lizza's grave. Ned spoke softly, "I go now, my love. But I will come to take you home. You will be safe here. Our daughter will grow strong like her mother. I will raise her good, my love. I promise you that." He then said a prayer of strength for himself and Christiana, for Jo and Auntie, who would dote on her until this war was over.

Later, Ned was to learn that apparently Lizza's appendix had burst the day she had died. No doctor was to be good enough to save her. Ned and the family were told, when he did arrive from

Gettysburg, that it was fatal. Even if he had lived next door, she still would have died.

Ned said sad goodbyes to all, and a very sad one for him on leaving Christiana. He knew she was in the best of care, but it didn't abate the pain that now was in and wracked his whole body. Up till now, Lizza had driven his every action and thought. She was strength. He often became tearful on the ride back to Virginia.

Chapter 40

A New Command as Colonel

Ned was in no hurry. It was time for both armies to go into winter camp. For some, rain and muddy roads, sleet and snow, and icy winds that would blow in over the Blue Ridge Mountains. For others, nor'easters would howl down on Virginia from the Atlantic Ocean.

Ned came to Rockville, Maryland, and sent a wire to General Grant that he was in route back to City Point, Virginia. He asked if any orders were additional upon his path there. In 24 hours orders came back that he had been turned down for Lieutenant Colonel by Grant, but, "...submitted for the rank of Colonel. It was voted on and passed in Congress. Congratulations, Colonel McDonald!" stated Grant. It was little consolation for his great loss, but he felt honored by Grant's submission.

Ned was to report to Washington, D.C., and be given a command of a regiment whose sole assignment was hunting down Mosby's men. The assignment from Grant said, "We have failed at every turn to squash this tiresome pest. Now, I look to you to end his free reign in the Northern neck of Virginia."

Well, I'm back where I started, Ned thought, but on the other side.

Ned knew it was no easy assignment laid before his feet. He would need good horsemen, good horses, seasoned veterans and men who could be in the same saddle for days at a time. Mosby had all these traits at his disposal. Ned would need to handpick his regiment, surely Grant would cede this to him. The first Massachusetts cavalry had been sorely outmaneuvered in their attempt over the months and Mosby still moved at will.

Ned got approval from Grant to handpick his men and company commanders. In Washington, he was given full access to records of all of the cavalry's men and their ranks. With this information, he began a meticulous selection process. He chose men from General John Kilpatrick's ranks, many from General George Armstrong Custer's, and even from his old commander Sheridan's elite company. In a short 30 days, Ned was calling his men together outside Rockville, Maryland.

He had some of the best mounted men in the Union Army. They looked the part. These men were seasoned veterans. Ned had an unlimited source of horses from the stables in Arlington, Virginia, an ideal location for replacement mounts for his men. He was given the choice of having his men directly ordered by General Grant.

In his command tent, the night before the regiment's first inspection, Ned felt the full gravity of his assignment. He had been given everything to achieve the goal. Now it was up to him to step up and do it. Mosby was no easy adversary, as the years had proven out. To Grant, Mosby and his Raiders constant raiding of supplies, intercepting communication, and causing great distress to Washington, D.C. now necessitated an end to the marauders.

The new Colonel had chosen well. He had three company commanders over the ten lieutenants who were to command his smaller marauder squads. There were 500 men with each lieutenant having a 50-man squad. Ned felt this gave him good coverage with the ten groups and the advantage of having 50-man squads, whereas Mosby's squads typically only had 25 to 40-man squads.

In addition, Ned would try a new tactic. He knew almost every place that would and could house a Mosby squad. So, he would begin south of Warrenton and push north, spread squads out at half-mile intervals with the squads in all covering a 5-mile swath. Like driving deer through thickets. It was his hope that he would create a sense of insecurity for Mosby's men and let them not feel the ability to roam at their leisure.

With the initial push, he felt he could sweep into the net at least 75 to 100 men. And after reaching the Potomac River, they would sweep south and keep this up until they flushed Mosby out for a battle, or moved him on, or ultimately shut him down. Ned believed that Mosby and his men would seek the mountains eventually, or perhaps even at the start of this flushing movement. Either way, he wanted them to keep on the move and make their host families feel uneasy and unsafe.

Ned schooled his men on how they would hide and where and how to look for those who were hunkered down. This was easy for Ned, since he had done it many times as a Mosby man. Normally, those looking for him passed by when they could have practically reached out and touched him.

With winter closing fast on Virginia, it was shut-down time for armies, but not for Mosby. He preferred the winter when he would raid in the dead of night in the coldest weather. Ned's men were adapted to his tactics. He had set the date of mid-December for the first sweep north. Although many of his men were a bit anxious, Ned had been meticulous in preparation. During the time of their preparation, Ned kept scouts north of Warrenton to keep tabs on the activities of Mosby and his men.

South and west of Warrenton, military action continued. The Petersburg siege with minor battles flared up. General Custer still battled Early's cavalry. Nashville, Tennessee was still being contested. Fort Fisher, North Carolina, with great naval presence, tried to dislodge the garrison there. In Saltville, Virginia, over two mountain ranges away, General Stoneman began the engagement of General Breckinridge.

So, winter had not shut down all activity and Ned was about to heat up his own. In his command tent, the wind was heard outside. The chill continued to increase. The thoughts of Lizza, he could not suppress. They would come at him in surprising times. He could be riding in front of his men in an exercise and she would take over his mind. It took great will to push it away.

Now, on the very verge of his new command pushing north, Ned questioned his best thoughts. It was more than being unsure of his ability. Such nagging questions as to whether the war was right, his participation in the war and wanting it so desperately to be the right cause, and the reason he went to the Union. Repatriation, the reasons he left Lizza, went over and over in his mind; it was time lost, precious time he could have spent with her. With her gone now, the notoriety and the promotions and accolades seemed to pale, as he pondered these things this cold night in Virginia. The more he mulled it over, the more he was confused.

Ned thought of those he had come to know these past years. Events flashed faster and faster. He fell into a fitful sleep and awoke hours later very restive and vexed over the last eight hours of mixed emotions. He tried to shake these things, but it was to no avail. The state he was in was not that of the leader he had grown to become.

He got up, dressed, and went to Jake. He saddled and tacked him up. Ned called his first company commander, Captain Nelson. Ned informed him that he was in charge of the regiment until Ned returned. That they would continue to drill until he returned and that the shove off date and time were to be rescheduled at a time not yet determined.

Ned added, "I am going to do a final scout before we commence."

"But Colonel, Sir," the Captain said, "We have had scouts for two weeks up ahead with the information we need."

Ned responded, "Yes, we have, but you forget, I know Mosby like no one else. I can possibly see things differently than they and come to a whole different take on what I see versus what they see. I want to be sure, Captain."

"Yes sir, Colonel," the Captain replied, "But should you not have a good man with you?"

Ned appreciated the comment, but responded, "It's better by myself, Captain. You forget this is how I came into this war."

"Yes sir," the Captain said.

Ned continued, "I'll be at most a few days. Have the men sharp for my return."

Trying to be positive, the Captain replied, "Yes sir, as they are now, Colonel. They all are most anxious to be in the saddle."

Accepting the thought, Ned said, "I know, Captain. Just a few more days."

"Yes sir, Colonel," the Captain uttered.

Chapter 41

Trying to Regain Balance

Ned took off north. He needed to think. Clear these phantoms that kept creeping into his head. A few days would not hurt the overall mission. Ned knew already where he was headed, but he didn't know why. He was going to the Taylor's. He was drawn for a reason he didn't know. All he knew was that was where he was going.

As Ned arrived, Sarah greeted him halfway from the road gate. She didn't look herself, not the bubbly young girl he had come to know. Ned dismounted and unsaddled Jake. He put his saddle on the porch, as Jake chose to munch on some scrub grass next to the fence line.

Sarah then just blurted out, "Sister took her life, Ned." It caught him by surprise. "Sis took her life. She killed herself in prison."

Ned dropped his head, and said, "Oh, no, Oh God, no. When Sarah?"

Sarah responded, "I guess two weeks ago, but mom found out only yesterday."

"Where is your mother, Sarah?"

Sarah said, "In the rocker in the parlor. She just rocks and rocks. She doesn't answer me, she just rocks."

Ned entered the house and went into the front parlor. Jean was staring out the window and rocking slowly.

"Jean," Ned called out to her.

Jean didn't answer him or even turn.

Sarah was now at his side and she said, "See, as I told you she just rocks."

Ned walked to the chair and stood in front of her, then knelt to look at her. He said softly, "Jean, its Ned."

Jean kept up the same rocking. Ned reached to stop her and she got angry and forced it forward and back, so he let go of the rocker.

Ned tried again, "Jean, I am so sorry. I'm here because I felt the need to come. I didn't know why."

She stopped the rocker and then stared at Ned without a word. He waited for her to speak, but she just stared and started to rock again. Ned looked to Sarah, who was still at the doorway and stood watching. She shrugged her shoulders.

Ned spoke, "I'm going to stay a few days, Jean, and we will talk later." With that he left to take care of Jake. He spent the rest of the evening talking to Sarah and learn more about what had happened.

"Mama just became eerie, Ned, after you left. She talked about strange things. We thought she had lost her mind."

Ned, again trying to show his feelings, said, "Sarah, I'm so sorry."

Sarah responded, "No need to be, Ned. Sis was always worried more about herself than the rest of us. Mama said she always wanted to be the doted on daughter and when I came along, she lost that. She always tried to make sure I was put in my place. I could never be good enough for her. I'm sorry she's gone, I really am Ned, but more because of what she's done to Mama. Once again, a selfish choice of hers."

Ned was taken back by the words of Sarah, but saw quickly a now mature young woman. That night Sarah and Ned heard the rocking chair down in the parlor as it lulled them to sleep.

Ned heard a rap at the bedroom door as the morning light shone through the window.

Ned said, "Come in."

Jean stepped through the door and said, "I hope you slept okay, Ned. I am sorry for yesterday."

Ned politely responded, "Its okay, Jean."

Jean replied, "No, I'm very sorry. It is not okay, but it has been a blow, Ned. Just one more family member dead for this damned war."

Ned nodded in agreement.

Jean continued, "My daughter is dead, Ned, but I actually lost her many months ago. This is enough. Don't you agree?"

Ned offered, "Yes, I do, Jean!"

Jean forced a smile and asked, "How long can you stay?"

"Just a bit," Ned replied, "I'll come down after washing up. I have much to tell you."

"Very well," Jean said, "I'll have some eggs and biscuits and coffee ready. Is that good?"

"Sounds great, Jean."

After breakfast, Ned went on for some two hours updating Jean and Sarah about all that had taken place since he left. The discussion included not getting to see Molly because of Lizza's death and the grief it brought, his promotion, the assignment that he was given directly from Grant and the misgivings he felt about his part in this war.

Ned specifically said, "I feel I have done a terrible thing for my part in this war. And I mean for my part as both a Rebel and a Federal. It's so muddled, Jean. I'm really lost. I'm not sure about anything anymore."

Trying to console, Jean said, "None of us is, Ned. We seem to just have to go along with the tide, in and out with no control over the events of our lives."

Ned appreciably replied, "That's exactly it, Jean. And now I've been given a post, by the highest in command, to complete a mission for which he believes I am the most suited. And yet, here I sit away from my command, trying to decipher my feelings. Jean, I am just so tired."

"I know, Ned," Jean said in her motherly tone.

Sarah came to him and put her arms around his neck from behind his chair. She said, "We love you, Ned."

He answered, "I know you do, but you see, I have those who really love me on both sides of this war and I am afraid to lose anyone of you. I don't even know what I believe anymore. I do know I only believe all this is wrong and I don't want to take another man's life, even if it's in the name of war. I've done and seen enough. I don't like what I've become. I've believed in honor and duty and all the trappings of war. The ancient wars that I've read about do not bear out the words they so gloriously profess of on the battlefields. Their aftermath tells a different story altogether."

Ned was now in tears. He was angry. He tried to verbalize his feelings, "This war has taken and tore apart my family and friends, and on a scale too great to fathom."

The words of Elizabeth, years before, were coming to haunt him. She had said almost the same words he had.

Though the day was long, Ned was able to get some much needed rest.

Jean and Sarah would go to Washington to claim their Molly's body and bring it home for burial. She had a neighbor agree to take her. Ned offered, but she told him if he would dig the grave and stay and mind the house, she would like that.

Ned answered, "Of course, Jean. I'd be honored to do both." Ned knew about the family plot. Jean told him to dig it to the left of Grandma Taylor. He assured her it would be ready upon their return.

Chapter 42

A New Beginning

It had only been two hours since Jean and Sarah had left the house for Washington when Ned heard a knock at the door and then the door open.

A voice echoed through the house. "Jean, it's Rose, my dear!"

Ned came around the corner.

"Oh Ned, it is you," Rose said. "What a most pleasant surprise!"

"Hello, Rose," Ned replied, "How are you?"

Rose said, "I came to see if she'd left."

Ned responded, "Yes, Rose, not two hours ago. I just found out last night after my arrival. I was compelled to come. I had a sense of urgency to come, Rose. I hadn't a clue why, but I came."

"I know she's glad you did, Ned," Rose said.

Ned added, "I am, too, Rose, although I was on the cusp of a new assignment."

"Oh," she said.

Ned then confessed, "Yes, except I've lately had reservations of my part, past and future, in this war. I have been recently promoted."

Rose proudly said, "I noticed, Ned. Colonel."

Ned, warming up some, responded, "Yes, and Grant submitted it. He has given me a regiment to hunt down Mosby."

Rose shot back, "Do tell!"

Ned then retreated some, "Rose, I can't! Not that it's Mosby. I can't be a participant in this war any longer in my loss of Lizza now!"

Rose questioned, "Lizza, Ned?"

Ned answered, "Yes, Rose, she died many weeks ago."

Rose continued, "For that I'm greatly sorry, Ned. How?"

Ned somberly answered, "She had an internal rupture. My only consolation, Rose, is I got to her for her last hours on earth."

"Again, I'm so sorry for your loss," Rose replied.

"Thank you, Rose," Ned said.

Her eyes truly hurt and they showed it. Rose had lost a teenage daughter just before her incarceration by the Federals.

Rose then added, "Ned, can we sit and talk? I would like to talk over some things with you that might help. At least I hope they will. I know that at our last meeting here I played games that men and women play with one another, but I am much different. Oh, I can play the part well if I so choose. But, I am far from that charade now."

They sat and she began to tell her story. Rose was of Irish dissent, Catholic, born in Maryland, had good schooling, and was a voracious reader.

Rose went on, "Ned, I have a keen sense of self and I have a sense of propriety. I grew to appreciate this country and our past and its future course. I was in the inner circles of Washington, a socialite for sure, albeit one by marriage. However, I saw its usefulness. Long before the first report from cannons, I could see an unfortunate trend in Washington, D.C. You see, dear Ned, when the North assumed the government over the South as its exclusive possession, it sought to establish an unmitigated tyranny for liberty. True civil liberty cannot exist where rights are on one side of a geographical line and the power on the other. Even the ex-president and statesmen from northern roots claimed that we see a political party presenting candidates for president and vice president selected for the first time from the free states. Their avowed purpose was electing them by suffrage of one part of the Union and to rule over the whole United States. They could not have reflected on this course seriously, for if they had, they would know of its folly, to believe our southern brethren would submit and be governed as such. But they have, with intent, done so."

Ned looked and listened to her with great amazement. He saw her as a seductive, beautiful woman and now assessed her very differently than earlier. He was even more taken by her. She spoke with clarity and knowledge gained from years of observation of this country from the inner sanctum of its workings.

Rose continued, "Ned, Lincoln's Black Republicans, as they are known, are a sectionalist party bent on twisting and bending our Founding Fathers' intent, and in many cases dismissing it all together. That party wants a strong centralized government, to squash states' rights completely, 180° from the Constitution.

Then she asked, "Do I bring to you, Ned, a different view? It's not radical, dear Ned. It's the foundation of Monroe, Madison, Jefferson, Adams, and Washington. They foresaw these things. Yet, Lincoln aims to dissolve it part and parcel. And what they seek is political apostasy. They have again, I tell you, overthrown the Constitution and its guarantees, and substitutes in their place elective despotism."

Ned was reeling with the thoughts and consequences that Rose presented to him. He asked, "Slavery, Rose? What of slavery as an institution?"

Rose responded, "Slavery is but a single cry for their agenda. Don't you see, Ned, Washington, Jefferson, Adams, Franklin, Madison, Monroe, Hamilton, Jackson, Clay and Webster all warned of sectionalism parties geographically. But, we repeat the warnings to no heed. They only but admonish us and we are labeled enemies of the Constitution, while we are the very ones who uphold its principles. Nay, Ned, it's not slavery. It is an iota of the North's revamping of this country."

Ned was mesmerized at what he was hearing. He thought, here sits a woman as embedded in her beliefs as was Elizabeth. And here I am straddled on the fence like the cow caught half way over, trying to get the lush grass on the other side. Yet he was a participant of equal zeal in both armies and with no real understanding of their inner workings and to their ends.

Rose reached for his hand and squeezed, and then laid her other hand on top and said, "Ned, I know you are struggling so about all this, but as you have come to understand in your capacity of the soldier, you have really been but a pawn used by both the North and the South. Yes, even your and my people of the South! You have come to a crossroad, Ned, and you must choose."

Rose continued, "I came to it months ago, when my service to my new government of the South could not use me any longer. Perhaps long before that as I lay languishing in the prison, seeing my eight-year old daughter become worse and worse. I was made to feel as if I had no concern for her. That, Ned, is when I knew the North and the South, when it was expedient for them, used me as a clarion call for the rally of their cause. Yes, even my beloved Dixie. So, I cling to the Founding Fathers design. That is my rock, Ned, it is our hope as it was then. I have seen a course for me to move to a new territory and I will. I intend, in the near future, to move far across the Mississippi River."

Ned smiled at those words. They rang of past hopes, or were they?

Rose went on, "Ned, you must come to your own conclusions, but you must take care of the demands put upon you first. You must address your capacity for which you are charged as a Colonel in the Union. If your questions of which you are asked deter you from your duty, you must ask for dismissal from those duties or suffer a possible strict court-martial and imprisonment."

Ned knew Rose was right, at least about this. He had lost his conviction of duty and for that alone he needed to step down, even with the arrows that Grant would suffer for his recent appointment. But, if Ned knew one thing about Grant, it was that he held forth right honesty above all else. Ned knew he must send a wire to Grant at Petersburg asking to be relieved of his commission in the Union Army.

Rose still held Ned's hand and looked at this young man, who intrigued her on so many levels. She saw in his eyes his mind mulling over her words, rearranging thoughts of the past from so many different people and his own discernment.

Rose understood only too well and said, "Life is short, Ned. You know this all too well. Changes in our lives are created for growth, not to diminish or hold back. You, yourself, know a battle ebbs and flows. Changes in strategies must be formed to win the day. So, it is in your individual life." Rose reached and laid her hand on his cheek and added, "Ned, this chapter of your life is over. I know you know this. Shed the old skin and move forward with a shiny new fresh one."

Ned smiled and laid his hand on hers. He then took both of her hands in his, looking at them and tracing her fingers, Then said, "Rose?"

Rose immediately replied, "Yes, Ned?"

Ned continued, "You have come into my life at a point that could not have been more pivotal, for without you, I may have stumbled terribly to suffer consequences that could have been detrimental to my very existence. I can only believe you were of divine guidance."

Appreciative, Rose answered, "Yes, I believe that, Ned, and I also believe that you and I have yet a purpose together. Just perhaps, Ned, just perhaps!"

Ned looked at her and said, "Tell me more, Rose, I crave your words and your voice."

So, Rose went on into the late night and early morning, when both became uncontrollably weary with sleep. She finally said, "Ned, we must sleep."

Ned went to his bed and Rose collapsed on Jean's bed. As Ned awoke late that morning and was on the way to dig the grave for Jean's eldest daughter, he passed the door where Rose went to sleep, but the door was open and she was gone. He went to the front door and sure enough her carriage was gone also. He assumed she left for the comfort of her own bed.

In about two hours, Ned finished the digging and went back to the house. He readied himself to go send the wire of his desire to be relieved of duty and of his officer's commission. He would return the next day to receive his reply.

There were no feelings of regret on the ride back to the Taylor's house and he had also noticed that not once had he seen hide nor hair of Mosby's men. He thought it strange for it had crossed his mind several times that he was alone in Mosby-land. Mosby's men were those who would hang him if he were caught, but somehow that was of little concern, because he felt he could out run any of them should they see him.

On the other hand, he did think hard and long about the intensive time with Rose yesterday. But, his mind also wandered in thought to Aunt Bev, Jo and Christiana, and even of Elsa, Elizabeth and Bessie. All of them were important to Ned. He wondered what they would think.

After an uneventful trip, Ned came to the house. He sat in Jean's rocker and considered his life and where he had been, and where he would go. The war, for him, was over. At this point, nothing was resolved in his mind, except that war caused death needlessly to mostly young men barely able to shave a sparse beard.

For Ned, life was about to start a new chapter. Even though he didn't know what the future held for him, somehow that didn't matter. It only mattered that things were new and different, he was somewhere else. Maybe someday he would come back to Virginia, but for now it held death in its very winds.

He wished Rose were here. She inspired him. She had a magnetism to her that was undeniable in both her roles as a seductress and mentor. He felt some guilt in his feelings of her in this way. But, it felt good to not feel pain in remembering Lizza on her deathbed.

Ned didn't know it, but Rose was in her rocker in her room contemplating Ned. She had feelings that stirred in her and they had taken away bad memories of her dead husband and teenage daughter's death. Also, gone were the nagging memories of the old capital prison that left indelible marks on her and her now 10-year-old daughter, Rose, who was her namesake.

"I can't entertain such a man," she said aloud to herself. "I am 50 years old, he but maybe 31 at best." She didn't know. A pang of guilt shot through her, but also the excitement of the younger Rose of years ago. It plucked her fancy. He is scrumptious, though. She smiled at the thought, then, out loud, again, she told herself, "Behave, Rose."

Ned could take it no longer. He wanted to see Rose. He rode over to the Brewster's where she stayed still cloaked from the Federals.

Someone downstairs called out, "Oh Rose, you have a caller!"

"Just a moment," Rose said. She knew no one, but Jean or Ned who would call, so she quickly attended to her person, took two looks in the mirror, and glided down the stairs in her best entrance.

In her nicest voice, she said, "Why, Ned, isn't this a surprise. I certainly didn't expect you. I left you to sleep and I needed to return so Lynn here didn't worry. Lynn Brewster, I surmise you know Mr. Ned McDonald."

Lynn responded, "Yes, Rose, he was roundabout several years ago. Ned, it's good to see you again."

"As you, Mrs. Brewster," Ned replied.

Rose promptly asked, "Lynn, may we use the parlor?"

Mrs. Brewster answered politely, "But of course, Rose."

Rose added, "And Lynn, you are quite welcome also."

"Oh! I think not, Rose. I need to attend to the kitchen," she said as she smiled and left.

"Come, Ned," Rose said, as she moved with great grace and sat on the settee.

Ned began, "Rose, I sent the wire of my resignation and I'll go for the reply tomorrow."

Rose inquired, "How do you feel now that you've done it?"

Ned answered, "Good, it's a relief of sorts. I believe it will be a complete relief upon receiving confirmation of my request."

Facing Rose directly, Ned continued, "Rose, I've thought nothing but of our long talk yesterday."

"And…" she said.

He went on, "I find great merit in it and its veracity most complete."

She smiled and laid her hand on his and said, "Thank you, Ned."

He took her hand and said, "No! Thank you, Rose. You have opened my mind and your words rang true."

"And you've come to tell me this?" she inquired. "Thank you, Ned."

"Yes, in part," he replied.

"In part, Ned?" she questioned.

He quickly answered, "Yes, but truth be known, Rose, I wanted your company."

Rose wanted his also. She said, "And I am glad you've come for both reasons, for I, too, have thought about what I imparted to you yesterday and that you might find truth in it. But, I also have thoughts about you as a man. I mean to say, as a woman who looks at a man in interest." She paused and then said, "Please, forgive me, Ned, that was crass and most untactful."

"No, it's not, Rose," he said excitedly, as he held her hand tighter but with tenderness. "Rose, I'm not good at these things, but I am drawn to you. I would hope that the difference in our years will not hinder us at any point."

She replied, "Well, I have thought of it, too, and I will not if you will not."

Ned smiled. "Consider it, gone."

"Gone it is," said Rose and then added, "Well, isn't all this a surprise, Ned, but a very welcome one indeed. In the future, we will certainly cause people to talk. You know they must. But that's down the pike. We are just beginning this, aren't we?"

Ned responded, "Yes, Rose, you are correct. Rose, I feel new. I came here expecting, I'm not sure what, but I found newness, not a nagging baggage that sat on me as an oxen yoke."

Rose quickly added, "I, Ned, feel the same, for my losses have yoked me for way too long. I've prayed for a man to come to me. I just never expected one such as you. The women will surely try to steal you from an aging woman."

Ned laughed, "Rose, Cleopatra herself would not achieve such a feat."

Their eyes met and wavered, not only seeing a new path for each, who only days before saw before them a darkened path ahead with no real light.

Becoming a bit more practical, Ned said, "I have loose ties to complete, Rose. I have many a letter to write to explain my position and my choices. There is Elizabeth in Richmond and I have Elsa and Bessie, Auntie and Jo. It will be hard for them. They are all strong Unionists. But most of all I have my daughter, Christiana to be concerned with. She is not a year old."

Understanding, Rose replied, "Ned, I feel your friends and family, with seeing a heartfelt letter, will maybe feel some disappointment, but will not cease in their love for you. As for your daughter Christiana, Lizza's and your child, she must be foremost in your mind. While only a mere baby, she warrants 100% concern."

Ned appreciated her words and added, "I have, Rose, been concerned with her. I miss her horribly, but I know for these last months that she was best near family in Pennsylvania for personal attention and safety, and feeling secure. Rose, if all goes as we foresee, how are you prepared to accept a mulatta child?"

Rose responded, "Well, Ned, I'll ask the same question. How are you prepared to accept a young girl of mine from another man?"

Ned knowingly nodded his head and offered, "I understand, Rose."

"You see, Ned, these times have created much different looks upon families. But on some was it not so different? You see, my father married three months after my mother died while giving birth to me. Did he love this new woman when they married or was it convenience to sustain? I do not know, Ned, but he adored her till the day she died, two months before his death."

235

Ned gave Rose a soft kiss on her cheek and lingered there as he slid his lips to hers, and so the pact between the two was temporarily sealed.

Rose then spoke, "My life, for sure, Ned, has been full and robust in many avenues I've traveled down. I want a man to adore me for me and I to adore him without distractions of politics or government obligations as my first marriage."

Ned said, "I will give that to you, Rose."

They hugged one another as they sat enjoying each other's company.

Ned gently said, "Rose?"

"Yes, Ned," Rose answered.

It was then that Ned slid to his knees as he looked up at her and said, "Rose, will you honor me with allowing me to be your husband until the time ceases for me?"

Her eyes filled with tears and she answered with joy, "Yes, Ned! Yes, I will be your wife!"

Chapter 43

Another New Beginning

The wire sent back from Grant regretfully granted his request to be relieved of duty and his officer's commission.

"You're free, Ned," Rose said gleefully.

Ned responded, "Yes, I had reservations, but it does feel good! Now I need to go see my daughter."

"Yes," Rose replied," and I, Ned, must advise Richmond that I did not die in North Carolina as all thought and of my intent to move west. And, also, put an article to be posted in Washington to the effect of my leaving this war to those who find it fruitful and enjoyable. I am nervous, Ned, and to be honest, quite relieved over the putting to bed these past years."

Ned and Rose had summed up that Christiana would stay with Jo and Auntie until they found a place to put down roots, and then he would send for her. He had, in the back of his mind, hoped that it was a place they might want to come and live also.

Ned was leaving to the north now as a civilian. He was as he came years ago, a man on a mission with his horse, only this time, a mission to a quite a different end. Ned and Rose would be married upon Ned's returning.

The morning broke with clouds and darkness and a biting cold out of the mountains. Ned thought about leaving on a better day, but, instead, decided to get on the road.

This was a goodbye that was emotional for Rose. She had, all her life, remained in control of her emotions and it had served her well. For once, now with Ned, she unabashedly spoke and cried her love for him and for him to be safe and return to her.

Rose added, "I will not, for an iota of time, cease to pray for you my love, and your safety until you are back in my arms."

Ned whispered in her ear, "Rose, I will be unsettled in my soul until I am once again in these arms." Embracing, they gave one another a passion-filled kiss.

Rose stood, shivering in the whipping wind, as Jake and Ned went north to Chambersburg, Pennsylvania. Ned, to Rose, was a love she had so longed for all her life and, finally, at the autumn of her years, she found him and would experience it fully in every capacity. She went into the warm house and wrote a letter sending for her daughter to come to Virginia. She then lay on the bed and curled up to cry in joy over the life that had come to her.

With a comforting feeling, all those months in prison and her daughter's death were cleansed away, so she might live a life far from this cauldron of despair. She had lost years, it seemed, hoping for a separation of the South from the North. Now it looked that it was gone. Far west was a new life with a man to love and be loved by.

Jake and Ned crossed over the Blue Ridge Mountains to the Shenandoah Valley. They entered Maryland and then into the Cumberland Valley up to Pennsylvania. Ned stayed the night in Williamsport just over the Potomac River into western Maryland. It would be a long day to Chambersburg, Pennsylvania, over 40 miles, so Ned and Jake left before daybreak.

The wind whipping down the Cumberland Valley cut deeper than in Virginia. Jake was squinting his eyes at the icy blast in his face. Ned just saw daylight when, at a T in the road to the west not 100 yards away, he saw at least 25 men on horseback. They were not Federals, for their attire was too sporadic.

One of the men saw Ned at the same time. Ned and the man just looked at each other. Then, it possessed Ned. He had never put the spurs to Jake, although since the army, he had worn them.

Ned spoke sharply, "Go, Jake!" He touched Jake with the spurs and Jake responded as if he had been shot out of a Columbiad cannon.

At the same time, all 25 men tore down the road to the T after Ned. It was Mosby; they had been on a raid into Maryland, as they had many times before. Pistol shots were fired. Ned laid low and let Jake run. He gave him all the reins length. The road was straight and long up ahead. He was in their view. He had to change that.

A road came up on the right. Jake slowed enough to negotiate the 90° turn, built speed and went over a rise in the road. Then Ned saw it and said, "Oh, God." The road dead-ended into a gated pasture. A gate made only for a man as to keep cattle in. Jake slid to a halt and Ned looked back He saw them closing fast behind him.

The narrow road sat a foot below the pasture ahead with fence down each side. Ahead, the gate was about 5-foot high and 4-foot wide. For them to get into the field and away, Jake needed to jump the 5-foot gate, 60-feet ahead at the dead end.

Ned said to Jake, "Well, big man, what you think? It's do or die."

Ned then yelled at the top of his lungs, "Jake, get it! Jake!"

Jake was galloping. Ned let him do what came natural for such a horse. Jake checked up a little, cocked his body, as Ned stood in the stirrups, and then up Jake flew tucking his front legs tight against his chest. Ned grabbed his mane for balance. Over they went, as Jake held his back legs out straight to clear the gate and then touched down.

Ned, relieved, said, "Whew! Ole boy! We did it, or you did it!" With a pat on his neck, they flew off across the pasture down a hill and out of sight. On the side, there was an easier jump to get out of the field and they hit the road north again.

The Raiders cussed and fumed at the escape. "There is only one horse and rider capable of that jump," said Mosby. "I knew that was McDonald. The profile looked too familiar."

Mosby yelled, "Let's go!" and they were off to find him, if they could, by the long way around.

Ned knew Mosby was not a man to be bested. He would follow and catch up to him if at all possible. So, he put as much distance between them as he could by setting Jake at a good pace. By now, Jake was endurance tested and was a good battle horse.

It was past dark as Ned road up to the house outside of Chambersburg. As he climbed off Jake, it was Jo who greeted him with great affection and joy to see him.

Then came Auntie, so overwhelmed to see him, she said, "We had no idea you were coming, Ned. What a wonderful surprise!"

Ned responded, "I had none either, Auntie, until just a few days ago. So much as happened in less than seven days. I must tell you."

So, arm in arm, each one to a side, they went into the house.

Auntie offered, "Ned, sit here, eat this. I had just dished it up."

Ned was starving, but said, "Auntie, not yet, I'll be back. I have to take care of Jake."

Thirty minutes later, after putting Jake in the barn, watering him, giving him fresh straw, laid thick to sleep on, and fresh food, Ned was ready to eat.

After eating, Ned remarked, "Boy, that was good, Jo!"

She replied, "Don't thank me. Auntie made it."

"Thank you, Auntie," Ned said.

Pleased, Auntie said, "Not at all, Ned. It belongs in an empty stomach." She continued, "Tell us, Ned, we are dying to hear what you teased us with."

Pausing, Ned said, "Well, I'm not with the army any longer. I've resigned."

A hush came over the room.

A surprised Jo said, "You resigned, Ned? Your commission?"

Ned firmly responded, "Yes, I've seen enough, killed enough, and cannot and will not do it any longer."

Auntie was clearly agitated. "What do you mean, you will not do it any longer?"

Jo then said, "Yes, Ned, tell us."

"Well," he stammered, taken aback at their reaction. "I have decided that I cannot contribute to this wholesale killing that this war has caused."

Auntie forthrightly commented, "You now come here, nephew, with this carefree attitude of 'you've had enough,' when this rebellion requires every good man to squash it? Don't get me wrong, nephew, I don't want you to die, but sweet Jesus, to walk out on your country so cavalierly. I'm sorry, I don't understand."

"Neither do I, Ned!" Jo almost shouted.

Ned politely responded, "This war will be over soon. That's clear. And I have reached a decision that I can live with. I'm sorry that you two don't agree with me."

Auntie yelled, "You're right, I don't!" and slammed her fist on the table and continued, "Were my husband as you, I would not be a widow, but I would have him a dead hero for his country than an alive coward as you!" As she ended her words, she glared at Ned, daring him to say a word.

He looked at Jo, as she glowered the same look. Ned cast his eyes down, not knowing what to say. Then, with disappointment, he said, "I wish to see my daughter."

Auntie's aunt was flustered at witnessing the scene and quickly said, "This way, Ned."

As Ned entered the room with Christiana, he heard Auntie say, "He's nothing but a damn coward. He became yellow."

Ned, for the moment, forgot the two.

The aunt said, "Shush, Ned, she's sleeping."

He peeked under the canopy veil. Her pert nose and full head of hair were beautiful. He lightly put his finger in her palm and she reacted by closing it on his finger while still asleep.

The aunt softly commented, "She's such a good baby, Ned. She hardly cries. She eats good and she smiles at everything. She's alert to everything around her."

"She's grown so much already," Ned said.

The aunt responded, "Yep, she's going to be a tall one, Ned. Yes, sir, I believe a tall girl."

Ned apologetically said, "I am sorry for the scene like that in your house."

"Oh, Ned, forget it. They will cool down. They know that you're no coward," the aunt said

"Thank you, dear lady," Ned replied.

The aunt responded, "It's okay, my boy."

After being with Christiana for a short while, Ned said, "I need to go see Lizza."

"Why yes, of course, she answered.

At Lizza's grave, Ned shared, "I've come to see you and Christiana. Oh, Lizza, she's so beautiful.

Ned continued, "I will be taking Christiana to see those mountains and rivers that you wanted to see. I'm going to find a piece of land looking at both. Then I will bring Christiana. I will raise her to be strong to go with her beauty. This I can say to you, Lizza, Yes, she will live to see many changes and have a chance at the life you didn't have. I will make sure."

He talked to Lizza for an hour, oblivious to the cold, kneeling down all the while. He told her of leaving the army and of finding a woman. Ned said that he hoped she would approve of her and that she was a woman who could give Christiana much in the way of being a woman, to move through life with ease, be properly educated and have your charm. She is capable of holding her own, not only with strength from me, but from being reared in the art of words. He told her that he would always love her best; no one could extinguish her from his memory. Then he prayed out loud and arose and returned to the house.

"I will leave in the morning," he told Auntie and Jo still sitting at the table. "I would appreciate your continued care of Christiana. I will, in a few months, maybe a year, come for her. I am moving out west. When this war finishes, there will be a mad rush of folks that way. I suspect I want to be there before it happens. Much opportunity lies out there."

Ned took all the money that he had in his saddlebags and spread it on the table. He said, "This is all I have right now. Hopefully, it will be enough for a while to take care of my daughter. I will send more with my last pay from the army when I receive it. Now I am tired and need sleep."

Auntie said, "Ned..."

"No, Auntie, I've heard quite enough. Like I said, I leave at first light."

"Ned, please, we... " Jo began.

"Jo, no," Ned said. And then he left for the back room, the place he stayed on his last visit. Jo and Auntie looked at one another, knowing all too well what damage their quick tongues had brought.

At early morn, before first light, Ned went to see Christiana. Auntie was rocking her. He knelt as she was handed to him. He held her close and committed to memory her smell and her soft cheek. He spoke quietly to her, promising to return for her. He then kissed her on the forehead and then each cheek. He said to her, "Soon, I will return for you my daughter. Thank you, Auntie."

She responded, "Ned, you take good care of yourself. This little one needs you."

He replied, "I will." He left, walking to the barn where he lost control and cried as he saddled Jake, preparing to leave.

With Jake's reigns in hand, he walked once more to Lizza's grave. He knelt again and told her, "I love you, Lizza. I will be back for our daughter." He bent to kiss her grave, then mounted Jake. He now felt the cold of the morning. The light flurries were soon to fall thick. Without looking back at the house or giving Auntie and Jo another chance, he clucked for Jake to move out.

Chapter 44

Unexpected Trouble

Before he passed through Chambersburg, the snow fell heavy. Ned pushed Jake faster. Within hours this might be over a foot of snow. With over 20 miles covered and almost 2 feet of snow on the ground, Ned stopped in Hagerstown, Maryland. He stabled Jake and found a room and commitment for a meal after laying down a watch for payment. It seemed a good deal with the way the snow fell, almost 3-feet before morning. At daybreak, the sun shone strong and bright. The landscape was pristine white and the snow would begin to melt soon.

The morning was the warmest since leaving Rose. Ned saddled Jake and they pressed on in the deep snow. There were snowdrifts in many places, some only inches deep and others up to Jake's chest.

Trusty Jake did his duty as always. After crossing the Potomac River just below Shepherdstown, the snow had not been nearly as heavy. It was easier going for Jake. Ned traced the Potomac River to Harper's Ferry. He looked down at the town. Over to the east, on the Maryland Heights, he saw a band of men.

He pulled out his French made binoculars. There were Mosby's men still in Maryland, perhaps even on the way back to Virginia. Ned could not help it. He fired his revolver in the air to taunt. The band of riders stopped and looked. He waved his hat above his head in circles. He saw that they had seen him. He got Jake to rise-up on his hind quarters while striking the air with his front feet. Ned continued to wave his hat.

"Down, Jake." Ned saluted and disappeared from their sight. He didn't know it, but before he disappeared from the area, several very long shots at him and Jake were taken with carbine rifles.

Soon Ned began to think of Grant's letter of acceptance of his dismissal. It said, "I am regretful of your decision. I will lose a valuable soldier and tool with which to apply my trade. You have done yourself proud with valor, endurance and devotion to duty. I can only hope, but have no doubt for your success in the future, in whatever endeavor you may enter. I hold no rancor over your decision. Each man must always be truthful with his own self. If our paths are able to cross again, I shall greet you with a special, warm affection." It was signed, Ulysses S. Grant. These words he would never forget, nor would he of his family's words of his cowardice and yellow streak.

As they continued their journey, the pace of Jake and Ned was more leisure. Home to Rose was not far away. Ned was close to Leesburg, Virginia, the last leg back. However, he was unaware of Mosby and his men. He had become lax and had not kept alert all the time. Mosby and his men crossed just north of Harpers Ferry, over the Potomac River, raced along its course and crossed at a bridge just past Point of Rocks, and again crossed the Potomac that now was the confluence of Potomac and Shenandoah rivers.

They intended to catch Ned after two misses and one act of dismissal and disregard. Ned's pace was so carefree that Mosby had actually beat Ned and Jake to Leesburg. They had sighted him and drew up the snare to catch him. They lay low and watched his direction out of Leesburg.

Ned was on the road to Salem. Mosby knew that they could go an adjacent road, then cut back to catch him at a crossroad. Mosby had at least six men hidden at each corner of the crossroads.

As Ned and Jake cantered down the road, he felt good not having to worry about war. It seemed peaceful this far north of all the conflict. Then, the silence was broken. Pistol shots pierced the air from every direction. Ned looked everywhere as men on horseback closed in on him. There were six men ahead and behind on the road. He looked east and west; they closed in.

Ned looked to each side; there seemed to be nowhere to go but up steep wooded hills. He saw one small path going down a ravine. He went next to the road and followed it until he ran out of ground. It dropped away 50 foot at least. Six men had followed and the others were directly above him on the road looking down at him. All 25 pistols were aimed at him and Jake.

A voice called out, "Will you give it up, McDonald? If not, we will end it here, right now for you."

Ned spitting venom at being caught and so very stupid, said reluctantly, "I will give up."

The voice said, "Very well, throw down your gun and be escorted up to the road. Ned dismounted in front of Mosby, being encircled by the rest of the band.

"Well, McDonald, we have met again. I thought I would not be given such a pleasure after losing you in Maryland."

Ned responded, "Yes, well, I thought the same, Colonel."

Mosby continued, "I thought my fortune most welcome at spying you above Harpers Ferry."

Ned replied, "Yes, again, I became complacent."

"Yes, to our gain, right, McDonald?" Mosby quipped.

"Yes, I would think it would seem so, Colonel," Ned uttered.

Mosby happily went on, "Well, it seems to be a conundrum, McDonald. I gave you a chance to assess your allegiance, but you determined that by your escape from prison and then your stamped commission as a federal officer. And to your credit, you moved quickly to Colonel. Oh! Yes, McDonald, I knew of your actions and even that you have a regiment to the south."

"Had a regiment!" Ned emphasized.

Mosby retorted, "Had?"

Ned answered, "If you have learned so much about me, Colonel Mosby, you would have learned that I resigned my commission with a letter of acceptance of that resignation."

Mosby demeanor became confused and he said, "You resigned? As of when?"

Ned replied, "Many days ago."

Mosby responded, "How convenient, McDonald."

Ned said, "Not at all, Colonel. It was given by me for reasons that you would not understand."

Mosby cattily remarked, "So, you think me not able to grasp ideas, McDonald?"

Ned answered, "Not it all, Colonel. You think only as a soldier, and that is a limitation in and of itself."

Mosby laughed. "Mount up, McDonald. We have much to discuss, and I care not to pursue it on this road. Your fate is to be determined, but first we talk."

Jake and Ned were surrounded tightly as they went down the road south and on to Mosby's hideaway. Ned was cursing himself silently at the situation he now found himself in. To him, the trip to Mosby's site seemed to be about him 18 miles. Ned was blindfolded during the ride to the location. After they removed the blindfold, Ned was placed on a straight back chair, with all the men stationed around the room against the walls. He looked around. It was a nicely appointed 20' x 30' room with a large fireplace, heavy curtains, shiny wood floors and carpet rugs.

Then Mosby spoke, "Well, McDonald, I must now decide what I am to do with you. You said that you were no longer a federal officer. If you are not, then you are no longer to be considered a prisoner of war and thus entitled to certain rights of protection. Isn't that true?"

Ned nodded in agreement.

"Well then," Mosby said, "Is it not true that when you were arrested by me and sent to the Provost who then incarcerated you, that it was done. That is until the veracity of your claims of being loyal to the Confederacy and not a spy, was followed by your escape. After your escape, you were not only repatriated, but were then commissioned a captain in the Federal Army. All of that might mean that you were spying when I arrested you."

Ned replied, "Yes, all you say is true, Colonel. I do not dispute a word."

Mosby quipped, "You do not?"

Ned answered, "I do not!"

Mosby went on, "You seem most flippant, McDonald."

Ned answered, "Not at all, Colonel. I simply tell the truth. The truth also is that I've been on both sides of this war, with convictions equal to both at that time. I questioned both as to truth and right. In reckoning of both, I've come to the realization that for me this conflict is a no-sum game, both sides lose. The best and brightest that both have brought to bear have been lost forever. The sadness, in that alone, is enough to blanch at further bloodshed. Colonel, have you... have you not had enough? All of you, I ask the same question?" Ned looked around the room at men he had once served with and said, "Gentlemen, I have!"

Not a word was spoken. Finally, Mosby spoke, "McDonald, it is true that we have seen much blood and many revered ones lost, but such is the cost of change. I cannot rest until I see every federal ousted from southern soil."

Ned looked on a face of conviction that was once as one with him.

Mosby then said, "If it be that we are to lose this fight, I will, at that time, decide my course. As for now, I'll remain as are all these men here, committed to the cause!"

Ned politely, but firmly added, "The cause is all but dead, Mosby. Can't you see it? Needless blood will be shed until the hour of surrender because of thoughts like yours. The North has overwhelmed a predetermined end. It was ordained long ago, Colonel Mosby. You have put up the good fight with bravery, dedication and gallantness, but you are blinded about the end. The Southern Army fought against odds that were of the 300 Spartans. If the Confederacy had the resources as the North, the North would have lost years ago. But they didn't, and now they have even less."

Mosby angrily responded, "Enough, I've heard quite enough from you!" Ned just shook his head in dismay.

Mosby replied, "Your fate, McDonald, that's what now must be decided. I will leave it to these men, some of whom you rode with, some you have not, but each one knows your deeds on both sides. I will have no vote in this. There are 24 of them. You need 16 votes for you to live, any less and you hang today. Do you understand?"

Ned quietly answered, "I do, Colonel Mosby."

Mosby then said, "I will allow one question from each person upon which you will give a direct answer. If there is no question, I will be given thumbs up or down. Again, it will take 16 thumbs up for your life to be spared. Ben, what do you say?"

Ned knew Ben Palmer well, always natty in his outfit, black derby hat, good looks, dark hair and a mustache.

Ben said, "McDonald, I have known you well, your courage displayed many times. You even came for me at risk of your own life when my horse was shot down from underneath me." And he added, "For that alone," and then Ben shot out his arm with his thumb up.

Ned nodded his head as if to say thank you!

Mosby continued, "That's one, Ned. John what say you?"

John Corey Meer was an intense man, same dark features, goatee, dressed like a rebel cavalry man should. While in complete reckless abandon in a charge against a foe, he would begin to cry when he would peak at his most angry times and shake. But you wanted him in a close fight. He was like a lion.

John said, "McDonald, I know you well. I was glad to call you friend and fellow Raider. I hurt when I heard of your commission in the Union, but I cannot forget you as a Raider as we rode together." He also shot out thumbs up.

Mosby went on, "Two, McDonald. Walter?"

Walter Godsden had been in the original group chosen by Mosby that winter at Fredericksburg. He had been shot and captured by the Federal's, and then escaped. His treatment by his Federals, as usual, was not by the rules of war for Raiders.

"Thumbs down," Godsden said, "definitely."

Mosby continued, "One death vote."

Godsden looked away and did not even make eye contact with Ned.

Mosby turned to another, "Frank, what say you?"

Frank Rathbone at one time had saved the only cannon the Raiders had. He had put his life in such peril in saving it that they called him affectionately, grapeshot, for the type of load put into a cannon when close firing upon a charging infantry. It was meant to take out dozens or more with one firing.

Frank said, "McDonald, I have mixed feelings on this thing we now vote. I remember a time a young boy took a shot at you from an alley on the raid. We went after him to disarm him. We had the intent to kill him if necessary. He stood defiantly pointing his rifle at us and you stepped forward and I shall always remember your words, 'Boy, if you kill me, your memory of it will haunt you all of your life. Please don't pull the trigger!' He looked and looked at you. Then he started crying. You then took the rifle and knelt and hugged him. I was moved greatly by the compassion of that scene." And for that, Frank snapped out thumbs up.

The voting continued around the room. The vote was now 15 to 8, one vote would decide Ned's fate as to live or be hanged before dark that very day.

Mosby turned to Tom Booker and said, "Tom, what say you?" Tom Booker was a hulk of a man, a big bonded Virginian. He had such a thick mustache that it muffled his words as he spoke. His yell on the charge was booming and sent chills down even Raiders backs.

"McDonald," he said in his deep baritone voice, "I have known you well. I, with great zeal, voiced words of support about you to others who doubted when they sent you to Richmond. I was angry when I found out differently. I have seen you in action on numerous occasions, too many to remember, and I thought only a man who had nothing or no one at home could give up everything in harm's way as you always did. I saw no equal, then or now, as you did then. So, now I ask why such a man has reached such a point as you have so stated about war and those who fight and their causes being carelessly sought after. My question is, have you someone who has so changed your thoughts, and who are they to you?"

Ned paused and then softly responded, "Yes, I had married and fell in love with a slave girl. She has died but a few months ago. Our daughter is in Pennsylvania. She is not a year old. That is when you saw me, I was in route to see her mother's grave and our daughter."

Eyes got bigger around the room! Mosby had not told anyone after he found out about Lizza on that night at the Taylor's. Mosby was silent.

"I, now, am engaged to an older woman, whom I came to love. That was my destination when you caught up with me." Ned played his last card. He had to. He could take no chance and every Confederate man, woman, or child knew Rose O'Neill Greenhow. They all knew how she was an icon at the war's beginning; a rallying call to stand up against the tyranny of the North.

Ned continued, "She lives in the Northern neck here in Virginia."

Mosby shot up with, "I know every family here in the neck!"

"If you did, Colonel, you would know she's been here for some time," Ned responded.

"Her name? What is her name, McDonald?" asked Mosby.

Ned directly answered, "Rose Greenhow."

Mosby quickly responded, "Rose, McDonald, died in North Carolina."

"No she did not," said Ned politely.

The rest of the men talked amongst themselves in disbelief saying, "Rose? It can't be."

Lee Haverson, who voted for Ned to hang said, "I saw her the day she got off the boat from her release from prison. They brought her down the Potomac to the Chesapeake Bay, then up the James

River. I saw her in Petersburg before going to Richmond. They say President Jefferson Davis even came to see her instead of her to him at the Ballard hotel. She was a heroine and still is."

The final vote was not taken. Mosby then said, "McDonald, you will take us to her then, now!"

Ned was blindfolded once more.

Mosby added, "Now, McDonald, where to?" Ned's blindfold was removed once they were out of Mosby's area of hiding. He led them the most direct way, once he had gotten his bearings.

Finally, Mosby, the 25 Raiders and Ned reined up in front of the Brewster's.

Mosby said when they stopped, "The Brewster's, Bingo!"

Immediately through the door came Rose. She had seen Ned at the lead of what she knew to be Mosby and his men. She played down her alarm and summoned her cool collected demeanor as she had all through her time in the Washington, D.C. prison at the start of the war.

Mosby said to Ned, "You will not say a word or I will shoot you down where you sit, McDonald."

Mosby rode to the porch some 60 feet in front of the rest of the men. He knew her face. And asked, "Mrs. Greenhow, is it?"

Rose answered, "Yes, I am. Colonel Mosby, is it?"

"Yes, I am," he replied. "I do not wish to trouble you but you catch me off guard. I had heard that you had drowned."

Rose responded, "Well, yes, it had been rumored, but as you can see, Colonel, I'm most sound and alive."

"Yes, of course," Mosby said, stumbling over his words. A competent lawyer before the war was now at a loss for the very words that made him successful.

Rose continued, "I must ask you, Colonel…"

Mosby replied, "Yes, Mrs. Greenhow?"

"Colonel, why have you escorted my betrothed to me as you have?"

Mosby was again taken aback. "So, McDonald and you, dear lady, are engaged?"

Rose queried, "Yes! He did not tell you?"

Mosby responded, "Why…why, yes he did."

Rose went on, "Did he also tell you, Colonel, that he is no longer a participant in this war that takes away forever our best and brightest?"

"Why, yes, ma'am, he did," Mosby uncomfortably said. He was taken back at her words, since she was once a leader of the South's most ardent fire-eaters and now talks of pacifism.

Rose asked, "Colonel, is my love under arrest?"

Mosby responded, "No, Miss Greenhow, he is not. I thought it imperative to see that the words he spoke were the truth. After his actions in this in the past spoke different."

Rose then said, "I can assure you, Colonel, I am still a good southern woman, even if I now see things differently. And I can assure you that we both pose no threat to the Confederacy. We, in fact, find our beliefs even stronger than at the outset of the war. We just choose a different path to show it."

"And what path would that be?" Mosby asked her.

Rose replied, "A path of understanding and strength to those who have suffered so very much in this hell we find ourselves. The North is a tyrant. Our constitutional rights that we were given have been disregarded and trampled on. But, we have come to the brink of destruction. As good southern people, we now must be ready to steel ourselves to save and rebuild the dignity that only southern folks can bring to bear. We must endure to the very end and rebound."

"You speak as if we have lost already," Mosby said.

"Colonel, if you will but look around, you will see it. If you do not see it now, surely you will soon enough." Rose's words were heard by everyone present. With that they all edged closer to the porch.

Booker, after hearing all that was said, spoke up. "I have yet to vote." All looked at him as he did. Booker shot his arm up with the thumbs up.

"Well, Miss Greenhow," Mosby said, "It seems I will be leaving your fiancé to your care," Ned dismounted.

Mosby spoke up, "McDonald, I would have hanged you back there if you fell one vote shy. You know me and if you had lied about your betrothed Miss Greenhow, or if she were anyone else, I still would have imprisoned you to our care. However, if this dear woman finds you worthy of her Rebel affection, then I must not find charge with you."

Rose appreciatively responded, "Thank you, Colonel. May God protect you and your men." She then put her hand out to the Rebel Colonel. Mosby took it and thanked her. Each man, in turn, came in like kind and paid homage to the Rebel heroine.

Chapter 45

Beginning New Lives Together

Once inside the house, Rose threw her arms around Ned. And then said, "You shall not bring such a scene to me again," as she pushed away enough to see his eyes. "Do you hear me, Ned McDonald?"

"I do, Rose. Nor do I want to find myself in such a position. I became relaxed on the last leg here. I should have realized earlier that he would be so affronted at what I did to him. Especially, doing it twice."

Rose told him, "I was never so shaken at seeing you with them. I've been in some tight spots, Ned, but knowing those men as I do, I figured I could do nothing to save you. I thought surely they had brought you to here, after which they would kill you."

She laid her head on his chest, as Ned stroked her long black hair that draped past her waist.

"Tonight, my love, I'll tell you more about me. I feel compelled to do it, so you will feel no regret ever about marrying me. The lady of this house is away and will be with good friends until tomorrow. We were all at Jean's this morning. She buried Molly, but I didn't stay long. I came back in hopes that you would arrive."

Ned responded, "Lucky for me you did, Rose."

She answered, "I should say so."

Ned said, "Rose, I am sorry I missed Molly's burial."

Rose agreed, "Yes, Jean wanted you there, but decided to go ahead. There was maybe a score of folks to be with Jean and Sarah. Come Ned, you must be hungry."

While eating, in between bites, Ned asked, "Rose, have you told Jean of our engagement?"

"Not yet," answered Rose, "I wanted to share the news together with you by my side."

"Then let's do just that now, before it gets too late!" Ned announced. He finished eating and they went to share the news with Jean and Sarah.

"Well, I'll be," Jean said, "I don't know what to say. I guess I underestimated you Rose. You move faster than I thought." She broke into laughter and hugged Rose with great excitement.

"Damn!" said Sarah. Everyone was shocked at her word.

Jean responded, "Sarah! Whatever has possessed you?"

"Mother, I'll never be able to marry Ned. Someone always is at the head of the line."

Everyone laughed, even Sarah.

Ned bent to hug his forever admirer. "Sarah, if ever I could give to you I would, as I told you. The years that separate us at your age are great."

"Oh darling," Rose said, "perhaps you may get Ned yet. He will still be handsome when I pass away."

Again, it brought humor to all.

The betrothed, also, explained to Jean of their move to the west to begin their lives anew and away from the war. Jean insisted she be allowed to host the wedding before they leave.

Ned and Rose briefly looked at each other then back at Jean. In unison, they nodded and said, "Yes, of course!"

Back at the Brewster's now, Ned told Rose of his visit to Chambersburg and the cool reception over his leaving and no longer contributing his part to the war. But also about the thrill and joy of seeing Christiana. Rose smiled and beamed at Ned's shine on his face at his speaking of her as he did. She, too, had known the joy and pain of motherhood. She had eight children. Five of her children had died, two boys and three girls. And she still had three living, Lila, Rose and Florence. So, she had suffered both pain and wrenching loss, yet the great joy of motherhood.

Rose lovingly commented, "I see your love for your daughter, Ned. It gives me great happiness to see that special look on your face."

Ned comfortably responded, "Yes, I feel it for her, Rose. And although my family feels as they do now about me, they will take the best care of her until I can properly do so." Ned squeezed her hand.

Rose then said, "Ned, you know my stance, as it has been of proslavery and of the South, but I have softened some in many areas. Only because I have looked at my life and those things I have done, of which I'm not proud, yet I would do them all over again. I did this because of fervent beliefs. Your daughter's a mulatto child. Yet, I find understanding in that because your wife's daughter lives, because of the love you had for a Negro woman. It was a love you deeply felt. And I know, if time went back, you would choose it again."

Ned said, "Yes, I would."

Rose continued, "I, at one time, could not imagine falling in love with a man who had a child with a Negro slave and even unto marriage. Yet, I find my thoughts on the matter of no consequence, in the way I look at you and the love I have for you, or the feelings I have at the proposition of rearing Christiana.

Ned nodded, "Yes."

Rose went on, "You see, Ned, life tends to soften with an aging soul. My life was about prestige from the time mama sent sis and I to live in Washington, D.C. after daddy was killed in Rockville, Maryland, on the plantation. I sorely longed for it, but I soon found that to survive with comfort, I had to be assertive and, in my youthful beauty, I found it could be used to that end and so I did. Entering into the circle of notables, and listening carefully to the men and their opinions of laws and politics, these assets gave me much in the way of desirability."

Ned listened to Rose. Her life was most certainly complete, once being a confidant of John C. Calhoun. He was arguably the finest man in word and thought ever produced in America. She was the closest of friends with Dolly Madison, wife of a framer of our Constitution. Dolly was the first lady to entertain in a manner that would be emulated for decades to come and was a confidant to James Buchanan, the single president.

Rose continued, "Ned, I was, for 20 years, the Socialite Madame in Washington. I entertained the elite in my home and these were always at the finest events."

Ned was impressed, as he listened to Rose with great interest.

Rose went on, "In addition, I have always tried to help my husband's career. But he was not up to that effort. I did love him, but it was a marriage mostly of convenience that drove me in those years. His breeding was the best of Virginia gentry. But, alas, he suffered a tragic death. So, I continued in the same manner. The intrigue of it all seemed necessary to my existence. So sad, it seems to me now, that it was so."

Rose spoke uninterrupted for three hours, giving Ned insight into the woman that he had come to love, and now even more so.

"Rose," Ned said after she finished, "As you well know, I have not the desire of such things and yet you have seen a flame of desire for me. For that I'm thankful to God. I can only give you my devotion of love for surely to come will be trials and hardships if we are to go westward."

Rose kissed his hand that she still held and said, "I welcome it all, my love. And now I have something to tell you about some security for us. In early years of the war, I speculated in stocks and in railways. I have a substantial monetary fund that is ours, so we will never be without."

Ned's surprised face humored Rose.

"Yes, my love," she offered, "We will be fine! We can be in a business of our choosing where we decide."

Ned didn't know what to say.

She continued, "Now nothing more to be said of that. It's ours, my dear. Do you understand me?"

Ned responded, "Yes, Rose, I do."

Rose then added, "I have also sent for my daughter, Little Rose. She will be here in a matter of days. She's now almost 12. Also, I have sent a letter to my other daughters of my upcoming marriage. They will adore you, my love. My oldest daughter's husband is in Wheeling, West Virginia. He, believe it or not, is a Union officer."

Ned laughed and said, "Who would believe that Rose would have such Union baggage."

"Yes, I know," Rose replied, "But the ones I love the most are Union affiliated."

They retired into the parlor and sipped Madeira in front of the warm fireplace. They entertained each other with antidotes of the war years. After midnight, Rose excused herself to freshen up.

After 30 about minutes, Ned heard Rose call, "Ned would you come up the stairs."

Ned went to the hall and looked up the stairs at Rose in only her black linen wear. Her long black hair, draped down her front, with her ebony skin in bright contrast showing her low deep cleavage. The candle she held lit up her personage to the most perfect sight to look upon. He was mesmerized.

She said invitingly, "Come, my love. I'm in need of your touch! Are not you of me?"

He happily responded, "Yes, Rose," which was all he could muster.

She quipped, "Then why do you keep me waiting in such anticipation here?" She lowered her hand even more as if to beckon.

Rose's face, to Ned, was a beauty beyond compare as he stepped up the stairs to her arms. Rose and Ned fell into a long embrace. Rose had years of experience in bringing pleasure to men. She had loved many men, even the ones she needed to seduce for information during the war. Ned's inexperience was her challenge, of which she was most capable. The art of lovemaking was made known to Ned that night and Ned's youth was her reward. They lay under the quilts in full committed alliance, sealed with love and ecstasy.

Later, Rose spent much of that night unable to sleep, staring at Ned in the moonlit room. She was overtaken listening to his breathing, fully appreciating what had come to her, even so in the autumn of her life.

Over the next several days Ned and Rose discussed their options of where they would go to live and just how far west they should go. Ned visited Molly's gravesite; he knelt and said a prayer over her.

Ned and Rose were married in a small ceremony held at Jean's home. Jean set everything up, including the Reverend. It was a brief, quiet service with only Jean, Sarah and the Brewster's in attendance.

Jean and Sarah had prepared a lavish dinner for the wedding party after the nuptials. Rose was radiant next to her new husband as Ned was beaming with pride over his new wife. Soon now, Little Rose would be in Virginia with them to join this new family. Sarah was looking forward to someone near to her age to be with or at least until Ned and Rose moved away.

Chapter 46

More Trouble from the Past

The Mosby raider, Gadsden, who voted for Ned to hang, had become agitated more and more as each day went by that the turncoat, as he called Ned, had escaped the noose. So, unbeknownst to Mosby, he wrote to the Richmond War Department telling of Ned's location, that Mosby had caught him and then let the fugitive go.

On a frigid morning after the wedding, Ned heard the plaintiff calls of Jake. He knew this call of warning that all was not right. He peaked out of the heavy curtains toward the stable. He saw nothing. He looked east and west, then north.

Ned said to Rose, "I'll be right back, Rose. I need to check on Jake."

She answered, "Fine, Ned. Put on something warm or you'll catch your death out there this morning."

Ned put on his heavy wool sweater, along with his oil duster and buttoned it up. He put his hat on and threw a long scarf around his neck. He pushed the door open and immediately was set upon by over 20 Confederate soldiers led by a major, name Dixon. Ned tried to pull himself back into the house, but there were too many for him to fend off.

Rose came to the commotion at the door and yelled, "What is the meaning of all of this? Unhand my husband!"

Ned was pinned to the ground by five men. He couldn't even look up. His face was shoved into the floor.

"I said let him up, Major! I demand his release now!" shouted Rose

"I'm sorry ma'am. You are Rose Greenhow?"

"No, Major, my name is Rose Greenhow McDonald."

"Yes, ma'am, and be that at as if it may, I've been instructed to apprehend Ned McDonald and escort him back to Richmond to be imprisoned."

Rose demanded, "By whose orders, sir? By whose orders?"

"Ma'am, it was by the Provost Marshal in Richmond and signed by the War Department."

At that moment, Gadsden stepped through the door and said, "Major, that is the right man!" Gadsden had come to assure Ned's identity.

The Major responded, "Very well, lift him up and shackle him good. We want no more escapes."

Rose empathetically stated, "Then, I shall accompany you to ensure his safety."

"I cannot allow that ma'am," replied the Major. "He is now under my care. I will assure you of his safety while I'm in charge."

As they shackled Ned, he told her to please be calm. Rose was most riled at seeing him manhandled so harshly.

Ned continued, "I'm fine, Rose. Please love, be at ease."

Rose came back, "Don't fret, Ned. I will go to Jefferson Davis myself. I will be on the heels of you. I shall see the President before they shut the cell door on you!"

As Ned was carted away, Rose donned her warmest cloak and ran to the barn. She wished she had help in harnessing Jake to the buckboard. Her skills were limited, but Jake was most capable and deciphered her intentions, even if Rose's rein work was somewhat confusing.

She stayed well back, but followed the escort for Ned all the way to Richmond. She nearly froze to death, but pushed aside all her great discomfort for his rescue. As the escort party went right through Richmond's outer defenses, Rose was delayed slightly, but was able, as usual, to use her womanly virtues, still honed to a razor's edge.

Chapter 47

The Possible Aid of a Friend

Rose raced down Broad Street towards President Davis' home, the Grey House, as it was called by the Confederacy. It was painted grey, a 3-1/2-story home with a portico porch at the rear of the house looking down on terraced gardens and Shockoe Valley. The front of the house had a modest entryway. Rose had come here many times after her release from prison in Washington, D.C. Davis had looked upon her as an absolute hero; even giving her a large stipend of $2,500, which was a small fortune, for her aid in the first Bull Run battle, and for her work after the battle.

Rose had visited the home and was entertained by Jefferson and Varina, his wife, while in Richmond. Davis even thought so much of her abilities that he sent her as an emissary to solicit aid from England and France, of which she spent one whole year, but without much success other than lip service

It was 4:00 p.m. when she pulled up at the Davis' home. The sentry had known of her, but thought, as most, that she had died. She was asked her business and told to wait while a message was passed to the officer of the guard. He was in the same capacity as years ago when Rose visited the President and Varina. Upon seeing Rose, he recognized her.

Rose said, "I'm not a phantom, Lieutenant."

The Lieutenant responded, "I can see Mrs. Greenhow, but how?"

Rose replied, "Lieutenant, it's a long story I can readily assure you, but I am at present most hurried with a great need. Is it possible to be presented to the Davis family?"

Politely responding, the Lieutenant said, "I will announce you, ma'am. I'm sure they will be eager and relieved to know you are very much alive. Come wait inside."

The house felt so good and warm as she waited, thawing out. Rose had grown accustomed to the cold and realized how frozen she was once she felt warm air.

In the background, Varina Davis could be heard yelling for Jefferson, "Come quick, hurry to the front door. At the most haste, come now!"

Varina's footsteps were heard upon the wood floors coming at an almost double-quick pace. In her excitement, she slipped and almost fell while coming around the corner. Her eyes caught the sight of Rose, and said, "Oh! My dear, Lord! It's true!" as she hurried to embrace Rose with great joy.

Varina and Rose, in those early years in Richmond, had become good friends. Neither was totally accepted in the elite circles. Varina, although deeply connected to Virginia in earlier generations, was not the Richmond ideal. Even though she was raised in the South, she was not a true Virginian. Also, her dark complexion was quite exotic and different.

Rose was southern born and bred, but not a Virginian. Though, in earlier years she circulated with social graces, her exploits were so eagerly publicized and marginalized her. Even the name Greenhow, highly regarded for generations, could not diminish what the elite snobbish Richmond women thought of them behind their backs. The two notable women were drawn to one another; both were well educated, had keen minds of politics, and were observers of the times. They were natural friends.

"Rose, my heart soars from the depth of despair of which it sank at the news of your death."

Rose apologetically responded, "I am sorry, Varina. At that time, I thought that my failure in France and England needed bolstering and that, if all thought I had died in the waters off North Carolina, perhaps I could serve in a capacity under a guise I would create. But alas, I failed at that. This war is advanced beyond my abilities. But, for the reason I am here. Dear friend, my life has taken a dramatic change much to my joy, yet at the moment it lies with much angst. I need to ask a great request from your husband and my President."

"But of course," the President's wife replied, "Yes, of course, but what is it?"

As she finished her words, President Davis came into the front hall and said, "Rose? Rose, is it you?"

"Yes, Jefferson," answered Varina.

Jefferson excitedly said, "Rose, what a blessed moment. We all were terribly stricken with grief at the word all of the South received, but you're here!"

"Yes, Mr. President, I am sorry for not being able to secure aid," Rose responded.

"Nonsense, dear Rose!"

"Jefferson," Varina interrupted, "Our Rose is in much need of your help."

"Oh? Do tell Rose," the President replied.

Rose began as they still stood in the hallway. "I have met a man of whom you know, at least I believe you do. We have married and he has brought much love into my life. He is at this very moment being put shackled into Richmond's prison."

Jefferson looked confused. "Rose, what is his name?"

Rose said, "Ned McDonald."

"Ned McDonald," he repeated.

"Yes, Mr. President.

The President asked, "He was accused of treason while with Mosby, he escaped, and is being imprisoned once again?"

"Yes, Mr. President." Rose continued, "He also helped the Union and advanced to the rank of Colonel, but he resigned that commission and came to a decision that he felt that this war was a no-sum proposition. He had lost many family members. He had fought bravely on both sides, all the while trying to make sense of it all, but he finally gave up. Ned desired to not participate in something that he could not believe in."

Jefferson Davis listened as Rose went on pleading her love's case before him, the highest rank of the Confederacy. He then said, "Come in please, let's sit, Rose."

Rose asked, "Please, Mr. President, I ask his release into my care. I assure you that he has no interest in any subversive activities, for any side."

Varina, seeing the great anxiety in her dear friend, went to her and put her arm around Rose. She took her hand while giving a pleading look to her husband, but she said not a word for he had not asked her thoughts. Varina knew not to voice her opinions, except only when asked. She was not President, he was.

The President said, "Rose, what you ask of me is not a small request. We, the South, are ever in your debt for your bravery and suffering at the Federal's hands, but this what you ask of me?"

Rose responded, "Mr. President, if I were not sure of Ned's worthiness, I would not have aligned my life with him and agreed to wed him. He is a man of great worth. His heart is of the kindest. He saw in me a love he desired, even though, as you know, the most ardent of Southern pride."

"Yes, of that I'm sure, Rose," The President replied.

Rose again asked, "Please, I beg of you, release him to me. If you seek to prosecute him on said charges, he will be available to answer to any and all of them." Then Rose put her hands together pleadingly.

Jefferson Davis was in deep thought over what Rose had asked. He began to pace the room with his hands behind his back. Varina assured Rose with subtle pats and squeezes of her hands.

The President then said, "Rose this is a delicate situation. We are all critically strained with uncertainty looming large before us. First, Rose, you will stay here with us. I will not have you trying to find lodging in the city."

Varina agreed out loud, "Yes!"

Second, I will have Ned, your husband, brought here to me this very night, I wish to discern with my own mind and eyes of his countenance."

Rose's face showed great relief and she said, "Thank you, sir."

The President responded, "Rose, please, I am Jefferson to you unless in mixed company." Rose beamed and nodded her head in acknowledgment. "Lieutenant!" he called out.

"Yes, sir!" the Lieutenant sharply replied as he quickly appeared.

The President ordered, "Lieutenant, you will make necessary the arrangements to bring Ned McDonald here to me this night."

"Yes sir," was the response.

"Oh! And Lieutenant, he will not be manacled and shackled."

The Lieutenant quickly replied, "Yes sir, Mr. President,"

Rose's special friend, Jefferson, offered, "Now relax, Rose. I cannot, if what you say is true of Ned, have him taken from your arms."

Tears weld in Rose's eyes. "I do love him so, Jefferson."

An understanding Jefferson added, "Of that I can readily see, Rose. Please, you ladies converse. I must lie down. My head aches terribly."

At that the door opened and a guard said, "Mr. President, General Robert E. Lee, Sir." Lee walked by the Sergeant.

The President responded, "Lee, I forgot about your coming."

Lee replied, "Mr. Davis, I can come back if it is not a good time."

The President said, "No, in fact, come into the other room. I've come upon something that I would like your thoughts about."

The two men left the room and shut the door.

Chapter 48

The Decision

Ned had been thrown into a cell similar to the one before when he first came to Castle Thunder. He was punched and kicked a few times, but nothing like before. The door opened. Three men came in. Ned thought, here it goes again.

An officer said, "Stand, McDonald. Put these fresh clothes on."

"No thanks," Ned said sharply.

The officer said, "You've been requested to appear at the President's house."

Ned's immediate thoughts were not positive. He had no idea that Rose had shadowed his route to Richmond.

The officer continued, "Well then, use this water to wash the blood off of you."

As they arrived at their destination, Ned stood looking at the President's house, having guards on each side of him and two behind. The Lieutenant sent to fetch Ned motioned him up to the porch. He looked at Ned and his black eye and the big bump on his other cheek.

Ned asked, " Lieutenant, what's this about? "

The Lieutenant dismissed the escort detail.

One from the detail asked, "Shall we wait, sir?"

The Lieutenant responded sharply, "I said, dismissed!"

Ned looked around puzzled. He was shaking from the cold, as he had been relieved of his coat he wore this morning. His teeth were chattering at the subzero temperatures.

As the door was opened, the Lieutenant said, "Relax, McDonald. Come in."

Ned went in and looked around. A servant gave the message to Varina that Ned had arrived and then to Jefferson Davis and Lee. Varina and Rose walked into the hall.

"Rose," Ned said as he saw her.

"My love," she said as she made no waste of time getting to his arms. Varina watched her good friend feel great relief to be in Ned's arms. Rose touched each wound on his face.

Ned said, "I'm fine, Rose, really I'm good!"

They kissed and hugged unabashedly in front of Varina.

Varina quipped, "If you don't stop, Rose, I believe I shall become jealous."

Rose realized the situation and said, "Oh, forgive me, Varina. Varina, this is my husband Ned McDonald. Ned, this is the Confederacy's First Lady, Varina Davis."

Ned said, "Mrs. Davis, I'm honored."

"As am I, Ned," Varina responded as she put her hand out. Ned took it and bowed.

Varina said, "Well, Rose, you certainly have maintained good taste in men. You failed to tell me how handsome he was."

"Yes, isn't he," Rose said as she sidled up next to Ned with her arm in his.

Varina invitingly said, "Come you two, let's make ourselves comfortable."

Ned hesitated to sit since his clothes were so dirty.

Varina understood and graciously offered, "Nonsense, Ned, you can freshen up soon enough." Varina called to a servant and instructed him to secure suitable clothes for their visitor.

The servant looked Ned over, sizing him up in his mind for a few seconds, and replied, "Yes, Mrs. Davis. Right away,"

Varina, smiling, said, "That man is uncanny at finding sizes in all matter of clothes and fabric."

After 30 minutes of small talk, Jefferson Davis and General Robert E. Lee walked into the room. Everyone stood.

"Please," Davis instructed, "Sit."

Ned stood almost at attention looking at Robert E. Lee's impeccable appearance in his uniform, gray hair and beard. At 6-feet tall, 170 pounds, a more regal man was not to be found. To Ned, the fact of his skill in leading and inspiring men was evident even now.

Davis appreciated that Ned was taken with Lee and said, "Ned McDonald, General Robert E. Lee. General, Ned McDonald."

Ned saluted instinctively. Lee returned it.

"Please, McDonald, sit," said Lee.

Though no longer a solider, Ned was in awe of the man he had never met and only seen briefly, but had admired so very much. Lee was a man who had once been his commanding officer.

Lee spoke out, "Well at last, Mr. McDonald, I meet the man that so impressed General J.E.B. Stuart and Colonel Mosby. You know, sir, many believed you were a myth. You and your horse, mere phantoms."

Ned said only, "Yes, Sir."

Lee went on, "You were well thought of by our very best commanders and, I am sad to say, by the Federal's best commanders when you were in their employ."

Again, Ned blushing and chagrinned at the same time said, "Yes sir, General."

Lee added, "Mr. McDonald, I should like to very much meet your horse Jake. Jake, isn't it? "

Ned responded, "Yes, General, Jake."

Rose spoke up, "Jake is stabled outside, General Lee." Ned looked at Rose and smiled with relief that Jake was fine.

"Well, Rose, you seem to have been a phantom of sorts also," said Lee. "It is a relief to see you alive."

Rose answered, "Yes, General Lee."

Lee continued, "Seriously, Rose, it's so good to see you again."

Rose replied, "Thank you, General Lee."

Jefferson began, "Well, I have inquired of the General as to his thoughts about Ned's incarceration for said treason acts against the Confederacy and our most esteemed Rose and her request. First, business is, Ned, the general and I would like to hear in your own words of the actions that caused you to leave the Confederacy and then the Federals. And before you begin, I'd first like to have it said that you were only granted an audience on this matter because of our debt to your wife, Rose."

267

Rose nodded, as did Ned. Rose looked at Ned with love and her eyes assured him to go on.

Ned began, much as he had told Jean, the Taylor's, Rose and Auntie. He built slowly with nervousness and then went into a full-blown oration of passion to the questions that Jefferson and Lee wanted answered. Ned stopped after an hour of uninterrupted oration. As he finished, Rose leaned to kiss his cheek and hold his hand.

"Well," Davis said. Ned looked briefly at Varina, as she smiled an understanding look at him. Davis said, "I feel your passion to be sure."

"As do I," Lee seconded.

Davis continued, "But now the question about Rose and her request. I am going to defer to General Lee at this time. He was your commander in the field. I am too close a friend of Rose, as is Varina, to be impartial. General Lee, if you please."

Rose had detected that, even before they came into the room, this would be the way their fate would be decided.

General Lee began, "I realize, first, that you were a volunteer, scout volunteer, was it not?"

"Yes sir, General."

"So you had the capacity to leave at any time and take your services with you. When you left to the Union had you participated in the act of espionage and had you begun collecting information when you were arrested by Colonel Mosby that first time? Your answer is?"

Ned quickly responded, "No sir, General, I had not begun."

Lee responded, "I thought not!"

It was the truth, but the real truth was he was intending to! Lee knew this as well as Ned. Everyone looked at Lee.

Lee said, "Well then, we have not a problem as I see it. No reason for a treason trial."

Everyone sighed relief.

Lee continued, "However, we have a problem still and that concerns what good Rebels feel over a severe affront from you to the Confederacy. Your safety comes into question. It seems you may not find safety in most places in the Confederate states and Rose is forbidden, until the war ends, to go into northern states. You see what I'm alluding to?"

"Yes," said Rose," We have been thinking much about this."

Lee said, "Well, this is a problem you must solve, because I am deciding not to imprison Ned and not to seek charges against him."

Rose stood, as everyone did, and went over to kiss Lee's cheek. "Thank you, Mon General," in her best French accent.

Lee responded, "Trés bien!"

Varina then spoke up, "Welcome to our home, Ned."

Ned responded, "Thank you, Mrs. Davis."

Lee interrupted, "I know it is very cold, but I am most curious. Could I implore you enough to introduce me to this famous horse, Jake?"

"Yes, indeed," agreed the President.

Both Davis and Lee were the finest of horsemen, most notably Davis. He, like General Grant, knew good horse breeding and was quite keen on the subject. Ned was given an overcoat and the men folk disappeared into the cold night.

"Rose," Varina asked, "Where will you go? I have a great deal of worries for the both of you."

"So do I, Varina. I am not sure where we should go, maybe to England until this blows over. I made many friends in London and Paris, but I am not sure Ned is up to such a move. He seems very insistent on going far west, but whatever we decide it must be fairly soon. We cannot hide out here, with you in Richmond."

Varina said, "My dear friend, you may stay here as long as you deem it necessary. Do not trouble yourselves over that. Jefferson feels as I."

Rose positively responded, "That's very gracious, Varina. We will see."

"Come, Rose," Varina said, "Let's prepare your room and get it heated up."

Rose then added, "Varina, you must please help me get Little Rose here to Richmond. She's probably already in Virginia now."

Varina answered, "We will do it tomorrow."

Rose excitedly said, "We will at all costs. Thank you so very much!"

Chapter 49

Jake and the Jefferson Davis Family

Jake stood chewing his hay with much enjoyment as the three men entered the President's livery. One of the guards had brought Jake in out of the bitter cold and had him stabled.

Lee stretched to pat Jake's neck and said, "Fine, very fine animal. Yes, indeed. He's all and more of what is said about him."

"Well, Ned," spoke Davis, "I suppose I cannot make an offer."

Ned quickly responded, "No, Mr. President. I would take no amount for him. He's like a close brother. He knows me and I know him. We are a team. He is the result of my father's efforts and love of horses."

Davis interrupted, "I would consider it an honor if you would let me, at some time, experience his gaits."

Ned said, "Jake do you hear the President. He would like to see what you're made of. What do you think?"

Jake, with enthusiasm, shook his head up and down and all three laughed, as the cold air exhaled into the rafters.

"Tell me, Ned," said Lee. "You have ridden him solely through the whole war up till now?"

"Yes sir, General," Ned responded.

Lee replied, "I am quite amazed, and he never came to lameness?"

"No," said Ned. "Never."

Lee went on, "He never needed prolonged rest?"

Ned answered, "No sir, General."

Lee continued, "I am stunned. All the miles, all the terrain covered, truly an amazing feat by any horse."

"Amazing indeed," the President agreed. "Well enough, let's retire to the warmth gentleman."

"Agreed," said Lee.

Once inside, the President and Lee agreed that in the morning each would take the measures to absolve Ned from the charges levied against him. Ned gave special thanks to both great men. Then they excused themselves to discuss the intended visit of General Lee. Ned went into the room off the hall and sat down till Rose returned.

In came the oldest Davis child. "Hello, I am Margaret, I am pleased to meet you."

Ned stood. "Hello, I am Ned McDonald."

Margaret asked, "You are Miss Rose's husband?"

"Yes, Margaret," Ned replied.

Margaret said, "They will be down presently. They are preparing the bedroom. May I get you anything, Mr. McDonald?"

"No. No thank you," Ned answered.

Margaret then asked, "May I sit and entertain you until they return?"

"Why yes, of course," Ned replied.

"Thank you," she said as she sat on the soft chair and spread out her dress to her satisfaction. She daintily put her hands in her lap.

Ned guessed the young Margaret about eight or nine, dark hair and big brown eyes. She radiated confidence that he would like to see in Christiana one day.

"So, Mr. McDonald, I have heard of you and your steed. They say that to be able to accomplish your deeds that Jake must have powerful wings."

Ned laughed. "No, Margaret, but if he did, I would be the first to know. He does run like the wind racing down out of the mountains though."

She continued, "Other children, especially Jefferson Junior and his friends, love to hear tales they tell of you. I must say, Mr. McDonald, it does sound like great fun!"

Ned replied, "It is, Margaret."

Margaret responded, "I should like to meet your Jake!"

"Well, Margaret, perhaps in the morning I will introduce you to him."

Margaret then asked, "And do you suppose I could meet him first? I mean without my brother."

Ned answered, "I think that might be arranged, Margaret."

She smiled and lifted up, sitting even straighter. She replaced her hands, as if totally satisfied of going one up on her brother. She continued, "I like Miss Rose and Little Rose. Miss Rose said that Little Rose would be here in a few days."

Ned said, "I hope so, Margaret."

Margaret quipped, "Yes, we had great fun when last they were here in Richmond."

At that, Varina and Rose entered the room. Varina said, "Well, I see my little hostess has you well entertained."

Ned responded, "Yes, Mrs. Davis, she has indeed. We have had a good conversation."

Margaret excitedly answered, "Yes, mother, and Mr. McDonald, in the morning, will give me a special audience to meet Jake."

Ned said, "Yes, if that is okay with you, Mrs. Davis."

She answered, "Yes, of course, but Margaret you will have to take Jefferson Junior."

Margaret, a little upset, said, "Oh, Mother! Can not I have a special audience?"

"Well," Ned interjected, "I would love to give both a private introduction, Mrs. Davis."

Mrs. Davis replied, "Oh, very well, Margaret."

Margaret responded," Oh, thank you, mother."

Mrs. Davis then said, "Now, off to your studies."

Margaret answered, "Yes, mother," and then she curtsied to Ned.

Mrs. Davis said, "Thank you, Mr. McDonald. I need to learn my history." Margaret said, "I'll see you in the morning."

"She is such a little lady," Ned said, "And very charming."

Mrs. Davis, responded, "Thank you, Ned. She is growing so fast. She was a steadfast rock for me when little Joseph died." A tear came quickly to Varina's eyes. "It still pains me," she told Rose and Ned. "He was Jefferson's favorite you know. He fell right out there off the portico, 10 feet. So precious, he was only five years old. Now we have little Margaret and I see little Joseph's special smile in her. Well enough," Varina quickly said.

The next day Ned, at his word, gave two private audiences to Margaret and Jefferson Junior, both satisfied that that's the type of horse each wanted.

Chapter 50

Planning for Their Future

It was after 1:00 p.m. as Ned and Rose sat alone in the parlor. He told her that he had two missions to accomplish before he left Richmond. "Soon, Rose, I need to see Elizabeth and Bessie, then I would like very much to pay my respects at General J.E.B. Stuart's grave."

Rose wholeheartedly agreed, as she would like to go to the gravesite also. But she then asked Ned, "Do you deem it wise to visit Elizabeth and Bessie on the heels of your acquittal on the chance that she is a well-known sympathizer for the Federals? Why she has not been arrested, as I was, is beyond me. This war might be over if I had been allowed to do what she has done here in Richmond."

Ned said, "You're right, of course, Rose, but she was instrumental in maybe saving my life. I might've died like Jesse Wharton when you were held in prison. It's because of her that you and I had a chance to meet."

Rose gently replied, "I realize that my love, truly I do, and as grateful as I am to her for that, you should not risk being seen associating with her."

Ned knew she spoke the truth, but felt a nagging to see her and Bessie, he felt she still was with Elizabeth. It would be a closing of that chapter for Bessie to know that Ned was there for Lizza at the end of her life. Ned decided not to push the subject any longer and said, "Rose, I would like to go to the Hollywood Cemetery tomorrow."

The cemetery was a fairly new one and it was named such for the profusion of holly trees and in keeping with rural gardens, it was quite beautiful. Four years of war had quickly filled it up with Confederate soldiers to lie at rest with past President John Tyler, Lieutenant General James Longstreet's three children, who died of scarlet fever all within weeks of each other, and President Jefferson Davis's little five-year-old son. Also, there were General George Pickett of the infamous Gettysburg. Pickett's charge and his division, had almost been annihilated and slaughtered. They agreed, as well, to go together and pay respects to little Joseph Davis' grave.

After seeing and paying respects at the Hollywood Cemetery, Ned still felt the need to see Elizabeth, but, as Rose had said, it was wiser not to, at least not now.

The evening was spent in much conversation of where the exiled couple could go together until at least the war ended. Rose suggested San Francisco, where she had been many times with her previous husband. Although it was Federal, it was far enough away from being associated with the war by either side.

Ned began to ask about the Bay City. It had been years since Rose had been there. She told of its great potential for growth and how it had achieved much in that regard with each visit she made. "It's got its own special kind of beauty, Ned, unlike Virginia and our mountains. I will say that after a spell there each time, I longed for the East and my family. My children were little and still needed me."

Ned said, "Rose, I want to, at all costs, stay in the state of Virginia at least as for now. I cannot tell you why or where we should go to live, but I feel the strongest compulsion to remain here. It's just recently come over me, yet I still feel a pull to move west. I hope you can understand what I'm trying to say."

Rose agreed and replied, "I think you, like me, want to be near when the end to this war comes. No matter the outcome. There will be many who will possibly need our help."

Ned said, "Exactly. It's an overwhelming feeling Rose. I don't know what I will be able to do, but I must stay."

Rose responded, "Then stay we do, at least for now."

She related to Ned that Varina had an acquaintance whose mother lived west of Petersburg and that, if necessary, Varina and her children could go there if Richmond became untenable at any time. The mother had passed away and a daughter lived there alone in a big house that sat on the Lynchburg road going west out of Appomattox Courthouse about 1/4 mile. The family, the Coleman's, had lived on the land for over 60 years. They settled the land after coming from Scotland. Their daughter, Lisa, tried to maintain it, but recently lost her husband, who succumbed after coming home from the Cold Harbor Battle. Her children, two over 15 years old, had died the previous winter.

Rose said, "It might be where we can go to stay out of the army's way."

Ned agreed. The war had not been pushed in that direction. He suggested that Rose find out from Varina if this was still an option and, if so, they could head that way as soon as Little Rose arrived.

Rose assured Ned she would do so. "I like the thought of it the more we talk about it," she said.

Little Rose finally arrived after much changing of plans. The mother and daughter reunion was emotional. Little Rose adored her mother. She had the same facial structure and was gifted with wit and personality, just like her mother.

Ned was quickly taken with her as she was with him. Now the family was together albeit Christiana. Ned felt good. He liked the aspect of a core family. He was in love and felt loved. After Lizza had died, he had a feeling that he never wanted to feel again.

Varina then verified with Lisa Coleman Chalmers, which was her full married name, that, yes indeed, she would welcome the exiles to come live and help maintain the house and land. Varina had given Lisa a brief history of Rose and Ned, and it did not bother or offend her in the least. She simply said, "Send them as soon as they see fit to come."

Within 10 days, Rose, Ned, and Little Rose would take the Danville train southwest out of Richmond, then take the Lynchburg Petersburg train west to the Appomattox Courthouse area. It would be an easy day's travel unless railroad tracks had been ripped up by the Federal cavalry units.

Goodbyes were said and much sorrow was felt over leaving friends once more for all involved. It was an all too often scene played out over and over during the years for untold numbers of displaced families, and the losses were uncountable. Winter was closing fast giving way to spring, yet winter still gave last gasps of a cold hold on the two armies entrenched around Petersburg.

Ned lay next to Rose the night before going to Appomattox. Rose had long fell to sleep. She lay next to him with his arm keeping her close. His mind wandered like a careening carriage out of control. All the years that have gone by, the happiness, the sorrow, and the hopes played before him in his mind. And the left-over business with Auntie, Jo, Elizabeth and Elsa. For the first time, he felt frozen; not acting on his need, he felt fear. Fear had never entered Ned over the years. Now he felt it, fear that he would lose Rose and Little Rose, fear that he would never see Christiana again.

He felt vulnerable. He wanted to talk with his mother. She always put things in perspective and soothed his concerns. How could he feel this fear after all that he had experienced? He lay there quietly, speaking silently to his mother and asking for her words to come to him. After becoming too tired to remain awake, he fell into a deep sleep.

There was a voice, "Ned!"

Ned was stirred awake or at least he thought he was.

The voice continued, "My son!"

Ned responded, "Mama?"

The voice went on, "My son! Calm yourself. Trust in yourself. Be the man your father and I raised you to be. Ask your heavenly father for help. He will not fail you son. You have come far with much to be proud of and satisfied with. Yet, you have so much more to do, my son. Keep your mind clear. Be at ease. Your father and family are here with me. Lizza is with us. She and her memory will guide you in Christiana's rearing. Be not afraid my son. Those that you have concern for will be calmed over your choices."

Ned's mother's face filled his mind's memory. She looked more beautiful than ever before.

He said out loud, "I love you, Mama,"

Rose awoke. "Ned, are you all right?"

He replied, "Yes, my love!" His mother was gone, but forever her words would guide him. Ned answered, "I'm fine, Rose. Please go back to sleep."

Chapter 51

Moving to the Future

The train pulled into Appomattox Station. Awaiting them was Lisa. She was above average height of 5 foot 7 inches and weighed about 125 pounds. She wore her long blonde hair pulled back and her blue eyes were alert and discerning. Her warm smile eased all concerns of their coming here.

Lisa welcomed them, "Hello! I am so happy to see all of you. I am hopeful that you will find my home comfortable and make it yours until such time you feel, as Varina put it, your compass of direction changes."

"Thank you, Lisa," Rose said putting her gracious self first and forward. "Ned, Little Rose and I are most grateful for you opening your home to us."

Lisa responded, "I'm happy to have your company. I've lost my husband and two sons in the last year. Now all I have is Eve and her son, Cain, my two slaves left by my husband. I gave her freedom, but she felt committed to me being here alone. Her five-year-old had been very sick. Her man, Adam, died two years past. So, such has been my lot. Yet, now you have graced me with help."

Ned smiled as Rose stated, "Lisa, we will help where you need it. I hear from Varina your farm needs attention."

Lisa laughed, "I believe it's past attention."

They loaded their luggage onto the buckboard wagon. The station to the Coleman acreage was only a short one and a half miles.

The Coleman house was comfortable. It was a two-story, classic column house, and there were three outbuildings and a stable. It sat in the 250-acre clearing, straddling the Lynchburg Road surrounded by heavy forestation. It was clearly in disrepair. Ned had his work cut out for him.

The house inside was well cared for between Eve and Lisa. They kept up appearances and settled in awaiting spring with its warm breezes and dogwood blossoms in this beautiful Virginia countryside, untouched by the war. To Rose, this area reminded her of Montgomery County, Maryland, near the foothills of the mountains.

Nearing winter's close, Jefferson Davis tried peace talks with the North but to no avail. Then, in February, the South lost the last part in Wilmington, North Carolina. The last of Early's Army in the Valley was lost. In March, Jefferson Davis signed a bill in the Confederate Congress to enlist black men.

Through the last vestige of cold weather, Ned repaired fences, the roof on the stable, and leaks in the roof of the main house. For several months, they enjoyed some semblance of a peaceful life. The company they provided for Lisa was most appreciated.

Rose worked on another book. It was to accompany the one she finished writing in Europe, which became a bestseller in England and the British Isles, called *My Imprisonment*. This one was to be named *Imprisonment and Beyond*.

Ned and Rose grew more in love as the days passed. It was a love she never thought possible. All the years before she had sought prestige, elevation of status and all that these encompassed. It was her very nature. Now it was about soul-searching, love, and the little pleasures that life had to offer. As she put it lately, life's small little treasures. Her thoughts were vocalized in nightly conversations. She began to soften. She called herself a revised Southern woman. Her life had become simpler and one of appreciation. People of the past might ask, who is this woman that spewed such venom with a passion held but by a few? All she knew was that she felt content for the first time since her father had died and as a young girl back in Maryland.

Lisa had introduced Rose and Ned to the surrounding folk, the Tibbs, the Floods, the Pattersons and the Wrights. They all came to Lisa's to be entertained with stories and good company. Ned enjoyed watching Rose so easily fit in with folks of the countryside. It was true as they said that she had grace for people of all stature.

Then came news of the inevitable spring campaign, the Battle of Five Forks. The word was General George Pickett was caught off guard at a Shad Planking Festival while General Sheridan, Ned's old Commander, made a surprise attack and Pickett lost terribly. It was called the Confederacy's Waterloo.

Only a few days later, Grant took Petersburg and one day later Richmond fell to Federal troops.

Ned confided in Rose after the news, "Lee will come our way. He has to get food, supplies and a railway south to hook up with Johnston in the south around North Carolina. I know Grant. He will be on Lee's heels and try to end it before Lee gets south."

Ned got a map from Lisa and laid it on the table. Rose and Lisa sat and watched him look at the area between Petersburg and Appomattox Station.

"Yes, Lee will try with great effort to get here where we are. The war will come here. I guess we and the McLean's chose the wrong area of land to await the end of this war," Ned concluded.

The McLean's had sold their house outside of Centerville, Virginia. The house sat on the hill overlooking Bull Run Creek. They had found themselves smack in the middle of the first Battle of Bull Run, the first real battle of the war. Wilbur McLean moved his family here to Appomattox thinking it was far and removed enough from war's wrath, and yet now here it was seemingly steaming directly at them.

Ned saw that Lee had nowhere to go but here to Appomattox.

"Well, Rose, your call, but I say wait here. I believe Grant will overtake Lee and his beleaguered force well before they get here. I also believe it is now only days before this war comes to an end."

Rose stood staring at the map, especially with her relatively late change of thoughts on the war and the South's independence. It was a great sadness to see what she also knew was inevitable. She knew of the South's indomitable spirit at Petersburg, of men starving and dying of disease, yet they remained at their posts. It hurt her to know so many Southern boys died in vain.

Elsewhere in thought, Ned laid his hands on either side of the tall window facing west. The winds from the East blew dry remnant leaves across the ground. As Ned wondered about the future, he could not help but think how capriciously his life, for the last five years, had been blown about by the Virginia winds. Gazing at the beautiful Blue Ridge Mountains, Ned could not foresee that, one day in the future, those same Virginia winds would blow him and his family across the Mississippi.

About the Author

C.R. Clark is a 9th generation American and feels blessed by God to be so. His ancestry lost several from families, starting from the 1750s, that fought for freedom in the Revolutionary War, the American Civil War and World War II. What is not lost on Clark is the price paid by so many in different creeds.

Receiving his higher education in Iowa, he lived the majority of his life in Virginia. The appreciation of the meaning and the cost of war was deeply etched by walking battlefields that abound in Virginia, which was called, 'The seat of the Civil War.'

Clark is a voracious reader and student of the 19th century, thus has chosen to write on and about. He feels this era is misrepresented and misunderstood to new generations. Possibly a museum of interest and thought might be sustained by his work.

C.R. Clark is an Elder in the Restoration Church of Jesus Christ of Latter Day Saints and 6th generation ordained Elder. He believes in the *Book of Mormon* given to Joseph Smith the martyr and the *King James Bible*.